Seanan McGui  a California-based author with a strong penchant for travel and can regularly be found just about any place capable of supporting human life (as well as a few places that probably aren't). The Toby Daye novels are her first urban fantasy series, and the InCryptid novels are her second series, both have put her in the *New York Times* bestseller list. Seanan was the winner of the 2010 John W. Campbell Award for Best New Writer. She also writes under the name Mira Grant. She is the first person to be nominated for five Hugo Awards in a single year. You can visit her at www.seananmcguire.com.

Also by Seanan McGuire

Toby Daye novels

Rosemary and Rue

A Local Habitation

An Artificial Night

Late Eclipses

One Salt Sea

Ashes of Honor

Chimes at Midnight

The Winter Long

A Red-Rose Chain

Once Broken Faith

SEANAN McGUIRE
THE WINTER LONG

A TOBY DAYE NOVEL

corsair

First published in 2011 in the United States of America by DAW Books
First published in Great Britain in 2016 by Corsair

1 3 5 7 9 10 8 6 4 2

A CIP catalogue record for this book
is available from the British Library.

ISBN: 978-1-4721-2014-4 (paperback)

Printed and bound in Great Britain by
CPI Group (UK) Ltd., Croydon, CR0 4YY

Papers used by Corsair are from well-managed forests
and other responsible sources

MIX
Paper from
responsible sources
FSC® C104740

Corsair
An imprint of
Little, Brown Book Group
Carmelite House
50 Victoria Embankment
London EC4Y 0DZ

An Hachette UK Company
www.hachette.co.uk

www.littlebrown.co.uk

This book is dedicated, with love and gratitude, to Tanya Huff.

Thank you for making so many things possible.

ACKNOWLEDGMENTS:

Welcome to *The Winter Long*.

This book was one of the first I fully plotted, back when this series was a glimmer in my eye and a fantasy for the future. Everything I have done with October's world to this point has been for the sake of getting here, to the book that you now hold in your hands. I am incredibly excited to be at this point, to have gotten this far into Toby's story—and make no mistake, there's still so very far left to go.

Thank you for reading. Thank you for trusting me to tell you this story, which has been with me for so long. Thanks to the Machete Squad, who are a constant in my life, and who keep me together when things get hard. Thanks to Amanda and Michael, and to Aislinn (welcome to the world, my skeleton girl; we are going to have a lot of fun). Thanks to the Disney Magic Bitches, who have endured another unnumbered series of Disney excursions, including possibly the best birthday party I have ever had, and to my darlings, Vixy, Amy, Brooke, and Shawn, who knew I was a scorpion when they picked me up.

My editor, Sheila Gilbert, is the best I could have wished for, and my agent, Diana Fox, is still my personal superhero. Thanks also to Josh Starr at DAW, who is the most frequent target of my random mid-week phone calls, and to my cover artist, Chris McGrath, for bringing Toby so beautifully to life. And thanks to the crew here on the ground: Christopher Mangum, Tara O'Shea, and Kate Secor.

My soundtrack while writing *The Winter Long* consisted mostly of *Night Visions*, by Imagine Dragons, *Queen of Spindles*, by Talis Kimberley, *Baptized*, by Daughtry, endless live concert recordings of the Counting Crows, and random episodes of *Welcome to Night Vale*. Any errors in this book are entirely my own. The errors that aren't here are the ones that all these people helped me fix.

Now grab your coat. It's going to get a little chilly in here.

PRONUNCIATION GUIDE
THROUGH THE WINTER LONG

All pronunciations are given strictly phonetically. This only covers races explicitly named in the first eight books, omitting Undersea races not appearing or mentioned in book eight.

Afanc: *ah-fank*. Plural is Afanc.
Annwn: *ah-noon*. No plural exists.
Bannick: *ban-nick*. Plural is Bannicks.
Barghest: *bar-guy-st*. Plural is Barghests.
Blodynbryd: *blow-din-brid*. Plural is Blodynbryds.
Cait Sidhe: *kay-th shee*. Plural is Cait Sidhe.
Candela: *can-dee-la*. Plural is Candela.
Cetace: *sea-tay-see*. Plural is Cetacea.
Coblynau: *cob-lee-now*. Plural is Coblynau.
Cu Sidhe: *coo shee*. Plural is Cu Sidhe.
Daoine Sidhe: *doon-ya shee*. Plural is Daoine Sidhe, diminutive is Daoine.
Djinn: *jin*. Plural is Djinn.

Dóchas Sidhe: *doe-sh-as shee*. Plural is Dóchas Sidhe.
Ellyllon: *el-lee-lawn*. Plural is Ellyllons.
Gean-Cannah: *gee-ann can-na*. Plural is Gean-Cannah.
Glastig: *glass-tig*. Plural is Glastigs.
Gwragen: *guh-war-a-gen*. Plural is Gwragen.
Hamadryad: *ha-ma-dry-add*. Plural is Hamadryads.
Hippocampus: *hip-po-cam-pus*. Plural is Hippocampi.
Kelpie: *kel-pee*. Plural is Kelpies.
Kitsune: *kit-soo-nay*. Plural is Kitsune.
Lamia: *lay-me-a*. Plural is Lamia.
The Luidaeg: *the lou-sha-k*. No plural exists.
Manticore: *man-tee-core*. Plural is Manticores.
Merrow: *meh-row*. Plural is Merrow.
Naiad: *nigh-add*. Plural is Naiads.
Nixie: *nix-ee*. Plural is Nixen.
Peri: *pear-ee*. Plural is Peri.
Piskie: *piss-key*. Plural is Piskies.
Puca: *puh-ca*. Plural is Pucas.
Roane: *row-n*. Plural is Roane.
Satyr: *say-tur*. Plural is Satyrs.
Selkie: *sell-key*. Plural is Selkies.
Shyi Shuai: *shh-yee shh-why*. Plural is Shyi Shuai.
Silene: *sigh-lean*. Plural is Silene.
Tuatha de Dannan: *tootha day danan*. Plural is Tuatha de Dannan, diminutive is Tuatha.
Tylwyth Teg: *till-with teeg*. Plural is Tylwyth Teg, diminutive is Tylwyth.
Urisk: *you-risk*. Plural is Urisk.

ONE

December 20th, 2012

For you there's rosemary and rue; these keep
Seeming and savor all the winter long.
Grace and remembrance be to you both.
— William Shakespeare, *The Winter's Tale.*

THE WOODS WERE DARK, filled with strange shadows. They twisted and swirled independent of any light source, making the space beneath the towering sequoias look treacherous and wild. Not much in the way of illumination could trickle all the way down through the tightly-laced branches to ground level; the few streaks of moonlight that had managed to reach us were washed out and thin, managing to seem almost darker than having no light at all. Everything was permeated by the smell of redwood sap and the sea.

We had arrived as a group, May, Jazz, and Quentin packed into the backseat like sardines, me behind the wheel, and Tybalt sitting rigidly next to me. He didn't really like cars under the best of circumstances. He liked them even less when there were multiple other passengers, since that meant he couldn't respond to an accident by yanking everyone safely onto the Shadow Roads. Call it a quirk brought on by being several hundred years older than the internal combustion engine.

I had parked the car in the mostly deserted Muir Woods lot, where May, Jazz, and Quentin had promptly gone on ahead, choosing retreat over dealing with my mood. This left Tybalt with the unenviable duty of trying to coax me into a party I had no interest in attending. I don't *like* parties. Someone always tries to assassinate someone I actually like, and there are never enough of those little stuffed mushroom caps.

Right: this had gone on long enough. I stopped at the edge of the first trail leading up the slope, digging my heels into the dirt and refusing to be budged. "Nope," I said. "I said I'd come; I came. These are the woods. I have entered Muir Woods. Now I'm going home. You have fun, I'll see you when you get back."

"Once again you underestimate my ability to move you, while simultaneously overestimating your ability not to be moved." Tybalt caught my wrist, tugging me forward.

I dug my heels in deeper. "You're the one who's overestimating things here," I said. "I don't want to do this. I told you I didn't want to do this. I told *everyone* I didn't want to do this. Can we just go do something else? See a movie? Go out for a nice dinner? We could go back to the house and watch some BBC Shakespeare. I won't even smack you for criticizing their pronunciation . . ."

Tybalt released my wrist and stepped back, looking at me with exasperated fondness. "October," he said. "Do you consider me so easily bribed as all that?"

"I was hoping?"

He raised an eyebrow.

"Everyone else will be here," I said, trying another angle. "We'll have the house to ourselves."

"Ah. That does put a different spin on things, and

were the matter mine to decide, it might even sway my response in your favor." My Cait Sidhe boyfriend shook his head, the moonlight glinting off his tabby-patterned brown hair. This late at night and this far from any human residences, neither of us was bothering with a human disguise. Not that he was in any way unattractive when he was pretending to be mortal—far from it—but I preferred his real face, complete with the malachite-banded green eyes that were currently narrowed in amusement over my predicament. "Alas, the matter is out of my hands. I will deliver you to the Queen, or we will both face her wrath."

I crossed my arms and scowled at him. "Arden isn't all that wrath-y. She used to be a bookstore clerk."

"She is, as you say, 'wrath-y' enough. She is a queen. That is sufficient to lend teeth to whatever wrath she chooses to express." Tybalt leaned forward and took hold of my wrist again, effortlessly unfolding my arms as he resumed trying to tug me into Muir Woods. "Come. The sooner we arrive, the sooner we can depart. Besides, you dressed for the occasion. Shouldn't you take the time to at least pretend to enjoy it?"

I scowled, but I couldn't pretend he wasn't right about the last part. We *were* dressed for the occasion, thanks to my having raided my old bedroom in my mother's tower, and his possession of a seemingly endless supply of leather trousers. He was wearing a pair in tawny brown, accented across the legs with strips of darker brown that managed to imply a tabby's stripes without turning into a costume from the latest revival of *Cats*. His cream-colored poet's shirt was unlaced enough to be tempting, but still modest enough not to cross the line into romance novel territory, and his brown leather vest and boots matched the stripes on his trousers. He looked basically amazing. No one could have looked at him without seeing the King of Cats he truly was.

I don't clean up quite as well. My dress was one-shouldered and long enough that I had to lift it whenever I was stepping over anything—I wasn't looking forward to climbing up the side of the hill between us and the Queen's knowe. The whole thing was made of spider-silk, which would have put it well outside of my price range if it hadn't been commissioned for me when I was still living with my mother. It gleamed in the moonlight like liquid silver. Stronger colors have a tendency to wash me out, thanks to my complexion: I'm naturally pale, made paler by my primarily nocturnal lifestyle. My hair is the kind of straight that refuses to take a curl, and a shade of no-color brown that's moved a thousand boxes of Clairol. Veins of pale gold run through it, courtesy of my increasingly strong fae blood.

Still, I had to admit the dress was a good cut for me, and it fit like it had been stitched yesterday. May had done my makeup, choosing subtle metallic shades to make it look like my fog-colored eyes were actually worth gazing into, and my hair was pinned into an artfully messy updo, woven with strands of black opal that matched my necklace and earrings. No one could say I hadn't at least attempted to get ready for a formal ball.

That didn't mean I had the slightest intention of actually *going*.

Tybalt apparently realized he wasn't going to make me move, because he stopped pulling on my wrist and stepped closer, placing a finger beneath my chin and tilting my head back until our eyes met. "Do you truly intend to waste all the work of preparing for this event? You look astonishing, October. Perhaps I am a proud man, but I did so look forward to seeing others seeing you and realizing that they had overlooked your beauty while allowing their eyes to be clouded by the woman who once ruled in this demesne. Smugness excites me. I was even more excited about the prospect of taking you home after the ball, and showing you exactly how much I appreciate that you have chosen me over all of them."

"Flattery will get you a lot of places, kitty-cat, including into my pants, but it's not going to get me to go to that ball."

Tybalt nodded, smiling broadly enough to show the point of one sharpened incisor. "Oh, I know. But did you know that there is one place that flattery will always get me?"

I raised an eyebrow. "Where's that?"

"Past your guard." He dropped my wrist. Before I could object, his arms were locked around my waist, and we were falling into the shadows, where everything was cold and black and there wasn't any oxygen.

We fell for what could have been forever. Intellectually, I knew it was only a few seconds. That didn't help as much as it might have. My body had enough time to notice that I'd stopped breathing and send up an objection, and then we were back on solid ground, and the air around us no longer felt like it was made of pure ice. It was no surprise when I opened my eyes and found myself looking at the door to Arden's knowe. It was standing open to the night air, and the trees around it were lit with pixies and fireflies. Of the two, the fireflies were more unusual—they're not native to California.

"Dirty pool!" I pushed away from Tybalt, who let me go without a fight. I glared at him. At least he had the decency not to laugh at me, although I could tell it was a struggle. "That was dirty pool and it wasn't fair, and you should be ashamed of yourself!"

"I am abashed by my own behavior," he replied, deadpan. "I will spend a lifetime fighting to redeem myself in your eyes."

"Damn right you will." I glared at him as I adjusted the strap on my gown and reached up to check my hair for frozen patches. We'd been in and out of the shadows too quickly for any ice to form. Bully for me. I lowered my hand and sighed, finally giving up on the glare as I asked, "So what you're saying is that we really have to do this."

"That is *precisely* what I'm saying." He offered me his arm. "If milady would do me the great honor of allowing me to escort her into the Yule Ball?"

"I hate you," I said, slipping my hand into the bend of his elbow.

"I know."

This vital exchange complete, we walked together past the guards at the door—who were smirking, having clearly eavesdropped on us the whole time—and into Arden's knowe.

The door led to an enormous entry hall. The walls and floor were polished redwood, seamlessly flowing from one into the next, while the ceiling consisted almost entirely of stained glass panels representing a stylized, star-filled sky. Some of the panels were open, allowing us to see the actual sky beyond, a twilit wonder of purple mists and multiple moons. We had crossed out of the mortal world and into the Summerlands when we passed over the threshold. The seamlessness of the transition said something about how many people had come and gone through those doors since Arden had reopened her knowe. Like most things, passage between the human and fae worlds is easiest in places where it's been done before, and the more often, the better.

No artwork or tapestries hung on the walls, which had been carved into a series of bas-relief panels retelling the history of the Kingdom of the Mists. Arden's resident crafters had been hard at work since my last visit: panels had been added showing the death of Arden's father, King Gilad Windermere, and the overthrow of the false Queen who had followed him on the throne.

The carvings of me were pretty flattering, even if they did get my nose wrong.

There were holiday decorations strung across the hall, anchored to the point where wood met glass, rather than being allowed to obscure any of the carvings. Wreaths of holly, ivy, and mistletoe competed with ropes of woven redwood branches, and everything smelled of sap and green things. My eyes were only for the hall itself. "It's beautiful," I murmured.

"Yes, it is," Tybalt agreed, following my gaze to the nearest panel. "The artisans of the Divided Courts are capable of some monumental things, when they rouse themselves to try."

"That was almost complimentary."

"I'll take more care in the future," he said gravely, and began walking again, pulling me with him down the hall to the main receiving room.

If the entry hall was large, this room was vast, easily the size of the false Queen's ballroom, which had previously been my gold standard for "why do you need this much space." It continued the redwood-and-glass theme, now accessorized with people. Lots and lots and *lots* of people. At first glance, it seemed like the entire Kingdom had shown up to celebrate Queen Arden Windermere's inaugural Yule Ball. Second glance confirmed that if it wasn't the whole Kingdom, it was certainly close.

I started to step over the threshold, on the theory that it was best to get this sort of thing over with quickly. Tybalt's sudden refusal to move pulled me to an unexpected halt. I turned to blink at him. I was still blinking when the herald to the right of the door announced, in a remarkably carrying tone, "Welcome to Sir October Daye, Knight of Lost Words, in service to Shadowed Hills, and to His Majesty, Tybalt, King of Dreaming Cats."

Another herald blew a quick fanfare on what sounded like a brass horn. I turned back to the room, gaping at the crowd, which was now largely concerned with staring at us.

"Oh, sweet Titania, I am going to murder someone, and I'm not all that picky about who it's going to be," I said in a low tone.

Tybalt laughed, and we walked together into the chaos of the Yule Ball.

There are four major holidays in the fae calendar, the fixed points in the year around which everything else revolves. Beltane and Samhain represent the transfer of power between the Unseelie and Seelie Courts. Back in the days when every fiefdom had two regents, they would have traded places on those nights. Yule and Midsummer are more general holidays, meant for everyone to celebrate. Hosting one of those two parties is a pretty big deal. Since the false Queen of the Mists had never been much into throwing the kind of shindig that would attract common ruffians like me and everyone I knew, we hadn't had a Kingdom-wide Yule celebration since King Gilad was murdered.

It looked like Arden was working overtime to make sure everyone knew that things were different now. A band played on one side of the room, and space had been cleared for the dancers, while tables had been provided for those who would rather sit and talk. Hobs and Brownies circulated through the crowd with trays of drinks and finger foods. I suppressed a shudder. The last time I'd been dragged to one of these large seasonal parties, my old enemy, Oleander de Merelands, had been disguised as one of the servants. She'd poisoned several people that way, and she'd drugged me. Not one of the high points of my career.

That had been a different time, in a different knowe, and Oleander was dead. I allowed Tybalt to hand me a tall flute of something that bubbled like champagne, but was the pale purple of lilacs. I sniffed it. It smelled, perhaps predictably, of blackberries. "Let's find Sylvester," I said. "I need to present myself to him before things get too hectic."

Unsurprisingly, Tybalt made a face. "Must we?"

"Yes," I said firmly. "We must." Sylvester Torquill was my liege, and had been for most of my adult life. Civility said that if we were both at the same party, I should find him and make sure he knew I was there. Tybalt wasn't bound by the same rules of fealty and propriety, which was a good thing, since he would have committed murder if he'd been forced to deal with Sylvester as often as I did.

Tybalt counted Sylvester as ... not an enemy, quite, but definitely someone he wouldn't think twice about leaving behind if the situation required it. That was because of me. They'd been almost friends before I came along and complicated things. Yet somehow I couldn't feel too bad about it, since the "complication" had involved Sylvester refusing to let Tybalt stay with me when I was sick and on the verge of dying. Tybalt took that sort of thing personally.

He wasn't the only one.

"Must I be pleasant?" he asked.

"Yes, unless he starts something." I scanned the throng. "He'll probably be near the refreshments. Come on, I think I see an ice sculpture this way." Keeping my arm linked through his, I plunged into the crowd. If he didn't like it, tough. Turnabout was fair play.

He didn't fight me. He understood where my duty lay, just like I understood about his. Faerie is a feudal society: Kings and Queens, knights and lords and ladies. I'd earned my title. It was the only way for someone like me to get the honor, since changelings—human-fae crossbreeds—can't inherit titles from our parents. It would have been a moot point in my case anyway, since my mother, Amandine, is untitled. I guess people figured that since she was Firstborn, she didn't need a title to get respect. I did. Part of having that title was maintaining it, doing all the things that a good little changeling knight was supposed to do. And as much as I didn't want to be at the party, it was nice to have an event that justified me and Tybalt attending together. Being a King of Cats meant that Tybalt's responsibility to his people had to come first. Sometimes I didn't see him for days. Other times . . .

I'd been in relationships before. One of them had been serious enough to result in my now-teenage, now-mortal daughter, Gillian. But what I had with Tybalt was something special.

The crowd fell away as we emerged into the bubble of empty space between the dance floor and a refreshment table laden with sparkling sugar desserts. Towers of cookies and less recognizable confections surrounded a huge gingerbread reproduction of Arden's knowe as seen from the Summerlands: a palace that was half redwood forest, half fairy-tale dream. There were even tiny lights inside, shining through the stained sugar glass windows.

"Whoa," I said.

A pointy-eared man with hair the color of fox fur was standing near the table, speaking earnestly to a slender woman of evidently Chinese descent. He was wearing the blue and gold of Shadowed Hills, as perfectly groomed as any fairy-tale prince. Her dress looked like it had come from fourteenth century China, or a reasonable facsimile thereof, except for the silver circuitry patterns stitched into the wine-colored fabric. They turned when I spoke, and their smiles were radiantly bright.

"October!" said Duke Sylvester Torquill of Shadowed Hills, my liege lord and lifelong friend. He stepped forward and enfolded me in a hug. I hugged him back, closing my eyes briefly as I breathed in the reassuring dogwood flower and daffodil scent of his magic. It was something that was uniquely his in all the world, and it had meant comfort to me since my childhood.

When he released me, I moved back a step in order to dip into a curtsy, at least pretending that I had retained some of the manners I'd had drilled into me. "Your Grace," I said. "It's a pleasure to see you."

Sylvester laughed. "Oh, stop that. You and I both know that you're not cut out for being respectful. I think it's bad for your health."

"Entirely possible," I agreed, straightening and turning to his companion, who was still smiling brightly as she waited for my attention. "Li Qin."

"Hello, October." Li Qin was the current regent of Dreamer's Glass, the Duchy that occupied much of the South Bay Area. Her only official claim to the land was a sort of "finders keepers" situation, since the previous Duchess had disappeared under mysterious circumstances, leaving Li Qin holding the keys. I knew exactly where Duchess Riordan was: stranded in Annwn, one of the deeper, sealed lands of Faerie. She wasn't going to be coming back any time soon.

Every race in Faerie has its own magical talents. Li Qin's race, the Shyi Shuai, bend luck. It was easy to wonder how much of Riordan's predicament had been helped along by the woman who now held her fiefdom. It was also difficult to care. Riordan had dug her own grave; let her lie in it. Maybe my attitude toward "rightful rulers" is a little case-by-case, since I had no trouble with Li Qin holding Dreamer's Glass, but I'd had major problems with the false Queen holding the Mists. Then again, Li Qin was a better regent than Riordan had ever been. If the line was drawn at "do your damn job, and I won't mess with you," well, there are worse standards to uphold.

"You look lovely tonight," I told her.

She brightened. "As do you."

"With that out of the way, I have a pressing question for October." Sylvester turned to me and bowed. "I know you have come here with an escort, but may I have this dance, my dear?"

Tybalt scowled. He didn't object. Having my liege offer to dance with me was a great honor, and one that I had no way to politely refuse. I pulled my hand from his elbow. "I'm a terrible dancer," I said.

Sylvester's smile grew. "Perhaps. But as you're still sworn to my service, it would behoove you to indulge me."

I handed Tybalt my drink, which he took without comment. "Fair enough." I curtsied before slipping my hand into Sylvester's extended one. "Tybalt, Li Qin, if you'll excuse us?"

"Only momentarily," said Tybalt.

"We'll talk later," said Li Qin, still smiling.

I turned back to Sylvester. "I'm all yours," I said.

"No, you're not," he replied, as he tugged me gently with him onto the edge of the nearby dance floor. The dancers parted to let us in, recognizing the necessity of making way for a Duke. "But your loyalty remains mine to command, and that's more than sufficient for me."

I wasn't sure how to answer that. I settled for focusing on the dance, my hand resting lightly on his arm, his body guiding me through the steps. I've never been much of a dancer, but he made me look like I almost knew what I was doing. "So who else is here?" I asked finally. "We just got here."

"Yes, I know," he said. "Your squire, your Fetch, and the rest of your household arrived a quarter of an hour ago, and the party started at sunset. You're very late. That's something of a relief, actually."

"It is?"

"Yes. It means you try to avoid everyone's parties as if they were filled with flesh-eating monsters. I'd begun to worry that you only avoided mine."

"Be nice to me, I've had a hard night." I wrinkled my nose at him. "I meant 'who else from Shadowed Hills is here'?"

"Ah. You meant, 'did Luna come?'" Sylvester's expression darkened. He spun me out and back in again, timing the motion to a flourish in the music that I hadn't seen coming. "She stayed home with Rayseline. She didn't feel it was meet for her to come out and celebrate the longest night of the year when our daughter would not be able to join the celebrations."

Rayseline Torquill was Sylvester's only child. She was currently deep in enchanted slumber, caused by an elf-shot arrow that had been intended for me. I felt a little guilty about that, but only a little. She *had* been trying to kill me, and she *had* killed her ex-husband—who'd been my boyfriend at the time—as well as wounding my little girl so badly that the only way for me to save her had been for me to turn her completely human.

Part of me knew that Raysel deserved whatever horrible dreams she was getting from her fevered brain. The rest of me loved her father too much to ever say that to his face. "Well, tell Luna I said hello," I said awkwardly, trying not to let my dismay interfere with my dancing.

"I will. As for the rest of my household, we've loaned the better part of the staff to Queen Windermere for tonight's fete, and all but the most essential of my knights and guardsmen are in attendance." He smiled. "You really do look lovely tonight. I remember when your mother had that gown made for you."

"Me, too," I said. "It's a good thing she invested so heavily in spider-silk when I was a kid. I've never really had much fashion sense." Spider-silk is a uniquely fae material, and once it's been cut and tailored to fit someone, it fits them forever, no matter how much they grow or shrink.

"I don't know about that. You wear that dress in your own way, not as your mother would, and I'm proud to have seen you grow into the woman you've become."

I reddened, blinking at him. "What brought that on?"

"Nostalgia, perhaps? It's good to see you. That's all." The dance was coming to an end. He guided me out of the crowd and back to where Li Qin and Tybalt were waiting for us. "You have honored me with the pleasure of this dance."

"You have honored me by asking," I replied, reclaiming my drink from Tybalt, who remained silent and stone-faced. This time I actually drank some. It tasted like blackberries, with a crisp, almost floral aftertaste. I turned to Li Qin. "Sorry about that."

"Never apologize for dancing," she said. "It's something everyone should enjoy, as often as they can."

I grimaced, trying to make it look like a smile, and changed the subject. "So who all's here from Tamed Lighting?"

"Everyone but Alex, since he still can't go out at night. Even April, although she's having trouble with some of the local redwood Dryads." Li Qin sighed. "They're a little snobby where she's concerned, and she doesn't handle it as well as she might."

"Are we talking tears or declarations of war?" April O'Leary was the Countess of Tamed Lightning, and the world's only nonorganic Dryad. Her tree had been destroyed to make room for a housing development, at which point her adoptive mother, January, had transplanted her into a computer server to save her life. The result had been a quirky, slightly alien individual with a strange sense of humor. She was doing an excellent job with her County, so far as I knew. That didn't mean she was equipped to do an excellent job with a bunch of leaf-brained tree huggers who thought she was an abomination.

"A little bit of both," said Li Qin. She sounded aggravated on April's behalf. It was a natural response. Li Qin was January's widow, after all.

There was a soft displacement of air behind me, accompanied by the smell of redwoods and blackberry flowers. I knew who was there even before Sylvester offered a shallow bow and a mild, "Your Highness," to the new arrival.

I turned, already smiling, to face our new Queen in the Mists, Arden Windermere.

She was wearing a flowing gown in a shade of frosted white that matched the blackberry flowers woven through her purple-black hair. Her mismatched eyes—one brilliant blue, one mercury-silver—were striking enough that she didn't need makeup to set them off. She looked like the Queen she was. She also looked profoundly uncomfortable. I guessed that was natural. Arden had been living outside Faerie for her entire adult life, spending more than a century hidden in the mortal world. She'd been back for less than six months, and in that time she'd become Queen and taken on responsibility for a whole Kingdom. Being surrounded by so many of her subjects at once had to be hard on her nerves.

"There you are," she said, and grabbed my hands, pulling me with her into a gateway that suddenly opened in the air. The world shifted around me as her portal deposited us outside. I yanked my hands away, as much to get my balance back as in protest of her treatment.

We were standing on a slanted rooftop, the shingles beneath our feet ripe with healthy green moss. Redwood saplings had rooted on some of them, straining toward the Summerlands sky above us. I looked around. Adult redwoods grew on every side, some of them ascending from the forest floor far below, others growing from the palace on which we stood.

Arden herself was sitting on the roof when I looked back to her. I blinked.

"Uh, Your Highness?"

"What took you so long?" She hugged her knees, looking up at the moons overhead. "I thought you'd be here earlier."

"I don't like parties." I paused. "And . . . I'm guessing neither do you."

"I don't know how to behave at something like this." Arden shook her head. "Everyone's looking at me, expecting me to be their Queen, and I just want them to tell me how long I'm expected to stay before I cut and run. I could barely make it through staff meetings at the bookstore without losing my cool. How am I supposed to be in charge of something like this?"

Cautiously, I moved to sit beside her. "Well, I don't know," I said. "You've been doing pretty well with the whole Queen thing. I can't imagine throwing one party would be that much harder."

"Then why don't you do it and report back?"

I frowned a little, leaning on my hands as I looked at her. It occurred to me that Arden didn't have that many *friends*. There was Madden, the Cu Sidhe from Borderlands, but . . . that was it, so far as I knew. She'd gone from being a bookstore clerk to being Queen essentially overnight, and she'd been outside Faerie since she was a child. When would she have had the time to make friends? "I'll tell you what," I said. "I hate parties. You hate this party. I'll pretend to like parties if you'll pretend to like *this* party, and maybe together we can fool the rest of the Kingdom."

Arden gave me a sidelong look. "Really."

"If nothing else, people will be incredibly impressed

that you got me to stay for an entire Yule Ball, rather than escaping at the earliest possible opportunity."

There was a long pause before, slowly, Arden smiled. "Will you sit at the high table with me during the banquet?"

"On one condition."

"Name it."

"Tybalt comes, too."

Arden's smile grew. "Deal."

TWO

SITTING AT THE HIGH table with Arden wasn't so bad. Tybalt found the idea hysterically funny and was on his best behavior, while my squire—Quentin Sollys—not only joined us, but ate with a mannerly precision that put the rest of us to shame. It helped that he was the Crown Prince of the Westlands, the High Kingdom to which Arden and the Mists swore fealty, and had been trained on things like "which fork do you use with the second salad course" when he was in diapers. I caught Arden watching Quentin out of the corner of her eye, trying to mimic his motions. I smiled but didn't say anything. Her own training had been disrupted by the years she'd spent in hiding, and if copying off my squire's metaphorical homework helped her, that was fine.

May and Jazz sat near the front of the banquet hall, where they could make faces at us throughout dinner. I smirked and made faces right back, earning me a few amused looks from Sylvester, who was seated with them. For the first time in a long time, I was totally relaxed, sure that nothing was going to ruin my good mood.

I should really learn to stop being optimistic.

The Yule Ball went until nearly dawn. Dinner was followed by more dancing, several musical performances by vocalists from around the Kingdom, and even an animal act with a phoenix and a flammable falconer. It was all good fun, and I was a little sorry to see it end. But no party can last forever, and eventually Arden moved to stand in front of her carved redwood throne, holding her hands up, palms facing outward. Bit by bit, the crowd quieted, everyone turning to face their Queen.

"The Kingdom of the Mists has known great turmoil and tragedy since the death of my father, Gilad Windermere. I am truly sorry to have failed you for so long by allowing a pretender to hold my throne while I hid from your eyes. I will not fail you again. This is the longest night of the year, and the night when we make our pledges unto Faerie, swearing we will never freeze, never falter, but will continue to turn the wheel around. We will keep dancing. By the root and the branch, by the rose and the thorn, we will do our best in service to our unseen Lord and Ladies."

The room cheered. Arden smiled but didn't lower her hands.

"Now, before the night is done, I must make certain appointments . . ."

I'm not ashamed to say I tuned out as she began reciting proclamation after proclamation, all of them impeccably memorized and dead boring. Li Qin was named as official protector of Dreamer's Glass until such time as Duchess Treasa Riordan could be found. Etienne's impending marriage to his mortal lover, Bridget Ames, was recognized and sanctioned by the crown. This person got permission to use that land. This other person was given leave to take a squire. The head of Arden's guard, Lowri, was recognized for bravery. I started silently reviewing the contents of the pantry at home, trying to work out whether I had enough cereal to get me through the week.

Tybalt's elbow introduced itself to my side, none too gently. I managed not to yelp, turning to glare at him instead.

"*What*?" I hissed, voice dangerously low.

He didn't answer. He just jerked his chin toward the front of the room.

I turned to find Arden looking at me, a mixture of amusement and annoyance warring for possession of her face. I winced. A path had opened through the crowd between us. That had happened every time she'd called someone to the front of the room.

Tybalt elbowed me again, clearly trying to urge me forward. Swell. I'd been summoned, and I didn't even know what for.

Please not another County, I thought as I walked to where Arden was waiting. *Or a Barony. Or a puppy. Or anything else I'd have to be responsible for.* At least I didn't have to worry about getting saddled with a Duchy. The only one that was even halfway available was Dreamer's Glass, and Arden had already given that to Li Qin.

"October Daye, sworn to Shadowed Hills, you have done a great service to the throne of the Mists. I, and my household, stand in your debt." Arden's tone was calm and measured, as if there had been no delay at all between her calling my name and me getting a clue. "Your fealty is sworn to another, or I would offer you a place in this Court, to be yours forevermore."

"Uh, yeah," I said. "I'm pretty attached to Shadowed Hills. Um. Sorry."

"And Shadowed Hills is pretty attached to you," she said. "I attempted to convince your liege to release you. He refused."

I shot a startled glance to Sylvester, who was standing to the left of the crowd. Then I smiled. I should have known he'd never let me down.

Arden was speaking again. I wrenched my attention back to her. "But I cannot allow a debt to go unacknowledged," she said. "October Daye, let it be known that on this day, you are recognized as a hero of the realm, with all the responsibilities and privileges that includes. You will be offered safety and succor in any noble household. All doors will be open to you. But all dangers will be laid before you, and we'll call you as soon as we need something large and monstrous slain." She smiled. "You're already doing that part. It won't be a big change."

"Uh." I stared at her.

Arden raised her eyebrows. "Uh?" she echoed.

"Uh," I said again, before I grimaced and managed to say, "I'll try really hard not to disappoint you?"

"I don't think that's the standard response, but you know what? Good enough for me." Arden tapped me on the left shoulder. "Congratulations, Sir October Daye, Hero in the Mists."

The applause of the crowd escorted me all the way back to where Tybalt was waiting for me. He didn't look surprised. In fact, he was smirking, which told me he'd already known this little curveball was coming. "I hate you," I informed him, and kept walking. With Arden's proclamations done, the party was breaking up. The sun had finished rising in the mortal world. If we left now, we could be out of the parking lot before the human rangers started showing up for work. That would mean fewer questions all around since, technically, Muir Woods State Park was closed after sunset.

The fact that human law said the park was closed wasn't a big deal: most fae don't have a lot of respect for human law. Still, the hour was a good reason for me to hustle my little changeling butt out of there. If enough people got out before being seen by humans became a risk, we were more likely to escape without somebody getting arrested and Arden needing to have some poor innocent park ranger's memory wiped.

Sometimes I think it must have been nice to be alive in the days where everyone knew that Faerie existed. Sure, bands of angry humans sometimes tried to kill us with iron and fire, but nobody questioned where we wanted to celebrate the seasons.

Tybalt followed me to the entry hall, where May, Jazz, and Quentin were waiting. May was holding a large canvas bag that smelled suspiciously like sugar cookies. When she saw me, she beamed, held the bag up as if for inspection, and announced, "I raided the kitchen!"

"Of course you did," I said, with a weak smile. "I just got named a hero of the realm. Like, the actual title accessory pack kind of hero, not just 'you do heroic things, gold star and try not to die.'"

"You were already a hero of the realm to us," said my squire. He sounded so sincere that I couldn't even poke fun at the statement. Not that I wanted to. Quentin and I have been through a lot since Sylvester first tried to use him as an errand boy. I refused the message he was supposed to give me, but I kept the messenger. It's all part of my larger pattern of picking up strays.

Jazz yawned as she asked, "So are we getting out of here? Please? Because if we're not leaving, I'm going to go sleep in one of the trees." She was a Raven-maid, a form of skinshifter, and one of the few diurnal races in the primarily nocturnal landscape of Faerie. Things like Yule were hell on her internal clock.

"We're leaving," I said, turning for the exit. We were just in time: I could hear footsteps behind us, signaling the start of the exodus. "Sun's up, and this is a pretty popular commuting route. If we want to make it home by a decent hour, we need to head out now."

"Oh, thank Oberon," said Jazz. "I can sleep in the car."

My skirt made descending the hiking trail connecting Arden's knowe to the main park difficult. I gathered it as high as I dared, exposing my calves, knees, and sensible black flats as I picked my way down the side of the mountain. Tybalt took the lead, offering his hand to help me keep my balance. I didn't object. We'd both been working on accepting help more easily, and it was starting to pay off, at least as far as I was concerned. Jazz nearly fell twice before saying something unpleasant in a language I didn't know, pulling the feathered band out of her hair, and transforming into a raven. She perched on May's shoulder after that, and we made the rest of the descent in silence.

"Did everyone have a nice time?" I asked.

"I ate so much sugar that I think I qualify as an annex to Willy Wonka's factory," said May.

"I liked eating at the high table," said Quentin. There was a hint of wistfulness in his tone, matched by a temporary strengthening of his Canadian accent.

It made sense that eating at the high table was something he'd have missed, coming from the family that ruled the entire continent. I flashed him an understanding smile. Quentin smiled back, and we kept walking.

Muir Woods was peaceful this early in the morning, empty of both the human tourists who would fill it in a few short hours and the swirling shadows that Arden and her illusionists had used to dissuade any illicit nocturnal hikers from setting foot inside. The redwoods stretched on toward forever, and everything smelled of sap, fresh running water, and the green.

This time, it was Tybalt who stopped at the edge of the parking lot. "I must return to the Court of Cats," he said.

"My absence from last night's Yule festivities was forgivable, for it is a great joke for me to be invited to the gatherings of the Divided Courts, but my people need my attention for a time. Will you be well without me?"

"You mean will I pine and die wishing you were there? I think I'll pass. Although you really owe me that 'showing me how much you appreciate my choosing you' thing." I dropped my skirt and leaned up to give him a quick kiss. He slid his arms around my waist, pulling me closer and deepening the kiss into something more. The taste of pennyroyal and musk lingered on his lips, a sweet reminder of his magic.

"Get a room," said May, and kept on walking.

I laughed, pulling away from him. "Okay, when my Fetch starts lecturing us on public displays of affection, that means it's time to stop. I'll see you tonight?"

"Count on it," said Tybalt. He turned and walked back toward the trees. The shadows at the edge of the wood spread for him like a curtain, and he was gone.

I smiled a little goofily as I followed the others to the car. Quentin was draped over the hood, making exaggerated snoring noises. May was just standing there, watching me tolerantly. Jazz had apparently fallen asleep; she was stretched across May's folded arms, still in raven form, not moving.

"Did you have a good Yule?" May asked.

"Not that it's any of your business—"

"It's *totally* my business."

"But yes." I unlocked the car, peering quickly into the backseat before I opened my door. "Quentin, stop faking being asleep and get in. You're not fooling anyone."

My squire grinned as he straightened up. Then he yawned and climbed into the front passenger seat. His eyes were closed by the time I slid behind the wheel.

May got into the back, setting Jazz on the seat next to her long enough to fasten her seat belt. Then she scooped her avian girlfriend back into her arms. "We're good," she said. Having significant others who spent a substantial amount of time as animals—mine a cat, hers a raven—meant we had adjusted the "everyone must wear a seat belt" rule to apply only to people who were currently in a seat belt-friendly form.

As expected, Quentin turned the radio to the local country station as soon as I started the car. Then he closed his eyes again, rolling as far to the side as the seat belt and a seated position would allow, and went to sleep. I smiled as I glanced at the rearview mirror. May was slumped over in the back, cradling Jazz like a stuffed toy.

"Peace at last," I murmured, and started down the mountain separating Muir Woods from the nearest outcropping of human civilization. Don't get me wrong: I was as tired as the rest of them, maybe more, since I was the one who found parties the most draining. The flip side was that escaping a party felt like a stay of execution, and that, combined with the comfort of being back behind the wheel of my faithful VW bug, meant I was more than awake enough to get us home.

We were almost to the base of the mountain when I realized none of us was wearing a human disguise. I swore under my breath and grabbed a handful of shadows from the roof of the car, gripping them between my nails as they tried to squirm away like eels. The smell of copper and freshly cut grass rose as I chanted, rapid-fire, "The trees they do grow high and the leaves they do grow green, many's the hour my own true love I've seen, many's the day I've watched him all alone, he is young but he's surely growing."

The spell, which had been building with each word, burst around me like a soap bubble, accompanied by a brief spike of pain at my temples. I breathed out, my shoulders relaxing. It was a simple blur, but it would do the job; as long as I didn't get pulled over, we should be able to pass any cursory inspection by the other drivers on the road.

A "simple" blur. Two years ago, I wouldn't have been able to manage a blur spell at all, much less cast one on a carful of people, and I would have paid for the attempt with a lot more than a momentary pang of magic-burn. Then again, two years ago, I was more human than fae, and still trying to force my magic into a mold it was never designed to fit. It turns out that when someone isn't Daoine Sidhe, yet keeps trying to scale their workings to Daoine Sidhe specifications, things sometimes go wrong. Who knew? Now, I was more fae than human—it was hard to say how *much* more, it being a matter of reading the balance of my blood, and not something that could be resolved with a scale—and I was more confident in the magic I *did* possess than I'd ever been in my life.

I blamed my years of uncertainty and confusion on my mother. She raised me to think I was Daoine Sidhe like Quentin and Sylvester, a blood-working descendant of Titania. The joke was on me. I was Dóchas Sidhe the whole time, only two generations removed from Oberon himself, and my skill set, while similar, didn't follow the same rules.

Quentin started to snore for real. I grinned to myself and changed the radio station to 80s rock, letting the dulcet tones of Simple Minds fill the car as I hit the gas. Next stop, San Francisco.

Traffic was normally heavy at this hour of the morning, but we were saved by the season: everyone who could be off the road was off the road, using vacation time and sick days to stay home with their families or catch an early flight to Maui. I concentrated on the drive, and in what felt like no time at all, I was turning into the driveway of our two-story Victorian home.

Coming home to an actual house and not a rattrap of

an apartment still felt like a gift every time it happened. Sylvester and Luna Torquill had been in the Bay Area for a long time, and they'd been investing in mortal-world real estate practically from day one. The house had originally been his. Technically it still was, since we'd never bothered to transfer the title, but in reality it was mine, and it would be mine for as long as I wanted it to be. It was *home*. I hadn't realized how much I'd wanted one until I had it.

"Wake up, sleepyheads," I said, turning off the engine and releasing the blur spell at the same time. "I do door-to-door service, but I'm not carrying you to bed."

Quentin mumbled something in sleepy French. I poked him in the arm.

"Wake up, go inside, and go to bed," I commanded. "Come on, move it."

"'M up."

"You're lying." I twisted to look into the back, where May was yawning and unfastening her belt. "Are you going to be able to coax Jazz back to human form?"

"She's pretty easy to coax. She doesn't like to sleep as a raven in the bed," said May, cradling her still-sleeping girlfriend. "I'm always afraid of rolling over and squishing her, so I won't cuddle when she does that."

"Firm but fair." I jabbed Quentin again. "Up. Now."

"I'm up." He sat up, opening his eyes, and glowered at me petulantly before pushing open his door and shambling toward the house like something that had just crawled out of its grave. May followed at about the same pace, Jazz's head resting on her shoulder. I swallowed a laugh, yawned, and got out of the car.

The cats and Spike, my resident rose goblin, met me at the door, complaining in their individual ways about being left alone, neglected and unfed. By the time I finished scooping food into their respective dishes—Purina for the felines, fertilizer for the animate rosebush—

everyone else was gone, vanishing into their respective rooms for the next several hours.

"You're on your own," I informed the pets, and turned to head for the stairs.

Going up a flight of stairs in my dress was about as much fun as doing anything else in it had been. The downside of wearing real formal clothing to a ball, rather than spinning an illusion and calling it a night: I actually had to worry about taking care of the thing. Spider-silk is difficult to tear, stain, or even seriously wrinkle, but it needs to be treated properly if you want it to keep looking its best. I went into my room, closed the door, and began the unnecessarily complicated process of getting ready for bed.

Fifteen minutes later, my dress was hanging in the closet, my hair was in a ponytail, and I was stepping into a pair of sweatpants. A little rummaging in the laundry hamper produced a nightshirt that wasn't too filthy to wear.

"Bed," I moaned, and pulled the blackout curtains over my windows, converting the room into a pleasantly artificial night. With this last chore accomplished and no demands on my attention scheduled until sunset at the earliest, I flopped full-length onto the mattress. I lay there starfished for about half a minute before I remembered how to control my limbs and started squirming under the covers. It would have been nicer to be going to bed with Tybalt, who always provided a pleasant source of warmth and a soothing purr, but sleeping alone had its advantages: for one thing, no one was trying to steal the covers. I nestled myself into a changeling burrito, sticking my head under the pillow for good measure.

The doorbell rang.

I pulled my head from under the pillow and turned to look at the clock, automatically assuming that I'd been asleep for hours and just hadn't noticed. According to the digital readout, it wasn't even eight o'clock in the morning. I'd been in bed for less than ten minutes.

The doorbell rang again.

"Oh, someone's getting murdered today," I muttered, rolling out of the bed. My bathrobe was on the floor near the door. I grabbed it and tugged it on.

The doorbell rang a third time as I was going down the stairs. "I'm *coming!*" I shouted, draping a human disguise around myself with quick, irritated motions of my hands. I would normally have worried about waking everyone else. Under the circumstances, I was more concerned about the doorbell waking them up if I didn't get it to stop ringing.

I wrenched the door open and snarled, *"What?"* with a ferocity that would have made the Luidaeg proud.

Sylvester, who had been raising his hand to ring a fourth time, froze. I did the same, and for a long moment, we stared at each other.

He was wearing a human disguise, and had traded his party finery for a pair of tan slacks and a white cotton shirt with buttoned cuffs. He would have fit in with an amateur theater production of *The Great Gatsby*.

"What the . . . ?" I blinked, relaxing as confusion replaced my anger. "What are you doing here? Why were you ringing the doorbell? Don't you have a key?"

"October," he said. There was something odd about the way he shaped my name, like he hadn't said it aloud in years. "You're here."

"Yeah. Look, it's the start of the day. What's going on?" I stepped to the side, gesturing for him to come inside. "You want some tea, or coffee, or something?"

"You are inviting me in?" He looked so perplexed that I was starting to wonder if something was really wrong.

"Um, yeah."

"Ah. Then, yes; tea would be a delight." He stepped

over the threshold. I moved to shut the door behind him and froze, the scent of his magic tickling the back of my throat.

He smelled like smoke and rotten oranges.

This man wasn't Sylvester Torquill.

THREE

THE WORLD SEEMED to slow down, turning crystalline around me. I automatically flipped the deadbolt as I finished closing the door, moving carefully and deliberately, like I was in a dream. Shutting myself in with my personal bogeyman wasn't the smartest thing I'd ever done, but I didn't think it would make a difference in the grand scheme of things. We weren't both going to walk away from this. I was unarmed and effectively alone as long as the others were asleep — and I prayed they'd stay asleep. There was a chance Simon didn't even know I had roommates. They'd be safe. Whatever he did to me, I just hoped it would be quick, and quiet enough that he wouldn't wake anyone else before he left. I had no illusions about being able to defeat him. There was no way in the world Simon Torquill would have appeared on my doorstep if he didn't feel like he somehow had the upper hand.

I turned to find him studying the hallway walls, his hands folded politely behind his back. His face was visible only in profile, still softened and humanized by the illusion plastered over it. I guess he didn't dare release it. Most people couldn't catch the taste of his magic just by walking past him, but any child of Faerie, however weak, would be able to smell the rot lurking inside him if they were standing nearby when he dropped the spell.

I'm not most people. I've always been incredibly sensitive to the scent of magic, and I knew exactly who he was.

He really did look exactly like Sylvester, even down to the design of his human disguise. It made sense: they were identical twins, after all. They had the same sharp jaw, the same fox-red hair and golden eyes. But where Sylvester's eyes were kind, always ready to smile or forgive, this man's eyes were hard. He'd seen things, *done* things that even a hero of Faerie should never be called upon to witness.

"You've done an excellent job with the place," he said. "It's more untidy than I would have expected, given your upbringing, but it's still good to see someone *living* here. I assume you haven't moved the kitchen?" He took off down the hall, moving with the proprietary speed of someone who knew exactly where he was and believed he had every right to be there. I followed him, trying to swallow the dust-dry feeling in my throat as I scanned everything around me, looking for things I could use as a weapon if necessary.

If necessary. Ha. As if there was any chance weapons *weren't* going to be necessary. I was alone in my hall with Simon Torquill, the man who'd turned me into a fish for fourteen years. I'd been lucky to survive our last encounter. Here and now, even changed as I was by the things I had experienced since then ...

I couldn't win this. I didn't have the power.

Simon stepped through the swinging door to the kitchen, which swung shut behind him, briefly blocking his view of the hall. That was my chance to run, either for the front door or for the stairs, where I could grab my phone and call for help. But that would put May, Jazz, and Quentin in more danger. Even if I screamed for them to get out of the house now, they'd never go if they thought I was in trouble, and they'd be risking themselves for nothing. Simon could cast a spell before anyone would be able to reach me. I knew that from bitter experience, even if I didn't know why he was there.

I stepped into the kitchen.

"Ah, good," said Simon, who was putting a kettle on the stove. "I found your tea, but is there honey? I wasn't sure."

"Look in the basket next to the toaster," I said. It was too domestic and peaceful to be real. I glanced around, hoping for a second that I'd see Karen, the oneiromancer daughter of my friend Stacy, come to help me through my nightmare. There was no one there but Simon and me. I was awake, Oberon save and keep me.

"There it is. Very good." Simon held up two mugs. "Would you like a cup of tea?"

"No, that's okay." I dug my nails into my palms, fighting the urge to grab a knife from the dish drainer and start screaming for him to get out of my house. "I'm not a tea drinker. I keep it around for company."

"Oh, yes. You're more of a coffee girl, if I remember correctly."

I opened my mouth to say that no, I wasn't even drinking much coffee these days, and paused, eyeing him. "You're not even trying, are you?"

"Excuse me?" Simon turned to face me. He had a squeeze bottle of honey in one hand. It was shaped like a bear. Somehow, that struck me as unutterably hysterical.

"I said, you're not even trying. You haven't done *anything* to make me believe that you're Sylvester. You can drop the illusion, *Simon*. I know who you are."

He blinked, disappointment flashing in his eyes. "I never claimed to be my brother, you know," he said. "I actually thought you were inviting *me* inside."

"I'd kiss the Luidaeg before I'd do that."

"And she'd let you, assuming the stories are true."

"What stories?" I asked, unable to stop myself.

"The ones that say you've finally decided to start finding allies, learn your place in this world, and grow into your potential." Simon dropped a teabag into his cup before taking the kettle off the stove and pouring water over it. There hadn't been time for the water to boil—the stove wasn't even on—but it came out hot and steaming all the same. "It's been a great relief. I'd been worried that you were going to break your mother's heart."

"What the hell are you talking about? Don't talk about my mother. You don't have any right to talk about her."

"October, believe me. If anyone is allowed to talk about Amandine, it's me." He added a generous amount of honey to his tea, releasing the illusion that had made him look human at the same time. The smell of smoke and rotten oranges filled the room. The change did nothing to make him look less like his brother. Raising an eyebrow, he asked, "Well? Will you do me the same courtesy?"

"I don't want to do anything for you," I said, through gritted teeth. I released my illusion all the same. It was a small thing, and antagonizing him wasn't going to do me any good.

For a moment—less than a second, but long enough for me to see—his expression changed, arrogance and calculating coldness turning into something that looked almost like longing. The moment passed as quickly as it had come, and he nodded. "Yes, this is much more what you should have been from the start. I'm sorry, my dear, but Amy did you no favors when she spun the balance of your blood from gold into straw on the wheel of her powers. It seems you've done better for yourself, now that you've taken the spindle in your own two hands."

"You know, as metaphors go, you probably couldn't have chosen a much creepier one."

"Sometimes 'accuracy' and 'creepiness' go hand in hand." Simon sipped his tea, made a face, and added more honey. "You're surprisingly calm. From the reports I'd heard, I expected you to attack me as soon as you realized who I was."

"I've learned some self-control," I said. "I can't beat you. I know that."

"So you're giving up in the face of a greater adversary?"

When he put it like that, it stung. That didn't make it the wrong decision. "You haven't attacked me yet. I figured I'd wait for you to make the first move."

Simon sighed. Then, slowly, he put his tea and the bear-shaped bottle of honey down on the counter, seeming to stretch the action out so that it took longer than was strictly necessary. Finally, he turned back to me, spread his hands, and said, "I am not the enemy you think I am."

I stared at him. "What?"

"I know you've painted me as some great bogeyman, some terrible threat, but —"

"You kidnapped your brother's wife and daughter, you stranded them in a realm of eternal darkness that drove Rayseline out of her mind, and you turned me into a *fish*." I didn't mean to argue with him. The words came out anyway, dragged forth by years of anger and fear. "You *laughed*. You turned me into a fish and you left me there to *die*. How dare you tell me that you're not the enemy I think you are? You are *exactly* the enemy that I think you are."

"It's true. I did those things. But, October, if you'd just listen to me —"

"What do you want, Simon? What are you doing here? I didn't invite you here. I never wanted anything to do with you. Now tell me what you're trying to accomplish, or get out."

"October." His tone was chiding, the sort of voice you'd use for a wayward child or an unruly pet. "Is that any way to treat a guest?"

"You're not my guest!" My temper finally snapped. I lunged for the dish drainer, fumbling for the knives.

Simon's stasis spell caught me before I was halfway there. I froze, arm outstretched, one foot off the ground. Gravity no longer seemed to be a factor. The smell of smoke and rotten oranges was heavy in the confined kitchen air.

"I'd hoped we could do this in a more civilized manner," said Simon. I heard the faint clink of his mug against the counter as he picked up his tea, followed by footsteps as he walked around me. He stopped where I could see him. "You are your mother's daughter. I mean that in the best way and the worst way at the same time. She always inspired contradictions."

Held by his magic, all I could do was glare, and rage silently against the horrible symmetry of his intrusion. The last time my life had seemed to mean something, Simon Torquill had come and taken it all away from me. It made perfect, horrible sense that he would do it again.

"I never wanted you to hate me, October. Far from it. I wanted to be . . . I wanted to be a part of your life, but I was never given the chance. That's why I did what I did. That's why I saved you."

Wait, *what?*

He must have seen the question in my eyes. Simon sighed, and said, "Forgive me. I didn't think about what fourteen years would do to your mortal life, because I never had a mortal life to lose. I honestly didn't think you'd remain enchanted so long, either. Amandine's work went deeper than I realized. But you won yourself free, in the end, and—" He stopped, mouth working wordlessly, like something was preventing whatever he wanted to say from getting through. The smell of smoke grew stronger.

For a second, it felt like the bonds holding me suspended in the air were slipping. I tried to move, and they snapped tight again. Simon raised a chiding finger.

"Please don't fight. I don't want either of us getting hurt." He shook his head. "It seems my geas is still intact, despite its not having been renewed in years. I cannot speak the name of my employer. Let me say, instead, that I was paid to do what I did. I was promised something I could not resist, and I was instructed to steal my brother's wife and child. They were to be returned as soon as ... my employer's ... goals had been met. I didn't know those goals included your death. I swear, on the root and the branch, I didn't know. Even if I'd been willing to kill you, I wouldn't have been able to meet your mother's eyes after I had slain her child."

He reached for my face, hesitating for only an instant before completing the motion. His fingertips caressed my cheek, and the spell that held me wouldn't even allow me to shudder.

Simon looked at me, eyes pleading, and said, "I transformed you to save you, and then I ran. I had no way of knowing I'd be branded a traitor by the one who had set all these things in motion or that, in my absence, Luna and Rayseline would remain captive. I swear. On your mother's name, on my sister's grave, I swear it."

It was strange, but I almost believed him. He sounded so earnest, and so sad ... and that did nothing to change the fact that I was held suspended in a stasis spell in my own kitchen, and that I couldn't stop him from touching me.

He took a deep breath. "October—" he began. He never had the opportunity to finish.

"Hey, fucko!" Jasmine's shout was loud enough to wake the dead. It would almost certainly wake anyone else in the house who was still asleep. I guess there's something to be said for having someone naturally diurnal around. She charged into the kitchen and into my field of vision, my old friend the aluminum baseball bat clutched firmly in her hands. She had it raised like she was going to hit a home run, using Simon's skull as the ball.

Simon turned toward her, raking the fingers of his free hand through the air. The smell of smoke and rotting oranges rose around him in an instant, thick and cloying. Jazz made a sound that was half human, half challenging raven, and swung her bat. Simon swept his hand down, pointing at her, and said a word that was less language and more the sound of water on rocks.

Jazz screamed as she fell. I could live to be older than Oberon himself, and I would never be able to forget that sound.

The echoes of Jazz's scream were still ringing in my ears when Simon turned back to me, eyes blazing with a strange combination of fury and sorrow. "I didn't want it to happen like this," he said, and followed the statement with another of those horrible, misshapen words. The smell of rotting oranges grew stronger, all but obscuring the smell of smoke.

I don't know what I did. I don't think I could have done it if I'd understood what needed to be done; I wouldn't have known where to begin. But I was angry, and I was scared, and when he flung his spell at me, I reacted on instinct alone. The stasis spell was an inconvenience, and so I pushed it aside as I snatched the shape of his magic out of the air and flung it back at him as hard as I could.

The spell burned my hands, and I fell as soon as the stasis broke, hitting the kitchen floor in a heap. Somehow, that didn't matter. Simon screamed, a shrill, agonized sound, and turned, running for the hall. There was something wrong with the way he was moving, but that wasn't my concern; not right here, not right now. All my attention was reserved for Jazz, who was crumpled in a heap on the floor, her hands webbed together and covered in shining scales, her face mercifully concealed by her hair.

She wasn't breathing.

"Oh, sweet Maeve, no." I scrambled to her side and rolled her onto her back, trying not to look at the twisted outline of what had been her face. The raw pink slashes of newly formed gills scarred her neck, lying flat and unmoving against the skin. I didn't know where to start looking for a pulse, and so I didn't bother to try; I just braced my hands on her chest and shoved downward, calling on what little I remembered of CPR as I tried to force her to respond. "Come on, Jazz, *come on!* You're not allowed to die on me!"

She didn't respond. I heard the front door slam. I kept doing chest compressions; I couldn't think of anything else to do. There was a scuffing sound from the direction of the hall. I turned, hands still moving, to see May standing frozen in the kitchen doorway.

"Toby . . . ?" she said.

"Simon was here I thought it was Sylvester but it was Simon and he put me in a stasis spell only Jazz came in and he hit her I don't know what he hit her with I think it was a transformation spell I broke the stasis but I wasn't fast enough and now she won't wake up!" The words tumbled out in a rush, undisciplined and wild.

May stared at me for a split-second. Then, pulling herself together with an almost visible force of will, she walked over to kneel by Jasmine's side, sliding her hands beneath mine and taking over the chest compressions before I could tell her not to. "You said you broke Simon's spell. How did you do that?"

"I . . . I don't know." It had just happened, too fast for me to really pay attention to anything beyond survival. "I just reacted. He was throwing another spell at me, and I knew I couldn't let it hit me. I wouldn't be able to help Jazz if he knocked me out or turned me into something."

"Instinct is a wonderful thing. It doesn't care about the lies our parents told us, or the ones we tell ourselves." May kept working. Her voice was unbearably calm; she sounded like an undertaker's assistant preparing for the biggest job of her career. "We don't have much time. Close your eyes, and listen to me."

"May—"

"Oberon's balls, Toby, close your eyes and *listen to me*." The facade of calm broke on her last words, showing a vein of raw, terrified need beneath it. "She's not breathing, okay? But she's not dead. I know dead, and she's not there yet. You can save her, but only if you listen. Only if you do exactly what I say. *Please*."

I gaped at her, and then closed my eyes, too dumbfounded to argue. I felt May pull her hands away as she stopped the chest compressions, and then her fingers closed around mine, pressing them to Jazz's torso, so tight that they almost hurt.

"What does Simon's magic look like?"

"It doesn't *look* like anything. It's magic. Magic is invisible. But it smells like smoke and rotten oranges." Traces of it were still hanging in the kitchen air, turning it foul and horrible.

"That's just the surface. Look closer. What do you see?"

I frowned, brows knotting together, and tried to concentrate on her question, rather than the deadly stillness of Jazz's chest beneath my hands. Magic doesn't look like anything, unless it's the glitter of pixie dust or the wispy smoke that sometimes follows the Djinn. Magic is intangible, smells and sounds and flavors on the wind. Nothing that lasts. Nothing that makes a mark on the world around it. Simon's magic was smoke and oranges, and it lingered in the throat like a bruise, but it was still transitory, just like everyone else's.

"Try *harder*," May said sharply.

Right. I screwed my eyes more tightly shut, trying to think. What does magic look like? What would *Simon's* magic look like? The smell of it was horrible and rancid; it would have to look a lot like that, all slimy lines and angles—but sharp ones, precise and exact. He might be a bastard, but he was never sloppy. Gray-and-orange lines, twisted together into a tight, complicated net of knots and hidden snares that would catch you if you weren't careful. The more I considered it, the more it seemed like I *could* see it, wrapped around the body under my fingers, pulsing with a sluggish, sickly light.

Sounding distant now, May said, "You see it." It wasn't a question.

I nodded slowly. The lines of it were getting brighter as I focused on them. "It's like a web," I said.

"Where's the weak spot, Toby? Every web has a weak spot."

That was easy. "Over the heart."

"Good." She shifted my hands to the side, pressing them over Jazz's heart. "You can see the weak spot, Toby. Now break it."

"What? May, I can't—"

"Break it."

There was no arguing with her tone. Wincing, I hunched down, and focused on the lines. I still wasn't certain they were real, but they were brighter now, either because I was closer to them, or because I was achieving a state of serious delusion. The smell of my own magic was starting to rise around me, summoned by my tension. Oddly, the copper and cut grass smell of it just brought the lines into even clearer focus, making it harder to dismiss them as a fiction.

"Let go," I said.

May pulled her hands away.

Moving my fingers with careful deliberation, I slid them under the network of lines, hooking them into two of the knots. My head began to throb, the pain beginning at my temples and then radiating outward. The web lifted up with little resistance, almost clinging to my hands. I tugged until it was a few inches off Jazz's body, and then pulled as hard as I could, forcing the strands apart until they reached their bearing limit. The throbbing in my head got worse as the smell of smoke, mixed with copper, sizzled in the air around us.

The net snapped with a backlash that was only half physical, but which sent me tumbling backward, smacking my head hard against the kitchen floor. I groaned, as much from surprise as from pain, and lay still for a few seconds before pushing myself upright again, expecting to see May flung sobbing across her girlfriend's body.

I saw no such thing. May had pulled Jazz's head into her lap and was stroking the other woman's hair. She was crying, yes, but they were relieved tears; the smile on her face made that as plain as day.

"Jazz?" I asked. The pain from my head's introduction to the floor was fading. The pain from breaking Simon's spell wasn't. It was almost a relief to have my limits so clearly delineated.

"She's going to be okay," said May. She looked up, smiling brilliantly. "If you can move, come over here."

If I could move? That didn't sound encouraging. I moved my fingers carefully, and found they still responded to my commands. If anyone noticed that I had a headache—something I tend to telegraph by wincing a lot—I could blame it on my impact with the kitchen floor. Blunt force trauma excuses a lot of things. I got onto my hands and knees and crawled over to them.

Jazz remained supine on the floor, eyes closed . . . but

they were *normal* eyes, set in a normal face. What little I'd seen of her before I ripped the net away told me that this was a great improvement. I glanced downward. Thin red scabs ringed her neck, but the gills were gone. Her chest was moving normally, rising and falling in slow, shallow hitches as she breathed.

"She's alive?" I whispered.

"She's going to be fine," said May, still smiling through her tears. "All you had to do was listen to me."

"But . . ." I pushed myself into a standing position, reeling a little as my head throbbed in time with the motion. "I don't even know what I *did*."

"You know the trick with the dresses? The one where we'd take something the false Queen had transformed, and then you'd pull on the spell until it turned into something else?"

I nodded. I quickly regretted the motion.

May didn't seem to notice. Her eyes were back on her girlfriend's face. She was looking at Jazz like she was some sort of miracle. Considering what had just happened, maybe she was. "You finally figured out how to unravel fresh spells the same way you reweave them. That's what you did. That's what you did for me."

". . . oh," I said. I didn't really understand, but I wasn't sure that mattered. Jazz wasn't going to die, and she wasn't going to spend the next fourteen years of her life living in a fishpond. Those were the important things.

"Thank you," whispered May.

Those words—those forbidden words—were enough to finally shock me out of my shock. I straightened. "I need to go," I said.

"Go? Go where?"

"Sylvester. He has to be told that Simon is back. He has to . . . I have to go."

"Wouldn't it be faster to, you know, *call him?*"

Yes: yes, it would have been faster. But I needed to

see him. When I tried to picture Sylvester's face, I kept seeing Simon's instead, with those cold, hooded eyes staring at me, daring me to challenge him. I needed to see my liege. I needed to tell him what had happened, and let him put his arms around me and tell me that he would keep me safe this time. Even if it was a lie, it was a lie I needed.

So I told a lie of my own. "They're identical twins, May. He may have gotten into Shadowed Hills already; who would stop him?" I shook my head. "I need to go to Shadowed Hills. I can't know I'm actually speaking to Sylvester unless I can taste his magic."

"At least take Quentin with you. He's your squire."

I started to take a breath to argue, paused, and tried pleading instead. "Jazz can't be moved yet. You'll need help if Simon comes back."

"I'll call Danny." May shook her head. "Take him. I get that you don't want to leave us alone, and I get that you don't want to put Quentin in danger, but you're forgetting that I remember what Simon did to you. I remember it like he did it to me. I can't let you go alone."

I paused a second time. May and I mostly tried not to talk about our shared memories these days. It was too confusing, for both of us. But she knew better than anyone else in the world what Simon had done. She'd gone through it, too, in her way. "If he's awake, I'll consider it," I said finally. "Now, I'm going to get some clothes, grab my weapons, and ward the crap out of this place. Stay inside. Don't answer the door for anybody. Do you understand me?"

"I do," she said. "Toby . . ."

"Don't tell me to be careful. We both know that's not going to happen."

"I wasn't going to tell you to be careful." Her eyes narrowed, mouth twisting in a vengeful line. "I was going to tell you to get the bastard who hurt my girlfriend."

"Oh, don't worry," I said. "I will." Maybe it was foolish of me to make promises I couldn't be sure of keeping, but Simon Torquill had done more than enough to earn whatever he had coming to him. He'd come into my home; he'd hurt my family. He'd gone too far, and this time, finally, he was going to pay for everything he'd done.

FOUR

CAGNEY AND LACEY were curved on my pillow like sleeping commas when I opened the bedroom door. Either the chaos in the kitchen hadn't filtered up the stairs—unlikely, given Jazz—or the cats hadn't cared. I leaned over and pulled the pillow out from under them, sending them sprawling. They opened their blue Siamese eyes and squalled, protesting this rough treatment.

"I needed you awake, and I don't have time to be polite," I snapped, throwing the pillow on the floor. I started yanking off my nightclothes, letting them fall where they landed. "Simon Torquill was just here. That name doesn't mean anything to you, but it'll mean something to Tybalt. I need you to tell him I've left for Shadowed Hills, and that he should find me as soon as he can."

The cats stopped complaining and simply looked at me, assuming the classic sphinx poses practiced by felines around the world. I shook my head.

"He's at Court. I've intruded enough there recently." I knew he'd be angry at me for leaving before he could join me, but this was part of the balance we had to strike.

Sometimes, I had to take care of myself, no matter how much it upset him, just like sometimes, he had to take care of me, no matter how much it upset *me.*

The cats kept staring at me. I shook my head again, digging through the mess on the floor until I found a pair of reasonably clean jeans. "I don't care how mad he's going to be. He can be mad at me. Just tell him, all right? Tell him Simon is back. Tell him Simon came to the house. Simon hurt Jazz. Tell him . . ." I hesitated. None of the things I wanted to say felt right, and so I shook my head and said, "Just tell him to hurry."

Cagney meowed once, a sharp, almost disdainful sound. Then she jumped off the bed and ran out the bedroom door. Lacey followed her. I looked after them for a few precious seconds. They were both indoor cats; I'd never caught them outside the house. They still had a way of getting to Tybalt when they needed to. The Court of Cats is open to all felines, and they all know how to get there. He would hear. He would find me.

I got dressed as fast as I could, yanking on my shoes and belting my knife around my waist. After a moment's hesitation I grabbed my sword from where it hung on the closet door. I still wasn't good with it, despite Sylvester's many patient hours of training, but it would keep the fight farther away from me, if it came down to that. The way I was feeling right now, anything that kept the fight at a distance was a good thing. The last thing I put on was my leather jacket, shrugging it over my shoulders and taking a small degree of reassurance from its familiar weight.

"I can do this," I said. "He isn't going to be there, and even if he were, he's not the bogeyman. He's just a man. I can beat him."

They may have been lies, but even lies have power if you repeat them often enough. I took a breath to steady myself, turned, and opened the bedroom door.

Quentin was leaning against the hallway wall, already dressed to go, with his own sword belted by his side. He raised his head and looked at me coolly. His bronze hair was wet and slicked back from his face, a concession to the shower he hadn't had time to take. "I thought you might forget to wake me, so I got ready," he said. There was no quarter in his expression: he knew damn well that I'd been thinking about leaving him behind, and he wasn't having it.

Tough. "I didn't wake you because you need to get some sleep. As your knight, it's important for me to look out for your health."

"You didn't wake me because you don't want me coming with you."

"Oh, right, silly me. I didn't want to drag my squire into pointless danger."

Quentin narrowed his eyes. "You would have woken me before you knew I was the Crown Prince."

That made me pause, but only for a second. Quentin was my squire, yes, but he was in the Mists under a blind fosterage: no one was supposed to know who his parents were, and even though I'd known him for years, I hadn't learned their identity until recently. It turned out that was because they were the High King and Queen of the Westlands—a Kingdom better known as "North America" in mortal circles. He was going to rule a continent one day. Assuming he stayed alive that long, which was by no means guaranteed while he was living with me.

In the end, I decided to go with aggressive honesty. My headache was enough to make anything else seem like too much work. "Guilty as charged. I didn't wake you because I don't want you anywhere near Simon Torquill, okay? This is the man who turned me into a fish for fourteen years. Now he's trying to feed me some bullshit line about how he did it to 'save me,' which means he's delusional on top of everything else. So, yeah, you're staying home. I'm not going to be the girl who gets the Crown Prince killed."

"I'm still your squire. That comes first until my training is finished," Quentin shot back. "I'm not staying behind. You know I can follow you. Do you really want to make me do that?"

I glared at him. "I hate you."

"I know."

"You will do exactly what I say at all times. That includes backing off if I say something is too dangerous for you. Do you understand?"

"You're my knight," he said, almost cheerful now that he knew he was getting his way. "I do what you tell me to do."

"That'll be a cold day in Mag Mell," I muttered, and stalked toward the stairs. "Come on. We need to ward this place to kingdom come before we get on the road."

We walked down the stairs side by side, our shoulders brushing the walls. I managed to swallow most of my relief—I wasn't going out there alone—but I couldn't swallow my dread. The only place I knew for sure that Simon *wasn't* was the house. By leaving it, I exposed myself to him, wherever he might be lurking. I took some small comfort in knowing that the spell he'd thrown at me had hit him. Hopefully, the bastard was a pigeon or something by now.

May and Jazz were no longer in the kitchen. My former Fetch had dragged or carried her unconscious girlfriend into the living room, and was busy warding the windows while Jasmine slept on the couch. May looked around when Quentin and I appeared in the doorway.

"I didn't wake him up on purpose," she said. "He must have heard the noise from the kitchen, same as I did."

"I'm a little insulted that you all thought you could have a major fight in the house and not wake me up," said Quentin.

"You're a teenage boy. You could sleep through a nuclear bomb. Now go ward the front door and the mail slot against intrusions."

"Don't try to leave without me," he said, and ran off to do as he'd been told.

I watched him go, managing to keep my expression mostly composed until he was out of sight. Then I turned back to May, allowing my fear to show. "He's not going to let me leave him behind."

"No, he's not." She muttered a line from what sounded like a They Might Be Giants song, waggling her fingers at the window as she spoke. The smell of cotton candy and ashes filled the room, layering on top of the traces of her magic that had already been present. She turned back to me. "That's good. You'd worry about him just as much if you let him out of your sight, and you're not exactly rational where Simon is concerned."

"He tried to turn your girlfriend into a fish!"

"I'm not exactly rational where Simon is concerned, either," she said wearily. She walked back across the living room and perched on the arm of the couch, reaching down to stroke Jazz's hair. "I'd be the worst kind of backup possible right now—the kind who just wants to go home and take care of someone she loves. But that doesn't mean I want you going out alone."

"I told the cats to find Tybalt," I said, feeling somehow ashamed of myself for wanting to run before any of my allies could put themselves in the line of fire for me. I couldn't handle it if they got hurt. Not by this. Not by *him*.

"That's a start." May looked up, meeting my eyes. There was nothing soft in her face, not now; in that moment, she looked like an avenging angel. "Find him. Hurt him. Please."

"I'll do my best." Footsteps in the hall behind me signaled Quentin's return. I turned as he skidded into view. "Ready?"

Relief suffused his features. "I thought you'd try to sneak out while I was distracted."

"Nah. What kind of knight would I be if I didn't endanger your life for no good reason?"

He smiled—a brief, forced expression that died as soon as he looked past me to Jazz's sleeping form. "A bad one," he said.

"I guess that's true. May? Call if there's any change."

"I will," she said. "Open roads. Kick his ass."

"You got it," I said, and went.

Quentin and I paused by the back door long enough to spin human disguises and drape them over ourselves like shrouds. Fear and anger made the casting faster than usual, even though the spell itself made my head throb. Strong emotions have always fueled my illusions that way, even back when I believed I was Daoine Sidhe, when illusions were supposed to be part of my birthright.

"How many traffic laws are you planning to break?" Quentin asked, as we walked out to the car, checked the backseat for unwanted passengers, and got inside.

I fastened my belt, stuck the key in the ignition, and bared my teeth in the semblance of a smile. "All of them," I said, and hit the gas.

Quentin seemed to have been expecting that answer. He grabbed a handful of air, singing a verse from a song about boats—the kid had an endless supply of songs about boats—as his magic rose and burst, filling the car with the smell of steel and heather. I felt the weight of his don't-look-here spell settle over us as we reached the end of the driveway. It was a more sophisticated illusion than the one that made us seem human. It would keep us from being pulled over or ticketed during the drive, and all I had to do was remember that most of the other drivers couldn't see me, which could make avoiding a collision a little more exciting than usual. It was a worthy tradeoff, especially considering the land-speed records that I was about to break.

On a good day, with no traffic, it takes about an hour to get from my house in San Francisco to my liege's knowe in Pleasant Hill, the mortal suburb that conceals the fae Duchy of Shadowed Hills. There was traffic. Not as bad as it would have been during rush hour, but enough that despite breaking every posted speed limit and a few rules of common sense, it was still almost ninety minutes later when we reached the parking lot at Paso Nogal Park. I pulled into the first available parking space, nerves rattled from the drive, and unfastened my seat belt.

"Quentin, I want you to stay close," I said, twisting in my seat to look toward my squire. "We don't know where Simon is. No unnecessary risks."

"Okay," he said. The scent of steel and heather wafted through the air as his don't-look-here popped around us.

"Good." I started to reach for my door. My hand found empty air. It took a few precious seconds for me to realize someone else had gotten there first, wrenching the door open; then a hand was closing around my upper arm, hauling me out of the car.

My first instinct was to reach for my knife. Fortunately, my eyes were faster than my hands; I had just closed my fingers around the hilt when I recognized my captor, even if I wasn't accustomed to seeing him this disheveled. I stared at him. Tybalt stared back, the banded green of his eyes muted by the illusion that made him seem human.

"Are you hurt?" he demanded.

"Hello to you, too, Tybalt." I breathed in, tasting his heritage, just to be sure. Simon might have been able to make himself look like Tybalt, but he would never have been able to pass himself off as Cait Sidhe; not to me, not to my particular set of skewed magical abilities. I relaxed as my magic confirmed that yes, this was Tybalt. There were other Cait Sidhe in the world, but he was the only one who would be looking at me with such a perfect mix of terror and exasperation.

"Why didn't you wait at the house?" He let go of my arm. "I came as soon as the cats reached me, but you had already gone."

"Look at it this way," I said. "If I wasn't there, Simon had no reason to come back."

That was the wrong thing to say. Tybalt's face contorted with sudden fury, washing everything else away. "He found you once," he said, voice low and dangerous. "He should never have been allowed to come near you again."

"But he did, and I survived," I said. "Now come on. We need to tell Sylvester his brother's back in town." I took a breath before adding, "He probably wants to get his hands on Simon, and he may have some idea why Simon would come back to the Mists. I think that's the sort of thing we need to know." And I could confirm that Sylvester was who I thought he was. If I'd been Simon, the first thing I would have done was replace my brother. Most people aren't as sensitive to the scent of magic as I am. He could have gotten away with it, as long as he'd distracted Luna and kept me—and my mother, I suppose—far away from Shadowed Hills. Simon might have had ways to cross the Bay Area faster than I could manage in a car. He could be the acting Duke by now.

Tybalt stared at me for a moment. Then, with a shake of his head, he moved to follow me up the hill that would lead us to the entrance to Shadowed Hills.

Quentin moved faster than either of us, although he kept his word and stayed close, never roving more than a few yards away as he went through the complex series of steps and turns necessary to unlock the door into the knowe. I slowed down until Tybalt and I were walking side by side, then reached over and slid my hand into his, lacing our fingers together.

"You have no idea how terrified I was when Cagney and Lacey came to the Court of Cats and told me you'd been attacked," he said, voice pitched low to keep it from carrying to where Quentin was now running circles around a hawthorn bush.

"I have some idea," I said, ducking under an oak branch. "I'm sorry. I couldn't wait."

"It would have been safer to take the Shadow Roads."

"That assumes you'd be available immediately. You were, but that's not the point. I couldn't wait when there was a chance that Sylvester was in danger." I dropped his hand long enough for us to run our own circles around the hawthorn.

When we were done, Tybalt reclaimed my hand. "That argument has merit. A pity it's not the real reason you made this journey."

"No, it's not," I admitted. "I just . . . I need to see him. I keep closing my eyes and seeing Simon's face."

"That, I can appreciate. You cannot, however, force me to like it."

"No, I can't. But I can be glad you're here now." I paused before chuckling to myself.

Tybalt gave me a sidelong look. "What is it?"

"Just thinking. The last time Simon Torquill came into my life, you and I were what, enemies? Adversaries? Definitely not friends."

"I was certainly not sleeping with you at the time," said Tybalt, the ghost of a smile flitting across his lips.

I managed not to grin in relief. That smile, brief as it had been, was all I could have asked for. A smiling Tybalt was a Tybalt who was still capable of stepping back and looking at the situation rationally. I loved him, but even I could find him frightening when he was fixated on vengeance. Not that Simon didn't deserve a little vengeance;

it was just that I wanted him alive to answer my questions when it was over.

We passed the final obstacle to find Quentin waiting by the door in the burnt-out old oak tree, an expression of polite disinterest on his face. I let go of Tybalt's hand and approached the door, murmuring, "Didn't hear a thing, did you?" to my squire as I passed him.

"Nope," he said, without hesitation.

I smirked, raised my hand, and knocked.

Only a few seconds passed before the door was opened by a black-haired teenage girl in the livery of Shadowed Hills. Half the livery, anyway: she was wearing a proper page's tunic, but her breeches had mysteriously vanished, replaced by blue jeans and tennis shoes. Quentin stiffened with automatic dismay, his own training doubtless providing a running inner commentary on how inappropriate her attire was. I just smiled, amused despite my exhaustion and the events of the day.

"Hi, Chelsea," I said. "Can we come in?"

Chelsea Ames was a full-blooded Tuatha de Dannan, and the daughter of the head of Sylvester's guard, a man named Etienne. She was going to be an immensely powerful teleporter when the potion that was currently blocking her powers wore off. For the moment, however, she had no magic at all, so it was no real surprise when she frowned at me, unrecognizing.

"You are . . . ?" she asked.

"Toby," I said. My human disguise used to look more like my true face. That was a while ago. I indicated my companions. "This is Quentin and Tybalt. You know us all. Now please, can we come in? I need to talk to the Duke."

"Toby!" Her confusion fled, replaced by delight. "Wow, I didn't know you were coming over today! Um . . . the Duke's asleep. That whole daylight thing, you know?" She stood aside to let us enter the knowe.

"Oh, don't worry," I said, unable to keep a note of grim certainty from creeping into my voice. "He'll want to see me."

The look on Chelsea's face as she closed the door told me just how disturbing I sounded. "I, um ... you guys wait here, okay? I'm going to go get my dad." She took off without waiting for an answer, running down the hall and skidding out of sight around a corner.

Chelsea and I met under strange circumstances—something that's true of me and all the teenagers in my life. Chelsea's mother had raised her knowing that she was a changeling, but not knowing exactly what that meant, and when Chelsea's powers activated, Bridget had had no idea how to cope. Etienne might have been able to help, but he'd been unaware of Chelsea's existence. Lots of complications later, Chelsea was purely fae—a consequence of my having burned out her human blood in order to save her from her own out-of-control teleportation—and her parents were finally living together. It seemed to be working out for them so far, thank Oberon. Bridget would not have taken being permanently separated from her daughter well at all, and that would have been unavoidable if she had chosen not to stay with Etienne.

Sometimes I think Faerie is overly hard on the children it creates when it brushes up against the mortal world. And then I pause and realize that it's even harder on our parents.

"She's a good choice for daytime door duty," I said, as I released my human disguise. Tybalt and Quentin did the same. "She's full-blooded fae, but she hasn't gone nocturnal yet."

"She's a *terrible* choice for door duty," said Quentin. "She doesn't know any of the proper forms, she can't see through illusions or even know for sure when someone's wearing them, and did you see what she was wearing?" He sounded most offended about the last part.

I smiled at him, shaking my head. "My little conservative."

"I may disagree with his assessment of the young lady's attire, but I cannot argue with her lack of powers," said Tybalt, slowly. "If she cannot see someone's true nature, how is she to bar your enemies from entry?"

"Oh, that's never been the point of door duty here." I started walking. If Etienne wanted to talk to me, he could come and find me. "If an enemy showed up, she'd let them in. Probably offer them tea and scones or something, too."

Tybalt blinked at me. "I . . . what?"

"Sylvester is a retired hero. He doesn't get to have much fun these days, and most of what he does get is interrupted by his knights insisting that he's not supposed to risk himself without really good reasons," I said. "An enemy making it into the knowe isn't a problem. It's a treat. An enemy making it *out* of the knowe, on the other hand . . ."

"I will never understand the Divided Courts," muttered Tybalt darkly.

"If it helps at all, neither will I," I said.

The halls of Shadowed Hills were built to house an army, with smooth marble floors and high ceilings that could accommodate any number of aerial or oversized fae. I've seen Giants walking there, shoulders a little hunched, but heads still not hitting the ceiling. One thing was for sure: I didn't envy the Hobs and Brownies whose job it was to keep the chandeliers and stained glass windows glittering.

Ropes of roses and holly circled every window, acknowledging the season while steadfastly refusing to abandon the flowers that had given the Duchy much of its reputation. Luna, Sylvester's wife, was a Blodynbryd, a rare form of Dryad tied to roses instead of to a single tree. She was also one of the greatest gardeners in Faerie, thanks to a combination of her innate nature and centuries of practice. The roses, and all the other flowers in the Duchy, were hers.

We walked until we reached a filigreed silver gate that led to a solid wall instead of a hallway or a courtyard garden. I stopped, turning to Tybalt and Quentin.

"Sylvester will forgive me for intruding on his private quarters," I said. "I'm not so sure he'd forgive me for bringing company. Will you wait out here, and trust that I'm not going to find a way to get myself killed while I'm waking the Duke?" Assuming it was Sylvester in there, and not his brother. I had every confidence that if I screamed, my boys would come for me.

"You're planning to wake a man who once defeated an entire Goblin army with a sword, despite his arm having been broken in an earlier engagement," said Tybalt dryly. "I believe waking the Duke is an excellent way to get yourself killed, should you startle him."

"Then I'll do my best not to startle him," I said.

Tybalt sighed. "We will wait here."

"Good. I'll be back as soon as I've told Sylvester what's going on."

I turned to the gate. It looked delicate, like I could have peeled it off the wall with one hand. Appearances can be deceiving. This was one of the few doors in the knowe that was supposed to be locked to anyone who hadn't been formally invited to use it, and the enchantment that was woven into the metal of the gate itself did a pretty good job of enforcing that restriction. Gently, I reached out and rested my fingers on the latch.

"Hey," I said. I was speaking to the knowe, and not to either of my companions. In Faerie, sometimes, intent is everything. "It's me, October. I really need to see Sylvester. It's important. I know you're only supposed to open for family, but he *is* my family, just not by blood. Will you please let me in?"

The latch turned under my hand, and the door swung inward of its own accord, dispersing the seemingly solid wall like it was mist and revealing a small, circular garden under a deep purple Summerlands sky. I glanced back at Tybalt and Quentin, flashing them what I hoped was a reassuring smile, before stepping through the gate onto the cobblestone garden path. I heard the gate swing shut behind me, and when I turned to look, there was nothing there but an ivy-covered garden wall.

"Right," I said, and turned again, starting down the path.

Some of Luna's gardens were showy and elaborate, intended to serve as living jewels in the crown of Shadowed Hills. This garden was private, and its design supported that. The only flowers were roses, and they were more subdued than the riotous flowers that grew elsewhere in the knowe. Most of them were striated in yellow and blue, the colors of the Duchy itself. Marble benches ringed the garden, allowing for quiet contemplation. There were several cobblestone walking paths, including the one that I was on. They came together to circle a decorative fountain before they branched out, leading to smaller, freestanding silver gates.

This was only the third time I'd been in this part of the knowe. The first time, I'd been coming to warn Sylvester about an attempt on Luna's life, and I'd been elf-shot for my troubles, nearly dying on the cobblestones I was walking along. I looked down, trying to find traces of the trauma in the stones under my feet. It wasn't there. Even when I breathed deeply, looking for traces of the blood, it wasn't there. There was no sign that anything bad had ever happened here. But I remembered, and I walked a little faster as I tried to outpace that memory.

If I remembered correctly, the gate to my right would lead to Rayseline's quarters. I turned left, walking up to the gate and stopping, unsure how to proceed. "I don't suppose there's a doorbell somewhere on this thing, is there?" I asked, only half rhetorically. The gate didn't answer me. I sighed and reached for the handle.

As soon as my fingers touched the metal of the gate it began to chime, quietly at first, but louder and faster with each passing second, until it was like I was standing in a forest of wind chimes. I yanked my hand back like I'd been burned. The chiming continued.

Then, with a final loud chord, the chiming stopped, the handle turned, and the gate swung open to reveal a tall, redheaded Daoine Sidhe in breeches and a sleeping shirt, squinting slightly in the twilight of the garden. An empty bed was partially visible behind him. I stepped forward and breathed in, catching the reassuring scent of daffodils and dogwood flowers. Only then did I allow my shoulders to unlock. I tried to settle my expression as I let out my hastily taken breath and bowed.

"Good day, my liege," I said. "I'm sorry to disturb you, but it was genuinely important."

"October?" He sounded confused, and when I straightened, I saw that he looked even more so. Then the confusion passed, replaced by growing wakefulness, and worry. "Of course you wouldn't disturb me if it wasn't genuinely important. Is someone hurt?"

I thought of Jazz. "Someone was, but I fixed it," I said. "Sylvester . . ."

He raised a hand, cutting me off before I could finish the sentence. The worry in his expression deepened, turning slowly into a deep, burning fury. "I can smell him on you," he said, voice honed to a razor's edge. It could have drawn blood. "I should have known that if he ever came back here, he would come for you first."

"My liege?" I said, reeling a little. When Oleander had come back, I hadn't been able to convince *anyone* she was in the Kingdom. She'd managed to halfway convince me that I was losing my mind. It seemed almost perverse for things to be so much easier this time.

Then again, I *had* been throwing Simon's spells around like they were softballs. It made sense that some of the stink of him might have clung to me, and if anyone was sensitive to the smell of the man's magic, it was his twin brother.

Sylvester turned his cold, furious face toward me. I quailed, and he blinked, looking briefly surprised before his fury melted into resignation. "I'm sorry, October. I didn't mean to frighten you. I just . . . I didn't think he'd really come back. Not like this. I'm so sorry. Can you forgive me for not being there?"

"You had no idea it was going to happen today," I said, still shaky. My headache wasn't helping. I heal so fast these days that I had become unaccustomed to lingering pain.

Sylvester stepped through the gate, pulling it closed behind him. The glimpse of the darkened bedchamber I had seen when the door opened disappeared, replaced once more by the empty air. Without another word, he stepped forward and folded me into a hug. I made a sound that was somewhere between a sigh and a sob and simply let him hold me, enjoying the safety and comfort of his arms. I lost my mortal father when I was seven years old. Sylvester had been the closest thing I'd had ever since.

"I am so sorry," he said again, when he finally let me go. He started down the cobblestone path, and I followed, walking with him to the first of the marble benches. He sat down, motioning for me to sit beside him.

I sat.

"I knew he'd return one day. There's too much for him in this Kingdom for him to stay away forever, and my brother has never been anything if not stubborn. Even when we were children, when his magic still smelled like smoke and mulled cider, he would have his way no matter what the cost." Sylvester shook his head. Something like grief was lurking in his eyes. "He should never have come near you."

"He said he transformed me to save me," I said hesitantly. "I think there's something wrong with him."

Sylvester's laugh was thin and bitter. "Oh, I *know* there's something wrong with him. There's been something wrong with him for a very long time. But . . ." He hesitated.

I frowned, eyeing him sidelong. "I don't like the tone of that silence."

"You have to understand, October, that time is different for the pureblooded."

"I know that." I'd always known that. From my mother's inability to remember that my birthday was something important to the sad way most purebloods looked at changelings, like the fact that we'd die someday meant we were as good as dead already.

"Yes, but . . ." Sylvester hesitated again before he said, "I admit, I've often wondered about the nature of what he did to you. Transforming you into a creature with a long lifespan, using a spell you could someday break yourself . . . I think he may be telling the truth, disturbing as it is to consider. He may have transformed you as he did because the alternative was killing you, and he didn't want to be responsible for your death."

"Why the hell not? He'd already kidnapped Luna and Rayseline. It's not like he could have done anything to make you angrier." And he'd *laughed*. I remembered that so clearly. Simon and Oleander, laughing while they watched me gasp and struggle to breathe the air that had become poisonous to my body. How could that have been an attempt to *save* me?

"It's not my wrath that he was worried about. Not in

that moment." Sylvester looked at me sadly. "Did you come here alone?"

"No. Quentin and Tybalt are waiting in the hall."

"Good. That means you'll have someone to rant at when I finish telling you what I'm about to tell you."

I blinked. "What are you talking about?"

Sylvester paused for a moment before he continued. "Have you never wondered why the doors in Shadowed Hills are willing to acknowledge you as family, or why Luna could enter your mother's tower uninvited, despite the wards Amandine has put in place over the years? I know you believe the knowes are alive, and I don't think you're wrong, but they're normally inclined to follow their own rules."

A horrifying picture was starting to form at the back of my mind, assembled from things people had said to me over the years. Arden's confusion when I said my mother was married to a human; Oleander's visit to the tower, all those years ago, when she'd taunted Amandine with her relationship with Simon. The way Sylvester cared for me . . . and then the last piece of the awful puzzle fell into place as I recalled Simon's own words about my mother in my kitchen only a few hours ago.

"You're not serious," I half-whispered.

"I'm afraid I am," he said.

"I want to hear you say it." My tone was suddenly challenging. I didn't try to rein it in. "Say it! I won't believe it if you don't say it."

"You are my niece, October, in the eyes of the law, if not the substance of your blood." Sylvester looked at me solemnly. "My brother took Amandine to wife long ago. Things were different then. *He* was different then. And no matter how much he changes, no matter how much he has changed, I truly do believe that he still loves her."

"You are *not* serious." I jumped to my feet, beginning to pace back and forth. "Why are you telling me this now? You don't think this is something I should have known years ago, like, I don't know, *before you sent me after him?* This is not okay! This is the new dictionary definition of not okay!"

Sylvester sighed, shaking his head. "I didn't expect you to take this well, but I had expected you to take it a little bit better than this."

"You think I'm overreacting? You're telling me your brother was *married to my mom*, and you thought I was going to do anything other than exactly what I'm doing right now?" I glared. "This is not okay."

"According to fae law, my brother is still married to your mother," said Sylvester, sounding apologetic.

I stared at him.

Under fae law, a pureblood who has an affair with a mortal isn't even cheating on their spouse. Showing bad judgment, maybe, but that's it. Which meant that marrying Dad wouldn't have required my mother to divorce Simon, because the marriage wouldn't have counted under fae law. It was just a dalliance taken uncomfortably far. It wasn't *real.*

"This isn't happening," I said.

Sylvester stood. "I'm afraid it is."

"Simon Torquill is my *stepfather.*"

He nodded.

"That's just . . . that's not okay."

"No, it's not. But I believe it may be why he chose to transform you, rather than killing you. My wrath means nothing to him. Your mother's, on the other hand . . . there is nothing in this world he wants or yearns for more than Amandine's forgiveness."

"Forgiveness for what?" I asked.

Sylvester turned his face away.

I groaned. "So great, he did something so bad you won't tell me about it even now, and now he's back in the Kingdom, where he can get to her." I shook my head, pushing my shock and anger aside in the face of something much more immediately important. "Oak and ash, Sylvester, we have to warn my mother that he's coming." Amandine would have no idea. She wouldn't be prepared. And Firstborn or not, if he took her by surprise . . .

Sylvester shook his head. "Your mother is the last person he would bring to harm, in this world or any other. He loves her. He has always loved her."

"He's your brother, and he kidnapped your wife and his own niece," I snapped. "Why the hell would his estranged wife be off the list of people to hurt?"

"Perhaps because he and Luna have never cared for each other," Sylvester said. "Why he would hurt Rayseline, I don't know." The fury sparked in his eyes again, just for an instant; long enough that I had to struggle not to look away. "I would love the opportunity to ask him. In private."

I swallowed hard and said, "We don't know why he's here. We don't know what he wants. I want to know that my mother is all right. Please."

Sylvester sighed. "All right," he said. "If nothing else, he may have gone to see her. If he has been and gone, perhaps she can tell me where to find him—and if she won't agree to do that, I may be able to find a trace of his magic to follow. And then . . ." He didn't finish the sentence. He didn't need to.

For the first time in my life, I found myself in the awkward position of actually feeling bad for Simon Torquill.

FIVE

WE STEPPED BACK through the main gate. Tybalt and Quentin were standing on the other side of the hallway, next to the wall, and talking in low, intense voices. Tybalt glanced up, seeming to realize that they weren't alone anymore. Quentin did the same a heart-beat later. Both of them went quiet, stepping apart. Quentin looked at me anxiously. After that first moment, Tybalt didn't look at me at all. I sighed and filed that away as something I could ask about later. I had a huge file of things to ask about later, and I almost never re-membered to ask any of them.

"I should get a secretary," I muttered.

"What's that?" asked Sylvester.

"Nothing." I turned to the boys. "Do you want the short form or the long form? Never mind, scratch that, you're getting the short form right now, and you'll get the long form later, probably over alcohol, ice cream, or both. Simon Torquill was married to my mother. Is still married to my mother under fae law. That means he's family, and that means he can enter her tower without her giving direct and immediate consent. She's probably not in any danger, since she's Firstborn, but she's also confused, so he might be able to get around her defenses. I want her warned at the absolute least, and preferably moved here. Any questions?"

They both gaped at me. Quentin recovered first. "So are you going to call him 'Daddy' now? Can I watch? From behind a safe Plexiglas barrier, like they use on *MythBusters*?"

"No more TV for you," I snapped. "And I will call Simon Torquill 'Daddy' right after I do something else that's never going to happen, ever. I *have* a father." He was long dead and forgotten to almost everyone in the mortal world, but he wasn't forgotten to me.

"What do we do?" asked Tybalt.

I could have kissed him for that. *Would* have kissed him for that, if it wouldn't have required time I wasn't willing to spend right now. "Sylvester tells his people Simon may be on his way, and that they shouldn't trust his face—Simon has the same one. They need to make him cast a spell. They need to trust his magic. We head for Mom's tower. If she's there, we warn her. If she's not there, I try to negotiate with the wards and convince them to keep Simon out." Modifying a spell that had been cast by one of the Firstborn would be easy, right?

Probably not. Even though the spell was my mother's, it would be like sticking my hands into live current. I still had to try. Amandine was so bad at taking care of herself these days, and Simon was . . . well, Simon. There was no telling what he'd do if he got his hands on her.

For just a moment, I tried to picture the man he must have been in order to get my mother to marry him. I couldn't find any path between that man and the one I knew.

"What if Simon's there?" asked Quentin.

Sylvester smiled that thin, alarming smile again, and

said, "If he's there, my brother and I can finally have the reunion I've been dreaming of for so long."

I shuddered. There was no way to interpret his words that didn't end in blood and screaming.

"We can manage without you," said Tybalt.

"Ah, yes," said Sylvester, raising an eyebrow. "Because a half-trained squire, a knight with an abnormal sensitivity to transformation spells, and a King of Cats, that's the appropriate way to handle my brother, whose magic has been honed to a killing edge by many, many years of villainy. Whatever was I thinking?"

"Okay, can we fight with Simon, instead of with each other?" I asked. "Pretty please?"

"That is my intention, assuming we can find him," said Sylvester calmly. He continued, "Amy will listen to me, if she's there, and may respond to me when she doesn't respond to you. I'm sorry, October. I know she's your mother, but there are centuries of history between us, and those may be enough to pull her back into the present day, if only for a moment."

Tybalt spoke before I could. "I do not like you," he said, looking straight at Sylvester. His voice held the perfect, bald honesty that has been the birthright of the feline kingdom since time began. He stepped up to stand next to me, putting a hand possessively on the back of my arm. His gaze remained fixed on Sylvester the whole time, making it clear who the show of ownership was directed at. "I think you are too comfortable here, in your marble halls, and have forgotten what it means to fight for what is yours. But if you insist on coming, at least you'll be one more person between Simon and October. Are you sure your men can hold your wards against a member of your own family without you here to bolster them?"

I turned to gape at Tybalt. Sylvester was already nodding. "They are well-trained, and they know their jobs. October was one of them for a reason, after all."

"Fine. We will wait for you outside in the garden, where October may shout imprecations at her leisure." One corner of Tybalt's mouth tilted upward in a smile. "I believe she'll be calling both of us some rather inventive names."

"You've got that right," I muttered.

"Very good." Sylvester nodded to me, and then to Quentin, before turning and heading off down the hall at a rapid clip.

"Come along," said Tybalt, turning to head in the other direction. He kept his hand on my arm, using it to steer me. "We have much ground to cover."

I was startled enough that I allowed him to pull me for several steps before I stopped, becoming a dead weight against his hand. He turned his head to look at me, expression mild.

"Are you going to begin the shouting while we're still inside? I ask only because I advised your liege that we'd be in the garden, and I know how you hate disappointing him."

"Sylvester has been lying to me for my entire life," I said. "To say I'm not happy with him would be an understatement, but I don't need you at each other's throats—"

"October." Tybalt didn't take his hand off my arm. "There is no love lost between Sylvester Torquill and myself; there may never be any love there to lose. But I have no objection to his presence, if he will protect us from his brother. Forgive me if I would do whatever needs doing to keep you safe. If you cannot forgive, please understand that I'm never going to change my ways in this regard. Perhaps not in any regard touching on your safety."

I blinked at him, glancing reflexively to Quentin.

He shook his head. "I'm not getting involved with this one. He's your boyfriend. Also, I think he's pretty much right, but I'm not sure I'm allowed to say so, what with the whole squire and loyalty thing in the way."

"Why did I let you people outnumber me?" I demanded. I turned, starting to walk in the direction Tybalt had been trying to push me. I kept my chin high, trying to show that I was *choosing* to walk this way.

"Because somewhere in that lovely skull of yours is a glimmer of self-preservation, fighting against all odds to remain intact and keep the rest of you breathing," said Tybalt, hurrying to keep up. He still didn't take his hand off my arm. Matching his steps to mine, he continued, "This does raise an interesting question of protocol, however. I had regarded Sylvester as the closest thing you have to a father figure. However, if Simon has a legal claim to the role, I may have to approach him as your eldest male relative."

I opened my mouth to swear at him, and paused, walking in silence for several steps before I asked, "Is this your way of distracting me from the fact that we're going to wait on the lawn when my mother may be in danger?"

"Yes," said Tybalt calmly. "Is it working?"

"If you mean 'is it making me want to kill you with a brick,' then yes. It's working." I sighed. I might be furious, but it was good to know there were some things I could always count on where Tybalt was concerned. It was even better to know that Sylvester was going to be with us, serving the dual purposes of providing backup and keeping himself in my sight. Upset as I was with him, I didn't want to think about him here, at Shadowed Hills, where I wouldn't be able to do anything to help him.

"I know you're worried, but Amandine is Firstborn," said Quentin. "I'm pretty sure she can take care of herself."

"Amandine's not so good at paying attention to her surroundings right now, and she *married* Simon," I said. "Maybe she can take care of herself, but is she going to realize she needs to? Because I'm afraid she's just going to open the door and invite him back into her life."

"I doubt even your mother would be so foolish," said

Tybalt, and opened the door to the back garden. For a moment, we all just stared.

". . . whoa," I said.

Luna had clearly been preparing the grounds for winter, even if she was spending the bulk of her time at Rayseline's bedside. Most of the roses were covered by canvas sheeting, and the hedges had somehow been teased to even greater heights than in the summer, twisting into strange, elegant shapes. The roses that weren't covered didn't need to be; they were flowers of pure snow white and brittle, translucent ice blue, impossible in the mortal world, and impossibly beautiful even in the Summerlands.

Quentin was less reserved than I was. "Snow!" he shouted, our troubles forgotten as he dove straight into the nearest snowdrift. The spray he kicked up hit me in the face. I yelped.

"Hey! Be careful! That stuff is *cold*." I looked mournfully at the white expanse of the lawn. "It didn't even occur to me that it might be snowing in the Summerlands."

"It may not have been five minutes ago," said Tybalt. He gave me a concerned look. "Should I go inside, and see if I can locate a Hob to give me directions to the winter wear?"

"No," I said, turning to face him as I finished my scan of the gardens. "I need to talk to you."

Tybalt frowned, watching me silently. I fought the urge to bite my lip. He looked so serious, and so worried, like he knew that whatever I was going to say, it wasn't going to be something he wanted to hear.

Tough. "Did you *know?*" The words were strangely fragile when exposed to the light like that.

Tybalt blinked. "Did I know?" he echoed.

"Did you know Simon and my mother were married? Have you been keeping this from me? Have you been doing the same thing everyone else has been doing, and *protecting* me?" I spat the words at him like a mouthful of snakes, all twisting and venomous. "I need to know the truth, and I need to know it now."

"No," he said, and I didn't hear any lies in that word, only rock-solid conviction. "I swear to you, October, I did not know. My association with the Torquill line goes back centuries, but it was broken after the Great Fire of London, when they ran and left me behind in a city full of ghosts. I never even knew that Simon had married, and to be quite honest, I did not *care*. He is beneath my notice, save for where he endangers you."

I searched his face, looking for any hint of dishonesty. I didn't find it. I relaxed, the tension going out of my body. Tybalt put an arm around me, and I leaned close, grateful for his warmth.

"I won't claim never to have lied to you, but I have not lied to you since we decided to try taking this relationship seriously," he said quietly. "I love you. Lying to you would be a mistreatment of what that love means."

I laughed, a cold, jagged sound. "None of the other people who say they love me seem to feel that way."

"Then they are not very good at loving," he said. "We will go to your mother. We will see that she is fine. If Simon troubles her, perhaps that will pull her out of the fog. We know she can rise, when she feels the need."

"I know," I said. "I'm just worried."

"That is because you are a good daughter." Unspoken was the fact that he didn't think Amandine was a very good mother. I loved him even more for that—both for thinking it, and for not saying it out loud.

She did the best she could with me. It's just that what she wanted for my life and what I wanted were always different things. I would have broken myself trying to be the daughter she wanted me to be. In the end, I did the only thing I could have done—the only thing that stood any chance of saving us both. I ran away.

I leaned closer to Tybalt, resting my head against his shoulder as I watched Quentin, who was apparently half Snow Fairy, kicking his way through the glittering yard. "We really need to take him skiing," I said.

Tybalt snorted. He pulled me closer and pressed his cheek against mine, only to draw back and look at me disapprovingly. "You *are* cold," he said. "Can I convince you to reconsider your position on properly outfitting yourself for this expedition?"

"Mom's tower isn't far, and it'll be closer if I have genuine need to get there," I said. "I'll be cold, but I'll live." The Summerlands are the last layer of Faerie to remain accessible. They're both larger than the mortal world and smaller, following some strange set of physical laws that no one has ever been able to adequately explain. My friend Stacy's oldest daughter, Cassandra, is majoring in Physics at UC Berkeley, in part because she'd like to be able to figure out how the Summerlands can bend space the way they do.

Living in the mortal world makes it easy to forget that Faerie doesn't follow the same laws. Maybe that sounds a little pat—I mean, my boyfriend is a cat in his spare time, and my sister was originally the physical embodiment of my impending death—but those things are normal to me. Unlike snow in California, and land that can expand and contract like a rubber band according to the needs of the people who use it.

The one thing that never changes is the size of a claimed demesne. Shadowed Hills had set boundaries and borders. No matter what happened, it remained the same size. Technically, the same could be said about my mother's tower, but it was a pretty small chunk of real estate: the tower and grounds occupied a patch of land scarcely larger than the footprint of my own Victorian house. I guess that's one of the side effects of building upward, rather than outward.

The door opened behind us. I pulled away from Tybalt, turning to see Sylvester standing there with an assortment of coats slung over his arm. He had added a military-style greatcoat to his own attire, tan camel hair or something close, with patches on the elbows. "It occurred to me that you had not made allowance for the weather in your plans," he said. "I hope you don't mind if I reduce our chances of dying of exposure during the walk."

There was no point in arguing now. "No, coats are great," I said, shivering exaggeratedly before I held out my arms. "Gimme. Please. Before I lose feeling in my fingers."

"You chill too easily," said Tybalt, with an "I told you so" look.

"You love me anyway." The coat Sylvester had brought for me was patchwork wool in a dozen shades of red, trimmed with rabbit fur and large enough to fit over my leather jacket. Slipping it on was like enfolding myself in a giant fabric hug. I stuffed my hands into the pockets, enjoying the feeling of being completely surrounded.

"True enough." Tybalt's coat was of a similar style, if in a more masculine cut, and made of shades of brown and gray. He sniffed once, and then said, "These will do."

"You're darn right." I took the last coat from Sylvester—this one done in shades of purple—and held it up, shouting, "Quentin! Come put this on before you catch your death of cold! I need you to live long enough to be cannon fodder when Simon decides to attack."

"You're really inspiring, you know that?" asked Quentin, as he trudged through the snow to take the coat from my hands.

"I learned from the best," I said. "Come on. Let's move."

The boundary of Sylvester's land was always marked by a forest. We walked toward the trees, our feet crunching in the snow, and into a veritable winter wonderland. Everything was limned in glittering white. Most of the trees were leafless and dormant. Meanwhile, the scattered trees that always appeared brown and dead during the summer had come alive, putting forth frost-laced leaves and even delicate winter flowers. I glanced to Sylvester, who knew more about fae flora than I did.

He took the hint. "Luna planted some of these, of course; she took cuttings from others, for the winter gardens. They're all naturally occurring. They can lie dormant for years while they wait for a good snowfall."

"Huh," I said.

Quentin was ranging ahead again, too delighted by the snow to be sensible about staying with the pack. Tybalt walked to my left; Sylvester to my right. They didn't look at each other, and I was too tired from lack of sleep and too worried about my mother to play mediator. They were both big boys. They'd figure it out for themselves, or they wouldn't.

The wood ended at a meadow. That was normal. What wasn't normal was the dividing line that ran through the middle of the open ground, cutting it into two distinct landscapes. On our side, the Shadowed Hills side, everything was white and frozen. On the other side, as the land grew closer to Mother's tower, everything was growing resplendently green, completely ignoring the season. In Faerie, the king is the land, and that goes for anyone who holds dominion over even the smallest scrap of territory. The space between Shadowed Hills and Amandine's tower was unclaimed, responding in a general fashion to the kings and queens around it.

"Is there a reason Shadowed Hills is having a white Christmas?" I asked, glancing to Sylvester.

He sighed, and looked away. "Luna is . . . not well," he said, before beginning his march down the gently sloping hillside, toward that slash of improbable green.

I winced. "Right." I looked to Tybalt. "Mom probably doesn't even know what season it is." Actually, thinking about it, it was never anything but summer at her tower. That was part of why the snow had been such a surprise. I'd only lived in the Summerlands for a decade or so—no time at all, as Faerie measured such things—and most of that time had been spent as Amandine's shadow, living with her in her eternal summertime. It was easy to forget that some people were fond of cycles, if not of actual change.

"Amandine will be fine," said Tybalt, taking my arm in his. "If Simon wishes to challenge a Firstborn daughter of Oberon on her own ground that will be his funeral, not yours."

"Come on." I started after Sylvester, trying not to dwell on the word "funeral." Mom was Firstborn. That didn't make her immune to Oberon's Law. If she killed Simon, she could be in serious trouble, and while I didn't think she was a killer, it was always hard to tell what Mom would do. I'd never learned to read her the way I had most of the other people who made up my admittedly small circle of family and close friends. But in the years since I'd returned from the pond . . .

Fae madness isn't the same as human mental illness. Sometimes I wish the fae had maintained a language of their own, rather than stealing and sharing with mortals. Maybe then we'd have a better word for what the purebloods go through when the centuries of mistakes and magical backlash get to be too much. They go away for a time, receding into themselves and pulling a veil of fog over the world. It's the only way to give their brains the space to carve out a new worldview, something that can account for the changes that inevitably happen around them. Amandine had been skirting the edges of that fog when I had run away from her, tired of watching her flirt with an oblivion that would probably leave me dead of extreme old age before it let her go. Then Simon had transformed me, and by the time I made it back to my own body, Amandine was gone, burying herself in the fog with all the enthusiasm of a girl preparing for her first formal ball.

She might know Simon wasn't living with her any-more. But depending on how long they'd been together, she might not.

I walked a little faster.

Everything changed when we stepped across the invis-ible line dividing the lands influenced by Shadowed Hills from the lands influenced by my mother. The temperature shot up at least ten degrees, everything suddenly smelling of fresh green leaves and sweet potential. I pulled my arm away from Tybalt long enough to shrug out of my coat. He and Quentin did the same. Sylvester kept his coat on, but his was tailored, not borrowed from the general stock; it was probably enchanted to keep him at just the right tem-perature, regardless of the weather. We walked on until the bowl of the meadow began slanting upward again, and we stepped out of springtime into summer.

By any rules of normal geography, we should have been able to see Amandine's tower long before we reached that transition point. The Summerlands aren't big on rules. We stepped into the summer, and the land leveled out before us, and we were suddenly standing less than fifteen yards from the low stone wall that sur-rounded the elegant white needle of the tower. The stone glowed faintly against the twilit sky. Flowering trees and bushes crowded her garden, all blooming in a dozen shades of white and ivory.

"Think she's home?" asked Quentin.

"I don't have the slightest idea," I said, and started walking faster. The others fell back, allowing me to take the lead. The enchantments on the tower knew who I was; they'd always let me in, no matter what else might be going on. That could be important, depending on the situation ahead of us.

The gate swung open when I touched it. I left my fingertips against the wood, murmuring, "These three are with me. Let them in." Then I walked on, into my mother's garden.

Tybalt, Quentin, and Sylvester followed without difficulty. The enchantments were listening.

I hadn't lived in the tower for a long time, but the layout of the garden had always been simple, and I knew the way. I followed the path as it curved gently past the marble birdbath to the door, which was standing open. That was enough to make me stop, one hand going to my knife as I sniffed the air, trying to find traces of magic beneath the riotous perfumes of a dozen different types of flower, some of which never existed in the mortal world. I thought I smelled smoke. I couldn't be sure.

"Tybalt?"

"Yes." The smell of pennyroyal and musk cut through the layers of perfume as he transformed, and as a cat, he raced past me, up the shallow steps at the threshold, into the building beyond.

I tensed, waiting where I was. Simon was a powerful magician, but Tybalt was harder to transform than I was—most people are harder to transform than I am—and there's very little that can catch a Cait Sidhe when he's not trying to be caught. The tower was five floors, no more than four rooms to a floor. Some of the floors were a single large room, like mine, like Amandine's. He could search them and return in an instant. He could—

He reappeared on the steps, stretching back into human form, a blank expression on his face. For just an instant, I was certain that he had found her body in one of the tower's upper rooms, throat slit by the silver and iron required to kill one of the Firstborn, colorless eyes open and staring into the rafters.

Then he shook his head. "She is not here; from the scent markings in her room and parlor, she has not been here in days, maybe even weeks. There are no signs of a struggle. I'm sorry, October. Your mother is still missing."

It was almost a relief. I realized that even as I sighed, shook my head, and said, "We had to check. Did you smell anyone else?"

"Yes." His face hardened again. "Traces of candle smoke and rotten oranges. Simon has been here, and recently."

I turned to Sylvester to see how he was taking this news. He was staring at the tower, lips gone pale and bloodless as he pressed them into a thin, hard line. One hand was grasping the pommel of his sword. His knuckles were white, and I had to fight not to take a step away from him.

"I can't follow this trail. Our magic is not so attuned as it once was, and he is too far for me to follow. He could see our walls from your mother's land, and the wards would never tell me how close he had come," said Sylvester, voice pitched low. "He could have been here for days, watching us, waiting for the chance to strike. Oh, he is going to pay for what he's done to me and mine, October. On the root and the branch, I promise you that."

I glanced to Tybalt, who looked as alarmed as I felt. He stepped away from the tower, and the door swung shut behind him, leaving the four of us standing in my mother's garden, where the white petals from the blossoming trees were falling like so much unfrozen snow.

SIX

WE TRUDGED SILENTLY through the meadow between Mom's land and Sylvester's. Even when we stepped back into the snow, Quentin remained by my side, not running off to make snowballs or enjoy the weather. The quiet lasted until we were standing on the lawn of Shadowed Hills, with the doors waiting to welcome us into warmth and presumptive safety. Tybalt, Quentin, and I stopped. Sylvester took a few more steps before turning to face the rest of us.

"October—" he began.

I raised a hand, cutting him off. "Who would he run to? If he isn't here with my mother, where would he think he could go for aid?" He wouldn't be hiding with the changeling underground, of that I was certain: places like the one that had raised me were too far beneath him, even in his hour of need.

Sylvester frowned slowly, looking confused. "Are you that angry with me?"

"Right now? Yes. You've been keeping secrets from me. Things I needed to know." Like maybe before he'd sent me running after Simon, before I'd been turned into a fish and left stranded in a watery jail for fourteen years. "I love you. I always will. But right now, I'm pretty pissed at you. So can you just answer the question, please?"

"Simon was ... not well when he was last here," said Sylvester, picking his words with care. "He was separated from your mother. Luna disliked having him in our halls. He wandered the Kingdom, taking hospitality where he could find it."

"Did he go to January?" I asked.

Sylvester shook his head. "No. Tamed Lightning had not been founded yet, and as a titled, unlanded Count, Duchess Riordan saw him as a threat. Perhaps if he'd been willing to formally divorce your mother—but that would have required taking steps neither wanted taken."

I blinked, frowning. Fae marriages are complicated things, filled with rules about inheritance and succession that I never bothered learning. But fae divorces are simple. Unless there are children involved, all the couple needs to do is announce that they're no longer married. "Why didn't they want to get a divorce?"

"I don't see how this relates to where he would be if not here or at your mother's tower."

I bared my teeth. "Humor me," I half-snarled. "Why didn't they want to get a divorce?"

"Because that would mean admitting there was no hope for them. It may be hard for you to believe, but there was a time when we were all so much younger than we are now. My brother loved your mother as he's loved very few. He wasn't willing to give up on her. And maybe I'm a sentimental old fool, but I always took it as a good sign that your mother wasn't willing to give up on him, either."

There was something he wasn't telling me. I've had a lot of practice at being lied to, and I know how to recognize the signs. I narrowed my eyes. "What else?"

"What?"

"What else aren't you telling me?" He started to protest. I shook my head, stopping him before he could get a word out. "No. Maeve's teeth, Sylvester, I'm mad at you for keeping secrets, and you're *still doing it.* Why the hell would you do a thing like that? You know you're on thin ice right now."

"My dear, I've been on thin ice for a very long time, especially where your family is concerned." Sylvester ran a hand through his hair, sighing as he turned to look at the forest blocking our view of Amandine's tower. "There is so much history between your mother and me, between all of us . . . I don't even know where to begin. But there are also things that I promised her I would never tell you. I broke one promise to her. I won't break a second. I'm sorry. I truly am. I love you more than I can ever make you believe, but I gave her my word."

I stared at him. Finally, I asked the one question I was sure he would actually answer: "What promise did you break?"

"She came to me when she was pregnant with you. She asked me to stay away from her child, from her mortal life, until she chose to reenter Faerie on her own terms." Sylvester turned back to me. "I won't apologize for coming to get you before she could make you mortal, but that betrayal has been a wall between us ever since. She's never forgiven me. I don't think she ever will."

"Wait." I wanted to scream at him, to tell him he was one of the people I'd always counted on to never betray me. Unfortunately, right now, it was more important for me to be smart. Purebloods take promises seriously; it's part of why they hate saying "thank you," a prohibition that most changelings catch from their fae parents, like catching cooties on the playground. And the next step up from a promise is a geas, a binding enchantment compelling someone to do something—or *not* to do something.

Like, for example, never to tell certain secrets. Ironic, and annoying. "Simon said something while he was at my house. He said he couldn't speak the name of his employer, because his geas still held. Do you have any idea who might have hired him to kidnap Luna and Rayseline?"

"I have asked myself that question a thousand times without finding an answer. If I had even the faintest clue, I would have tracked that person down years ago and made them pay for everything they had done to me, to my family, and to you," said Sylvester, a new chill leeching into his words, until every one of them could have frozen me where I stood.

Or maybe that was just the snow we were all standing around in. I wrapped my arms around myself, trying to conserve warmth, and said, "Okay. So you don't know anything that can help us find Simon, and some old promise to my mother matters more to you than I do. Good to know where I stand."

"October—"

"We're leaving." I turned to head for the doors. Sylvester grabbed my arm. I stopped, slowly turning back to look at his hand. Voice level and calm, I said, "Let go of me."

"I would never allow anyone or anything to harm you. If you believe nothing else, I need you to believe that."

Except that he *was* harming me; he had been harming me every time he kept the things I needed to know secret from me. He just couldn't see it. "I *need* you to let go of me."

And then Tybalt was there, shoving his way between us, forcing Sylvester to let me go. The two of them stared at each other for a moment. A low growl was rolling through Tybalt's chest, making the hair on my arms stand on end. I glanced at Quentin, who was watching the whole scene with wide, frightened eyes.

"I speak to you now as a King to a Duke, and with the utmost respect," said Tybalt, in a tone that made it clear he could care less if Sylvester took offense. "If October is hurt because you kept a promise to her mother rather than upholding your duty to one who is your sworn vassal, believe me when I say that I will return here on my own, and I will make you sorry you ever allowed harm to come to her."

Sylvester smiled a little, eyes still filled with shadows. "Tybalt, if October is hurt because of what I didn't tell her, I'll leave the door open for you."

"Great. Since we're at the threats and dick-waving part of the day, I guess this is where we go," I said. "Sylvester, if you decide to change your mind about being an asshole, you have my number." I turned and stormed back into the knowe before he could reply, with Quentin and Tybalt close at my heels. Everything felt wrong. My stomach was a hard, cold knot of anger and dismay. The world—my world—was changing again, and I didn't like it.

I didn't like it one bit.

The halls of Shadowed Hills were deserted, which made sense, given the time of day: any sensible purebloods would be asleep, and most changelings who live in the Summerlands learn to keep pureblood hours. We were almost to the door before I heard footsteps hurrying up from behind, and turned to see Etienne walking toward us as fast as decorum allowed. He was wearing his uniform, but it looked a little more rumpled than I was used to, like he had finally allowed himself to relax a little bit. It was a surprisingly good look on him.

Etienne had always been the most hidebound of Sylvester's knights. We were all expected to wear ducal livery if we were standing guard, but most of us called it a day when we reached "presentable." Not Etienne. If he had to leave his quarters, his boots *gleamed* with polish, and his hair was styled until it looked shellacked. Not now. His tabard was only laced halfway down the sides, and his hair was mussed in that "straight out of bed" way endlessly imitated by fashion magazines and aspiring models. For the first time, I could understand what Bridget had seen in him. He looked like a man, and not like a Ken doll with a sword.

"October, wait!" he called, and walked a little faster, not quite breaking into a run. Running in the halls was against the rules, after all.

I stopped walking. Quentin and Tybalt did the same, and Quentin shook his head. "I've never seen Sir Etienne this unkempt."

"Me neither," I said. "I wish I had a camera."

Etienne, who was close enough to hear us, glared. "Show some decorum," he said. "It might serve you well in your future dealings with the nobility."

I wanted to protest that I didn't intend to have any future dealings with the nobility, but as I was standing between my boyfriend the King of Cats and my squire the Crown Prince of North America, that would have been a little disingenuous. "I've done okay without any decorum so far," I said. "I'll take my chances. What's got you out of bed in the middle of the day? Please tell me you're not going to ask me to babysit. I've got a sort of full plate right now."

"October, I would trust you to the ends of the earth with my child's life and safety; should she ever be endangered again, Oberon forbid, there is no one I would rather set upon her trail," said Etienne. "But the Fire Kingdoms will freeze before I allow you to babysit."

I snorted. "Shows what you know. I'm good with teenagers."

"Yeah," said Quentin. "She hasn't gotten me shot in *ages*."

"Aren't you helpful," I said, glaring at him.

Quentin beamed.

Etienne looked between us, apparently bemused. "Your method of communication remains as irreverent as ever," he said. "Chelsea woke me, but she has nothing to do with why I came to catch you. Is it true? Is Simon back in the Mists?"

"He came to my house," I said. "He tried to talk to me. When that didn't work out for him, he attacked Jasmine and ran. I'm going to the Luidaeg's now to ask her what we should do, but I wanted to check on Sylvester first."

"And because of their similarity in appearance, you felt the need to lay eyes upon him yourself, rather than using the telephone," said Etienne grimly. It wasn't a guess: he was the one who'd trained me, and he knew how my brain worked. "That makes sense, although it seems needlessly reckless. You shouldn't be involved in this. Let Sylvester handle it."

"Fuck. That. For one thing, I'm almost as mad at Sylvester as I am at Simon right now. For another, what do you want me to do? Wait for Simon to come back to the house and condemn us all to a new life in somebody's fish tank? Nuh-uh. I'm willing to be patient when patience is called for, but that isn't being patient, that's being stupid." I shook my head. "I'm going to the Luidaeg. She doesn't volunteer information, but at least with her, I know she's telling me the truth when she speaks."

"October—"

"I know Simon was married to my mom." Was *still* married to her, although I didn't want to say that out loud; it was too disgusting to waste time thinking about. "Is there anything *else* you people haven't been telling me?"

Etienne looked alarmed. He raised his hands, palms toward me. "Peace! I never spoke of it because they were separated, and I assumed you knew and didn't want to discuss it. It would have been unseemly to bring it up."

I stared at him, my anger taking on a new white-hot

form. "Oh, my sweet Maeve, you thought Sylvester took me as his knight because of *Simon*, didn't you? That was why you never believed me when I said I'd earned my post. You thought I was . . . I think I'm going to be sick."

To his credit, Etienne looked ashamed. "I learned better."

"Oh, oak and ash." I closed my eyes for a moment, breathing in deeply. The situation wasn't Etienne's fault. He hadn't done this to me. When I opened my eyes again, he was watching me warily, like I might bite. Forcing my tone to lighten, I said, "Look, I need to run, but once this is all taken care of, we should take the kids and do something fun. Hit Great America for the day."

"What is 'Great America'?" asked Etienne, dropping his hands back to his sides.

I smiled. "Ask Chelsea. I'm sure she'll be happy to explain." Great America was a local roller coaster park. There was no way Chelsea wouldn't know all about it, and no way Etienne would be able to avoid an outing once he'd mentioned the possibility. Maybe using his teenage daughter against him was mean, but hell, people used my squire against me all the time. Turnabout was just fair play.

"I will do that." His expression turned worried. "But please, I have to urge you, don't go looking for Simon on your own. Whatever he intends can't be good, especially not for you."

"I won't be alone," I said, glancing to Tybalt, and then to Quentin. "I'll have a King of Cats and a damn fine Daoine Sidhe illusionist with me. We'll be all right. Also, I have no intention of fighting fair." I didn't say anything about my having thrown one of Simon's spells back at him. My fingers still ached when I thought about it too hard. It wasn't something I wanted to discuss with anyone until I had discussed it with someone who might actually be able to tell me something useful.

Etienne shook his head. "You are too cavalier about treating with the sea witch," he said. "It makes me fear for your safety."

"Like the Dread Pirate Roberts so often said, she'll most likely kill me in the morning," I said. I grabbed a handful of shadows, weaving a human disguise around myself as I continued: "Until that happens, she's a pretty good ally to have. Hug Chelsea for me, okay? And we'll talk about getting together soon."

"I think I would like that," said Etienne, inclining his head.

"Good. Open roads." With that, I turned, and beckoned for Tybalt and Quentin to follow as I exited the knowe.

The moment of transition between Faerie and the mortal world was jarring as always. Paso Nogal Park was deserted this early in the morning, and we didn't see anyone else as we made our way along the narrow walking path that wound down the side of the hill. Leaving Shadowed Hills was always easier than getting in. Maybe there was a deeper meaning to that, but if so, I didn't want to think about it too hard.

At least my headache was almost gone. I always deal better with emergencies when I'm not actively in pain.

Tybalt put a hand on my shoulder when we reached the bottom of the hill, pulling me to a stop. "This is where I take my leave of you," he said.

I turned to stare at him, all the tension I thought I'd lost in the snow flooding back again. "What?"

"I said—"

"I heard you." I turned again, tossing Quentin my keys. "Go get in the car. You don't need to hear this."

He was a smart boy. He took off running, and he didn't look back. I focused my attention on Tybalt.

"*Why* are you leaving me?"

"Duty." The word was grim. "I need to notify the Court of Cats that there is danger in the city, and set them to watching for Simon. I'll ask them to watch your house as well. He won't take us by surprise a second time." He smiled a crooked smile, clearly trying to get me to do the same; clearly trying to keep me from worrying.

"All right," I said. "Will you meet us at the Luidaeg's?"

"I will," he said.

The tension slipped away again. His logic was sound, and more, it didn't carry any hint of him going to track down Simon without me. "Then I'll call May and let her know where we're headed. If she doesn't pick up, we'll swing by the house instead, just to make sure she and Jazz are all right." If Simon had circled back, they could be in trouble. May couldn't be killed, and she would recover from most physical wounds just like I would. That didn't mean she couldn't be incapacitated. Jazz had no innate physical defenses, and she'd been unconscious when I'd last seen her. This time, I managed to force a smile. "So if we're not hanging with the sea witch, come save us."

Tybalt reached up and pressed the knuckles of his right hand lightly to my cheek. "You are very fortunate that I love you, for I doubt I could endure you otherwise," he said.

My smile grew. "I love you, too."

"Of course you do. I'm wonderful." With that, he turned and walked away, vanishing into the shadows beneath a nearby clump of trees.

"Okay. Now we move." I turned back to Quentin, who was watching me with concern. "What?"

"Nothing. I'm just . . . I never met Simon. He was before my time. How worried should I be?"

I hesitated. He needed to know what we were up

against—but I could explain just as well while we were moving. "Get in the car," I said.

He got.

Once we were safely on the road, heading toward the freeway, I said, "Remember Oleander?"

Quentin shuddered. "I don't think I could forget her if I tried."

"That's good. When you forget your enemies, you give them the power to come back and surprise you. Never forget her, or the things we learned from fighting her." Mostly what I learned from fighting her was that if someone really wanted to poison me, I'd need to be in a hermetically sealed bubble to prevent it. Then again, that was when I'd been more human; my body might just shrug off the poison if something like that happened to me now.

"So what does Oleander have to do with anything? She's dead."

"When she was alive, she was Simon's . . ." I hesitated, not sure how to finish that sentence. I'd always assumed they were lovers, but if he was married to my mother, would that really have been true? Yes, I finally decided. He'd fallen far enough that he would have been willing to cheat on his wife on top of everything else. "She was his lover, and his accomplice. She went to see my mother once, to ask if Simon had been allowed to see me. The way she looked at Amandine, and the way Amandine looked at her . . . there was so much *hate* there."

"Okay," said Quentin, sounding puzzled.

"Think about it. Oleander was the sort of person who killed kings for money, and she poisoned Lily just to frame me. Simon, though? Simon ran around with her on purpose, knowing what she was. Now what kind of a person do you think that makes him?" I shook my head. "I got stuck in the pond because everyone figured Simon had kidnapped Luna and Rayseline, and I was looking for proof. He caught me, and sploosh, it's fourteen years later."

"Did he?"

"Did he what?"

"Kidnap them."

"Yeah. He admitted it to me in the kitchen, before Jazz broke in on us and everything went to hell. Simon actually *said* he was responsible for Luna and Raysel disappearing." If I could find him, if I could restrain him somehow, I could find out exactly where they'd been kept. I was good with knives, and I didn't much care if Simon bled. Maybe knowing where they'd been would be the key to undoing some of the trauma that haunted Rayseline's mind. She could wake up more than just forgiven: she could wake up healed—

"Why?"

"Why what?"

"Why did he kidnap his brother's kid?" Quentin shook his head. "I just . . . I love my baby sister. I can't imagine being willing to hurt her, even if we were having some sort of a fight."

It was still a shock when Quentin mentioned his family so casually, like it was something I'd always been allowed to know. "I didn't realize you had a sister."

"Yeah." He smiled. "My fosterage began when she turned seven and was old enough to understand that I wasn't going away because I didn't love her anymore. Her name's Penthea."

"That's pretty." Traffic was moving fast enough that I had to keep my eyes on the road. That made the conversation easier to have; I didn't have to look at him. "He said someone had hired him, and that he couldn't say the name of his employer because the geas still held. So whoever it was not only paid him, they swore him to silence in the most literal way possible."

"At least that means we know it's not Oleander."

"How's that?" I skirted a brief sidelong glance in his direction.

Quentin shrugged. "If he'd been talking about Oleander, and their whole relationship was some sort of cover, the geas would have broken as soon as she was killed. Dead people can't maintain that kind of binding. Oleander's dead, so that means she didn't hire him."

"Great. Then we're looking for a living person, powerful enough to throw a geas on Simon Torquill, with a grudge against Sylvester, and . . ." I paused again. "And against me, or at least against Amandine. Simon said my death was one of his employer's goals."

"That might be why he fled the Kingdom. If he wasn't willing to kill you, and he was dealing with someone that powerful, that could have been the only way to prevent himself from being forced to go through with it."

"Yeah." I quieted, sinking into my thoughts. Who hated Sylvester that much? Who hated *me* that much? I couldn't think of anyone, and I wasn't sure I wanted to. The trouble was, I was going to have to figure it out, because until I did I had no way of knowing what had driven Simon out of the Kingdom, or what might have brought him running back, ready to "save me" again. Considering the way he'd saved me the first time, I wasn't sure I could survive a second salvation.

Quentin must have caught my mood. He leaned forward, turning on the radio and flipping through the stations until he found the one that he usually liked to listen to, playing modern folk and light rock from Canada. The Barenaked Ladies were offering to light up my room. He started to sing along, quietly at first, then louder and louder, until I couldn't fight my smile any longer. He grinned back.

"We'll figure this out," he said. "One way or another. I mean, what's the worst he can do? Be spooky at you until Tybalt kicks his ass?"

"There's the fish thing," I said.

"I'd like to see him try."

"You know, it's a funny thing, but after everything that's changed . . . so would I." I hit the gas a little harder, and we left Pleasant Hill behind us.

SEVEN

CALIFORNIA HAS LAWS about motorists using their phones while they're driving, and so I left it up to Quentin to call home while I focused on navigating San Francisco's daytime traffic. I've been nocturnal long enough that driving during the day stresses me out. The streets were filled with homicidal drivers and suicidal pedestrians: cars turned the wrong way up one-way streets, while people crossed against the light, seemingly unaware of the giant metal death machines bearing down on them. I found myself swearing steadily, hands locked around the wheel.

Quentin got off the phone shortly after our third narrowly missed collision. He grimaced. "How do people *do* this every day?"

"I honestly don't know," I said. "What's the news from home?"

"May says they're both fine, and Jasmine is awake and showing no ill effects from Simon's spell. Danny's there in case they need to move. He brought soup and orange juice. Apparently the right way to deal with the aftermath of a magical assault is by treating it like the flu."

He sounded so puzzled that I had to laugh. "Not the worst idea I've ever heard. What did she say when you told her we were heading for the Luidaeg's?"

"That it was a damn good idea, and that as soon as Jazz is up for it, she's going to have Danny take them to Muir Woods."

I nodded. "Good plan. Arden will take care of them." The traffic died as I turned onto a side street that was little more than a glorified alley, replaced by empty sidewalks and a deep, abiding silence. I forced my hands to relax, cutting my speed until we were gliding along, fast enough that it still felt like we were getting somewhere, slow enough that we weren't going to mow down any unsuspecting bicyclists or tourists who had wandered into the wrong neighborhood.

And this was very much the wrong neighborhood for tourists. San Francisco is a city of many faces, with financial districts, slums, and upscale retail neighborhoods existing side-by-side. Maybe it's the hills the city was built on, creating a series of minute geographical divides, but there are parts of San Francisco that feel like they should belong to some other city entirely.

Then there's the Luidaeg's neighborhood.

I knew we were getting close when first the cars and then the pedestrians dwindled to nothing, leaving us to drive alone down deserted, dangerous-looking streets. Everything around us seemed to fall into disrepair as we drove, and even the sky grew darker, dimmed by an omnipresent fog of the sort that the city is justly famous for. Broken glass glittered in the gutters, and crows perched on the telephone wires, croaking to themselves as we passed. This was the territory of the sea witch. All others had best beware.

Tybalt was waiting for us on the corner near her apartment, his hands jammed into his pockets and an impatient look on his face. I pulled up to the curb and killed the engine, smiling as I got out of the car.

"Been waiting long?" I asked.

"Not so long as you might think."

"Good." I started walking toward the Luidaeg's apartment. Tybalt fell into step beside me, and Quentin brought up the rear as the three of us turned into the alley that housed her door. Then I stopped, blinking.

The Luidaeg was sitting on her front step, a pint of Ben and Jerry's Cherry Garcia in her hand. She looked up as we approached. "Ah," she said, sticking her spoon back into the ice cream and standing. "There you are. You're late."

"I didn't know we had an appointment," I said.

"You never do. Come on." With that, she turned and walked through her open apartment door into the hallway beyond.

Tybalt and I exchanged a look. I shrugged, and we followed her inside. The door slammed behind us of its own accord. Apparently, we were going to be staying for a while.

It was hard to say how large the Luidaeg's apartment was, since I'd only ever seen the hallway, living room, kitchen, and bedroom. Several other doors led off the hall. One of them was presumably a bathroom, but the rest were anybody's guess. When you're an undying daughter of Oberon and Maeve, normal physical laws apply only as much as you want them to.

She hadn't bothered putting up her illusions before we came in. The place was spotless, with kelp-colored carpet and cream-colored walls. The air smelled of fresh seawater. If Yankee Candle could have figured out how to bottle that scent, they could have cornered the home fragrance market and put all their competitors out of business in a season. When we reached the living room, we found her sitting in an overstuffed easy chair, stirring her ice cream into an unrecognizable slurry.

"This is going to suck," she said, without preamble.

"You're here because Simon Torquill is back in town, and you want answers. I get that. The problem is, those answers are like a crunchy candy shell surrounding a chewy center of shit I can't talk about. Not won't, can't. As in, 'I am physically unable to tell you what you came here hoping to find out, and there's no way you can word the questions that will get us around that little glitch.'" She sounded genuinely sorry.

I paused, studying her. The Luidaeg didn't just sound sorry; she *looked* sorry. Her shoulders were slumped, and her eyes were fixed on her ice cream, like she couldn't bear to look at us. She seemed perfectly human, with her dark, curly hair hanging loose around her face, which still bore the ghosts of old acne scars. There wasn't even the faint glitter of an illusion to mark her as fae, but that was a reflection of how powerful she really was. Only one of the Firstborn could mask their nature that completely.

"Is this because of a geas?" I ventured.

"Ten points for Amandine's daughter," said the Luidaeg, and licked half-melted ice cream off her spoon before jabbing it viciously back into the container. She raised her head and looked at me. Her eyes were the pale green of sea-tumbled glass, and full of fathomless desperation. "I can't, Toby. You know I can't."

"I know." I worried my lip between my teeth for a moment before I asked, "Can I try finding some questions that don't break any of the rules, but that might help us out?"

"You can try," she said.

"Do you know where Simon Torquill is?"

The Luidaeg blinked. Then she shook her head. "No. He can hide himself from me, the bastard. Old magic, borrowed from your mother, no doubt."

I nodded slowly, tensing a bit. "So you can talk about Mom and Simon."

"That was never technically a secret." She sighed. "I never brought it up with you because, well. What good would it have done? Amy was off in her private fairyland, and Simon was Dad-knows-where. Telling you how they used to do the nasty wouldn't have helped you any, and it might have made it harder for you to sleep."

"Especially if you worded it like that," I said, wrinkling my nose. "Luidaeg ... Mom left him, right? She must have, since she got together with my father. So why didn't she divorce him? There was no land to fight over, and she never took his title. Sylvester said it was because that would mean admitting there was no hope for them, but that just ... that didn't sound right. Something was missing. What isn't he telling me?"

"It didn't sound right because it was only half the story. Fae marriage is a funny, funny thing," said the Luidaeg. "Easy to do, easy to undo, that was always the goal. Dad wanted us to enjoy the same happiness with each other that he had with my mother and with his pretty Summer Queen—and he wanted it to be just as fleeting. Give us eternity and we still measure our lives by the span of seasons." She looked at her ice cream, sighed, and put it aside.

"Some of us believe marriage is for longer than a season's time," said Tybalt mildly.

"Sure, and some of you believe a marriage that lasts longer than a month is some sort of crime against nature." The Luidaeg shook her head. "It's all easy, as long as you only have the people who are getting married to worry about."

I frowned. "Wait, what are you ..." My voice trailed off as a thought struck me. It was the sort of thought I didn't enjoy having, didn't *want* to be having, and would probably have paid a considerable amount to *stop* having. "Fae marriages can be ended at any point by the spouses saying 'we don't want to be married anymore,' unless there are children."

"Any children have to declare which parent they wish to follow, just like all us Firstborn had to declare which parent we belonged to," said the Luidaeg. There was an edge to her words, like they carried a meaning the rest of us hadn't picked up on yet. "It keeps lines of succession straight. But if the child is unable to choose, the marriage must endure."

"Oh, sweet Titania's ass, *please* don't tell me I'm like Arden and I have an elf-shot brother in a box somewhere," I moaned, pinching the bridge of my nose with one hand.

"No, that would be easier," said the Luidaeg. "You have a sister, and she hasn't been elf-shot, although whether she's alive or not is anyone's guess. Her name is August. She's been missing for over a hundred years, which means the only way your mother can divorce Simon is to admit that August is dead. Until that happens, August has a say in the separation."

I lowered my hand, staring at her. "A hundred years? You mean . . ."

"She disappeared just before the earthquake. Just before King Gilad died and this Kingdom went to shit." The Luidaeg's gaze was as dispassionate as the sea that she was named for. "The numbers all align, when you start looking at them properly."

"I am . . . I am not even going to ask you why you never thought I should know that I have a sister who's been missing since before I was born, and am instead going to skip ahead to asking again why you never told me my mother was *married* to the man who turned me into a *fish*. You say it would have made it hard for me to sleep. I say I still needed to know."

"Really?" The Luidaeg tilted her head. "Why is that exactly?"

I blinked at her. "What?"

"I regret saying this even before I have said it, but . . .

perhaps there is value in her question," said Tybalt slowly. "When you first returned to us, you were consumed by despair, and by the longing for vengeance. But what Simon did was not forbidden under any known reading of fae law—he turned a changeling into an animal. There are many who would say that a changeling is already an animal, and so he merely altered your breed. Had you been told, then and there, that Simon Torquill was your stepfather—could anything have induced you to rebuild your bridges with Shadowed Hills? Or would you have devoted your every waking moment to tracking Simon down and getting your revenge, no matter what the cost?"

"You couldn't have defeated Simon as you were; I frankly doubt you could defeat him now," said the Luidaeg.

"I like being your squire," said Quentin. "I'm kind of glad you didn't know any of this sooner."

I groaned. "*When* are you people going to learn that withholding information is not the way to endear yourselves to me?"

"I'm the only one here who withheld anything, Toby, and I did it because you never asked—and yes, because it was a little bit in your best interests, although I would have answered if you'd ever figured out what questions you needed to ask. I've always had a plan, and you've always been part of it." The Luidaeg shrugged. "You running off and getting yourself killed stupidly didn't have a good enough payoff for me."

"Okay," I said, pinching the bridge of my nose again. "We're not only getting off topic, you're making me want to throw things at all of you. So let's move on for right now and I can be pissed off later. Simon said something about having been hired to do what he did to Luna and Rayseline, and not expecting me to be a part of his job. Do you know who his employer was?"

"Yes," said the Luidaeg.

"Can you tell us who his employer was?"

"No." She opened her mouth like she was going to continue, and froze for a long moment, visibly struggling. Finally, she sagged back in her chair and spat to the side, looking disgusted. "Fuck. I can't tell you *anything*. I can't even get so far as animal, vegetable, or mineral. Simon's employer is off limits."

"Okay." I frowned, lowering my hand. "So whoever hired Simon is alive, and you can't say their name, right?" The Luidaeg nodded. "Did this person cast the geas on you themselves, or was it cast by someone else?"

"They cast it themselves," said the Luidaeg. She paused, looking both surprised and pleased. "I wasn't sure I could tell you that. Yes. This geas was created by the person whose name I can't say."

If learning this person's name was as important as I was starting to think it might be, we had a way of doing that. I just didn't want to suggest it until we'd exhausted all other avenues, since it would involve me sampling the Luidaeg's blood. The blood of a Firstborn is nothing to mess around with. No matter how strong my magic got, I was never going to forget how weak I was compared to them. "Could I create a geas powerful enough to bind you?"

The Luidaeg snorted. "No. You're a changeling. Even if you weren't, you'd have to get me to drink your blood if you wanted to bind me like that. And that's not going to happen any time soon."

"Who could?"

There was a pause as she sorted through the words that she was allowed to say. Finally, she said, "Any of my siblings, if I let them get close enough; any son or daughter of Titania. Oaths are a form of illusion, after all. Your squire would have a better chance of binding me than you would, because at least he has the Summer Queen's blood, if not her blessing."

". . . right." There were too many descendants of Titania to rattle off in a list; even if I named every single one

I knew, there were hundreds more within the Kingdom. It didn't help that she didn't formally claim all her descendant lines. Some of them were considered children of Oberon, thanks to the whole "fae children can only inherit from one parent" structure inherent in our society. "Is it someone I know?"

"Yeah."

The Luidaeg and I both froze. It had been a softball question, one I expected to have lobbed back at me with an immediate refusal; something to keep the conversation going.

"What do you—"

"You have to leave now." For a moment, I would have sworn I saw genuine fear in her face. The moment passed, but the memory of it lingered. "I mean it. Get out."

"Luidaeg—"

She pushed herself out of her chair. Her eyes were still green, and her skin was still tan and human; her form wasn't slipping, which was the most frightening thing of all, given how agitated she looked. I'd never seen her this upset without her fae nature beginning to bleed through. Her forgotten pint of Ben and Jerry's fell to its side on the floor as she stood, spilling ice cream everywhere. She ignored it, advancing on me.

"This is my fault. I know it's my fault. I should never have let you get so comfortable. You started thinking of me as harmless. I'm safe. I'm the monster at the end of the book, the one that you run to when the bigger monsters start threatening to eat you, but that's not right, Toby, that's *not right*, you forget yourself. You forget *me*. I am the scariest thing that has ever gone bump in the night. I am what you knew, at the bottom of your unformed child's heart, was lurking in the back of your closet. And what I am telling you, right here and right now, is that you need to leave, because I am afraid of what will happen if you don't."

I stared at her, fighting the urge to take a step backward. Something told me that retreating would mean showing weakness, and showing weakness would be a mistake. "I'm not scared of you. If you were going to kill me, you'd have done it a long time ago, and it wouldn't have been over a yes or no question."

"Toby." She said my name gently, and with a deep, centuries-long sorrow. "Who the fuck said I needed you to be afraid of *me?*" She took another step forward, dropping her voice to a whisper: *"Run."*

I stared at her for a moment before groping behind me until I found Quentin's hand. I trusted Tybalt to run, but Quentin . . . he was even closer to the Luidaeg than I was. If I was having trouble with this, he was going to be staggered. My fingers closed around his.

"I'm sorry," I whispered.

Then I turned and ran, dragging my squire down the hall with me as I fled from the woman who had become one of my staunchest and most trusted allies. I expected to hear things breaking, or worse, the sounds of pursuit, but all that followed us was the unmistakable sound of the Luidaeg sobbing like her heart was broken. It took everything I had to wrench the door open and keep going, rather than turning back to help her.

The door waited to slam until all three of us were standing in the alley, which was blanketed by a thick fog that should have burned off long since. We stood frozen, staring at each other, until Quentin asked in a small voice, "What happened?"

"I think . . . I think I found a loophole," I said. I sounded shell-shocked, like I'd just been through something much worse than a run down a short hallway. "She shouldn't have been able to answer that last question. She shouldn't have been able to tell me that it was someone I knew. That's why she threw us out."

"If she violated the geas, however accidentally, there

may be consequences," said Tybalt, dawning horror in his tone. "She was moving us out of the line of fire."

"We have to help her," said Quentin.

"Yeah, we do, and that means finding a way back *into* the line of fire. We need to know more about what we're dealing with here." I turned and started walking toward the car, digging my phone out of my pocket as I went. Much as I hated cell phones, they had their uses. The name I needed was halfway down my contact list.

It was the middle of the day, an hour when all good fae were snug in their beds like happy little monsters. My call went straight to voicemail. I hung up and called again. It went to voicemail again. I hung up and called a third time. We had reached the car by then; I unlocked the doors and peered into the backseat while I waited for an answer.

This time, I got it. "Hello?" Li Qin sounded groggy and half-aware, which made sense, given that I'd probably just hauled her out of a sound sleep.

"Li Qin, hi. I need a Library pass."

"Toby?" The grogginess faded, replaced by confusion. "Titania's teeth, Toby, it's barely past noon. What's going on?"

January had been Sylvester's niece before she was Li Qin's wife. Trusting that this meant I didn't need to explain the whole tangled history of the Torquills to her, I said, "Simon's back."

Li Qin gasped, all signs of bleariness vanishing from her voice. "What? Where? Is Sylvester all right? Do you need me?"

"No, although it would probably be best if you could check in on April. I'm not sure Simon knows about her, and I'd like to keep it that way." The backseat was clear. I got into the car. Tybalt and Quentin did the same, both of them watching me curiously. "Look, it's a long story, and I don't think this is the time to try explaining it, but

I really need access to the Library right now. The Lui-daeg can't help us, and I need answers."

"Right—of course. I'll wake Mags up. I'm sure she'll be fine with you coming over again. She liked you well enough last time you went to visit, and you didn't burn the Library down, which she appreciates." Li Qin hesitated before offering, "I can twist your luck . . ."

"I don't know if I'm ready to go that far just yet. I'll let you know." Every type of fae has its own gifts. Li Qin could manipulate probability, allowing her to arrange for great coincidences. The trouble was, the scales had to be balanced. The last time I'd allowed her to bend my luck, I had wound up disemboweled. Twice. That didn't mean I wouldn't take the help if it came down to it. It just meant that I had no desire to become reacquainted with my liver.

"Okay. Just . . . be careful, all right? Simon is a very complicated man."

"He turned me into a fish once."

"Yes. Complicated. The Library is still in the same general area, I believe; is Quentin with you?"

I glanced over my shoulder. "He's here."

"I'll text him with directions. You shouldn't text and drive."

I rolled my eyes as I twisted back into my original position. "Okay, wow. Way to slide in a 'safe driving' PSA when I'm about to risk my life doing stupid shit."

"There are some stupid things you don't have to do," said Li Qin primly. "Open roads."

"Kind fires," I said automatically. Hanging up my phone, I tucked it back into my pocket before starting the engine. "Li Qin's going to check in with Mags and then text Quentin with the current location of the Library." Mags was the current Librarian. She could grant and deny access. Even Arden didn't have that power.

"Much as I enjoy the dizzying whirl of your utter lack

of planning, might you explain why we're going to the Library of Stars?" asked Tybalt. He didn't sound annoyed; just baffled, like he was sure there was a perfectly reasonable explanation for my behavior that he simply hadn't figured out yet.

"There can't be that many people I know who are powerful enough to bind the Luidaeg and were here when Luna and Rayseline disappeared. There are even fewer who would scare her like that," I said, driving slowly as I moved through the fog. "If we check the Kingdom histories for around that time, maybe we can find the points of intersection, and figure out what the pieces are that we're missing. And if nothing else, at least we know that Simon won't be able to come after us there. We can regroup."

"Charming," sighed Tybalt. "Ah, well. At least it's a plan, rather than a knee-jerk reaction to a previously unknown threat. That's an encouraging change in your usual mode of operation."

"Jerk," I accused.

"Yes," he said mildly. "But your jerk, which I think buys me a certain measure of leniency."

My reply was cut off by the sound of Quentin's phone chiming. "I've got the address," he said. "We're cleared to enter the Library."

"Great," I said, and hit the gas. It was time to get some answers. If the Luidaeg couldn't help us, we were going to have to help ourselves. And maybe then, we could help her.

EIGHT

FOLLOWING THE DIRECTIONS on Quentin's phone brought us to the Library of Stars in less than twenty minutes, mostly via side streets and alleys where there was no traffic, but where a single trash bin could make the road too narrow for us to continue until somebody got out and moved it. We probably traveled about three miles all told, moving deeper into the heart of the city with every turn we took.

Fae Libraries—capital letter intentional—are strange things, both like and unlike their mortal equivalents. You can't just walk in and request a Library card; unless you've been invited by the current Librarian, you can't walk in at all. All Libraries are constructed in shallowings, space scooped out in the thin membrane between the Summerlands and the mortal world. The doors are hard to find and constantly moving, thanks to the enchantments built into the walls. The only way to get inside is to have a Library card, or to get one of the Librarians to give you permission. Prior to meeting Li Qin and being introduced to Mags, I had never seen a

Library. Now, it seemed we couldn't go six months without my paying a visit.

Last time we'd dropped by, the Library had been concealed behind a secondhand bookstore that had looked like it was on the verge of crumbling into utter disrepair. Despite the fact that the new set of directions had taken us into a completely different neighborhood, we found ourselves in front of that same filthy, rundown bookstore when we pulled up at the address that Mags had provided. Even the doorway had moved, bringing with it a wealth of splinters and ancient spiderwebs.

"Huh," I said, getting out of the car. Tybalt and Quentin followed. "Anybody want to bet that none of the neighbors have noticed this place?"

"I do not take what you call 'sucker bets,'" said Tybalt, wrinkling his nose at the condition of the store window. "I do, however, feel the distinct need to put on gloves before I touch anything."

I paused with my hand on the doorknob, looking back at him. "I don't remember you being this concerned with the condition of the place the last time we were here."

"You had just been exiled the last time we came to the Library," he said, in a reasonable tone. "I am taking this situation very seriously, and yet for once, we are not in such a state of immediate crisis that I am unable to appreciate the little things."

"We're in enough crisis for me," I muttered, and opened the door.

The inside of the bookstore was no better than the outside. A thick layer of dust mixed with glittering pixie-sweat covered every surface, rendering the spines of the books that were stacked in haphazard piles virtually unreadable. Not that I could imagine anyone *wanting* to read most of them; they were all in that awkward window between "new" and "vintage" where they didn't really hold any appeal for anyone. A mortal bibliophile might have squawked at the condition they were in, but since no human was ever likely to set foot in this store, that didn't really matter.

We picked our way between the stacks, all of us going quiet as we concentrated on not knocking anything over. Fae can see in low light, but that doesn't mean it's easy, and a little care was required to reach the faintly shimmering doorway on the far wall. It would have been entirely invisible to mortal eyes. I knew that for a fact; I'd been virtually human the last time I'd been here, thanks to a bad combination of goblin fruit and my own powers. I'd only been able to use the door because Tybalt had picked me up and carried me through.

Well, I was standing on my own two feet now. I took a deep breath and stepped through, crossing from the mortal world into the Library of Stars. There was a brief, dizzying dip, and then I was standing on the clean hardwood floor of the Library, surrounded by tall shelves on all sides. I stepped out of the way, letting Tybalt and Quentin follow me through.

We were still in a confined space surrounded by books, and the faint haze of pixie-sweat still hung suspended in the air, adding a golden sheen to everything it touched, but that was where the similarities between the bookstore and the Library ended. The bookstore smelled like mold and dust and decaying paper, just one step short of despair—and not a long step, either. The Library smelled like knowledge, that strange alchemical mix that only came from combining old books, leather bindings, and care. Lots and lots of care.

The source of that care was hurrying toward us, if the sound of footsteps was any indication. I turned to see Magdaleana Brooke—Mags to her friends, and to anyone who had trouble pronouncing that many vowels—come trotting around the end of a nearby shelf. Her wings were half-spread, leaving yet another overlay of pixie-sweat on the air behind her. "You're here!" she said, sounding almost surprised. Her archaic British accent made her sound like Wendy by way of Tinker Bell, which went well with the rest of her: short, blue-eyed, and red-haired, with a fondness for the long skirts and sensible shoes that suited her chosen profession.

"We are," I said. I hesitated. "You did text Quentin the address, right . . . ?"

"Yes, of course, after Li Qin called, but I didn't expect you to get here so fast."

"We were virtually in the neighborhood," I said. "I'm sorry we had her wake you up, but it's an emergency, and we needed to get started researching as soon as possible."

"You didn't wake me, actually," said Mags. Her wings gave a nervous twitch, spraying glitter over everything within three feet of her. "I was already up."

I blinked. "Really? I thought Puca were nocturnal." Mags' type of fae, the Puca, are almost extinct in the modern world. It wasn't difficult to believe that I might have missed a few things about them.

She shook her head. "We are, normally, but the Library is open whenever a patron requires the use of it, and as Librarian, I have to be on the premises to supervise. Li Qin isn't the only person in this Kingdom with a Library card, you know."

"She's the only one I've ever met," I said.

"That you know of," Mags politely corrected. "You still owe me a history of your mother, you know. You agreed to that the last time you were here."

"I know. I've been busy." I hadn't been, not really; I just hadn't wanted to come back to the Library. Books have never been my thing, and Mags' strange, bright eyes seemed a little too intense when she asked me about Amandine. I would pay my debt to her. Probably faster now that she'd reminded me of it. That didn't mean that

I was ever going to be comfortable among the high-stacked shelves of her domain.

"Luckily for you, I'm relatively patient." She looked from me to Quentin, and finally to Tybalt. "I do have to remind you, however, that the rules of the Library apply to everyone who walks in here, regardless of their race or title. There is no fighting in the Library. Anyone who starts a fight or responds to a challenge will be thrown out. You may think you can take me. You're probably right. But none of you can take the Library. Now come along, this way." She turned and started off into the stacks.

I glanced at Quentin and Tybalt, who looked as confused as I felt. "Any idea what that was all about?" I asked.

"Maybe she thinks you and Tybalt are getting ready to break up?" said Quentin hesitantly.

Tybalt snorted rather than dignifying that with a verbal response. I grinned a little and followed the trail of pixie dust that Mags had left hanging behind herself in the air. It only remained distinct enough to track for a few minutes, but that was more than long enough to lead us through the stacks to the wide open space that served both as a sort of "living room" for Mags and as a central study area for the people who were using the Library. I could hear her voice as we drew closer, quietly scolding someone.

"I guess she told us about fighting because whoever got her out of bed is still here," I said, and stepped around the edge of the last stack, moving out into the open.

Mags turned when she heard my sharply indrawn breath, which was followed by the sound of Tybalt's low, almost subsonic growl. Of the three of us, only Quentin was completely silent. He had gone statuary still. I glanced at him, and saw that his hand was at his belt, resting on the pommel of his sword. His lips were thin and tight with rage.

Simon Torquill looked up from the book he'd been studying, but he didn't otherwise move. That was probably the safest choice he could have made. As long as he was seated on the Library's antique, overstuffed couch, he was about as far from looking like a threat as it was possible for him to be. If he so much as wiggled his fingers in a way I didn't like, I was going to break all the rules against fighting in the Library.

"What is *he* doing here?" I intended my words to come out as a demand, angry and strident and powerful. Instead, they were a squeak, and I probably wouldn't have been able to hear myself if I'd been standing where Mags was.

Either she could read lips or she knew what I was likely to be saying, because she sighed, starting across the floor to the three of us. As she drew closer, she said, "Remember, there is no fighting in the Library. Simon Torquill has a Library card. He hasn't done anything that would cause me to rescind it."

I stared at her. "He turned me into a *fish*."

"Did he do it in the Library?" Mags shook her head, not waiting for me to reply. "I don't make judgments about the character of the people who come here. This is a neutral place, and for it to remain so, the rules have to apply equally to everyone, with no consideration for what they may have done outside these walls. Consider your own history. You've killed a Firstborn and overthrown a Queen. Against your record, turning someone into a fish is positively friendly."

I stared at her. Tybalt's hand on my shoulder saved me from doing anything I might have regretted later. As in "immediately," since we still needed access to the books.

"Even so, given their history, it would have been considerate to warn us," said Tybalt.

Mags frowned at him. "This is my Library," she said, in a colder tone than I had ever heard her use before. "You are guests here, using someone else's card as a pledge against your good behavior. Simon Torquill has his own Library card, and has been a patron for over a century. Exactly why should I be warning *you?* If anything, I should have refused you entry until he said he was done. Be glad that I'm more charitable than you appear to be."

I took a deep breath, trying to force my nerves to stop sounding danger bells in my head. When I was sure that I could speak civilly, I said, "We really do appreciate you letting us come here. The rule about no fighting in the Library . . . does it apply to everyone? I mean, is he going to attack me if I get too close to him?"

"Not unless he wants to be reminded that the Libraries are more than capable of protecting themselves when they have to," said Mags. She shook her head. "If you can't be civil, I'm going to have to ask you to leave. I'm sorry. Rules are rules."

"As long as he doesn't start anything, I can behave myself," I said, looking past her to Simon. He was still sitting on the couch; it didn't look like he had moved an inch since we walked in. I couldn't tell if that was arrogance — showing how little of a threat he considered us all to be — or if he was actually being considerate.

Fighting was forbidden inside the Library. For the first time, it occurred to me that this was something I could use to my advantage.

"Good," said Mags, folding her wings again. "Now, what is it you needed to research? Hope chests again? Did you lose another princess?"

"Probably — they're like loose change, we're always finding them between the couch cushions. But today's topic is 'people who were in the Kingdom twenty years ago, who could be commonly found in either San Francisco, Pleasant Hill, or the corresponding parts of the Summerlands, who would have encountered me, the Luidaeg, and Simon Torquill.' You got a book on that?"

Mags blinked at me, and for a split-second, I actually felt somewhat hopeful. This was a magical Library, after all, operated single-handedly by a woman with dragonfly wings who looked like a teenage girl, despite being a hell of a lot older than that. If miracles could happen anywhere, it was probably here.

"That's a bit more specific than we tend to carry on the general shelves," she said. "How about we start with the last Kingdom census, and see where we can go from there?" She turned and vanished back into the stacks before I could say anything.

"I think milady Librarian is anxious in our company tonight," said Tybalt. His voice was mild, but there was a dangerous edge to it. I knew that if I looked over, he would be staring at Simon, as fixated on his prey as any cat has ever been.

"Yeah, well, I'm a little anxious, too," I said. I bounced slightly on the balls of my feet, wishing Mags would hurry up. "I didn't even know we *had* a Kingdom census."

"They're not very useful," said Quentin. "They omit changelings as transitory, and it's really easy to lose track of people."

Given how easily we'd lost track of Arden and Nolan—the children of our rightful King—I could believe that without trouble. I shook my head, saying nothing as I started across the floor toward Simon.

To his credit, Simon didn't move. He remained exactly where he was, hands visible, no weapons drawn, unless you counted the large, leather-bound book that he'd been reading from. I stopped in front of him, cocking my head to the side in order to read the title.

Geasa and Bindings, it read. I raised an eyebrow and looked at Simon, waiting.

There's an art to staring someone down. It takes practice to find the right combination of bravado and unconcern, that line where "screw you" becomes "whatever." Once you find it, though, you can stay there forever. I maintained eye contact with Simon until his cheeks flushed slightly and he looked away, eyes dipping to the book in his lap.

"I thought there might be a method for dispensing with the trouble I currently find myself grappling with," he said. "As it turns out, bindings of this magnitude are surprisingly difficult to undo, unless you were the original caster." He looked up again, his veneer of superior calm settling over him like a cloak as he turned his head to study Tybalt and Quentin. It was too late. I'd already seen the man beneath the charade, and as I watched him, I realized something that stunned me.

Simon Torquill was afraid.

"I know the King of Cats of old, although he was a Prince when last we had any discourse," he said after a moment, inclining his head respectfully to Tybalt. I glanced to the side in time to see Tybalt bare his teeth in answer. "Your Majesty. I was unaware the Library of Stars had opened their doors to the Third Court. A pleasant surprise."

"I have always been an exception," said Tybalt tersely.

"Indeed, you have proven yourself an exemplary breaker of rules time and time again." Simon turned a smirk in my direction and said, "He may be too shy to tell you this himself, but there was a time when my parents were quite concerned about my sister's honor, all on account of this lovesick tomcat. Dear Rand and I were acquainted in Londinium, long before any of us dreamt we'd meet again in the Americas."

This time, Tybalt's snarl was audible. "Do not speak of your sister in my presence," he said.

I raised an eyebrow. "Interesting as it is to watch you

try to needle my boyfriend, you sort of sound like a soap opera villain right now. 'Gosh and golly, October, why don't you stand there while I reveal a bunch of dirty secrets that stopped mattering centuries ago.' His name is Tybalt now, as I'm sure you're aware, and whatever may have happened with him and your sister happened in another time."

Tybalt shot me a grateful look. Oh, he knew I'd ask him about it later—I didn't go into detective work because I was content to let questions go unasked, or unanswered—but this was neither the time nor the place.

Simon contrived to look offended. "I merely thought—"

"Either you're here to hurt me or you're here to help me," I said. Something about my tone seemed to get through; he fell silent and sank back a bit on the couch, watching me warily. "I have plenty of evidence that you're here to hurt me. You put me in a stasis spell and you tried to transform one of my housemates into a fish, which, I don't know if that's your go-to spell or what, but you should know that that one *really* bothers me, so I'd avoid it if I were you. Just to be sure that I don't accidentally hit you over the head with a lead pipe and bury you in a shallow grave in Muir Woods."

"Queen Windermere probably wouldn't mind too much," said Quentin.

"I assure you, I am not here to hurt you," said Simon gravely. "I acted in haste before. I did not expect . . . any of what happened in that kitchen, I swear. It was as much a surprise to me as it was to you."

"Kinda doubt that, since you came to me, and that was the first surprise of the day," I said, unable to keep a note of sour impatience from my tone. "It's been a day just *full* of surprises."

"I would agree," said Simon. "You are much more your mother's daughter than I had been led to believe."

"No thanks to her," I said.

Simon didn't comment on that. I guess having his stepdaughter insult his wife wasn't something he felt he needed to get involved in. Instead, he looked past me to Quentin, and said, "Since you are only known to keep company with two teenage boys, and this one lacks fangs, he must be your squire. Hello." He shifted his position slightly, making it somehow clear that I was no longer the focus of his attention. "I understand you were originally fostered in Shadowed Hills, in the care of my brother. That must have been a great change for you."

"Didn't you used to date Oleander de Merelands?" asked Quentin. He sounded every inch the sullen teenage delinquent, his usual courtly—and yes, princely—graces abandoned. I could have hugged him in that moment. If Simon didn't already know who he was, there was no need to give him reason to suspect.

As for Simon, he hesitated, stiffening, before finally nodding and saying, "I kept company with the lady you have named many times over the centuries. It was generally at the behest of our mutual . . . employer." He choked on the final word, as if even saying that much was difficult for him. After a pause that lasted only a few seconds, he managed to continue, "Our relationship was perhaps more intimate than my lady wife would have preferred, but as Amandine and I were unavoidably separated at the time, she and I have never been forced to discuss the matter. I was very sorry to hear of Oleander's death."

"Oh?" asked Quentin. "Why, because she didn't manage to take any of us with her?"

"No," said Simon. "Because I wanted to kill her myself, and hadn't had the opportunity to do so yet. You want me to be a villain: things are always easier when there's a clear villain, and I can fill the role admirably. I have before, and I probably will again. Please don't mistake villainy for evil. The two can exist side by side while remaining quite distinct. And Oleander, for all her good points—and she did have some, although they were regrettably few and far between—was evil."

For a moment, we all just stared at him. Finally, I blurted, "Why didn't Mom ever tell me about you?"

"I'm sure she had her reasons," said Simon, looking away. "Your mother and I . . . we didn't part cleanly. We both had our ideas of what needed to be done in order to resolve things we had left unresolved. Mine involved some choices she was not comfortable making. Hers involved, for me, too much safety and reliance on other people. She thought that just because she was Firstborn, the world would eventually realize she should get her way."

"Sort of hard for the world to realize that when she didn't tell anybody."

Simon smiled slightly, the expression tinged with clear regret. "Amy has always been fond of secrets," he admitted.

"Yeah, well, I'm pretty much done with secrets, so let me make myself perfectly clear," I said. "Tybalt and Quentin are mine. So is your brother. So is my Fetch and her girlfriend, and anyone else you look at and think 'gosh, Toby would be upset if I hurt this person.' You follow? Because I won't just be upset. I'll be angry. And you'll be sorry."

"Is everything all right over here?" Mags' voice broke in, and I turned almost guiltily to find her emerging from the stacks with the thickest book I'd ever seen clasped in her arms. Her wings were vibrating rapidly, sending sprays of pixie-sweat in all directions as she eyed the four of us. "Remember what I said about fighting in the Library."

"No one's fighting," I said. "Some threatening, yes, and maybe a little glaring, but there's been no fighting, I swear."

"Count Torquill?" said Mags.

Simon rose. He moved stiffly, like his left leg didn't bend right. "It's quite all right, Miss Brooke. My step-daughter and her friends were simply reminding me that I am not one of their favorite people, but as they did so in a calm and nonviolent manner, I can't really take offense. I think I'm done with my research for today, however, so if you'll excuse me, I'll be going."

"Wait!" The word escaped before I could prevent myself from speaking. Simon stopped in his tracks, turning to stare at me. Everyone else did something similar. Cheeks burning, I swallowed, and said, "Wait, please. I have to ask you something."

"Am I the villain, or am I the person you ask when you need information?" Simon asked. He didn't sound annoyed, quite, but he sounded like he very easily could be. "What do you want to know, October?"

"You came to my house."

"Yes."

"You said . . . you said you were there to help me."

"Yes, I did," said Simon, looking briefly frustrated. "But there are so many barriers on what I can say that I don't see how I can do that, unless you're willing to let me turn you into a tree and plant you someplace where you won't be found for a hundred years."

I stared at him. "The spell I threw back at you this morning. Is *that* what it was supposed to do?"

"I said I was going to help you, October," he said. "I didn't say you were going to appreciate it."

Tybalt started to growl again, low and deep in his chest. I glanced toward Quentin. If he'd been Cait Sidhe, he would have been making the same sound. As it was, he was glaring at Simon with such intensity that I was half afraid the other man was going to spontaneously combust. I put my arms out slightly, just enough that I'd be able to grab them if they tried to lunge. The last thing we needed was to get kicked out of the Library before we'd learned anything useful.

"The Luidaeg is under a geas, too," I said. "Did you know that?"

"I am aware," said Simon. "It is a surprise to hear you went to her. I expected you to be rather more timid, or at least smarter."

"She's my aunt," I said, like that explained everything. "She was able to get around the binding enough to tell me that the person who bound her was someone I know. Do you know who bound the Luidaeg?"

"I do," he said.

"Did the same person bind you?"

Simon looked at me for a moment, mouth moving as he tried to force words out past a tongue that no longer seemed to want to cooperate with him. Finally, he made a choking sound, and said, "I have to leave." Then he turned, still stiff, left leg barely bending, and made his way quickly into the stacks.

I stayed where I was, looking after him.

"Was there a point to that?" asked Mags. She sounded annoyed.

"We pretty much knew from the Luidaeg that they were bound by the same person, but I wanted it confirmed. And I wanted to see whether Simon would tell me the truth."

"But he didn't tell you anything," Mags protested.

"Sure he did," I said. "If he'd been lying to me, a 'no' would have cost him nothing." I turned back to Tybalt and Quentin. "Put on your studying shoes, boys. We've got work to do."

NINE

IT WAS DIFFICULT TO focus on research with the ghost of Simon Torquill hanging over us, an unwanted presence we could neither dispel nor deny. Worrying about the Luidaeg made it even harder, until focus seemed like a beautiful dream. I sat on the Library's antique couch with the bulky census open on my knees, running my finger down columns of names and trying to associate them with faces dredged from the dusty recesses of my mind. Quentin was settled next to me, going through a box of dusty sheets of loose-leaf paper that Mags had fetched from wherever it was that historical records went to die. He had refused to split the burden, insisting that his knowledge of the political divides within the Mists would be more useful than Tybalt's actual observation of the Court. I had refused to get involved, and in the end, Tybalt had ceded the point.

I sort of wished he hadn't, since in the absence of anything else that needed to be reviewed, Tybalt was pacing around the edges of the room-sized square where we were working. It was getting on my nerves, quite honestly, but my attempts to convince him he should maybe go elsewhere had met with disdain.

"Do you honestly believe that, after you have encountered Count Torquill not once but twice in a single day, I'll allow you to ask me to leave your side?" he had asked, eyes blazing. "I'm not sure how relationships are commonly conducted in this modern age, but I am absolutely certain that a proper suitor does not leave his lady to be turned into a fish because she would feel more 'comfortable' were he elsewhere."

That had settled the matter. Tybalt only got that formal with me when he was really unhappy. I was a little uncomfortable with his pacing, but as he would clearly have been *extremely* uncomfortable leaving me—even in the Library, where I was supposed to be safe—I didn't press the issue.

Mags came and went, mostly to make sure we hadn't started eating the books while she was taking care of her filing. I was still a little pissed about her not having warned us that Simon was there, so I didn't have much to say to her. Maybe it was unfair of me, but hey. I'm part of Faerie, and Faerie isn't fair.

"I've never heard of half these people," said Quentin glumly, picking up another stack of loose pages. The motion dislodged a patch of pixie-sweat, and for a moment, we were both distracted by sneezing.

When the air finally cleared, I wiped my nose and said, "If your records are anything like mine, I've got a partial reason for that: like you said, the census doesn't count changelings, and we're not *that* transitory. Devin isn't in here, and he was in the Kingdom before the 1906 earthquake. I'm not in here either, but Mom is, and she's listed as 'bride of Simon, mother of August.'" I shook my head, unable to keep the bitterness from my voice as I said, "All these thrice-cursed years of people withholding information from me, and all I had to do was drop by my local Library and ask for the phone book."

"Ah, but first you had to find someone with a Library card and earn their trust enough that they would share its graces with you," said Tybalt, as his pacing brought him close enough for conversation. "Sadly, 'all those years' were vital parts of your unintentional master plan. The Court of Cats will not be listed on those rolls either. We do not take part in the petty schemes of the Divided Courts."

"Like the census?" I shot him a venomous look. "Did I tell you recently just how good you are at not being even remotely helpful?"

"Ah, but you see, I am *exceedingly* helpful." He leaned in to kiss the top of my head. "As long as your aggravation has a safe target, you'll keep focusing on your work, and not become too frustrated to continue. I am the most helpful thing in this room."

"I resent that," said Quentin.

"Many men have resented me in their days, young prince," said Tybalt. "Be proud of the legacy you have joined."

"Tybalt, don't taunt my squire," I said. "Quentin, don't kill my boyfriend. Both of you, shut up and let me work."

Tybalt laughed and resumed pacing. I shook my head, sinking deeper into the couch. At least one of us was happy.

I'd managed to make it through the census of Golden Gate and halfway through the census of Dreamer's Glass before Quentin spoke again. "There are too many names," he said. "We're going to be here forever, and since we don't know for sure who Simon and the Luidaeg both know, we can't really eliminate anyone."

"And since there are no changelings on the list, we're missing a whole swath of potential candidates." I leaned forward, pinching the bridge of my nose. "We don't have time for this. We're not going to be able to figure it out this way, but I don't know what else to do."

"Do you really think it could be a changeling?" asked Mags. I looked up to find her standing at the edge of the workspace, another pile of books in her arms. "I mean . . . I'm not trying to sound dismissive or anything, but most changelings couldn't power a geas as strong as the one you described. It would burn their hearts to ashes in their chests."

"Chelsea Ames," I said. "She was a changeling strong enough to rip a door to Annwn in the walls of the world. You can't write changelings off just because most of us aren't that powerful. Some of us break all the rules, and that means there's no universally right answer."

"Maybe Mags is on to something, though," said Quentin. "We're looking at the census of the Kingdom's fae, right? Minus the changelings and the Cait Sidhe and I guess anyone who didn't feel like being counted."

"Right," I said.

"Yes," Mags said.

"Blind Michael isn't on here," Quentin said.

It was enough of a curveball that I paused for a moment, trying to adjust to this new information. It wasn't happening. Frowning, I said, "That doesn't surprise me—he didn't technically live in this Kingdom since he had his own skerry. What are you getting at?"

"I guess just that there are people who have contact with this Kingdom all the time, but manage to stay outside of it. What if Dianda cast the geas? Patrick is listed, but she's not. It could be almost anyone from the Undersea."

"No, kidnapping isn't their style." I didn't have to think about the words before I said them. The denizens of the Undersea might slit your throat or invade your lands, but they wouldn't kidnap your children. That simply wasn't how business was done down there. "Also, if

Simon's employer had been someone from the Under-sea, turning me into a fish wouldn't have saved me. It would have put me on the menu."

"It can't have been Blind Michael," said Quentin. "He doesn't fit the 'living' part of the description."

"Well, I don't think Acacia would have arranged to have her own daughter and grandchild kidnapped and imprisoned," I said. "She was too happy to see Luna again when we broke Michael's Ride."

Mags was staring at us, open-mouthed. I shot her a curious look. She recovered her composure enough to say, "I just—you people talk of the First as if they were commonplace, as if we should all be seeing them on a regular basis and having them over for tea. It's so strange. Even in my youth, the First were rare creatures, better left to someone else's story than drawn into your own."

"Mom's Firstborn," I said, with a shrug. "It makes me harder to impress." Now that Mags had pointed it out, the strangeness of the situation was visible to me, too. There was a time when meeting *any* of the Firstborn would have been a terrifying notion. Now it was basi-cally Tuesday.

"Your mother," said Tybalt thoughtfully.

"Yeah?" I frowned at him. "What about her?"

"She knows the Luidaeg, obviously, in the same way Acacia does; they are all of them sisters. She knows Si-mon. She must have, to have married him."

My eyes narrowed. "I don't like where this is going."

"I did not expect you to. That doesn't mean you can refuse to come along for the journey." Tybalt shook his head, expression turning grim. "She knows everyone we know to have been bound, and she has never kept any counsel save her own."

"I'll be the first to admit that I have issues with my mother, but she's still my *mother*, and you may want to back off on the whole 'your mother may have ruined your life' song that you're starting to sing," I said, a dangerous note in my tone. "I don't like it, it doesn't suit you, and you're beginning to piss me off."

"That doesn't mean you don't need to hear it," said Tybalt flatly. "Amandine is as strong a candidate to have spun this geas as any other. We cannot rule her out just because you do not want her to have done it, my little fish. If the world were that kind a place, it would be so different as to have never made us."

"Fine. *Fine*. I can deal with this in one phone call." I'd been looking for an excuse to pick up the phone anyway, although I couldn't bring myself to say that part out loud. I dug my phone out of my pocket and began pressing the keys in a spiral, moving outward from the center. When I reached the end, I spiraled back in, and chanted, "One's for sorrow, two's for joy, three's a girl, four's a boy." The smell of copper and freshly cut grass rose in the air around me.

"What's she doing?" asked Mags, sounding concerned.

"Calling the Luidaeg," said Quentin. I saw him shrug out of the corner of my eye. "Toby usually does that when she wants to ask questions that could get her dismembered. You get used to it. I'm surprised she hasn't done it already, since worrying about the Luidaeg is part of why we're here."

"I'm not sure I'd want to get used to it," said Mags.

I rolled my eyes as I raised the phone to my ear. There was no ringing: instead, there was the distant sound of waves, beating themselves endlessly against some unseen rocky shore. That was normal. The Luidaeg's phone isn't connected to any official "service," either mundane or fae, and it reacts differently every time I call it. I think the creepiest thing it could do at this point is actually behave like a normal phone.

There was a click. The sound of waves stopped, replaced by empty air. That, at least, was unusual. I frowned. Normally the Luidaeg answered her phone by yelling at me. "Luidaeg?" I said.

There was no response. I thought I heard someone breathing, but it was a thin, distant sound, and it could have just been air running over the receiver.

I tried again: "Luidaeg? Are you there? Is something wrong with the connection?" I could always hang up and recast the spell, if that was the case. The fragments of my magic were still hanging in the air around me, ready to be grabbed.

Still the silence, and the faint, distant sound of what could be breathing.

"Okay. I'm going to try again." I hung up, raising my head to look at the others. "Something was wrong with the connection. I didn't get her."

"That's weird," said Quentin. "That's never happened before, has it?"

"No," I said, barely keeping myself from snapping. Fear was beginning to rise in my throat, thick and cloying. I dialed again, this time in an X-shape. "Five's for silver, six for gold, seven for a little girl who dreams of getting old," I chanted. The magic rose, burst, and fell into the air around me as I raised the phone back to my ear.

Again, there was the sound of waves, followed by a click and silence. This time, I held the phone out to Tybalt, motioning for him to come closer and listen. Cait Sidhe have exceptionally good hearing. It's a part of their feline nature.

He leaned in, bringing his ear to the phone. Then he frowned, and plucked the phone from my hand without saying a word as he straightened up. Seconds ticked by. He raised a hand, motioning for the rest of us to remain silent. Finally, he said, "If this is some form of punishment for October having asked you things she should not have asked, say so now. Failure to speak shall be taken as consent for what you know will follow."

More seconds ticked by. He hung up the phone, tossing it back into my hands.

"Your squire has learned the necessary skills to drive in this mortal world, has he not?" he asked. There was a tight edge to his voice, like he was just this side of losing his composure. That was bad. When Tybalt loses his composure, things are always bad.

"I don't have my license, but I can drive," said Quentin.

I set the census aside as I stood, shoving the phone back into my pocket. "Why are we making Quentin drive? How freaked out am I supposed to be right now?"

"Someone was there, but it was not the Luidaeg," said Tybalt, stepping in close to me. I recognized this as preparation for towing me into the Shadow Roads, and zipped my jacket as he continued: "The tempo of the breaths was wrong. Someone else is answering her phone."

There was no way in this or any other world that that could be a good thing. "We need to go back to her apartment." I pulled the car keys out of my coat pocket and lobbed them underhand at Quentin, who plucked them from the air. "Get there as fast as you can. Call when you're at the alley." Don't be dumb; don't walk into a potential ambush. In short, don't be like your mentor, since I was about to run headlong into yet another life-or-death situation.

What can I say? I know my strengths, and I like playing to them. "Leaping before looking" is absolutely in my top ten Greatest Hits.

"I'll see you there," said Quentin.

I glanced to Mags. "Sorry. Not paying my debt about Mom today."

"I'm sure I'll be seeing you soon," she said, ingrained

politeness overwhelming the dismay that I saw written clearly on her face.

Then Tybalt's arms closed around me and we fell backward into the shadows, descending into the darkness that never broke. He let go of my waist as soon as we were through, his fingers locking around my right wrist, and together we ran down the Shadow Roads. I quashed my rising panic; it's hard to panic and hold your breath at the same time, and I wouldn't do the Luidaeg any good if I gave myself hypothermia by trying to breathe in a place where there was no good air, only the endless cold. Instead, I focused on trying to match my stride to Tybalt's, counting his steps instead of counting the breaths that I wasn't taking. It helped a little, and anything that helped me to survive the shadows was a good thing.

Tybalt and I emerged from the Shadow Roads and into the more mundane shadows of an alley near the Luidaeg's apartment. Her wards prevented him from getting us any closer. I hit the ground running—or tried to, anyway. I made it four steps before the lack of air and the glimmers of frostbite at my extremities brought me to a screeching halt. I caught myself against the alley wall, coughing the ice from my lips and out of my throat. Tybalt stood nearby, wary and watching. The Shadow Roads were hard on the Cait Sidhe, but it was a difficulty that they dealt with for their entire lives. Those same Roads were still new and cruel to me, and I was reminded of that fact every time we had to use them.

"If you can run . . ." he began.

"I can run," I said, and pushed myself away from the wall as I did just that. Tybalt paced me, close enough to leap to my defense if I triggered a booby trap, far enough away that we weren't going to trip over each other. Running that way was almost second nature for us these days. Anything that thought we were easy pickings would find itself in an awkward situation. With enough warning, we could even—

The thought died half-formed as we came around the corner and entered the Luidaeg's alleyway. Her door was right in front of us . . . or it should have been, anyway. I stumbled to a stop, eyes wide, and stared in disbelief.

The apartment door had been kicked in, knocking the rotten wood right off of its rusted hinges. Chunks of broken doorframe littered the front stoop. The Luidaeg had never seemed to be that worried about personal security—she maintained her wards, because that's just what you *do*, but she'd never given any indication that she expected to have them challenged. I guess being an immortal water demon from the dawn of Faerie makes you a little bit careless. The life that was likely to be endangered by anyone foolish enough to break into her home wasn't going to be hers.

"Blood," I whispered. "I smell blood."

"October . . ." Tybalt's hand caught my wrist. I froze. I hadn't even realized I'd started moving again. I couldn't take my eyes off that gaping hole where a door should have been. "This isn't right."

"Oh, you think?" I tried to pull my wrist away. He didn't let go. I turned to level a glare at him. "You need to let me go now, Tybalt. I smell blood. The Luidaeg could be hurt in there. She could need me."

"Or she could be dead, and you could be walking headlong into the grasp of whatever killed her." He frowned. "This is too strange and too easy and I do not like it."

"Neither do I." This time when I pulled away, he let go of my wrist. "We ran here because she might need us. I'm not going to run away again just because we were right."

"I know." His frown faded, replaced by a coldly predatory expression. I'd seen it on his face before, usually right before something got seriously hurt. "We will go slowly. We will stay together. And if I have to, I will drag you with me onto the Shadow Roads."

"Agreed," I said, and turned back to the hole that had once been the Luidaeg's front door. Everything about this situation felt wrong; everything I'd ever learned about self-preservation screamed for me to turn around and run. I drew my knife.

With Tybalt to guard my back, I walked forward, into the apartment.

TEN

THE HALLWAY WAS dark, although I couldn't have said whether the lights were off or broken. The Luidaeg's illusions were back at full strength, cloaking everything with filth and decay. I wanted to take that as a good sign—most people can't maintain illusions when they're dead—but this was the Luidaeg, and all bets were off. Maybe the clean, well-organized apartment she lived in was actually a horrible, rotting shell that she'd transfigured into something more livable, and now the transformation was falling apart. I didn't know. The Luidaeg had never told me, and suddenly my lack of information felt like it could be the thing that got one or both of us seriously hurt.

The smell of blood was stronger now that we were inside, although it was still weak enough that I couldn't be sure we were going in the right direction. I wasn't even sure whether it belonged to the Luidaeg. I breathed in deeper, trying to confirm, and almost gagged on the smell of rotting wood and decaying fabric. No more deep breaths for me.

The carpet made nasty sucking sounds as we picked

our way through the debris, making a silent approach impossible. Even Tybalt couldn't move without making noise. That would normally have been a little reassuring, since I find Cait Sidhe stealth slightly unsettling under most circumstances. At the moment, I wished there were something I could do to muffle our steps. Anything that might have given us an advantage.

But there was nothing. We walked down the hallway to the living room, where the moonlight filtering in through the grime-smeared windows illuminated a level of chaos that was unusual even for the Luidaeg. Her coffee table had been smashed down the middle, reduced to a pile of splinters, and two moldering cushions from the couch were split open. Muddy stuffing and rotten feathers were scattered around the room. Cockroaches skittered around the edges of the walls, disturbed by our motion.

I stopped, motioning for Tybalt to do the same, and closed my eyes as I broke my promise to myself and took a deep breath of the cloying, fetid air. I was looking for the source of the blood I'd been smelling since the street, and maybe traces of a bloodline that didn't belong to one of us. I was hoping for something that might lead us to whoever had done this, or maybe an early warning before someone dropped an illusion and attacked.

What I wasn't expecting was the way the blood slapped me across the face, so strong that it nearly knocked me off my feet. I gasped before I could stop myself, stumbling backward as my eyes snapped open. Tybalt was there to catch me by the shoulders, steadying me and keeping me from landing on my ass on the Luidaeg's floor.

"What is it?" he whispered, lips close to my ear.

"Blood," I managed.

"So you've said," he said. "What—"

But I had already turned my attention back to the room, swinging my head back and forth like a bloodhound seeking a scent until finally I found it and plunged forward, heedless of the trash and obstacles littering the floor. Let Tybalt watch my back; I needed to find the source of that blood. I needed to know if the Luidaeg was okay.

The smell of blood led me to the shredded couch, which was flipped over to create a smaller bubble of hidden space within the greater room. The Luidaeg was behind it, lying on the floor in a crumpled heap. Two more split cushions had fallen to cover her, mostly hiding her body under a veil of poly-foam blend stuffing. I threw them aside, almost grateful for the brief reek of mold that accompanied the motion. At least it was something to obscure the smell of blood, if only for an instant. The Luidaeg didn't move.

The Luidaeg wasn't okay.

"October?" asked Tybalt from behind me.

"Here!" I dropped to my knees on the carpet. The squelching noise my landing made had nothing to do with seawater. There was blood *everywhere* in this terrible little corner of the room, soaking into everything it touched. Grabbing the Luidaeg's head, I turned it until she was facing me. "Luidaeg? Can you hear me?"

My eyes had adjusted enough to the dark that I had no trouble seeing the long streak of half-dried blood running down the side of her face, dipping inward at the corner of her mouth before tracing the line of her neck and vanishing under the collar of her blood-soaked sweatshirt. A bruise had blossomed under her left eye like some sort of terrible flower, all bitter yellows and deep purples. More blood was matted into her hair, turning her normally wavy curls into a jagged mass of spikes and snarls.

"Oh, root and branch . . ." I whispered, feeling under her jaw for a pulse. She looked so much smaller than I had always believed her to be, her natural illusions withering and fading away. The Luidaeg had seen legacies born, seen empires rise and kingdoms fall. She was older than anyone else I had ever met, even Blind Michael. Along with her sisters, she had once been the terror of bog and fen, a mother of nightmares and a sister to screams.

But that was so long ago. Her brothers and sisters had been hunted and killed by Titania's jealous children, or by descendants of Oberon looking for an easy path to becoming heroes. Her fens had dwindled until she was nothing but a dockside squatter, and still she'd been re-membered. She'd become a monster to her parents' sur-viving children, and she'd made the role her own. She was too old and too much a part of our heritage to die.

She couldn't do that to me.

"Is there a pulse?"

Tybalt's voice snapped me out of my brief reverie. I searched her throat again, pressing my shivering fingers into the soft skin of her neck, and shook my head. "There's no pulse."

If she wasn't gone, then she was going, and there was nothing anyone could do about it.

No. The thought crossed my mind, followed instantly by a chilling resolve that wound through me like the Shadow Roads, freezing everything it touched. Maybe it was true that most people couldn't do anything about it, but I was Amandine's daughter. I was among the first of the Dóchas Sidhe. And this was *not* going to happen on my watch.

"Help me move her," I said, shoving my knife back into my belt and sliding my hands under her arms before I started to stand. Every shift of my position brought another of her wounds into view. There was so much blood.

Tybalt moved immediately around to lift her feet, ask-ing, "Where are we going?"

"Her room. Even if it's trashed, the bed's big enough

that we should be able to find a flat space to lay her out on, and I'm going to need room to maneuver."

"October . . ." He frowned at me, expression speculative, even as he began backing across the living room toward the hall. He knew me and my limitations better than almost anyone else, and he wasn't going to make me walk backward across a dark, cluttered room. "Are you preparing to do something utterly foolish, or simply stupid?"

"Remember that time I raised the dead?" In the basement at Tamed Lightning, just me and my knife and the body of Alex Olsen, who'd had information that I needed. I hadn't even known what I was back then; I'd thought I was just another Daoine Sidhe, one with an unusually high tendency to wind up bleeding all over the damn place.

Tybalt's eyes narrowed. "I recall something that might fit that description," he said. "I recall, for example, that I did not speak to you for quite some time afterward, since you had done something that should have been impossible."

"We know it's not impossible. Not for me."

"October—"

"I have to try!" I wasn't intending to shout. I did it anyway. My voice seemed to echo in the small, dark space of the hall. Tybalt looked at me, his eyes opening wide in surprise. I looked back at him, trying to make him see how desperate I was. "If there's anything I can do . . . she's been threatening to kill me since the day we met, and she's been saving me the whole time. I can be with you because of her. I'm here because of her. I have to *try*."

"I would never have asked you not to try," he said quietly. "I only need you to tell me what I can do to help you."

I smiled a little. "Just hold me up when my legs give out."

"My dear, that is something I will always be here to do."

We carried her through the junk-clogged hall to her bedroom door. It took some shuffling, but we managed to transfer her entirely into Tybalt's arms. The Luidaeg had never been larger than a human teenager. He held her easily, and I was grateful for her long, blood-matted hair, which hid her face from me.

The door to her room swung open as soon as I touched it, and the light of a thousand candles flooded out into the hall, seeming to chase away the clutter and the grime with its touch. Inside, the walls were lined with saltwater tanks rich with exotic fish and stranger creatures, things that were never meant to thrive in the oceans of this world. The pearl-eyed sea dragon she kept in the largest tank reared back when it saw us framed in the doorway, me with my bloodstained clothes, Tybalt with the Luidaeg in his arms.

I held up my hand. "Don't freak out," I said. "We're not the ones who hurt her. I just want to help."

The dragon glared at me, but it didn't break the glass of its tank and come rampaging out into the room, so I was willing to call that a victory, however small. I gestured for Tybalt to put the Luidaeg down on the wide expanse of her four-poster bed. Its frame was ornately carved with mermaids and seaweed, and it reminded me of the furniture Arden had kept with her during her exile from her own Kingdom. It's funny the things the mind throws up to protect itself from panic. Trivia suddenly matters more than anything else in the world.

The Luidaeg's head lolled like a dead thing's as Tybalt maneuvered her onto the mattress, setting a pillow under her neck to support it. He stepped back, glancing at me, and for a moment I could see the naked terror in his eyes, the fear he'd been hiding under bravado and efficiency. I managed another small smile, forcing it until the corners of his mouth relaxed, just a little.

"I won't do anything I haven't done before," I said.

"That's what I am afraid of," he replied.

Talk was just putting off the inevitable. I drew my knife for the second time before gingerly lifting her right arm and turning it until the underside of her wrist faced the ceiling. I winced. A deep cut had split her flesh, opening it to reveal the pale ice-blue of her bones. It ran parallel to the vein. That explained the blood. Someone had been trying to bleed her out, and they might well have succeeded.

I've said it before, and I'll say it again: blood magic is based on a potent combination of instinct and need. The two feed and inform each other, shifting their balance as the situation demands. Need something that the blood can give you badly enough, and there's a very good chance that you can have it ... if you're willing to pay the price. If you're willing to bleed for it.

There was a time when I would have taken care in injuring myself. That time was long past. I slashed my knife hard across my own wrist, hard enough that a few drops of blood spattered the Luidaeg's cheek, standing out against what was already there only because they were fresh and red, not brown and dried. The smell of cut grass and copper rose around me, bloody and aching, as my magic responded to the wound. I took a deep breath, gritting my teeth against the pain. No matter how fast I heal, pain will always hurt. I guess that's a good thing. It keeps me from getting more careless than I already am.

Gingerly, I placed my knife on the bed next to the Luidaeg's unmoving body, trying to remember what I'd done to resurrect Alex Olsen. It hadn't been that long ago. It felt like a lifetime. Blood ran down my arm and covered my fingers, dripping onto the duvet and leaving little red spots everywhere it hit. The wound itched, already healing, but it was too late; I had what I needed.

I raised my hand and caressed the Luidaeg's cheek,

wiping away the old blood in a veil of the new. My magic rose around me, cresting and filling the room with the smell of potential. It was up to me to sail this ship safely through the storm and into whatever port I could find, no matter what. I pressed my hand flat over the Luidaeg's heart, leaving a bloody handprint behind. Her skin was so cold it felt almost like it burned.

"Oak and ash and rowan and thorn are mine," I chanted, bringing my wrist to my mouth. "Salt and wind and witch-willow flame are mine." I licked what blood I could from the rapidly healing cut, and when that wasn't enough, I bit, cutting my own flesh with the jagged ivory edges of my teeth. It hurt as badly as anything I had ever done to myself, and that was exactly right, because this *should* hurt, this *should* cost. If it didn't, I would be lost.

This time, I got a solid mouthful of blood before the bleeding slowed too much to be useful. I swallowed, and it froze all the way down.

"Blood is blood and power is power," I said. "By the root and the branch and the tree, by our Lord and Ladies, live." I paused, and added more softly, "For Maeve's sake, live. What are mothers with no daughters left to live for?"

Nothing happened. My magic hung heavy in the room, the smell of it almost strong enough to be overpowering. "Live!" I commanded, and grabbed my knife. No time for chewing now; the ritual, if you could call it that, was too far along. I slashed the inside of my wrist open, cutting too hard and too deep for safety, and filled my mouth with my own blood. Then, before I could think better of what I was doing, I leaned forward and clamped my lips over the Luidaeg's, forcing my blood through them until some of it was forced down her throat by simple gravity.

The magic snapped solid with a painful flash, the blood suddenly rushing out of my mouth, and off of my body, like it was being pulled into a whirlwind. I could *feel* the heavy stickiness being pulled from my hands and arms, leaving them clean. I tried to pull away, and the Luidaeg's arms closed around me with impossible strength, holding me fast.

I didn't know what to do. I couldn't pull away; I couldn't breathe. So I bit her, and the cold strength of her blood filled my mouth, strangely devoid of memories. I swallowed it anyway, trying to use it to break free. It didn't work. Black spots were beginning to swim in front of my eyes as I struggled ineffectually against her hold. I could hear Tybalt shouting something in the distance, but he was too far away to help me; only the ghosts of his hands could reach me where I was, scrabbling uselessly at the edges of the world. I shouldn't still have been bleeding, but I was, and the Luidaeg was somehow taking it all.

There's only so much blood a body can afford to lose, and the hammering pulse of my heart warned me that I was rapidly running out. Then, abruptly, the Luidaeg let me go, and I was shoved away, collapsing like a rag doll into Tybalt's waiting arms.

"October?" He sounded closer now. That was a good thing, since he was holding me. I raised my head, and found him staring down at me. "What just happened?"

My headache, almost gone before, had blossomed anew like some perverse flower, spreading to fill my entire skull. I groaned as I forced myself to turn toward the bed, squinting against the candlelight. "I don't know," I said. "Hopefully, something good." My vision cleared and I sighed, half from relief, and half from simple exhaustion.

The Luidaeg was sitting up.

Whatever force had cleaned up the blood that had been covering me had done the same for her; her clothing, while torn to the point of uselessness, was spotless, and her hair fell in its usual heavy curls, shining and unsnarled.

She was staring in awe at her hands, looking at them like she'd never seen them before. Her wounds were gone. Even the bruise on her cheek had vanished.

"Hey," I said, trying to pull away from Tybalt and stand on my own two feet. I stumbled, and he caught me, lending me the stability I needed. My head was pounding. I did my best to ignore it. "Welcome back to the land of the living."

The Luidaeg raised her head, focusing on me. Her eyes were a clear, simple driftglass green. "What did you do?" she asked.

"Do?" I echoed. There were still black spots dancing around the edges of my vision. I tried to shake them away. Bad move; shaking my head just made the black spots double while my headache throbbed.

"Do," said the Luidaeg, holding her hands out to me like they were all the answer I could possibly need. There was a thin white line of scar tissue on her left arm, where the deepest of the cuts had been. I was willing to bet that, given time, even that would fade away.

"I . . . you weren't responding, but I thought there was a chance you weren't quite dead yet, and so I . . ."

"You brought me back." There was no mistaking the quiet wonder in her tone. "I was dead."

"Not quite."

"Yeah, Toby, I was dead." She shook her head. "I know what dead feels like. It's cold there. It's very cold. And I was dead." She wrapped her arms around herself, shivering hard.

"I couldn't let you go," I said. It was a small statement, too awkward to encompass everything that it meant: I didn't have the *words* to encompass everything that it meant. Then again, I *had* just brought her back from the dead, so she probably had some idea of what I was trying to say. "I just . . . I couldn't let you be dead."

"Thank you," she said. She sagged backward on the

bed. "I can't . . . I didn't stay dead long enough. The geas still holds."

"That's okay," I said. "I didn't . . . I wanted you to be okay not because you could help, but because you're my friend. I couldn't just let you die."

"There are people who won't be very happy with you for this." The Luidaeg closed her eyes. "You have to hide me. I can't stay where I am."

"Okay, Luidaeg. Just rest, okay?" I was saying "okay" so much that the word was losing all meaning. Maybe that was more accurate than I liked to think. It felt like the world was never really going to be "okay" again.

The Luidaeg sighed. "I can't tell you what's coming, Toby, even though I want to. But I can tell you one thing that might help."

"What is it?" I pulled away from Tybalt, moving to stand closer to her. Everything still smelled like my blood. That helped, a little, even if it wasn't enough to chase the black spots entirely away.

"Your mother," said the Luidaeg. "She told you to beware the Lady of the Lake, but to be more afraid of Morgane. Do you remember?"

I blinked. "I do, but I don't remember telling *you*."

"Your lover was a Selkie; he told me quite a bit, after he died," said the Luidaeg. "My name . . . my name is Antigone. But there was a time when they called me Viviane. When everything was swords, and stones, and so simple . . . your mother feared the wrong woman. I think I'm going to sleep now. I'll trust you to survive what's coming."

"Wait—what?"

Tybalt's hand closed on my shoulder. " 'Viviane' was one of the names for the Lady of the Lake," he said.

I stared at the Luidaeg. "You can*not* drop this on me and go to sleep. Luidaeg? Luidaeg!"

She didn't wake up.

ELEVEN

MY PHONE RANG. I stiffened, instinctively pulling away from the Luidaeg before I recognized the sound and pulled the phone from my pocket. "Hello?"

"I'm parked on the street," said Quentin's familiar voice. He sounded like he was scared out of his mind, which was only to be expected, given the circumstances. "Toby . . . the shadows that should be blurring the Luidaeg's alley aren't there. It's like she dropped all her illusions."

"She did," I said. "Come on in. Make it quick, we're not going to linger here long."

"Okay," he said, and hung up.

I lowered the phone. "Quentin's here," I said. "He says the normal defenses are down. I was sort of hoping he'd be smart and go straight for Arden instead of following instructions and coming here."

Tybalt chuckled. There was an edge of strain to his voice, but it was fading; I had saved the Luidaeg without killing myself in the process. He could stop worrying about me for a few minutes, at least until he figured out how much blood I'd lost. As long as I didn't try to stand up ever again, he'd never know. "He simply puts great stock in your ability to survive even the most ridiculous of situations. To be fair, you have yet to prove him wrong. Also to be fair, it is not as if seeking the assistance of the Queen is something you have encouraged him to do. It will take some time to adapt to the idea of the monarchy as an ally, not an enemy."

"Whose side are you on, anyway?" I demanded peevishly. I recognized my own relief, spreading through me and trying to make me giddy. I pushed it aside—we weren't out of the woods yet. We still didn't know who had attacked the Luidaeg, or whether they were coming back. Raising my voice, I called, "We're in the bedroom, Quentin. Did you crash the car?"

"I'm a better driver than that," my squire protested, steps coming faster as he hurried down the hall to the open bedroom door. "Did you see the apartment? The place is trashed. Where's—" He stepped inside and stopped, going statue-still as he took in the scene in front of him. Finally, quietly, he said, "Oh."

"Yeah, 'oh,'" I agreed. "She was almost dead when we got here." No need to tell him that "almost" was understating the case. "I managed to bring her back, but she's still in pretty bad shape, and she's not waking up. We need to move her someplace safe before whoever came here and did this to her realizes that they need to finish the job."

Quentin blinked, sky-colored eyes widening. "You think they'd know?"

"Whoever this was knew when the Luidaeg answered one question she shouldn't have answered," I said grimly. "They're going to know she's not dead. We need to move her before they come back. The only question is where."

"What of the Library?" asked Tybalt. "The place has its own defenses, and could no doubt protect her, if the lady Librarian was willing to let her inside."

"I don't think Mags would agree, and I don't know that the Luidaeg could handle any of the available Roads, or that we'd be able to carry her," I said. I hesitated before I continued, "Shadowed Hills is out—"

"For more reasons than I can list in a day," said Tybalt.

"—and so is my mother's tower. Whoever attacked the Luidaeg has Simon under a geas, and the tower recognizes him as family. He could just walk right in and take her."

"Maybe Patrick and Dianda could let her stay with them?" asked Quentin. "She's the sea witch. Unless her attacker was from the Undersea, she might be safe there."

"I think there's a better option," I said, looking at Tybalt.

His eyes widened minutely and then narrowed again, turning considering. Finally, slowly, he said, "You do not understand the scope of what you are asking me."

"Actually, I do," I said. "That's why I'm asking. A place where no one can go without permission, not even the Firstborn, because Oberon told them they weren't allowed. A place we can reach and our enemies can't. A *safe* place."

"A place for things that have been lost," said Tybalt slowly.

"Wait," said Quentin, as the penny finally dropped. "Are you talking about taking her to the Court of Cats? She can't hold her breath on the Shadow Roads if she's unconscious!"

"So we move her to a place where the Court is closer to the surface." I looked to Tybalt. "Will you do this?"

Silence. Then, finally: "Yes. But we must hurry."

I smiled. I couldn't help myself. "Okay, you two. Help me get her to the car." Thankfully, when I stood, my legs agreed to support my weight, and my headache was a dull enough roar that I could walk without crying. I was messed up, but I would heal. Hopefully.

Tybalt seemed to know that something was wrong, but since he didn't ask me directly, I didn't have to answer him. It was relatively easy for the three of us working together to carry her down the junk-choked hallway to the gaping wound of the door, and out into the cool afternoon air. I carried her feet this time, while Tybalt held her head and arms and Quentin walked near her hip, helping to keep her body from knocking against anything. Once again, Tybalt walked backward, leading the way.

My car was parked to fill the mouth of the alley. I don't think I'd ever been happier to see it, especially not after Quentin ran ahead, peered into the backseat, and called, "It's clear."

"Thank Maeve," I said, and started toward the car.

As soon as my foot left the Luidaeg's front step, there was a grinding, shifting sound from behind me, like rocks sliding into position. Tybalt stopped where he was, a nonplussed expression on his face.

"Well," he said. "That's one means of guaranteeing the security of your belongings."

I glanced over my shoulder. The Luidaeg's door was gone, replaced by an unbroken expanse of plain red brick. "I hope she can reopen that when it's time to come home," I said. "Now let's move."

Buckling a limp, unresponsive body into the backseat of my car was not something I'd rank among my favorite experiences, although it didn't make the list of the worst things I'd ever done, either. With a lot of shoving, swearing, and prayer, we managed to fold her into the vehicle and secure her with a seat belt, thus hopefully guaranteeing that she wouldn't fly out of a window in the event of an accident. I straightened up, swiping my sweat-dampened hair out of my eyes with one hand, and turned to Quentin.

"Keys, please," I said.

"You're going to make me ride in the backseat with the unconscious woman, aren't you?" he grumbled, digging the keys out of his pocket and dropping them into my waiting palm.

"Got it in one," I said. "We need to get the Lu—get *her* to our destination, and I need you free to focus on casting the best don't-look-here spell you've ever put together in your life."

"Promise you'll at least turn the radio to something decent?"

"No," I said. "Now get in the car."

Quentin sulked theatrically as he climbed into the backseat. He might have seemed flippant to someone who didn't know him, but I could tell how worried he was by the way he twisted in his seat as soon as his own belt was buckled, his eyes going to the Luidaeg's face. She had been his friend for almost as long as I had, and their relationship had always been refreshingly straightforward, unlike the relationship I had with her. She always threatened to kill me like she meant it; when she threatened to kill him, it was like she was saying "I care."

Then again, maybe she'd been threatening us both that way, and I'd just been too close to the situation to understand. I turned on the ignition, trying to push my own concerns to the back of my mind. She was going to be all right. I had saved her. I was a hero.

Speaking of heroism . . . "Quentin, do you know if Arden has the phones working yet?"

"They're not stable," he said. "April's got them doing all kinds of weird stuff with wires and fast-growing vines, but it's going to be a little while before they're consistently accessible via phone. Why?"

"I need to know if May and Jazz have reached her safely and brought her up to speed. I also need to let her know that someone beat the holy hell out of the Luidaeg, and damn near killed her." *Had* killed her, but that wasn't something I wanted to advertise. Ever. If I could raise the dead, that was going to be my little secret, at least for now. "If I were Queen, I'd want to be informed if something powerful enough to mortally wound a First-born was loose on my lands. You know. Just because I'm nosy that way." I scowled at the traffic around us. "Call May. I know her phone works in the Summerlands."

I hated to delegate something as important as bring-ing the Queen in the Mists up to speed, but even after we put a don't-look-here on the car, I was going to need to focus on traffic, or we were going to die. I always drive a little sloppily when I have a headache, and tempting as it might be to take the time to heal up after a serious in-jury, I couldn't afford the delay. I'd been awake for more than a full day at this point. Exhaustion was going to hit me sooner or later, and it was going to hit me hard.

That didn't mean I could stop. Not even for a second. Simon showing up in the Mists made everything per-sonal. The Luidaeg being attacked made it urgent. Some-one was going to pay for what had happened to her.

"Okay, I'll call May," said Quentin. "What do you want me to tell her?"

"Explain that the Luidaeg has been attacked, and that we're taking her somewhere safe, but we can't say where. Tell her I may not be available by phone for a while." I paused before adding, "And tell her what we learned about Mom. Arden can confirm it if she says you're full of shit." Arden knew my mother had been married to Simon—she'd been shocked when she met me, because she couldn't believe Mom would have a half-human child. So at least she'd be able to help May cope with that part. Everything else . . .

It was what it was.

While Quentin pulled out his phone and dialed, I glanced to Tybalt and asked, "Can you cast the first don't-look-here? You're better at them than I am."

"Only because you refuse to practice," he said, but raised his hands, sweeping them through the air in a grand gesture before saying, "My good lords and ladies, if you will attend to the stage, I would like to prepare you for an evening of wonders untold, and miracles such as the eye has never once beheld . . ." The smell of pennyroyal and musk rose and burst around us, perfuming the air inside the car. Quentin sneezed in the backseat.

I gave Tybalt a sidelong look, keeping most of my attention on the road. "What's that from?"

"Something a friend of mine used to say before curtain on each night's show." He smiled, the expression visible in the tension of his cheek and the way his lip curled upward. "He would be pleased to know that his magic lives on in the spells and wastrel charms of this modern world."

"May's caught up, and she called you some things I don't want to repeat," said Quentin, poking his head up between the seats. "She said to tell you that Jazz is awake and feeling better, even though she's still shaky, and that Arden has a really sweet guest room. We should go there for a vacation after all this is over."

"The day I get a vacation is the day the world ends," I said. "Still, you have done well, my squire, and as your reward, you may choose the radio station."

Quentin made a noise of wordless satisfaction, leaning farther forward as he clicked on the radio dial. The sound of Canadian folk-rock filled the car. I strongly suspected he'd convinced April to mess with my radio reception, since we seemed to get more folk music than was strictly normal, but it made him so happy that I didn't care that much. He pulled back into his seat, resuming his position next to the Luidaeg, and I drove on.

Quentin cast a don't-look-here on top of Tybalt's when we neared Golden Gate Park. It seemed like the safe thing to do.

The most common entrance to the Court of Cats appeared periodically in the alley next to the old Kabuki Theater. I don't know why Tybalt chose that location—I would have expected something on Market, in the actual theater district—but it was isolated enough to be safe, and with two don't-look-here spells shielding the car, I was able to drive right up to the mouth of the alley. I parked to block the sidewalk. A lot of people were going to find themselves jaywalking to the other side of the street without being able to explain why.

Once again, the three of us wrestled the Luidaeg's unmoving body out of the backseat. As soon as she was clear of all obstructions, Tybalt swung her up into his arms, holding her in a perfect wedding carry. He looked down at her sleeping face, and then back to where Quentin and I stood in momentary silence.

"I will be back," he said, and turned, carrying the Luidaeg into the alley like her weight meant nothing to him. I watched him walk away. Between one step and the next he was simply gone, taking the sea witch with him out of the world.

"Are you sure this is a good idea?" asked Quentin quietly.

"No," I said. "But it's the only one we have right now. She needs to be safe. Tybalt will keep her safe."

Quentin nodded. "Okay," he said. He hesitated before saying, "I almost expected you to say that we should take her to Shadowed Hills. That's where you always would have taken her before."

"I know."

Minutes slunk by like hours, and I had to fight with myself not to run into that alley and begin clawing at shadows until one of them opened and let me inside. Finally, Tybalt came walking back, empty-handed and wearing a shirt that looked almost exactly like his previous one, only minus the blood stains.

"She is safe," he informed us gravely. "I have advised my people of what must be done, and she will not be left alone. Someone will always be with her."

I bit my lip and nodded, unwilling to trust my voice. He smiled, very slightly, as he reached out and touched the side of my face.

"She wasn't elf-shot, October; she'll be awake and making your life miserable before you have a chance to properly miss her."

"I know," I said, and sniffled, fighting the urge to cry. "Let's get the hell out of here. We still have way too much work to do."

"If I may?" Tybalt leaned forward and tapped the collar of my shirt. I looked down at my bloody shirt, then back up again to him. "You need to change your clothing. Your house is five minutes' drive from here. You will feel better if you're not covered in someone else's blood. *I* will feel better if you're not covered in your own blood."

"I'd just like it if no one was covered in blood for a little while," said Quentin.

I paused before sighing and saying, "All right, I'll give. Let's go get me some clothing that can't stand up on its own — and then it's back to the Library, all right? Maybe we can still shake something out of the stacks. And if not, at least we're somewhere safe while we figure out our new plan."

"As my lady wishes." Tybalt sketched an elaborate bow before stepping around the car and sliding back into the passenger seat. Quentin ran after him, and I actually smiled as I got behind the wheel. Clean clothes would be a blessing. Getting the Luidaeg's blood off me would be even better.

Tybalt's estimate wasn't perfect: we pulled into the small covered garage next to the house about ten minutes after leaving the Court of Cats. Quentin was the first out of the car, as usual. What was unusual was the way he froze halfway down the path, shoulders going tense and back going ramrod straight. I was out of the car in an instant, hand going to my knife as I ran toward my squire and whatever threat had caused him to stop in mid-step. Tybalt was right behind me, and he would have been in front of me if the path had allowed him to pass without shoving me to the side.

Not Quentin, I thought fiercely. I couldn't be sure of raising the dead twice in one day—I wasn't even willing to count on doing it once under most circumstances—and I would throw myself in front of whatever bullet was coming for him before I allowed him to be harmed. It wasn't just the whole "Crown Prince" thing; that was a relatively new development. He was my squire and my friend and he would *not* be harmed if I could prevent it.

I stumbled to a halt as I pulled up alongside him, blinking at the back porch. Tybalt was more decorous about his confusion; he strolled to a stop, rather than skidding like the rest of us, and frowned in bewilderment. Normally, I might have teased him for looking so openly baffled. This time, I couldn't blame him.

The sight of Simon Torquill sitting on my steps with his arms full of roses was plenty confusing, after all. The fact that I was already able to tell him from his brother without thinking about it was worrisome to me, but that aspect of the situation was lost as I stared at the roses. He was holding at least fifty of them, long-stemmed and wrapped in a cone of tissue paper. Their petals were a dozen shades of blue and white, from the pristine shade of falling snow to the near-black color that lives at the heart of glaciers. Sprigs of a purple flower I distractedly identified as rosebay ringed the bouquet, protecting the roses from harm.

Simon stood, walking silently toward us. I shied back before I could think better of it, my shoulder bumping against Tybalt's chest. I felt his sternum vibrating from the slow, rumbling force of his growl. It was comforting. This time, if Simon decided to raise a hand against me, it wouldn't be me and one Raven-maid with a baseball bat against his transformation magic.

He stopped a respectful distance away from the three of us and held out his bouquet. When I didn't move to take it, he cleared his throat and said, "I would be most grateful if you would accept this small token of apology for the trouble that I have caused to you and yours."

"Aren't those flowers from Duchess Torquill's garden?" asked Quentin, narrow-eyed and wary. "It seems to me that giving someone a gift of stolen flowers sort of negates the apology."

"Shadowed Hills is my brother's land, and I have long had permission to walk its gardens and pick what I like from its soil," said Simon. His eyes never left my face. "My brother has barred me from his halls, but his lady wife has not yet barred me from her grounds. I think she hopes to trap me, like a spider traps a fly. I will not risk her succeeding, and so I say again that I would be most grateful if you would accept this gift from me. I doubt I'll be able to provide you with anything so lovely in the future."

"Why are you here, Simon?" I asked. My voice sounded thin to my own ears, and if my shoulder hadn't still been pressed to Tybalt's chest, I doubt I could have stood my ground without shaking.

"To bring you this," he said, holding out the flowers a bit more pleadingly. "They are yours. You have earned them, and they are the least that I can do."

This close to the bouquet, I could feel the chill rolling off their petals, like they had brought a little slice of Luna's private snowfall with them. "Roses and rosebay," I said. The combination tickled at the back of my mind, sorting through options until it finally reached the inevitable conclusion. I froze, straightening as I stiffened. "Get off my property."

Simon blinked. "What? But I—"

"Rosebay is a member of the same family as the oleander," I snapped. "They both mean 'danger' or 'beware' when they show up in a bouquet, and given that my mother's magic tastes of roses, it's pretty hard not to read your little gift there as a threat against my mom. Get the hell out of my yard or I'm calling the Queen."

"I always forget that Amandine took the time to train you," said Simon. He sounded almost embarrassed, like he'd committed some unthinkable error in judgment. "I apologize, October; I assumed you did not speak the language of the flowers, and included the rosebay in hopes that someone around you might translate. It was not my intention to distress you more."

"Perhaps you did not hear my lady when she bid you leave her grounds," said Tybalt, speaking in the tightly clipped tone that meant his mouth had suddenly filled with fangs. He had better control over his feline nature than most Cait Sidhe, but I knew from experience that his control could—and would—slip when he felt that the things he loved were being threatened. "If you do not heed her, you will wish that I had left you to your brother's tender mercies."

"I intend no insult to your mother and would have used another flower for my bouquet had I not considered clarity to be more important than discretion." Simon spoke hurriedly, like he was afraid of being chased away before he could get his message out. "I would never hurt Amandine. She is the only woman I have ever loved, and I was privileged beyond measure when she chose to be my wife. I am here to help you, not to hurt you. Please."

"We do not need your help," snarled Tybalt.

"Wait." Once again, the sound of my voice surprised

me. Was I really the one telling him to wait, rather than ordering him to rip Simon's throat out with his teeth? It seemed that I was. I stepped forward, finally accepting the offered roses. The tissue paper was thick enough that I didn't fear the thorns as I gathered them close and sniffed their cold perfume. It smelled like snow, like ice, and like the first stirrings of a storm, all overlaid with the sweet, familiar attar of rose. I looked up, meeting Simon's yellow eyes, and asked, "Why did you bring me flowers?"

"There is so much I can't say to you, October," he said. "The best I can do is work within my limitations, and try to prepare you for what's coming."

I hesitated. He sounded so lost . . . "The Luidaeg was attacked."

He started. I think that was the moment when I really started to believe that he was trying, however poorly, to help: he looked genuinely surprised, and more than a little bit afraid. "The sea witch? Is she . . . is she well?"

"She died." That wasn't the full truth, but it was close enough that I didn't have to fake the grief in my voice, or the tremor in my hands as I considered the magnitude of what had happened to her—and what I'd done. The roses in my arms seemed to be getting colder, threatening to freeze me clean through. "She died alone in her apartment, bleeding out on the carpet with no one to save her."

"That isn't possible," Simon said, staring at me. "I did not think . . . she can't die. She's the sea witch. She'll outlive us all."

"Firstborn are immortal, not unkillable," I said. "Hard to kill, I'll give you that, but wow did her attacker put in the effort."

Simon closed his eyes. "Then I am too late already. You should have let me make of you a tree, October. I am very good at making trees, and you would have had a little time. You would have been stronger still by the time you won free of the soil. That might have been enough."

"If you so much as whisper the first word of a transformation spell, I'll have your larynx in my hand before the second word can form," said Tybalt, with a chilling calm.

"I assure you, no further harm will come to her by my hand." Simon opened his eyes and then, to my utter shock, he bowed to me. "Sir Daye, you have done your bloodline a great honor. Your words and deeds will be remembered long after mine have faded into simple villainy. You have no reason to trust a single word I say as truth, but please believe me when I say that I am sorry I did not get to know you better."

"Uh, what?" I said.

"Good luck," he replied, before turning and walking away into the garden.

Tybalt growled, starting to step past me. I put out my arm, blocking him. He shot me a startled, almost injured look.

"Don't," I said. "He didn't threaten us. He even apologized, in his weird-ass Simon way. And he gave us something." I looked down at my bouquet of ice-white, glacial-blue roses. "He gave us a riddle to solve."

Tybalt didn't look happy, and I couldn't blame him, but he followed me as I unlocked the door and poked my head into the silent house.

May and Jazz were gone, of course, departed for Muir Woods in the back of Danny's cab. It still felt strange to come home and know that no one was there to meet us. I'd worked a long time to build a place for myself—a place, and the family to go with it. Now Simon was back, and it felt like everything was at risk. I still didn't know why he'd come here, or whether he'd left us any unwanted surprises. I turned, pressing my bouquet into the arms of my startled squire.

"Stay here," I commanded him. "Tybalt, you're with me."

Tybalt nodded, understanding my concern immediately. Quentin followed us into the kitchen, still looking utterly confused, but he didn't ask what was going on, and for the moment, that was good enough for me.

Side by side, Tybalt and I made our way from the kitchen to the hall. I gestured for him to check the living room while I started up the stairs, drawing my knife from my belt and holding it close to my hip. It wouldn't do me any good if Simon had hidden a monster in the upstairs closet, but holding it helped focus me a little, and I needed all the help that I could get.

This is your fault, I thought. *Quentin and Tybalt are in danger because of you. If you didn't let them stay around, they wouldn't be in harm's way. This is on you.*

The thought was unfair, and I pushed it aside almost as quickly as it formed. Maybe it was true, but if it weren't for me, Tybalt would still be lonely, Quentin would still be trapped in the spiral of pureblood superiority, and May wouldn't even exist. She'd be a night-haunt named "Mai," scavenging for the bodies of Faerie's dead, surfing from identity to identity without ever truly owning any of them. Jazz might have been safer if not for me, since it was her association with May that kept putting her in harm's way, but I somehow doubted she'd see things that way.

The upstairs hall was dark. I didn't turn the lights on, choosing instead to pause on the landing and sniff the air, looking for traces of blood or magic. I didn't find any, and so I started moving again, checking the rooms one by one for signs of a struggle or a spell. Light footfalls behind me signaled Tybalt's return, and I kept walking, feeling safer now that I knew I wasn't alone.

The upstairs was clean. I pulled my phone out of my pocket, bringing up the entry for May. Still staring at her room, I raised it to my ear. *Pick up,* I thought. *Come on,*

May, pick up. Just this once, do something because I want you to do it. Pick up the phone.

There was a click, and then May demanded, "Maeve's tits, October, what is it *now?* Please tell me you didn't do something you can't actually bounce back from, because I am so not up for pulling your bacon out of the fire right now."

I bit back a gale of completely inappropriate laughter. Oh, yeah, my nerves were fried. "Simon was on the back porch when we got home," I said. "I'm sorry to wake you, but you needed to know that the house is officially off limits until we catch him."

"I was already planning to stay at Queen Windermere's Hotel and Day Spa for the foreseeable future, especially after Quentin's cute little status update," said May without pause. Then she took a whistling breath and said, "He was *there?* At our house? Again?"

"He was," I said grimly. "Quentin brought you up to speed on the situation?" I was willing to let Simon go out into the world thinking that the Luidaeg was truly dead—it was better if we kept the knowledge of her survival close to our chests—but I wouldn't do that to May.

"He did, and sweet Titania, that's terrifying," said May. "Are you safe?"

"I honestly don't know," I said. "I'm just really, really glad you're in Muir Woods."

May actually laughed. "What a difference a monarch makes, huh? Six months ago you'd have gone for elective facial piercings before you went to see the Queen, and now you're happy to pawn me and Jazz off on her protection."

"It's amazing how quickly I can adapt to having someone on the throne who isn't actively trying to get me killed," I said. "Just stay safe, all right?"

"You know, I don't like that the pattern has become 'danger arises, get May the hell away from it,'" she said. "I want to help."

I hesitated before saying, "Maybe you can. This geas—it's on Simon *and* the Luidaeg, and the Luidaeg confirmed that the person who cast it is someone I know. We already know that whoever did it is still alive, or the geas wouldn't be active. So who knows me, Simon, and the Luidaeg, and has the power to bind one of the Firstborn? I've been trying to figure it out all day, and I'm coming up empty."

"Not quite empty," said Tybalt, from behind me. "You still have to consider the possibility your mother is involved with this somehow."

"He's right," said May wearily. "Tell kitty-boy I can hear him, and that he has a damn good point. Amandine is Firstborn, and she knows all three of the people who have to be checked off before someone makes the list. She's been sort of cuckoo for Cocoa Puffs for a while now, so there's an absolute chance that she could have done this."

"Why?" I asked. "What would she have to gain? And how could she have hurt the Luidaeg the way she did? Mom's not a fighter. She can mess with the balance of someone's blood, and yeah, that hurts like hell, but there's nothing in the Luidaeg for her to catch hold of."

"Maybe she didn't attack the Luidaeg," said May. "Maybe she hired or compelled someone else to do it, or maybe this isn't her at all. I'm just saying we can't cross her off the list because she's your mother. If anything, that puts her closer to this than almost anybody else."

I ran one hand back through my hair, wincing as my fingers snagged on several poorly placed knots. "Right. So you and Jazz will stay where you are, and stay safe. I'll take Tybalt and Quentin and go back to Mom's tower. It looks like I need to verify, once and for all, whether she's behind all of this."

"And if she is?" asked May. "Because let's face it, Toby, this is a pretty weak plan."

"It's what I've got." I dropped my hand. "If Mom is there, I arrest her for compelling the kidnapping of Luna and Rayseline Torquill, and I take her before the Queen to be held accountable for her crimes." Yes, I'd allowed Simon to walk away, even though he was the one who'd actually kidnapped them. I was going to be sorry about that later, I was sure. And yet the geas—which genuinely existed, since it also bound the Luidaeg, although I wasn't sure why Mom would have *needed* to bind him—had left him with little choice about his actions. Under those circumstances, it made sense to bring the mastermind to justice first, find out how much free will the underlings really had, and take care of things in the proper order.

May laughed unsteadily. "Sounds like you're going to have a fun night."

"I always do," I said. "Open roads."

"Kind fires, and Toby . . . be careful." She hung up, presumably to keep me from saying anything she didn't want to hear. I could understand the sentiment.

I put my phone back in my pocket. "Wait here," I said to Tybalt, before ducking into my room and yanking off my blood-crusted shirt, replacing it with a clean one. He was right: I did feel better with less blood on me. He smiled when I rejoined him in the hall, giving me an approving look. Together we walked downstairs and to the kitchen, where a clearly anxious Quentin was slapping together egg salad sandwiches with more force than strictly necessary. The roses from Simon were on the kitchen table. Patches of frost had begun to form around the bouquet, and some of the glacier-colored flowers looked like they were actually melting.

He whirled when he heard our footsteps. "Well?" he asked, gesturing toward us with his spoon, which was still full of egg salad. "Is everything okay?"

"It's all good," I said. "If Simon came into the house, he doesn't seem to have touched or done anything."

Quentin relaxed slightly. "Oh, thank Oberon. I don't want to deal with magical booby traps in my own home." He turned back to his sandwiches. "I didn't like standing idle, so I figured I'd start putting together something for us to eat. We've been running hard with no food all day. That can't continue forever."

"See, October, the Crown Prince's association with you has done him good after all," said Tybalt. "It has taught him to force-feed his elders, as they cannot take care of themselves."

"That's going to serve him well." My stomach growled, reminding me that Quentin was right: I hadn't eaten since getting out of bed, and I hadn't been in bed nearly long enough. I walked over and snagged a plate with one of the fully assembled sandwiches, carrying it with me as I crossed to the table and peered more closely at the roses. The chill coming off of them was enough to make me want to turn the heat up, but something told me that would just make them melt faster, and any message they might imply would be lost.

"Some of them are Duchess Torquill's own creations," said Quentin, as he went back to mechanically slapping sandwiches together. "Some were cultivars from the Snow Kingdoms, or from the deeper lands. People brought them along when all the doors were sealed."

"Makes sense," I said. That was how goblin fruit had been transported from the lands where it grew naturally into the mortal world. It was actually sort of nice to realize that we'd carried more than just deadly narcotics with us when we had to flee our ancestral homelands. "How long has Luna been growing this kind of rose?"

"As long as I've known her," said Tybalt.

"It's hard to grow roses from the Snow Kingdoms when it's not always winter," said Quentin. "They're really delicate. There are a few in the palace gardens back home, and *Maman* refuses to let me or my sister near them, since she's afraid we'll offend the Snow Kingdoms by picking flowers and turning prize blossoms into snow-melt."

"You mean like Simon has?" I asked. I stuck my finger into the water pooling around the bouquet. It was freezing cold. "Okay, so Simon mentioned the language of the flowers. Rosebay is a warning. White roses mean 'I am worthy of you,' which, fuck no, he isn't. Even if he weren't my stepfather. Blue roses mean . . ." I stopped, drawing a blank.

"Blue roses mean nothing, because they do not naturally occur in the mortal world, and the language of the flowers was borrowed, like so many other things, from humanity," said Tybalt. "They are a flower without a definition."

"Well, I'm just going to take a wild guess that roses made of ice are also outside the flower language, so . . . he gave me a bouquet that means both 'warning' and 'nothing.' What the hell, Simon?" I frowned at the flowers, taking another bite of my egg salad sandwich. There had to be something I was missing. Something—my eyes widened, and I swallowed my mouthful only half-chewed, to ask, "What if the point isn't the message, but the contents of the bouquet?"

Tybalt frowned at me. "What do you mean?"

"He's not saying 'beware, I am worthy of you,' or 'beware, no definition found,' he's saying 'beware' and giving me roses made of ice. Winter roses." I dropped the rest of my sandwich onto the table, whirling. "He's telling us that whatever's coming next, it's going to happen at Evening's old knowe. We need to get to Goldengreen."

"Are you sure?" asked Quentin.

I snorted. "Kiddo, I'm not sure of anything right now, but I'm sure we don't have time to waste standing around and arguing about it. Tybalt?"

"Yes?"

"Much as I hate to leave my car behind, it'll be faster if we take the shadows. Can you . . . ?"

He smiled a little. "You know, every time you request this of me, I laugh on the inside."

"Yeah, yeah, I know, once upon a time I freaked out at the idea of the Shadow Roads, and now I treat them like a faster version of the Monorail at Disneyland. The question stands. Can you get us both there without hurting yourself?" Tybalt was a King of Cats, but that didn't make him indestructible. He'd died twice in the past three years, and while he'd recovered both times—it turns out the old "cats have nine lives" myth got its start with the Cait Sidhe—that didn't mean I wanted to overtax him and go for a third.

Tybalt thought for a moment before he nodded. "Goldengreen is a friendly territory. I have passed through its wards before. I am more than willing to undertake this journey."

"Good." I offered him my hand. "Quentin, come on. We're heading for Goldengreen."

"I like field trips," he said, and grabbed my hand, and Tybalt pulled us both with him, into the shadows.

The Shadow Roads seemed a little less cold than usual, as if the lingering chill from my contact with Simon's roses was keeping the normal freeze at bay. That didn't make me any more likely to linger, especially not with my head still pounding and my legs still a little weak from blood loss. Tybalt ran and I ran with him, keeping a tight hold on Quentin's hand. The last thing I wanted to do was explain to his parents that I'd allowed him to become lost on the Shadow Roads for all eternity. Not to mention the fact that I would genuinely miss the kid if something ever happened to him.

We ran, as always, until I felt like there was no way I could run any farther; my lungs were going to give out, my feet were going to freeze solid, and I was going to fall. Then Tybalt's body gave a lurch, his hand very nearly ripping out of mine as he abruptly stopped moving. There was a moment of disorientation, during which I couldn't have said which way was up, and then Tybalt was pulling, and we were tumbling out into the empty air —

—some twenty yards above the cold black waters of the Pacific Ocean. I scrabbled to keep hold of his hand, and Quentin's, but it was no use; the wind ripped them away from me as we fell, and then I hit the water, and everything went black.

TWELVE

I OPENED MY EYES ON watery gloom, surrounded by waving fronds of the kelp that chokes the California coastline like the hand of a cruel regent. For a moment I hung suspended in the green, too stunned to understand what was going on. One minute we were running along the Shadow Roads, and the next, we were standing on thin air somewhere above the waves. And then we fell—

I jerked in the water, comprehension sweeping over me as I finally realized what had happened, and more importantly, where I was. I began to thrash, trying to follow the trailing kelp up to the surface. There was no way of knowing whether I was going the right way, but it was a fifty-fifty chance, and that was fifty percent more than I'd have if I stayed where I was. There was no sign of Tybalt, or Quentin. I may as well have been alone in the ocean.

Oddly, their absence helped: it gave me something to focus on beyond my own predicament. If they were hurt, or worse, they would need me to stay calm. They would need me to help them. Even with my hydrophobia threatening to rise up and slap me down, I clung to the thought that my boys needed me, and I kept on swimming.

Dammit, Luidaeg, why aren't you here to turn me into a mermaid again? The thought was almost dizzy, and I realized my vision was going black around the edges. All my runs through the airless cold of the Shadow Roads had been a sort of conditioning: I might not be a swimmer, but I could hold my breath for a surprisingly long time all the same. That was only going to get me so far, though. As I strained toward the surface, I was dimly, terribly aware that the end of the road was very close indeed.

Then something with all the grace and subtlety of a torpedo slammed into my middle, hard enough that the last of the air was knocked out of me and escaped toward the surface. I wanted to go after it, but I couldn't break away from the arm that was locked around my waist, dragging me toward some unknown destination.

I tried to focus through the black spots that were increasingly devouring my vision, and caught a glimpse of black hair, pale skin, and scales like blue-and-purple jewels. Something about them was familiar enough that I stopped fighting and closed my eyes, letting their owner carry me wherever she would.

The darkness had just been waiting for me to relax. It closed in, pouncing on the shreds of my consciousness like a cat pounces on a mouse, and the world went away for a little while.

"—by? Hey, are you dead? Wake up if you're not dead." Someone grabbed my shoulders, shaking briskly enough that my head flopped from side to side. I coughed, and water filled my mouth, summoned up from my throat and lungs. "Shit, she's choking." The voice didn't sound surprised, or particularly worried; this was more of a statement of fact than anything resembling concern.

Strong hands rolled me onto my side, and then someone gave me another shake, hard enough that I started coughing again. This time, I didn't stop until I was vomiting water all over the sand next to me. Someone helped me sit up enough that I wasn't throwing up on myself, which was a serious improvement. I struggled to catch my breath, breathed in, and resumed coughing. This time, no water accompanied the action. Thank Oberon.

"Oh, good, you're *not* dead," said a female voice. I started trying to sort through the options for who might have hauled me out of the ocean. I'd seen enough to know that I should know her, but the whole "nearly drowning" thing had put a bit of a crimp in my memory.

Everything was wet, and my body was one big ache, bruised by its impact with the water. My headache had become virtually an afterthought when held up against the rest of the pain. My leather jacket was like a lead blanket encasing my upper body, so waterlogged that it had probably pulled me almost to the seafloor before I woke up. I tried to roll toward the person next to me, and as I did, I realized I was covered in sand. That was a natural result of lying wet on a beach, but it was going to mean getting wet *again*, and somehow that was the final indignity. I braced my hands against the beach, shoving myself into a standing position, and turned.

Dianda was sitting on the beach a few feet away, her tail folded under her like something out of a Hans Christian Andersen story. She raised an eyebrow as she met my eyes, looking dubious. "Are you done with the barfing water and attempted suicide by ocean? I don't *mind* dead bodies in the Pacific, but you were right next to Goldengreen. That means you were trying to get in. And don't stress about my fins and your ears—I have the Cetacea maintaining a screen around this area, no one's going to see you."

I took a quick, borderline frantic look around. There

was a heavy fog covering the beach, leaving the two of us sitting in what appeared to be the only clear area. That must have been Dianda's "screen" . . . and we were inside it alone. "Oh, oak and ash, Dianda, where are the others?"

She frowned. "Others? You mean the Cetacea? They're farther out from shore."

"I don't mean your damn Cetacea, I mean Quentin and Tybalt!"

Dianda's frown slowly faded into an expression of blank neutrality. "October, you are the only one we found in the water. We wouldn't have been able to find you at all if we hadn't already been circling Goldengreen. I'm sorry. They're not there."

"Look again!" I hadn't been intending to scream at her, and yet somehow it happened anyway. My voice bounced off the nearby cliff wall and was swallowed by the sea.

"My people are still out there, October," said Dianda. "They're moving through the waves, they're looking for anything out of the ordinary, and if either of your friends are in the water, we'll find them. But you were half-drowned, and—"

"They're not my friends. They're my family."

"The sea doesn't care."

I looked at her bleakly, trying to make those words make sense within the context of the world. The sea didn't care. Tybalt, Quentin, and I fell out of the sky, and now only I was here, and the sea didn't care. I turned my eyes toward the gunmetal-gray waves of the roiling Pacific. Once again, the water had taken everything away from me. Because the sea didn't care.

"Why did we fall?" There was no life in my voice; it was a dead thing that fell between us like an accusation. That seemed somehow exactly correct.

"Because the wards of Goldengreen have closed," Dianda said. She rose, scales falling away, and moved to stand beside me, putting her hand on my shoulder. I didn't shrug it off. It would have been too much work. "Dean and most of his court are still inside, but all the doors are shut, and all the entrances are locked."

"How do you know?"

"Mary. She started screaming, and said that if we wanted to save Dean, we needed to get to Goldengreen before the doors froze shut." Grief rolled across Dianda's face like a wave, there and gone in moments. "We weren't fast enough. That's good for you, though, since I wouldn't have found you if we hadn't been beating at the underwater doors."

Mary was a Roane woman attached to Dianda's court. She had the gift of prophecy, even if she didn't always make sense—like most soothsayers, she spoke in riddles and metaphors more often than she did in simple, declarative sentences. The last time our paths had crossed, she'd foretold Connor's death. My eyes stung with salt that had nothing to do with the sea. I blinked the tears away, grasping instead for the burning ember of rage that was starting to burn in my chest.

"Who locked the doors?" I asked.

"Not Dean," said Dianda. "No matter who he swears his loyalties to these days, he would never, *never* seal the wards against his mother."

Her logic made sense. Dean had always been a dutiful son, and even if he kicked absolutely everyone else out of his knowe, he would have left a door open for Dianda. The rage was growing brighter in my chest, becoming a fire that warmed me even as it left ashes in its wake. "We came here because someone gave me a warning about danger at Goldengreen. I guess we needed to be faster, too."

"You think so?" Dianda's voice was frozen. I glanced at her. She glared at me. "You knew my son was in danger, and you didn't come sooner?"

"I didn't *know* anything, Dianda. We left the minute we figured out what the warning meant, and while we stand down here arguing about it, no one's getting in there to find out what's going on." I turned to face the cliff that stood between us and the mortal museum that housed the entrance to the knowe, so very high above us. "Do you have anyone who can get me up that cliff?"

"We're the Undersea. We don't fly."

"Right. Make yourself useful, then, and get back in the water. *Find my boys.*" Anger has always made my illusions come easier. I grabbed a handful of fog out of the air and twisted it into a human disguise, draping it over myself as I said, "I'm going to go find out what the hell is going on in Goldengreen."

"October, if they've been in the water this whole time, they're not—"

"Find them."

The Undersea prizes strength above all else. Dianda had been fighting to hold her Duchy since the day she received it. She looked at me and didn't argue. "All right," she said. "But what are you going to do?"

"I'm going to remind the knowe that I had a valid claim to it once, and I didn't abuse it," I said. "And then I'm going to go inside. Whether the knowe likes it or not."

"Take me with you."

"If the wards are sealed, I don't think I can talk it into letting two people inside. Find my boys. I'll find your son." I didn't wait for her to reply. I just turned and stalked across the sand, walking through the bands of concealing fog until I reached the base of the cliff. It wasn't quite sheer, and generations of San Francisco beachgoers had been able to find their way down. I walked along the rocky wall until I found a series of shallow steps someone had taken the time to hew out of the stone. That was as close as I was going to get to an engraved invitation. I brushed a little more of the sand off myself, and started to climb.

It was a cold enough, foggy enough day that even the exertion of climbing wasn't drying me off. My wet clothes got heavier and harder to carry with every step I took. I didn't take any of them off. The most logical thing to lose would have been my leather jacket, and that was never going to happen. So I climbed, wet and cold and furious, pulling myself hand over hand where the steps became too shallow to be anything more than suggestions, until finally—after what felt like an eternity—the slope turned gentler, and the last ten yards became almost reasonable. I straightened as I walked up the last few steps, and then I was standing on level ground, with scrub brush and sticker-plants tugging at my calves and ankles. I turned. The San Francisco Art Museum was about two hundred yards away, sitting serene on the edge of the cliff I'd just climbed.

I paused, turning again, this time to look at the water. There were no signs of Dianda and her people—or of my boys. If Tybalt and Quentin were out there, I couldn't see them.

Maybe I was never going to see them again.

The thought was chilling, even in comparison to the cold seawater soaking through my clothes. I forced it away as hard as I could, trying to bury it beneath the layers of my exhaustion and my determination to get into the sealed knowe. We fell because someone had locked the wards. That meant that everything which came after our fall—everything I wasn't going to let myself think about—was that person's fault. The more I focused on that, the easier it became to shut away the things I didn't want to be true. Someone had *done* this to us. Someone was to blame. And whoever it was, they were going to regret messing with my family.

I stalked across the stubby field behind the museum

until I came to the ramshackle frame of an old storage shed. It had probably been intended as a place where tools and garden supplies could be kept away from the refined eyes of museum patrons, but the landscapers hadn't used it in decades. Some of them even said it was haunted. Yet somehow it remained, even as they kept their rakes and weed killer in safe, well-lit closets. It should have been torn down as an eyesore. The same spells that birthed the rumor of its haunting kept that from ever happening.

The door was locked, sealed with clever charms as well as a more mundane padlock. I produced a set of lock picks from inside my jacket, flicking through them until I found the pick and wrench I wanted. Holding the pick between the first two fingers of my right hand, I pressed that palm against the cool tin door.

"You remember me," I said quietly. "I never forced you to go against your nature, or tried to wrest you away from the owners you'd chosen, and when I couldn't be the Countess you needed, I found you someone who could play the part. I've tried to be a friend, when I could, and I've tried to do no harm when friendship wasn't possible. Now I'm here because I need a favor. I am begging you. If you have any power over the spells that hold your wards in place, let me in. I need to know what's going on. I need to know why the doors are locked. Please."

The smell of my magic rose unsummoned in the air around me, and brought with it a stinging, subtle undertone that wasn't a smell or a sound or any of the other impressions I would normally associate with magic: it was just magic, pure and simple and older than anything I encountered in my daily life. It was even older than the Luidaeg in its way, or maybe just more primal. It was the knowe.

I pulled my hand away from the door, steadying myself as I knelt and started working at the lock. There was some resistance at first, and still that soft, stinging sensation filled the air around me, now laced with the distant sensation of a heart beating. I took a deep breath, trying to focus despite what I could only assume was the close attention of the knowe. I had been insisting for years that the knowes were alive; I had even received proof of various kinds, some more blatant than others. But this was the first time it had really felt like a knowe was *looking* at me—more than that, *seeing* me, and knowing me for something distinct and apart from the rest of Faerie. It wasn't a comfortable sensation.

The padlock clicked and came open in my hand. The sensation of being watched faded in the same instant, and the shed door swung open without my needing to touch it. I straightened, tucking the lock picks back into the waterlogged inner pocket of my jacket. "Thank you," I murmured, and stepped through.

The transition between the mortal and fae worlds has always been marked, for me, by a moment of disorientation. In those instants, up is down, hot is cold, and everything hurts and heals at the same time. Transitions like that used to be painful, back in the days when I was more human and further from Faerie. Since Mom spun the balance of my blood closer to Dóchas Sidhe, the pain had faded, although the disorientation remained.

As I stepped through the door into Goldengreen, I felt as if I were suddenly human again. The disorientation was worse than it had ever been, spinning the world around me like a top and yanking away my personal gravity at the same time, leaving me in a state of vertiginous free fall that barely managed to distract from the pain freezing every nerve and burning every inch of my skin. My blood boiled and iced over at the same time, trapping me in a limbo of agony that felt like it would never end. I was going to die here, alone in the spinning, painful dark.

It was the pain that allowed me to fight through the

rest of what was going on around me. I've become very acquainted with pain over the course of the last few years, especially where my own body is concerned. This was external pain, being forced on me by someone else, and I refused to let that be what took me down. I fought against it, trying to feel my way through the waves of agony until I struck the cool bedrock of my own self.

My hands hit the floor of Goldengreen's entry hall a split-second later as I landed in an unsteady crouch. The vertigo popped like a soap bubble, leaving me winded and feeling like my skin had been scrubbed from the inside, but intact. Under the circumstances, I'd take it.

Slowly, I raised my aching head and considered the dim, empty hall. No pixies clung to the rafters, and no many-legged shadows scuttled in the corners; the bogies were gone. There was no way that could be a good sign. None of Goldengreen's usual inhabitants were coming to greet me. I straightened, one hand going to the knife belted at my waist, and listened.

Every place is silent in its own way. I had been in Goldengreen when it was completely deserted, and I knew what its silence sounded like. This was quiet, but it wasn't silent; not quite. Voices were coming from somewhere, so thinned out and diffused by distance that they might as well have been the whispers of the "ghosts" that haunted the entry shed.

I took a careful step forward, still listening. The courtyard was the center of Goldengreen's social whirl, and normally, if someone was talking but out of sight, I would find them there. The voices didn't seem to be coming from the courtyard this time. I allowed that to embolden my steps, and sped up as I walked down the short span of hall between me and the courtyard doorway. When I got there I stopped, trying to let my eyes adjust, hoping that what I saw wasn't really true.

Shortly after I had become Countess of Goldengreen,

my friend Lily, the Lady of the Tea Gardens, had been murdered by Oleander de Merelands. I had inherited Lily's subjects, a motley assortment of changelings and purebloods with nowhere else to go. They'd promptly set about making the knowe a home, transplanting trees and flowers from Lily's holdings to the indoor garden that had been established in the courtyard. They'd stayed with Goldengreen when I'd passed it on to Dean, partially because I'd vouched for him, but mostly, I knew, because they hadn't wanted to move the trees.

They weren't going to have to worry about that anymore. The courtyard looked like it had been hit by a localized but powerful tornado. Trees were on their sides, roots sticking up in the air like accusing fingers. Flowers had been crushed, rosebushes uprooted and flung against the walls. I was still trying to take in the damage when I realized that the pale branches extending from beneath one of the fallen trees weren't branches at all. They were fingers.

"Oh, oak and ash," I breathed, and bolted up the courtyard stairs until I reached the level where the fallen tree was splayed. It was one of Lily's willows, old and grizzled with years of survival. As I drew closer, I could see the scales on the pale fingers, and on the soft skin of the hand that they were attached to. One of Lily's former handmaids, a woman whose name I had learned and then forgotten, because we'd had nothing in common except for our love of an Undine who would never walk with either of us again. I tried to brace against the dirt and shift the tree off of her body, but it was no use; I didn't have super strength, and all I could do was force her deeper into the soil.

I dropped to my knees, following some half-formed instinct as I grabbed her wrist—not to check for a pulse, but to check the temperature of her skin. She was cool enough that I guessed she had been dead for at least an hour, maybe longer. So why was there still a body here for me to find? The night-haunts came for all the dead of Faerie. That was their purpose, and their one form of sustenance. They would never leave a body unclaimed for this long, and here—inside a knowe, where no human eyes would ever look—they wouldn't have bothered leaving a replacement. The night-haunts should have come by now.

Unless someone was keeping them out, along with the rest of us. I stood, looking uneasily around the darkened courtyard, which could easily hold another dozen bodies buried beneath the broken greenery. Was Dean in here? Or Marcia? Had I lost friends today?

You mean apart from the obvious?

Again, I pushed the thought down, burying it deep within my mind. If I started mourning, I was going to break. I could already feel the fissures forming, and when they gave way, I would be glad to fall into the abyss of my own grief. Right here, right now, I needed answers. I needed someone to blame.

I wasn't going to get any of that in the courtyard. Murmuring a quick farewell to the fallen handmaid, I turned and ran back down the steps to the door, heading into the hall and pausing only long enough to reorient myself to the distant sound of ghostly voices. They were coming from farther down the hall. I started toward them, slowly at first, and then breaking into a run that stopped only when I reached the door to what Dean called "the coveside receiving room." It hadn't existed when Goldengreen was mine, but knowes can rearrange themselves. The current Count was a mermaid's son. Of course there would be a seaside entrance.

Opening the door brought light back into the world. The spiraling stone stairway that descended toward the receiving room was lit by glowing abalone shells, which might have seemed tacky under other circumstances, but here and now were a welcome change from the unyield-ing dark. The voices were louder now. Moving cautiously, lest I attract attention I didn't want, I started walking down the stairs.

The voices continued to get louder. I felt a small knot of tension in my shoulders give way as I realized that one of those voices belonged to Dean Lorden. He was shout-ing something I couldn't make out, and he sounded ev-ery inch his mother's son: imperious and angry, and ready to kick the world in the teeth until it started giving him what he wanted.

If Dean was alive, maybe Goldengreen hadn't fallen quite yet. I still didn't believe he was the one who had sealed the wards—not against his mother, not against *me*—but he was fighting, and that made a huge differ-ence in his survival prospects. I sped up, taking the stairs as fast as I safely could, and wishing I dared to pull the "sliding down the banister" trick that had worked for me in the false Queen's knowe.

Then I came around the last curve in the stairs, and froze, staring at the scene beneath me.

The receiving room was large enough to seem like it couldn't possibly fit inside the knowe, with a redwood deck covering half the floor, while the rest gave way to sandy beach that yielded in turn to a small, private cove. The cliff wall extended down past the surface of the sea; I wasn't sure what the seaward entrance actually looked like, and I didn't want to know. Over a dozen of Golden-green's subjects were clustered together at the water's edge, all but one standing as close behind their Count as they could. Dean stood at the front of the motley little group, a trident in his shaking hands, aimed at the person in front of him. Marcia was to his right, holding a butcher knife. Her hands weren't shaking at all. She looked per-fectly calm, and like she was ready for whatever was go-ing to happen next.

In front of them on the sand was a woman who couldn't possibly have been there. Her skin was so pale that poets could have been forgiven for calling it "as white as snow," and her dark hair wavered between black and purple, casting off wildflower highlights when the light struck it just so. Her hands were empty, but you wouldn't have known it from the terrified expressions of the people standing in front of her.

It was impossible. It was unbelievable. It had to be some kind of a trick. And yet . . .

"Evening?" I asked.

She turned, smiling at me with those familiar blood-red lips, looking somehow satisfied.

"Hello, October," said Evening Winterrose, once Countess of Goldengreen. "It's been a long time."

THIRTEEN

"**B**UT...BUT YOU..." I stammered, before words deserted me and left me speechless, cold, and confused. Evening raised her eyebrows, giving me an impatient look as familiar as it was disorienting. This couldn't be happening. None of this was even remotely possible. I seized on that fact and wailed, "You're *dead!* You can't be here, because you're *dead!*"

"That was the rumor, and yet." Evening spread her hands. "Here I am."

She looked exactly like she had the last time I'd seen her, before her murder had yanked me out of my self-imposed exile and back into Faerie, like it or not. Her hair was down, falling to her waist in an inky wave, and she was wearing a dark brown velvet dress with a white lace accent panel down the front, cinched at the waist like something stolen from a production of *Wuthering Heights*.

"Here you are," I parroted numbly. Then I paused, eyes narrowing. "But this isn't possible. Whoever hired you gave you the wrong face to borrow, lady."

Evening blinked. "I beg your pardon?"

"I've had doppelgangers used against me before. If your employer wanted you to achieve your mission without attracting attention, they should have suggested you mimic somebody who'd been dead for a little less time. Like, I don't know, no time at all." I drew my knife, keeping my eyes on Evening as I called, "Dean? Everybody okay over there?"

"I've had better days," he said, almost laconically. "You're all wet."

"Yeah, well, I stopped off to talk to your mother. She's a little concerned about the locked wards on your knowe."

"The knowe is mine, not his, as well you know," snapped Evening. "What's more, the wards were closed by my hand, and because I needed to determine what had gone awry here in my absence. How did *you* get inside?"

I frowned, looking past her to Dean. "Is she telling the truth? Did *she* close the wards?"

"She came in through the cliffside entrance," said Marcia. "She just walked in like she owned the place. We were in the courtyard, and . . . and . . ."

"And I reacted to a home invasion—to vagrancy—as I saw fit," said Evening. "The law allows me to defend my home."

"This isn't your home!" snapped Dean. "I'm the Count here, and you're a trespasser who is sorely trying my patience!"

Evening started to turn toward him, the smell of roses and snow wisping through the air like the beginnings of a venomous prayer. I gasped. I couldn't stop myself.

Doppelgangers can steal faces. They can mimic a person to the point where that person's loved ones would never know the difference. But the one thing no one can mimic is the scent of someone else's magic. Even if they

share an element—roses are common, for example—
they'll never be able to get the exact balance right. A
person's magic is a glimpse into their soul.

"Oak and ash," I breathed, everything else forgotten
as I stared at the miracle in front of me. "Evening. How
are you alive?"

Evening stopped mid-turn and swiveled back toward
me, a smug smile twisting at the corners of her lips. "Oh,
now you believe that it's me? What have I done to earn
this honor?"

"Your magic started to rise," I said, taking a step forward. My waterlogged sneakers squelched unpleasantly.
"Roses and snow. You're you. There's no one else you
could be. But how . . . this isn't possible. You *died*. You
cursed me, and then you died."

"Did I?" She put a hand on her hip, Dean and the
others apparently forgotten now that she had the opportunity to needle me. That, too, was familiar. Evening
Winterrose had been the best enemy I'd ever had, always
ready with a taunt or a harsh word that would still somehow manage to set me on the proper path. "I cursed you,
yes, because I was afraid that ruffian Devin was going to
try something, and I needed backup. If you'd been answering your phone that night, I wouldn't have been
forced to go so far. But I seriously doubt that I *died*."

"The night-haunts came for your body," I said. "That
constituted proof of death to me."

"The night-haunts can be bribed, if you know what
they desire," said Evening, dismissing my evidence with
a wave of her hand. "As for the rest of it, I think it's fairly
clear that I'm alive. I was attacked in my apartment, and
wounded to the point where the night-haunts came. It
took me some time to recover. When I did, I returned to
my knowe to finish the healing process, and found it in-
fested with vermin. Perhaps now that you're here, you
can convince the vermin to leave."

"She means us, Toby," called Marcia. Her voice was surprisingly steady, given the circumstances. "We're the vermin, and she wants to kick us out of our home."

"Uh-uh, little girl," said Evening, half-turning. "This is *my* home. You're merely the raccoons that moved into the attic while I was away."

"Your curse nearly killed me," I said. "You're telling me you didn't even mean to do *that?* That you were never really in danger?"

"You know, October, it's considered rude to carry on multiple conversations at one time," said Evening, attention shifting back to me. "Yes, I was attacked, yes, I cursed you, yes, I lived. I'm terribly sorry if my brief convalescence has inconvenienced you in some way. It was only three years. Barely enough time for moss to grow, and yet I come back to find you puffed up on ideas of heroism, and these people living in my knowe. It's enough to make me sick. Things are going to have to change around here, starting in this room."

"It's not your knowe anymore, if it ever was," said Dean.

Evening sighed, tilting her head back until her face was pointed at the ceiling. "You see what I have to deal with?" she demanded. "Uppity changelings and mouthy mixed-bloods, and for what? To have the proper order of things restored? Faerie has become a madhouse, and I seem to be the only guard left on the asylum staff."

I frowned. Evening had never been particularly nice to me—"nice" wasn't really in her vocabulary—but she'd never been this outright cruel before. She'd always looked down on me for being a changeling, of course. That was normal among the purebloods, and I'd barely noticed it at the time.

Maybe my standards had improved since then.

"He's right," I said. "This is his knowe. Actually."

Evening lowered her head, turning a blank-eyed look

on me. "How do you reach that conclusion, October dear?"

"Goldengreen is a fiefdom of the Kingdom of the Mists," I said. "That has never been questioned, and you swear your fealty to the throne. When you died—and everyone believed you were dead, whether or not that was true—the County passed to me, as payment for services rendered. I passed the County to Dean Lorden, as part of a peace brokerage between the Kingdom of the Mists and the Undersea Kingdom of Leucothea. It was acknowledged by the then-Queen of the Mists, who was later found to be illegitimate, and then acknowledged again by Queen Arden Windermere in the Mists, after she officially took her father's throne. So by any line of title you care to follow, this knowe is Dean's. The High King might be willing to uphold your claim to the fiefdom, since you're not dead and all, but you'd have to ask him."

"I see," said Evening, sounding faintly stunned. Her eyes narrowed as she considered me. "You've changed a great deal in these past three years, October. I didn't expect it of you, not at this late date. You seemed bent on a life of glorious mediocrity, like your mother."

"Yeah, well, I owe it all to you," I said. My stomach was churning. I couldn't decide whether I wanted to laugh, cry, hug her, or throw my knife at her head. Evening was the one who'd helped me when I'd first returned from the pond. She'd been the one to take me to a motel and talk me through those horrible days when I didn't know what year it was or whether I would ever see my family again. She'd forced me back into Faerie by getting herself killed, and I both loved and hated her for that. Now here she was, standing in front of me, and I had no living idea what I was supposed to do next.

And then there was the body in the courtyard. Thinking of that pale, slightly curled hand reminded me of the sealed wards, and the feeling of being slapped out of the Shadow Roads by a stronger magic than that of a King of Cats running through his own domain.

My fingers tightened on the grip of my knife.

"I see," said Evening, apparently picking up on the gesture. "If that's how things are to be, then that's how things are to be. A pity. I had hoped we could do this without fighting. I did so enjoy being your friend, October." She raised her hand, the smell of snow and roses rising faster this time, until it filled the room.

I braced myself, preparing to grab whatever spell she threw at me and fling it back at her. It had worked with Simon; maybe I could do it again. To my surprise, she simply turned, flicking out her hands like she was trying to dry them off. Dean wobbled. Then, without fanfare, he and all his subjects—except, inexplicably, for Marcia—fell backward, into the water. Marcia cried out, dropping to her knees and trying to lift her liege's head out of the water.

Evening turned back to me and smiled. "There we are. You can be angry with me, attack me even, for the crime of leaving you, but you'll be leaving all these people to drown. Or you can play the hero, rush to their aid, and know that I will simply walk away unchallenged. The choice is yours." She started walking calmly toward me.

I gaped at her, unable to process what was happening. The Evening I'd known would never have—but as I was coming to learn, I didn't know a lot of people as well as I'd always thought I did. Marcia was still crying, an increasing edge of hysteria coloring her voice as she struggled to keep Dean from drowning. No one was helping the rest of them. No one was going to help the rest of them if I didn't do something.

"Damn you, Evening," I snarled, and ran past her to the water. Marcia was sobbing as I pulled Dean out of her arms and hauled him up onto dry land. "Get the next one!" I barked, pausing only long enough to check that he was still breathing before I splashed back out to grab the next of the floating bodies.

I heard the sound of footsteps on the redwood deck behind me stop for a moment, and Evening's voice said, "I'll be back later, to discuss the matter of my missing property. If you survived my binding, you must have found it." The footsteps resumed.

I had other things to worry about. Evening's spell seemed to have slowed the breathing of the people it affected, at least a little; that was the only reason no one drowned before Marcia and I could finish dragging almost a dozen unconscious fae back to safety. She bent forward, resting her hands on her knees as she struggled to catch her breath. I turned and looked back toward the stairs.

Evening was gone. That wasn't much of a surprise.

I walked down the stretch of beach to Dean and nudged him with my toe. "Wake up," I snapped. "I have no idea what's going on, but you need to open the wards before your mother starts attacking the walls with a kraken or something." I could feel the emotional collapse nudging around the edges of my consciousness, prodding me with the reminder of everything I'd paid to be standing here in shoes filled with water, trying to wake up a teenage Count. He was barely older than Quentin . . . I nudged him harder, trying to swallow the lump that was forming in my throat. "Wake *up*."

Dean groaned.

"Guess that worked," I said, and took a step back. "Hey. Count Lorden. Drop the wards, I need to talk to your mother."

"Wha'?" Dean opened his eyes, blinking at me. Then he bolted upright, feeling around in the sand until his hand hit his trident. He pulled it to his chest, virtually aiming it at me. "What happened? Who was that woman? Where is she?"

"What happened was—don't point that thing in my direction unless you want me to shove it somewhere that isn't medically recommended—that woman was Evening Winterrose, former Countess of Goldengreen, and she . . . she left." With no more fanfare than that, my knees gave out, dropping me onto my butt in the sand. My feet wound up back in the water. Somehow, that seemed like the least of my concerns. "She hit you all with some kind of knockout spell so that I'd have to choose between stopping her and saving you, and she left."

"Toby?" The voice was Marcia's, but it seemed very far away. The numbness that had been protecting me since Dianda dragged me out of the water was finally cracking into pieces and falling away, leaving me feeling naked and exposed to the elements. "Are you okay?"

"We fell, Marcia." I looked down at the sandy beach in front of me, and considered the virtues of lying down on it, never to get up again. "She closed the wards, and we fell out of the sky. I couldn't . . . their hands. I couldn't keep hold of their hands." A sob was threatening to rise and overwhelm me. I fought it for as long as I could, struggling to keep it contained, but it was too late. Too much had happened, and while maybe I could have stayed in denial for a little longer, the sight of Evening had broken some inherent part of my heart so quickly and so unexpectedly that everything else was tumbling uncontrollably downward. "They were gone so fast."

"I'm going to get my mom," said Dean, sounding alarmed. The sound of splashing followed his words as he scrambled to his feet and ran off into the water. I didn't raise my head.

Then hands were on my shoulders, and Marcia was asking softly, "Who fell, Toby? Whose hands couldn't you hold onto?"

I closed my eyes. "Quentin. Tybalt. They . . ." The rest

of the sentence wouldn't come. I started to sob instead, great, unsteady braying sounds. Silent tears were for smaller losses. This was too much, it was too big; it was going to consume the entire world. I leaned against Marcia, letting her put her arms around me, and just cried.

Evening was alive. Tybalt and Quentin were dead. The world made no sense anymore, and none of the places I should have been able to run were safe for me—not Shadowed Hills, not my mother's tower, and not home. All the work I'd done since I'd returned from the pond was for nothing. I was alone. I was always going to wind up like this: sitting in icy water and utterly alone, no matter how many people were standing around me.

Marcia held me until the tears ran out. She didn't try to make me talk after that first broken, half-comprehensible confession; she was too smart for that. Instead, she just knelt in the sand beside me and let me weep myself dry. I kept on sobbing after that. The sea could stand in for the tears that I could no longer produce. They were essentially the same thing, after all.

"Aw, shell and stone," said a new voice. I heard Dianda pull herself up onto the sand beside me, and Marcia unwound her arms from my shoulders. Her relatively gentle embrace was replaced by a rougher, wetter one as the Merrow's strong arms pulled me to her. "Toby, I'm sorry. We didn't find them. I'm so sorry."

I'd thought there were no more tears anywhere in my body. I was wrong. Dianda spoke, and suddenly I could cry again, doubling over until she was the only thing holding me upright. I had grieved before. I knew what loss felt like. But nothing, *nothing*, had ever felt like this.

"The sea will rock their bones in the cradle of the currents," said Dianda, with the sort of sweet, ritual lilt to her words that parents use when talking to children. It would probably have been comforting if I'd been a daughter of the Undersea, raised to that kind of loss and that kind of sea foam immortality. But I wasn't, and so I cried harder, causing Dianda to make a wordless sound of frustrated confusion and hold me even tighter.

Running footsteps on the deck caught my ear—some things can't be ignored after you've lived the kind of life I have, no matter how much I might want to shut them out—but I didn't raise my head or open my eyes. Dean had a security force, and he wouldn't be caught off guard a second time in a single morning. Let him deal with whatever this was. He was the Count of Goldengreen, after all.

"Toby!"

My head snapped up, eyes opening. The bright light of the cove room nearly blinded me for a few seconds. By the time it cleared, I had found the source of the voice, and the blurriness faded to reveal Raj, Tybalt's adopted nephew and future King of Cats, standing just outside the reach of the water. His glass-green eyes were wide, and his narrow chest was heaving from the exertion of his run. My heart sank. I was going to have to tell him. I hadn't even reached the point of fully telling myself, and I was going to have to tell *him*, because I was his friend and he was Quentin's friend, and I owed him the news from my own lips.

"Raj." I pulled away from Dianda, noticing distractedly that she was in her natural form, the jeweled sweep of her tail curled underneath her like a cushion, and staggered to my feet. The ritual words that should have been used to announce a death to a member of the family weren't there, they wouldn't come; they had fled into some dark and hallowed place where I was not allowed to follow. So, instead, I took a step toward him, and trusted the bleak, broken look on my face to say all the things that my lips couldn't.

Raj blinked at me, eyes widening briefly. Then, to my enormous surprise, relief washed across his features and he dove forward, risking the water in order to throw his arms around my waist and shout, "You're okay! You're— all right, you're soaking wet and that's horrible, but you're not hurt! I'm not going to get skinned when I come home without you!" There was a note of forced joviality in his voice, barely concealing real, concrete relief. "Are you done doing whatever it is you've been doing here? Because I'm supposed to take you back to the Court of Cats."

My stomach sank as I realized I had no idea what the funeral rites of the Cait Sidhe entailed. Maybe Raj was here to take me back to the Court of Cats for his coronation, since I was technically Tybalt's consort. "I . . . Raj, I don't think I can . . ."

"What?" Raj pulled away, frowning at me. He left his arms clasped around my waist, like he was afraid I was going to run away if he let go for even a second. "Are you doing something here that's too important to leave? Because it looks like you're going wading with mermaids, and you can do that later. You know, for somebody who hates fish, you spend a remarkable amount of time with them socially."

I stared at him. "What the hell is wrong with you?"

"What?" Raj frowned, gathering his princely imperiousness around himself like a cloak—although he still didn't let me go. "What do you mean, what's wrong with *me?* You're the one sitting in the water and refusing to come to the Court of Cats like a sensible person."

"I'm not Cait Sidhe, Raj," I said, frustrated. "I had no way of *getting* there, even if I'd wanted to."

"I know, which is why they sent me to find you." His princely stoicism wobbled, revealing first relief, and then something deeper, something he probably hadn't intended to ever let me see: grief, raw and bleeding like an open wound. "You couldn't get to the Court of Cats on your own, and we were so scared, Toby. They said you all fell into the water together, and then you were just *gone*." He lunged into another hug, burying his face against my sternum. I would have slapped most teenage boys for trying that, but the gesture was so feline that I couldn't view it as anything but what it so clearly was: a request for comfort.

I put my arms around him, lowering my face until my cheek touched the top of his head. "I'm sorry," I whispered. "I just . . . I can't, Raj. I can't go there yet. I don't know if I ever can."

"October." A hand touched my back. I raised my head to find Marcia standing next to me, a concerned look in her eyes. "I don't think you're listening to each other. You're both scared and shaken, and you aren't really paying attention to what's happening. You're too busy paying attention to what you're afraid of."

"What do you—"

"Tell Raj why you don't want to go to the Court of Cats." There was a note of command in her voice. I'd grown accustomed to taking orders from her during the time we spent together at Goldengreen: she might be thin-blooded and only a quarter fae, but she pretty much always knew what she was talking about.

I took a deep breath. "I don't want to go to the Court of Cats because I'm not ready to see someone else sitting on Tybalt's throne," I said. My voice was surprisingly steady, maybe because I was speaking the absolute truth for once. *The Luidaeg must feel like this all the time,* I thought, and continued, "I love you very much, and you're going to be a great King, but you're not him, and I'm not ready." And then there was Quentin. Losing him was going to hurt even more, and for a lot longer. Tybalt was the man of my dreams. Quentin was the son I'd never been given the chance to have.

This time when Raj pulled away, it was to stare at me with disbelief that shaded slowly into understanding.

"You think ... when you lost hold of them, when you fell, you thought they drowned, didn't you? You thought you were the only survivor."

"Dianda found me," I said. Hope was trying to awaken in the pit of my stomach, and I forced it to be still, refusing to let it come fully alive until Raj actually said the words that I could feel him dancing around. "Raj, what are you saying?"

"Uncle Tybalt thought the same thing," said Raj. "He managed to save Quentin. He thought he'd lost you."

I stared at him for a moment. Then I whirled, breaking the seal of his arms around my waist as I said to the people behind me, "I have to go."

"Yeah, you do," said Dean. "Don't worry about Goldengreen. I'll ask my mom to loan me some guards so that we can keep that woman from coming back."

"And I'll ask my son to tell me what in the name of Titania's talons he's talking about," said Dianda, in what for her passed for a reasonable tone.

Marcia didn't say anything. She just smiled, eyes bright and teary in their sheltering rings of fae ointment.

I turned back to Raj. "Take me to him."

"Do you have a towel or something?" he asked. "You'll freeze."

I managed to resist the urge to grab him by the shirtfront and shake him until a doorway to the Shadow Roads fell out. "I'll heal," I said. *"Take me."*

"Okay," said Raj. He took my hands and pulled me into the shadow formed by the bodies around us, and then we were falling down into the freezing, airless dark, and I didn't care.

They were alive. Nothing else mattered.

FOURTEEN

RUNNING THROUGH THE shadows with Raj was nothing like running through the shadows with Tybalt, despite the similarity of the empty space around us. We ran for what felt like an eternity, connected only by our hands. I'd gotten used to running side by side with Tybalt, guided through the darkness more than hauled. With Raj, it was back to square one: he pulled, and I came, because stopping would have meant a frozen death. We ran through a cold, lightless world, caught in the jaws of a winter that would never end. I just hoped we'd come out the other side.

The seawater soaking my clothes was freezing into sheets of ice that cracked and fell away as we ran. My strength was fading, and Raj couldn't be much better off. It was hard for Tybalt to take me on the Shadow Roads, and he was an adult Cait Sidhe, secure in his powers. Raj was just a kid. Carrying me through the shadows had killed Tybalt once; what was it doing to Raj?

I was dwelling on that thought when Raj yanked me out of the darkness and into the dimly-lit hall of the

Court of Cats. I threw my free arm over my eyes, squinting through the ice on my eyelashes as I tried to speak. It came out in a squeak. Raj pulled his hand away and dropped to his knees, retching. I stayed upright for a moment longer before I collapsed beside him, gasping for air.

"Let's not do that again for a long, long time," I wheezed.

"Okay," Raj shakily agreed.

The feeling was rapidly returning to my fingers and cheeks, accompanied by the pins and needles sensation of healing frostbite. It was intense enough to keep me where I was for a few more seconds, and to make me very grateful that Raj and I hadn't tried that particular run before I could recover quite so quickly from injuries. It definitely made me miss running with Tybalt.

Tybalt. The thought stiffened my spine. I pushed myself to my feet, demanding, "Where do I need to go, Raj?"

"Wow." He managed a wan smile and raised his hand, pointing off down the hallway. "You stayed still longer than I expected. Just go that way. He wants you to find him, you won't get lost."

"Okay." I hesitated. Every nerve I had was screaming for me to run until I found Tybalt and Quentin, but Raj looked so small lying there on the hallway floor . . . "Can you shift? I can carry you if you're in cat form."

Raj's smile was bright enough to make me feel bad about even those few seconds of hesitation. "Yeah," he said. The air around him blurred, the smell of pepper and burning paper lancing through the air, and he was gone, replaced by a young Abyssinian cat—but not, I realized as I stooped to gather him into my arms, by a kitten. He had grown into the length of his limbs and the size of his ears, making him a handsome creature even in this form. My boys were growing up.

"So you know, I'm putting you down as soon as I see Tybalt," I said, and started walking, slowly at first, and then breaking into a jog.

Raj purred.

The Court of Cats is a patchwork kingdom, made from the lost pieces of the world around it. Mortal buildings and pieces of disused knowes, they're all the same to whatever strange magic assembles and maintains the Court. The hallway where we'd landed was all aged, oiled wood, like something out of a medieval castle. As I ran, I passed through a white-tiled hospital and an empty, disused library, where the shelves were empty and the ceiling was so high above me that I couldn't even hear the echoes end. There were windows, but after the first two we passed, I stopped looking their way—the things they showed were too skewed, and they didn't help me get where I was going.

Raj curled loosely in my arms, showing admirable restraint for a cat; even when I tripped over a raised doorjamb or a bit of uneven brickwork, he didn't dig his claws into my flesh. Much. The few times he did, the smell of blood put strength back into my wobbling legs, allowing me to keep up my pace.

"Did you intentionally drop us on the other side of the Court or what?" I asked. Raj, who didn't currently have a mouth capable of forming human words, didn't answer me. That was probably for the best.

Then I ran out of a plain hallway that could have been ripped from my first apartment building and into a large, stone-walled room with fireplaces on three of its four walls. It felt old, like it predated the world I lived in. Two long wooden tables were set up in the center of the room, big enough to seat thirty people between them. Only two people were actually there. I stumbled to a stop, barely noticing when Raj leaped down from my arms and went padding toward the nearest fireplace. My knees wobbled. I reached out and caught myself against the doorway.

That was what finally caught their attention: the small, mundane sound of my hand slapping against the stone. Even a Cait Sidhe could make noise running, but no Cait Sidhe would be so gauche as to slam their hand against the door. Cats only make noise when they want to.

Tybalt heard me first. His head snapped up, exhaustion written clearly in the lines of his face as he turned. There was a moment when that was all that happened: apart from that one small thing, he might as well have been a statue. Then, slowly, his eyes widened, exhaustion replaced by relief. It didn't happen all at once; in fact, it was still happening when he stood—the movement attracting Quentin's attention, causing him to finally turn as well—and walked toward me, moving with a frozen stiffness that spoke of both caution and minor injury.

He stopped a foot or so in front of me, gathering himself, before reaching out to stroke my hair away from my cheek, tucking it behind my ear. His hand was trembling. I reached up to catch it with my own, and realized I was shaking, too.

"I thought . . ." he whispered.

"I know," I replied, and flung myself into his arms.

Up until that moment—up until he drew me close and his mouth closed over mine, and I could feel the hot reality of his skin through my still-damp, ice-cold clothes— part of me had been unwilling to believe that this was happening. I'd seen my share of dream realities, from Blind Michael's dangerous homeland to my adopted niece, Karen, and her ability to pull me out of sleep and into whatever fantasy she wanted me to witness. I knew how real unreality could be. But this . . .

No dream I had ever experienced had been realistic enough to recreate the feeling of Tybalt's hands around my waist, or detailed enough to show me the small scratches on his left cheek, abrasions that would have healed in seconds on my own skin. His lips tasted like salt. I pulled away, startled. He was crying. I raised my hand to touch my cheek.

So was I.

When we broke the kiss, I leaned my forehead against his shoulder and directed my next words toward the floor, which wouldn't blame me for anything that I might have to say. "I tried so hard to hold onto your hands, I really did, but the wind pulled you away, and I couldn't find you, I couldn't find either one of you . . ."

"Toby?"

Quentin's voice came from my left. I raised my head and found him standing there in his torn, salt-stained shirt, a pleading expression on his face and his hands twisted together in front of him. I put my hand on Tybalt's chest, pushing him gently away as I tried to step free of his embrace, and to his credit, he let me go.

"I'm sorry," said Quentin miserably. "I tried to hold onto you, and I tried to fall where you were falling, but it happened so fast, and then I hit the water and everything went away and I woke up here and I'm sorry, Toby, I'm so sorry, can you forgive me? Please?"

"Oh, honey," I said, moving to put my arms around him. "You didn't do anything wrong. You did the best you could, but there was *no reason* to think the wards were going to slap us off the Shadow Roads. Do you hear me? We were all surprised by something that shouldn't have been able to *happen*. It's not your fault you couldn't predict the unpredictable. You did amazing. You *lived*."

Now it was Quentin's turn to bury his face in my shoulder and sob, with no trace of teenage self-consciousness or dignity. He clung to the front of my shirt with both hands, and I just held him. What else was I supposed to do? I knew how it had felt for me to think that he'd been lost. I couldn't imagine it had been any easier for him.

Tybalt put his hand on my shoulder, not trying to pull me away from Quentin. I tilted my head back to look at him.

"What happened?" I asked.

"We fell," he said. He couldn't keep the bleakness from his tone, or prevent his fingers from tightening slightly, like he needed to reassure himself that I was really there in front of him. "I lost hold of you almost immediately. I thought . . ." He paused, chuckling bitterly. "I thought you would both be better swimmers, given your coastal upbringings. I stopped trying to catch your hands and positioned myself to strike the water at an angle that might allow me to retain consciousness."

The desperate misery that had been in his eyes since I arrived suddenly made a little bit more sense. If he'd allowed me to fall without trying to get me back, and then thought I was dead . . . I couldn't imagine living with that knowledge. I bit my lip and just looked at him, willing him to see the understanding I was trying to project. I would have done the same thing in his place. That didn't make it any easier.

"I lost sight of both of you for a few seconds when I hit the water. Long enough, I assume, for the undertow to have changed everyone's positions. I swam, trying to find you—I admit, much to my chagrin, that I was only looking for *you*, at least at first—but you were nowhere to be seen. I found Quentin tangled in the kelp. The tide was trying to take him, and I was losing strength, and so . . ."

And so, faced with the choice of drowning or finding me, Tybalt had made the only choice I would ever have been able to forgive: he'd saved himself, and in the process, he'd saved Quentin. "You opened a doorway to the Shadow Roads," I guessed.

"There are a surprising number of shadows at the bottom of the sea," he confirmed. "I thought I would carry your squire to safety and then return. I admit, there were ... complications ... that I did not anticipate."

"Uncle Tybalt flooded two hallways," said Raj.

I turned my head, my arms still wrapped around Quentin, and asked, "When did you turn human again?"

He shrugged.

"Fair enough." I looked back to Tybalt. "The water came with you, huh?"

Tybalt grimaced. "Yes. Quite a lot of it, as well as some rather surprised fish. I was unprepared."

I looked to Raj for translation. He shook his head and said, "It knocked him out. The noise was enough that a bunch of us came running and found them flat on their backs in the hall, with water *everywhere*. When they woke up, they both started asking where you were."

"You were dead." Quentin finally pushed away from me. I turned back to him. He looked at me bleakly. "I just ... I just *knew* that you were dead. That I'd have to be the one who told everyone in Arden's Court, and in Shadowed Hills, and everywhere, because Tybalt is Cait Sidhe, and they wouldn't listen to him. I was going to have to give your eulogy a hundred times, and I was never going to see you again."

"Hey." I put my arms around him again. It seemed like the only reasonable thing to do. "That didn't happen. You with me? I'm not dead, you're not going to tell anyone that I'm dead, and if I *were* dead, you'd still be my squire. Sylvester would take care of all the announcements after you told him what had happened."

Quentin hugged me for a few seconds more before pulling away and saying, "You'd better mean that."

"You're going to be a king someday," said Raj. "Shouldn't you get used to saying the names of the dead now, while you still have time to harden?"

All three of us turned to look at him. He squared his shoulders and looked defiantly back at me, and I realized how terrifying this must have been. His uncle, who was supposed to keep all the Cait Sidhe in San Francisco safe, broken by the loss of one woman. His best friend, equally broken.

They were my boys and they loved me, and I needed to be careful with them if I ever wanted to be worthy of them.

That was an unsettling thought, no matter how true I knew it to be. I stayed where I was, not going in for another hug, as I raked my salt-matted hair back from my face with one hand. "We're all okay now, and that's what matters," I said. My words rang hollow. Considering how much else we had to deal with, from Simon to Evening and whatever her plan was, us being okay was a small thing. It wasn't going to save the world. But in that moment, it was definitely enough for me.

Tybalt was the first to break the silence. "Where were you? What *happened?*"

"It's sort of a funny story, actually," I said, even though there was nothing remotely funny about any of it. I began to explain, beginning with Dianda pulling me out of the water and stopping when I successfully negotiated my way inside the wards at Goldengreen. I knew what I wanted to say, but the words refused to come. I realized I was shaking again, uncontrollably this time, as my entire body got into the act.

"October?" Tybalt sounded alarmed. I didn't exactly blame him. He wrapped his arm around my shoulders, pulling me toward one of the room's three fireplaces. "Raj, get her a blanket and some dry clothing."

"Yes, Uncle," said Raj. The smell of pepper and burning paper rose again, and he was in cat form before he finished going around the corner. I guess that was a faster way to move around the court.

Tybalt was continuing to pull me along with him. I gave up any pretense of resistance and let him tug me along, my teeth chattering. The analytical part of my mind identified the issue as shock, both physical and emotional, coupled with hypothermia and blood loss. My body recovers quickly from physical damage, but that doesn't mean it's easy on me, especially when I'm not sleeping or eating properly.

He got me settled on the end of the bench nearest to the fire, sitting down beside me and wrapping his arm around my shoulder as he tried to loan me the body heat that I so desperately needed. Raj came back in human form with a thick wool blanket, which Tybalt took and draped around me. I unclenched my hands enough to grasp the blanket and pull it tighter, trying to ride out the shock, which felt more psychological than physical. It had been a long day, filled with surprises that I hadn't been looking for and wasn't really equipped to handle.

"October?" Tybalt's hand touched my shoulder, pressing down to be felt through the heavy wool. "Is there anything else we can do?"

"The person who raised the wards on Goldengreen—the reason we fell into the sea—it was Evening." I kept my eyes on the fire as I spoke. That made it easier, somehow. The fire didn't have any opinions on the matter; it wouldn't judge me or think that I was seeing ghosts.

Tybalt went still. After a long pause, he asked cautiously, "Evening?"

"Evening Winterrose, the former Countess of Goldengreen. That's how she was able to control the wards—she's the one who designed most of them." I shivered again, turning to face Tybalt. Quentin and Raj were behind him, both looking faintly bemused. "She was the first person I saw when I got out of the pond—the first fae person, I mean. She was the one who helped me get my PI license back. I stopped running away from Faerie because I had to solve her *murder*."

To my profound relief, Tybalt didn't immediately tell

me I had to be mistaken. Instead, he blinked, a slow frown spreading across his face as he considered what I had said. Finally, he asked, "Could it have been a doppelganger, or someone else pretending the right to her face?"

"I tasted her magic; that's how I knew who she was. Even without the confirmation, I don't think a doppelganger could have convinced Goldengreen to close the wards like that," I said. "Dean was inside at the time, and the knowe has accepted him as Count. *I* couldn't have snatched the wards away from his control, but she was able to. So either she's incredibly powerful, or she's attuned to the knowe on a level that none of us can match."

"But you said you talked the knowe into letting you in," said Quentin.

I glanced his way. "That's also part of why I don't have any trouble believing it was really Evening. I don't think Goldengreen ever *liked* her very much. Remember how upset the pixies and bogeys were when we came to reopen the knowe? They were afraid, because they'd been treated badly." Evening had used pixies to power her lights. I would never forget their small, shriveled bodies, preserved behind the glass that had imprisoned them until they died. It was inhumane. And Evening, the real Evening, had done that.

I took a deep breath. "So, yeah. It was her. Evening Winterrose is alive." Saying the words out loud made them feel more real. My shock began to splinter, replaced by a slow, growing anger. "She nearly killed me with the binding she used to make me solve her murder, and she was never dead. That b—"

"What did you say?" Tybalt's voice was like a whip crack, tight with sudden tension.

I turned to look at him, frowning. "I said she nearly . . . oh." The blood drained from my cheeks as I finally put together the implications of my own words. I couldn't believe it had taken me so long to see it. The binding, the message in the flowers Simon brought to the house, all of it. "She bound me. She used the old forms, and she bound me so tight that I nearly died getting rid of the ropes she used."

"Simon is bound, as is the Luidaeg, by someone who knew all three of you, and who is still among the living," said Tybalt. "Does the once-Countess Winterrose fit this description?"

"She's still a Countess, she's just landless now," I said automatically, before nodding. "But yes. She and Simon were both frequent attendees at the false Queen's Court. That crazy bitch was one of the only people who could tolerate them. And the Luidaeg . . ." I hesitated, trying to remember exactly what the Luidaeg had said when I told her about Evening's murder. The sea witch couldn't lie. That didn't mean she couldn't talk her way around the truth, when she had to. "She talked about Evening like she knew her. I think they've met."

"So she fits the bill," said Tybalt.

"Yes," I said again. "The roses Simon brought—the *winter* roses, from Luna's *winter* garden. He wasn't telling us there was danger at Goldengreen. He was trying to tell us that *Evening* was the danger at Goldengreen. It was her all along."

The statement was simple. Its implications were anything but. I went still, trying to steady my breathing as I considered everything that it could mean. Finally, I said, "You know, the Luidaeg tried to tell me. All the way back when we first met, she tried to tell me. She kept referring to Evening in the present tense. And I never saw her among the night-haunts. How could I have been so *stupid?*"

"You're very good at being blind to what you do not want to see," said Tybalt, a trifle wryly.

I shook my head. "This is too big. I should have seen

it." I pushed myself away from the bench, letting the blanket fall as I stood, and began to pace. My water-logged leather jacket was heavy, but I didn't take it off. "I feel like I'm still missing something."

"The dead are walking," said Raj. "I didn't realize we'd be living in a fairy tale this week. I would have packed tights."

I stopped mid-step, turning to face him. "Say that again."

"What?" Raj blinked at me. "Do you have an objection to men in tights?"

"The first part."

"I didn't realize we'd be living in a fairy tale this week?"

"That's it. Shit. Oak and ash and shit and damn and we are so screwed. *So screwed.*" The Luidaeg always referring to her in the present tense; the way that she, and a bunch of other people, had called her "the Winterrose," rather than using her given name. It all pointed to a conclusion that I had never actually drawn, in part because it was impossible.

"Toby?" said Quentin, sounding uncertain.

"Just give me a minute here, okay? I can figure this out." I fumbled in my pocket until I found the damp rectangle of my phone, only realizing when my fingers touched the plastic that it might have been killed by its encounter with the Pacific Ocean. Still . . . "Quentin, when April modified these for us, did she make them waterproof?"

"I think so," he said. "I know she said she was making yours extra-durable, since she's, you know, met you."

"Works for me." I pulled up Li Qin's number, hit "connect," and raised the phone to my ear, waiting anxiously as it rang.

Finally, just as I was about to give up, Li Qin answered with a genial, "Hello?"

"Li, it's Toby. Also, wow, you should tell April her work is top-notch, because I'm calling you from the Court of Cats, which means she managed to design a phone that can connect through like, three completely different layers of reality, and that's after being dunked in the Pacific Ocean. Can you call Mags over at the Library and ask her to call me, please? And maybe convince her to give me her phone number? This thing where I have to call you to get to her is getting old."

"Yes, but you'd never call me if you didn't need me to reach the Library, so cutting myself out of the loop isn't in my best interests," said Li Qin, sounding bemused. "Are you all right? You sound worried."

I couldn't quite prevent a burst of jagged laughter from escaping my lips. "Oh, man, Li, you have no idea how loaded a question that is. I will explain everything later, assuming we live, but right now, I have to ask Mags something. It's super-important. Please, can you get her to call me?"

"I'll do my best," said Li Qin. The line beeped as she hung up. I lowered my phone, turning to face my bewildered companions.

"I think I know what's going on," I said carefully. "I mean, the pieces have been there for a while now—maybe even since the beginning, with the Luidaeg refusing to actually say that Evening was dead. But I don't want to tell you what it is until I'm sure."

"Because you don't trust us?" asked Raj, looking affronted.

"No," I said. "Because I'm terrified."

My phone rang.

I stared at it like I had never seen it before. Once I answered the phone and asked my question, everything was going to change. Or maybe that was the wrong way of looking at things. Once I answered the phone and asked my question, everything was going to be revealed for what it had been all along. And Oberon forgive me, but I genuinely did not want to see.

I answered the phone. "Hello?"

"Er, October? Li Qin called and said that you wanted to speak with me. Is everything all right?" Mags sounded faintly puzzled, but I was coming to accept that as the Librarian's primary method of dealing with the world around her. Even when she knew exactly what was going on, she sometimes seemed like she didn't have a clue.

"Not really," I said. "I have to ask you a question, and I need you to be really, really certain of your answer. It's sort of 'everything depends on this'-level important."

"Oh. Well." Now Mags sounded flustered rather than puzzled. "I can certainly try."

"Okay. Remember when I was having my little goblin fruit problem, and we asked to look at the book about the creation of the hope chests?"

She chuckled darkly. "How could I forget? That was the most excitement I'd seen around here in positively years."

"Well, I think this may turn out to be more exciting. The hope chest that the County of Goldengreen was named after was given to some lady with a totally unpronounceable name, and you said that her big parlor trick was 'playing Snow White.' Can you explain? Please?"

"Er. Do you mean Eira Rosynhwyr?"

"Yeah, that's the totally unpronounceable name I meant." I looked toward Tybalt. He was watching me talk, his face utterly devoid of expression. He knew what I was asking and why I was asking it, I could tell, just like I knew he would let me finish the conversation before he started demanding details. "What did you mean about playing Snow White?"

"Just that she was rumored to be nigh-impossible to kill, even for one of the Firstborn," she said. "She could suffer an incredible amount of damage and recover completely without outside aid, providing she was given time to sleep. She favored cold places for her recovery . . ."

No shortage of those in the modern world, where anyone could rent a walk-in freezer for less than a thousand dollars a year. "Okay. One last question. What does 'Eira Rosynhwyr' mean?"

"Uh. It's Welsh, it means . . ." There was a pause, and the rustle of pages. I didn't bother wondering too hard how it was that she had a book of names close at hand. She was the Librarian, and she was in the Library. She could have anything she wanted close at hand. " 'Eira' is a Welsh female name meaning 'snow.' 'Rosynhwyr' is a compound word. It doesn't have a direct translation—the closest I can get is something 'rose that has been frozen.' Why do you ask?"

"Because we're all too stupid to live, and that's why we're all going to die soon," I said slowly. "Mags, I need you to do me a favor now, if you possibly can. I need you to close the Library."

"What? October, I don't think you understand what you're asking me to—"

"I need you to close the Library," I repeated, cutting her off before she could fully launch into her explanation. "I have every reason to believe that Eira Rosynhwyr is not only alive, but in San Francisco right now, and she's not playing nicely with the other children. You need to defend yourself. Close the Library."

"I . . . what?" Mags sounded frightened now. Good. Fear might be the only thing capable of keeping her alive if Evening came to the Library on whatever strange errands were driving her. "I'll try. I've never closed the doors without changing locations before, and I can't change locations intentionally unless someone is actually trying to burn the place to the ground."

"If the doors won't close, call me," I said. "I'll show up with matches."

Maybe that was what finally convinced her that I meant business. "All right," she said. "Is there anything else?"

"Yeah. If you see a woman with skin as white as snow and hair as black as coal . . . run." I hung up the phone without saying good-bye, stuffing it back into my pocket as I turned to face the others. They looked at me with varying degrees of understanding—Tybalt, who knew best out of all of us how Faerie worked, looked resigned; Quentin looked faintly horrified; Raj, who had never known Evening, just looked bemused.

"Evening Winterrose is alive, and her real name is 'Eira Rosynhwyr,' and she's the Daoine Sidhe First-born," I said without preamble. "I don't know why she faked her own death, and I don't know why she bound Simon and the Luidaeg to silence, but I do know one thing."

"What's that?" asked Raj.

"We are *so* screwed."

FIFTEEN

A STUNNED SILENCE fell over the room. It lasted almost a full minute before Quentin said, "She's my *First*? How can you . . . I mean, wouldn't we know?"

"The Firstborn have proven remarkably skilled at disappearing from the lives of their children," said Tybalt, in a careful tone. "Most of us are not even certain whether those who founded our lines are alive or dead. Why should the Daoine Sidhe be any different?"

"The Luidaeg said the Firstborn all stopped using their proper names with their descendant races, going to honorifics instead," I said. "She never used Evening's name when we were talking about her. It was always 'the Winterrose.' 'Eira' means 'snow,' and 'Rosynhwyr' means 'the frozen rose.'" I was stretching the translation a bit there, but I didn't think Mags would mind.

"That's not proof," said Quentin. He was starting to look distressed. I guess finding out that your First is the kind of person who just might be your worst nightmare come to life isn't exactly easy.

"No, but it fits," I said. "It makes a lot of other things fit, too. Like the fact that *everyone else* who's died since I came back from the pond has shown up among the night-haunts, but Evening was never there."

"The people who died at ALH never joined the night-haunts," said Quentin stubbornly.

"Because their souls were digitized and uploaded to a locked server," I countered. "Evening should have been there. She wasn't. So why not? It can't be because she didn't want to see us. Devin and Dare joined the night-haunts, and they didn't want to see us either. Joining the night-haunts isn't a *choice*, unless you're not as dead as you want everyone to think you are."

"How was Evening killed?" asked Tybalt.

"They used iron," I said. "That's another thing: you need iron *and* silver if you want to kill one of the First." I hadn't known that when Evening "died," but I'd learned it all too well from Blind Michael. If I hadn't used both iron and silver when I killed him, he would have just gotten back up and kept coming after the people that I loved, no matter how badly I'd hurt him.

Evening had been shot with iron bullets. Her throat had been slit with an iron knife by Devin, the man who'd taught me how to survive in the tangled border country occupied by the local changeling population. I'd tasted the damage, ridden it far enough to be afraid I was about to share her death—but I hadn't *seen* her die, had I? Her heart had still been beating when I'd pulled myself out of the blood magic that had been letting me follow what I'd believed to be her final moments. Even her injunction to "find the ones who did this" had never mentioned finding her killers.

She had known there weren't going to be any.

"We're so screwed," I said again, softer this time. Tybalt looked at me with concern. I shook my head. "Evening was there when I was knighted. She knows too much about me and the way I react to things. We can't surprise her."

"Yes, we can," said Raj. "She won't have expected you to come here. No one expects anyone who isn't Cait Sidhe to come here, because our doors are generally sealed against all others. I don't care whether she's the Firstborn of the Daoine Sidhe or the Queen of France; she's not going to be able to follow us. You're safe as long as you stay here."

"The Cait Sidhe had three Firstborn where most races had only one," agreed Tybalt. "Our First worked together with Oberon himself to make this place a sanctuary for our kind. This Eira, no matter how powerful she may be, will not have the power to overcome a spell woven by three of her equals and one of her superiors."

"That would be swell if we were staying here, but we're not," I said. Tybalt frowned at me. So did Raj. Quentin was looking away, watching the fire, expression blank. I shook my head. "Look: you can't pull everyone I give a damn about into the Court of Cats while we wait to see what, if anything, Evening is planning. May and Jazz are still at Arden's Court. The Luidaeg is still asleep. Sylvester doesn't know why his brother is ... oh, root and branch." I stopped mid-sentence, a wave of bitter understanding washing over me.

"October? What's wrong?" demanded Tybalt.

"Simon admitted to me—*admitted*—that he was responsible for kidnapping Luna and Rayseline, but he said he did it because he was hired to by the person who'd geased him. She offered him something he said he 'couldn't resist,' and so he agreed. But whoever hired him also wanted me dead." I raked my hair away from my face with one hand, feeling strangely numb. "She wanted me killed. That was part of the deal. And Sylvester doesn't know. He knows Simon did it, but he has no idea that it was Evening who hired—we have to get to Shadowed Hills. We have to *warn* him."

"We don't even know that Evening is going there," said Tybalt. "And even if you're sure, can't we call? Sylvester will listen to you. He's learned the value of your words, even when what you say is a seeming impossibility."

"Yes—yes!" I seized on the suggestion, digging my phone out again and dialing the number for Shadowed Hills. It was ringing when I raised it to my ear. And it kept ringing, and ringing, until dread gathered in the pit of my stomach, whispering to me of disasters and double-crosses. We didn't know where Simon was. He could have doubled back, he could have—

The ringing stopped. "Hello?"

The voice was Sylvester's, and wasn't Sylvester's, all at the same time. The dread solidified into a hard ball of anger. "Simon. Why are you answering this phone?"

"Why hello, October. It's lovely to hear from you. I was hoping you would call. You don't call nearly as often as I would like. You should really move back home."

I hesitated. I'd identified him by name. If it had been Sylvester on the phone, he would have corrected me, and probably been horribly offended. So why was he talking to me like I didn't know who he was? "What the fuck, Simon?"

"Yes, I'd really like it if you could bring Quentin to lunch next week. That seems like a fair compromise."

"Simon . . ." The anger was thawing back into fear. It wasn't an improvement. "Are you in trouble? Is *Sylvester* in trouble?"

"Yes, absolutely." His tone didn't waver, remaining absolutely genial. It was the sort of tone someone would use if the threat was in the same room.

"Okay. Got it. We'll be right there." I hung up the phone, looking back to the others. "Simon's answering the phone at Shadowed Hills, and for whatever reason, he can't speak freely. It could be a trap. I have to go anyway. We need to get to Sylvester."

"Next time you have need to choose a liege, I beg you, select one closer to your place of residence," said Tybalt. He rubbed his face with one hand. Then he nodded. "All right. We stay together. We'll travel through the Court for as long as we can, to shorten the time spent in shadow."

"I don't think we can walk from San Francisco to Pleasant Hill," I objected.

"You won't need to," Tybalt said. "If the Summerlands are smaller than the world they encircle, the Court of Cats is smaller still. Those who walk here may as well be wearing seven league boots, for all the distance we will cover."

"How far can we get?" I asked bluntly. "Name a place, please."

Tybalt sighed. "There is very little poetry in precision."

"Yeah, but there's a lot of accurate risk assessment. How far?"

"To the coast. My Court ends at the water—but from there, we should be able to use the Shadow Roads with less strain. Even if it's only a few miles, those miles are ones where we will not be running through the darkness, unprotected."

I paused, really looking at him for the first time since I'd hung up. "This is about protection. You don't want to leave the Court until we have to."

"I've lost you once today," he said quietly. "Please forgive me, but I'm in no hurry to repeat the experience."

"No forgiveness needed," I said. "Lead the way."

So far as I know, there's never been a real map of the Court of Cats: it's an essentially impossible place, made up of pieces of so many other places that you'd need a genius cartographer to devote his life to mapping the

Court as it is *now*, and you still wouldn't have a map of the Court as it will be tomorrow. Tybalt and Raj pulled slightly ahead, scouting as they made sure that we were walking into stable hallways, places that were firmly connected to where we needed to go. Tybalt walked with the tight-shouldered prowl that I recognized from all the times I'd upset or annoyed him over the years. He was worried. I couldn't blame him.

Quentin lagged, bringing up the rear of our little procession. I caught Tybalt's eye before jerking my chin very slightly back toward my squire. Tybalt nodded understanding, and I slowed my steps enough to let Quentin catch up to me.

We walked side by side like that for several minutes, falling into the easy rhythm of one another's steps, before Quentin abruptly said, "She brought me here."

"What?" I glanced at him, sidelong, as I kept walking.

"The Countess Winterrose. She's the reason I'm in San Francisco."

I frowned. "But you were fostered at Shadowed Hills. Evening's never been connected directly to Shadowed Hills. She and Sylvester have known each other for centuries, and he thought of her as a friend, but she was an ally at best, and a political opponent at worst."

"I know. Sir Etienne told me about her when I showed up on Duke Torquill's doorstep—not literally, the fosterage process takes longer than that—but she was the one who started the process. My father had decided I needed to be fostered in order to make me a better king," he stumbled slightly over the word, which had only recently entered our shared vocabulary, "someday, and in order to protect me and Penthea. I was declared his heir before they sent me away. That way there was no point in somebody threatening or subverting her if they couldn't find me."

I whistled. "Okay, I know your parents are pretty cool and everything, but that? That is cold."

Quentin shrugged. "That's kingship. I'm not in any hurry to start taking up my duties as the Crown Prince . . . although I wouldn't wish those duties on my sister, either."

"Uneasy lies the head that wears the crown. I get that," I said. "What did Evening *do?*"

"She contacted my father," Quentin said, eyes fixed on the hall ahead of us. His accent grew stronger, like he was remembering a time when everyone around him sounded like home, and not like the California coast. "She came to our court. I'd never seen her before, and then one day there she was, during private audiences, standing in front of the dais."

"Are you sure it was Evening?" I hated to question my squire's memory, but under the circumstances, I would have questioned my own.

Quentin seemed to understand that, because he didn't look annoyed. He just nodded, and said, "I'm sure. She was like something out of a story, you know? I was a fairy prince being raised in a castle hidden on an island outside of Toronto, and she still looked like something out of a story to me. I kept expecting wildflowers to grow in her footsteps. But not pretty ones, not daisies or poppies or anything like that. Poisonous ones. Hemlock and blooming wolfsbane and other things that can hurt you."

"That sounds like Evening," I agreed. "What happened?"

"She told my father that rumors of my impending fosterage had reached her, and that while she wouldn't reveal her sources, she had come to plead the case for her home kingdom of the Mists. She told him Goldengreen wasn't really an appropriate place to foster a child, but that the Duchy of Shadowed Hills was an excellent place to learn humility and service." Quentin shook his head, frowning. "He should have told her 'no.' He should have said that if she knew I was going to be fostered, she was a danger to the line of succession, and refused to let me go anywhere near her. I was only a kid, and I knew that."

"That clearly didn't happen, since you're here," I said.

"That's my point. My father is a good king and a good man and he loves me. He sent me away *because* he loves me. So why would he send me somewhere that had already heard rumors about the Crown Prince being sent into blind fosterage?" Quentin turned to look at me, still walking. "As soon as she said 'send him to us,' he should have replied 'get out of my court,' and instead he asked his Seneschal to contact the Duke of Shadowed Hills and start arranging my fosterage. I was in Pleasant Hill, presenting myself at the old oak tree, less than a month later."

I frowned. "Evening wanted you here."

"Yes."

"But why?"

"I don't know." He looked back to the hall. "I was sad when she died, because I remembered her coming to my father's court, but it never seemed important, somehow. It was like it had all happened in backstory, and now the story had actually started."

"That's a really weird way of putting it," I said.

"I know," said Quentin, sounding frustrated. "That's the problem. It's like I always knew how strange it was for me to be a blind royal foster placed in a Duchy that was in the process of recovering from horrible tragedy. Duke Torquill was barely speaking to anyone when I arrived at the court. Duchess Torquill was a ghost, and some nights, Rayseline wouldn't stop *screaming* . . . why would my parents have sent me there? They had no good reason to banish me to a Duchy that was both provincial and chaotic, but they did."

"Because Evening told them to," I said slowly. I had never wondered overly hard at the exact timeline of

Quentin's arrival in Shadowed Hills. Maybe I should have: he'd been fourteen when I met him, and he'd been there roughly two years. Luna and Rayseline Torquill had been released from their own captivity two years before I came back to the Duchy. "How did she get Sylvester to agree?"

This time, Quentin's chuckle was almost bitter. "Toby, when the High King tells you to do something, you do it. Even at his absolute worst, Duke Torquill was never so divorced from reality that he forgot *that*."

"Apparently, reality has taken out a restraining order on me," I grumbled. Putting a hand on Quentin's shoulder, I asked, "Are you okay? Are you sure you want to stay with us if we're going to be potentially facing your First? You could stay here with Raj while Tybalt and I go on ahead. I wouldn't think any less of you."

"I'm your squire," he said, with the note of familiar stubbornness that I'd long since become accustomed to hearing in his voice. "Where you go, I go."

"Then perhaps you should both prepare yourselves for a long, cold transit," said Tybalt. I looked up. He and Raj had stopped in front of a plain oak wall, decorated only by a line of hardwood molding along the upper edge. It didn't match the hallway around us, or either of the rooms that it connected to.

I didn't know how anyone could lose a single wall out of their home, and I didn't really feel like taking the time to ask. "This is the border?"

Tybalt nodded. "My Court extends no further."

"Raj seemed pretty tired after just bringing me from Goldengreen . . ." I said.

"He was running alone," said Tybalt. "It will be different when he runs the roads at the same time as I do. My presence holds the shadows open as his does not, as yet. I can help him."

That made me feel a little better about allowing Raj

and Quentin to run separately — and after our encounter with the wards at Goldengreen, I wasn't sure that running in a line was any safer. "I'll trust you on that," I said, moving away from Quentin and stopping next to Tybalt. He held out his hand. I took it, holding on as tightly as I could without hurting either one of us.

"I'll never tire of hearing you say that you trust me, little fish," he said, and glanced to Raj. "This will be a fair journey. Do you know the way?"

Raj nodded. "Run for Albany, come up for air. Do the same in Orinda. Then dive down into the Summerlands, so that we come up on the grounds in Shadowed Hills, instead of in the mortal world."

"Good," said Tybalt approvingly. "We shall take a similar route. When you arrive, if you somehow manage to beat us there, wait among the trees. Do not approach anyone, even if you know them."

"And if you need to take more breaks than that, do it," I said. "I don't want anyone else getting hurt today."

Tybalt smiled at me. For just a moment, nothing else mattered, not Evening, not Simon, not the confusing snarl of overlapping threads that my life had become. Tybalt and Quentin were alive, and we were all together, and we were going to find a way to get through this, because that was what we *did*. We were unstoppable, as long as we were together.

"Take a deep breath," he said.

I did as I was told, and he stepped into the shadows, pulling me with him into the dark.

We ran in silence and in cold, as we always did, but this time, the trip was broken with flicker-flash impressions of the mortal world, cities flickering into view around us as Tybalt pulled me out of the shadows long enough to catch my breath and lose some of the thin coat of ice that was trying to form on both of us. I recognized the first city we ran through — Alameda, whose ports backed on the San Francisco Bay, making it the perfect target for a short hop. The second could have been any one of the genteel suburbs that thrived in the East Bay, where bedroom communities had become a way of life. It hadn't been that way when I was younger; Lafayette, Walnut Creek, and San Ramon had all started out as farming towns, filled with livestock and with hunger. Now they had housing developments named after the orchards that used to thrive there, and I couldn't tell them apart.

The third city we ran through wasn't technically a city at all. One second we were in the dark, cold reaches of the Shadow Roads, and the next we were running across the interstate, with cars zooming all around us. Horns blared as motorists reacted to our sudden appearance. I gasped, seeing headlights bearing down on me, and Tybalt yanked on my arm—

—and we were back among the shadows, racing toward a destination that I couldn't see, but which hopefully wouldn't come with semis trying to turn me into changeling paste.

We didn't run long after that, thankfully. I was tired, and I didn't imagine Tybalt was that much better, since he was the one providing most of the motive force behind our journey. We tumbled out of the darkness and into the light, landing in a snowbank with me sprawled half on top of him. I sat up with a gasp as snow managed to infiltrate the few parts of me that *hadn't* felt like they were half-frozen.

Beneath me, Tybalt groaned. I rolled away from him, and he pushed himself upright, glowering through ice-crusted lashes. The look didn't seem to be directed at me, and so I raised an eyebrow, beginning to scrape ice sheets off the outside of my leather jacket.

"That was thoroughly unpleasant, and I apologize most profusely for nearly getting us both killed," he said.

"The highway was a nice trick," I said agreeably, leaning over to brush the snow out of his hair. "How are you feeling? Heart still beating, not going to drop dead on me again?"

"No, I think not," he said. There was a thudding sound, accompanied by a yelp, as if two teenage boys had just been dropped into the same snowbank. Tybalt's glower faded, replaced by amusement. "It sounds as if our respective charges have also arrived safely."

"Thank Oberon for that," I said fervently, and stood, scanning the snow-choked landscape for a sign of the boys.

We had clearly landed in Sylvester's demesne: the snow was proof enough of that, since no one else I knew was currently hosting a winter wonderland. Trees stood all around us, gray-trunked with translucent blue leaves that looked like they would melt if I so much as touched them. There was a heap of snow near the base of one of the nearby trees. As I watched, two heads poked up out of it, both frosted with snow, one bronze-topped and one russet. I waved. Quentin pulled his arm out of the snow and waved back.

"We're not far from the knowe," I said, turning to offer Tybalt my hand. He took it, pulling himself easily out of the snow. "We should be able to walk to the back door from here, which is good, since I'm *freezing*."

"Perhaps the household staff can equip you with something better suited to the season, or at least warmer," said Tybalt.

"I'd settle for not having half the Pacific freezing against my back, really." Quentin and Raj were out of their snowbank and tromping across the clearing toward us. Quentin scooped a handful of snow off the ground without pausing. I raised my hand. They both stopped, blinking at me. "Drop it."

"What?" said Raj.

Quentin sighed and let his handful of snow fall back to the ground. I nodded.

"I know, I never let you have any fun," I said. "But look at it this way: he would have screamed bloody murder when you put that down his back, and then we would have been explaining things to Sylvester's guards." Probably including Etienne, which would make it a reasonably easy explanation. It would still take too much time. "You can start a snowball fight with Raj later, okay?"

"Okay," said Quentin.

"Wait, what?" said Raj.

"Both of you, come on." I turned, trying not to shiver as I gestured for them to follow me out of the woods and into the gardens that stretched behind Sylvester's knowe.

Nothing moved but us as we made our way through the silent woods, our feet crunching in the snow. Even Tybalt and Raj couldn't keep themselves from making noise as they walked, which was almost a relief, given the circumstances. We reached the woods' edge and continued on, into the frozen gardens. The hedge maze was a skeletal outline, easier than ever to navigate now that it kept no secrets for itself. The rosebushes Simon had visited to gather my warning bouquet were still in full bloom when we passed them, seeming no worse off for having been inexpertly pruned.

"Let me lead from here," I said quietly, moving to walk a few feet ahead of Tybalt. It wasn't much, but it was enough that I'd be the first person any member of the staff saw. That might buy us time to explain what we were doing, and why we hadn't come in via the front door.

As we passed the rose garden, I stopped. Someone was standing near the ballroom doors, someone tall and thin with fox-red hair. Unfortunately, with Simon in the knowe, there was no way for me to know for sure whether that meant safety or danger. Tybalt moved to stand beside me again. We had been spotted. There was no sense in trying to tailor the first impression when it was no longer ours to make.

The figure started toward us. We held our ground. As he drew closer, I could see that yes, he was definitely one of the Torquill brothers; there might be two people who shared that face, but thankfully, there weren't more. He was wearing a charcoal-colored vest over a white shirt, and he looked worried. At this point, that, too, could have indicated either one of them.

Then he took one more step, and the familiar scent of dogwood flowers and daffodil caressed my nose, bidding me to be calm. I relaxed. "Sylvester."

"October," he replied, sounding puzzled. "What are you doing here? You could have been hurt—"

"Your wards have never been set to keep me out, and coming through the woods was easier than using the mortal world, under the circumstances," I said. "We used the Shadow Roads to get here."

He blinked. "From San Francisco? That's too dangerous." His gaze flicked to Tybalt. "I would have trusted some of you to have more sense than that."

"I'm going to ignore the part where you just implied that you don't expect *me* to have common sense, and cut straight to asking if we can come in," I said. "It's cold out here, and I can't really feel my feet anymore. I'd like to get warm and tell you why we came, if that's okay."

"Your timing is excellent," he said. "I was just about to call you."

I hesitated, looking at him. Finally, as my stomach sank, I asked, "Do you have company?"

"Yes," he said. "It's a miracle. October, Evening Winterrose is returned to us. She's alive."

I closed my eyes. *Fuck.* "You know," I said, in as level a tone as I could manage, "that's what I was afraid you were going to say."

SIXTEEN

SYLVESTER WAS Daoine Sidhe. If the feeling of dreamy inevitability Quentin had described experiencing in Evening's presence was an artifact of interacting with your First and not the result of some spell Evening had cast on King Aethlin and his Court, I needed to choose my next words carefully.

Naturally, I didn't do that.

"She's dangerous and you need to get her out of here," I said bluntly.

"What?" Sylvester frowned. I looked back at him, trying not to shiver. "October, I'm afraid you may be confused. Evening Winterrose, former Countess of Goldengreen, *your friend*, is here. She's alive. It's a miracle."

"It's a miracle that nearly got us all killed a few hours ago," I said. "She tried to take back Goldengreen. She closed the wards, and we got slapped off the Shadow Roads into the ocean. We could have died. One of Lily's former handmaids *did* die when Evening started a fight inside the knowe. Are you following me yet? She's dangerous." I didn't tell him she was the one who'd paid for the abduction of Luna and Rayseline. I was going to have to sooner or later, but this didn't seem like the time. Not when Evening was already in the building. Either he'd call me a liar, or worse, he'd attack her—and I didn't want to see what would happen if he went up against his own First.

Sylvester's frown deepened. "This sounds like a terrible misunderstanding. All of you are shivering—you must be freezing."

"I'm not," said Quentin.

"Let's get you inside and have Jin bring you some warm clothes," said Sylvester, ignoring Quentin completely. "Once you're dry, you can meet us in the receiving hall, and you and Evening can work out whatever issues you're having. I understand her return is probably confusing for you, but, October, just think. This is a miracle. We have been blessed by the oak, ash, and thorn this day, for one of our own has resumed her dancing."

I glanced at Tybalt, who answered me with a small shake of his head. Whatever we did next was my call. Swell. I love being the person who decides whether or not we let the potential for dry socks lead us to our certain doom. "Oh, goodie," I said, and stepped past Sylvester, through the open door into the knowe.

Shadowed Hills has always been famed for its roses. Luna's mourning had turned the grounds to winter outside the doors. The end result made the entire knowe smell of something very close to Evening's magic, a mixture of roses and snow that put my nerves instantly on edge. I may be better at detecting individual magical signatures than most people, but even I can't smell a single flower through an entire garden of identical blooms.

Tybalt, Quentin, and Raj followed me inside, with Sylvester bringing up the rear. I studied his face as he shut the door, trying to make my scrutiny as unobtrusive as ever. His eyes were somewhat unfocused, but that could have been a function of concern mingling with the twin surprises of having Evening show up in his knowe and the rest of us appear in his backyard.

Wait. "How did you know we were here?" I asked. "I didn't call."

"If you'll wait here, I'll get Jin for you," he said, and walked away, leaving the four of us alone in the hall.

Raj was the first to say what we were all thinking: "I don't like this, and I think we should leave as quickly as possible."

"That will be difficult, since I am not presently capable of taking October through the shadows, and I doubt you are any more recovered than I," said Tybalt, giving his nephew a hard look. Raj flushed with embarrassment and looked away. Tybalt turned to me. "I am afraid, however, that we are not safe here."

"Yeah, I got that. I was expecting Simon. I wasn't expecting this." I looked at the closed door to the backyard and shivered. Going back out in the cold wasn't a great idea, either. It might get us away from Evening, but it also might result in our freezing to death. We needed to find another option. "Hey, Quentin?"

"Yes?"

"Is there a route through the servants' halls from here to Sir Etienne's quarters?" When all else fails, get someone else involved.

Quentin frowned, turning to look at the smooth hardwood walls around us. There were no visible doorways or tricks in the molding. He was silent for long enough that I was about to say we needed to move when relief washed over his expression and he walked forward three steps, tapping a complicated pattern on a perfectly normal patch of wall . . . which promptly slid open, revealing one of the narrow servants' halls that riddled Shadowed Hills like worms eating through an apple.

"This way," he said.

"You heard him," I said. "Let's move."

I waited for Tybalt and Raj to follow Quentin through the opening before I turned and pulled the back door open, wedging it in place with a chunk of hard-packed snow. By the time Sylvester returned, with or without Jin, the hallway would be empty again, and the wind blowing outside would hopefully confuse our footprints enough to make it hard to tell whether or not we had actually fled the knowe.

Tybalt gave me an approving look as I finally stepped through the opening in the wall. "I knew there was a reason I loved you," he said, voice low and underscored with a purring thrum that made my ears redden.

"Flirt later, flee now," recommended Quentin, as he closed the door in the wall. It fit seamlessly back into place. Anyone who didn't know where the openings to the servants' halls were hidden would have a great deal of trouble finding us.

"Who taught you to talk to your elders like that?" I asked.

"You did," said Quentin.

"Oh, right." I pulled my phone out of my pocket, turning on the screen to provide us with a little bit of light as we made our way along the passage. Purebloods can see in the dark, but total darkness isn't exactly friendly to my changeling vision. I held the phone up in front of me, ignoring Tybalt's amused smirk, and elbowed Quentin gently in the side. "Lead the way."

We traveled through the hallways of Shadowed Hills in silence, only my still-waterlogged sneakers making any sound at all. I stepped as carefully as I could, until the squishing noises coupled with the feeling of my toes in wet socks got to be too much for me and I took both my shoes and socks off, carrying them in one hand as we continued into the dark.

"This should be it," said Quentin finally, stopping in

front of a section of wall that looked like all the rest. He tapped the molding twice, twisted something I would have sworn was a carving and hence untwistable, and pushed aside the panel that came loose. The opening was covered by a tapestry, making it impossible to see what was on the other side. He started to step through. I motioned for him to stay where he was and stepped through instead.

It was the right decision. As soon as I pushed the tapestry aside, a hand grabbed my throat and slammed me backward against the wall. I reacted on instinct, catching the wrist that held me and bending it sharply to the side. "Etienne! Let go! It's me!"

Etienne blinked, the snarl on his face fading into simple puzzlement. He didn't let go of my throat. I didn't let go of his wrist. It wasn't a fair exchange; I wasn't cutting off his airflow. "October?"

"Yes! It's me! Let go!" The conversation was starting to feel repetitive. I heard the tapestry rustle as someone followed me out—probably Tybalt, given that I was obviously in trouble. Hurriedly, I added, "If you don't believe me, you're going to in a second, because Tybalt's behind me, and he's going to introduce you to your own lungs if you keep doing this."

"October." Etienne let me go. I returned the favor, and he stepped back, watching warily as I rubbed my throat and Tybalt emerged from behind the tapestry. "What are the two of you doing here? It's not safe."

"No shit," I said. "And it's not just the two of us. We have our mini-mes along for the ride."

"Hi," said Quentin, poking his head out from behind the tapestry. Raj's head followed a second later. He didn't say anything, just looked Etienne up and down before turning dismissively away to study the chamber in which we were all now standing.

I wanted to do the same—I don't like not knowing

where I am—but felt that it was important I keep my eyes on Etienne, who had, after all, replaced the customary "hello" with an attempted strangulation. He was staring at the boys now, his copper eyes wide and startled. Then he turned to me, and demanded, "Are you a fool? Why would you bring them here?"

"Uh, because this is where my liege is, and I wanted to warn Sylvester that Evening Winterrose wasn't dead—please tell me that's why you're so upset, and that we don't have something *else* to deal with today, because honestly, I am about at my 'threats with no clear solution' limit." I took my eyes off Etienne to check out the room around us, belatedly realizing that we might not be alone. It was a pleasant-looking sitting room, with large windows that were currently closed against the snow falling outside. A half-knitted blanket was thrown over a chaise longue, apparently abandoned in a hurry. "Where are Bridget and Chelsea?"

"I suggested they might remove themselves to someplace deeper within our quarters while I investigated the sounds coming from the walls," said Etienne stiffly.

"That would be me, since the people I was with are much better at stealth," I said. "You didn't answer my question. Why are you upset?"

"Because a dead woman has claimed this knowe, and I have no powers with which to fight her off," he said. "I will defend my fiancée and child to the death, but I cannot protect my liege if he doesn't want to be protected."

"Evening?" I asked. Etienne looked at me like I was stupid. "I'm serious. I need to know, for sure, that we're talking about the same dead woman. I've given up on dismissing anything as impossible."

He sighed. "Yes. The Countess Winterrose arrived an hour or so ago. She just . . . she just walked in, like the wards weren't there at all. The Duke went to meet her, as did I, and Grianne, and a host of others."

"And?"

"And?" He looked at me bleakly. "All of them agreed immediately that her return was miraculous, and that she was somehow entitled to the hospitality of the Duchy, even though she had entered uninvited, even though she made no explanation of what had happened to her. Men and women I have respected for decades, suddenly slavering like striplings seeking a crumb of praise."

"But not you," I said slowly.

"No, not me," he said. "I moved to the back of the group—no one seemed to see me go—and when I had the opportunity, I slipped away, back to my quarters, and locked the doors. I did not think," he added, making a sour face, "to lock the servants' doors. I am grateful for the reminder, even as I must ask you all to leave."

"What?" I blinked at him. "Why?"

Etienne looked at me like I had said something even more stupid than usual. "It is not *safe* here, October," he said. "But more, if you are here, there is a good chance someone will come looking for you."

"We knew it wasn't safe here before we came. I called before. Simon answered the phone. I'm guessing he came in with Evening, and then slipped away while everyone was distracted by her miraculous return."

Etienne stared at me, apparently too shocked to speak. Oh, he was going to love what I had to say next.

"As for someone coming looking for us, we left a false trail and we took the servants' tunnels. Sylvester will hopefully think we snuck out the back door. Besides which, we're cold and exhausted, and I'm not going to run off and leave Sylvester under some should-be-dead lady's spell. Even if she *was* an ally of mine, once upon a time." I took a deep breath, trying to figure out how to explain the next part of the situation. Finally, I settled for just blurting it out. "Also, she's the Daoine Sidhe First-born. I'm almost certain. Ninety percent certain."

Etienne blinked.

"Let them in, Etienne," said a female voice from the door at the back of the room. It had a faint Irish accent. I leaned around Etienne to see its source: Bridget Ames, his mortal lover and soon-to-be wife. She offered me a wan smile. "Hello, October. I think we can manage a few dry sweaters, if that's all that you need."

"Socks would be great, too," I said, holding up my soggy shoes. "I feel like I'm going to lose a toe."

"I'll see what we can do," she said, beckoning for us to follow as she turned and walked back through the door in the far wall, presumably heading deeper into the living quarters she shared with Etienne and Chelsea. I glanced to Etienne to see what he wanted us to do.

He sighed, shaking his head—but his fondness for her was unmistakable. There was a light in his eyes that I'd never seen before Bridget and Chelsea came to live with him, and it infused his voice as he said, "You've done it now. There's no way she'll let you leave until she's sure you're protected from the elements. Couldn't you have reminded her that you heal at a ludicrous pace, and left before you risked Sylvester's anger?"

"Nope, because now we need to grill you on why Evening's whammy got everybody *but* you," I said amiably, as I started after Bridget. "You said Grianne was there?"

"Yes," he said.

"So we know it doesn't just work on Daoine Sidhe." Grianne was a Candela. Her race was primarily claimed by Maeve, which meant she couldn't make a valid case for being a child of Titania—Oberon might have descendants by both Queens, but the Queens had never had any children with each other. Evening's ability to sway people to her side could move across the barriers of bloodlines. That wasn't a good thing. "How about Luna? Was she there?"

"The Duchess was not present, no," said Etienne, a bit

of the old, familiar stiffness slipping back into his tone as he paced me. Quentin, Raj, and Tybalt followed close behind.

I glanced over my shoulder, meeting Tybalt's eyes, and nodded once. He caught my meaning immediately, and stopped walking, putting a hand on Quentin's shoulder to signal my squire to do the same. Returning my attention to Etienne, I asked, "Did Evening say anything unusual when she walked in? Anything that struck you as odd?"

"October, the woman has been dead for years," he said, leveling a flat look on me. "I attended her memorial. I remember the wounds you took in the course of seeking to avenge her. *Everything* she said struck me as odd, because she shouldn't have been saying anything at all."

"I get all that, but did she say anything specifically weird?"

He sighed. "I don't know why I bother trying to use logic on you. It always ends poorly. I should save my strength for better pursuits." We were walking down a hallway now, close and homier than I was used to seeing in Shadowed Hills. I recognized most of the pictures on the walls from Bridget's home in Berkeley. They showed Chelsea at a variety of ages, sometimes with her mother and sometimes by herself. The most recent pictures added her father to the mix, smiling with awkward paternal pride. They looked good together. "She said 'I claim the hospitality of this house, according to the law as it was written, and none shall raise a hand against me.' It's an old form. I was not expecting it."

"It's a bad form," said Raj abruptly. I blinked as I turned to look at him. He scowled. "Uncle Tybalt makes me learn all the stupid ways your nobility has defined hospitality over the years, because he doesn't want me to get caught in something I didn't know I was agreeing to."

"That's smart," I said. "What makes that a bad form?"

"She's calling on a law that was written back when the Firstborn were trying to kill each other all the time, that's what," said Raj. "Back then, if you harbored a son of Oberon or a daughter of Maeve, you were pretty much asking some descendant of Titania's to kick your door in. So Oberon said they had to stop killing each other when hospitality was in force, and that anyone who claimed hospitality under that rule would be entitled to the full defense of a household for as long as the period of hospitality lasted. No matter what they did, if they did it while they were under hospitality, you had to defend them. It's an 'I have to put your interests above the interests of everyone I care about' clause, and it's *awful*."

I blinked at him. He shrugged.

"What? I pay attention."

"Sometimes I forget that you're a prince in training, and not just a pain in my ass," I said. "Do either of you know what the period of hospitality is?"

"Three days," said Etienne. The hallway ended in a swinging door, which he pushed open with one hand, waving me through. "After that, she can be asked to leave. Based on what I've seen today, the Duke will make no such request. If she is actually his First as you claim— and I'm not saying I believe you, just that I have learned to indulge your mad suppositions—he may invite her to stay on permanently."

"Of course it's three days," I said disgustedly. "It's always three days. Were long weekends the norm in Faerie or something?" I stepped through the door into the first room I'd recognized since exiting the servants' halls: a small kitchen with rows of pots dangling above the butcher block island that occupied the middle of the floor. I had taken refuge here once, when Connor and I had been forced to sneak into the knowe due to my having been branded a traitor.

Shadowed Hills had a tendency to rearrange itself to suit whatever it needed at the moment. Judging by the view from the low window above the sink, this kitchen was nowhere near the position it used to occupy in the knowe. Bridget was nowhere to be seen, presumably having exited through one of the other three doors branching off the kitchen. Chelsea was sitting at the island, a pair of outsized headphones on her ears and her attention fixed on a small laptop. Raj perked up and started toward her, craning his neck to see what was on the screen. Etienne cleared his throat.

I grabbed his arm before he could let Chelsea know she had company. "Let them sort it out," I said quietly. "Raj is a cat, remember? He'll want to know how she reacts." And if Etienne didn't let him get a reaction out of her, he was likely to start slinking around, trying to surprise her. My own relationship with Tybalt—back when it had been a simple game of cat-and-mouse, before it turned more serious—had given me plenty of proof of the indefatigability of Cait Sidhe.

Raj stopped directly behind Chelsea, almost resting his chin on her shoulder as he peered at the laptop. Chelsea leaned forward and tapped the space bar. That must have stopped the video, because she removed her headphones and said, without turning, "It's called *ReGenesis*. It's Canadian, you probably haven't heard of it."

"My best friend is Canadian, and Ellen Page is extremely attractive, for a human," replied Raj primly. "I have heard of it."

"Wow," I said. "Fae hipsterism. Hi, Chelsea."

Chelsea flashed me a shy smile. "Hi, Toby," she said.

"Have you met Raj?" I asked.

"Not officially." Chelsea turned on her stool, giving Raj a brightly appraising look before sticking out her hand and saying, "Hi. I'm Chelsea Ames. Nice to meet you."

Raj looked nonplussed as he took her hand and gingerly shook. "My name is Raj. I am the Prince of Dreaming Cats, and an associate to October."

"Are you related to Tybalt?"

"He is my uncle."

"Cool." Tybalt had been involved in the rescue party that had finally been able to bring Chelsea home. She twisted back around on her stool, saying, "Mom went to dig out some sweaters. She said something about you looking like a drowned rat? I don't think you look like a drowned rat, but you can borrow my hairbrush if you want. Your hair is sort of a mess."

"Brushing my hair has been low on my priority list so far today," I said, amused. It was almost relaxing to deal with someone who had no idea what the fae community in the Mists had been like four years ago—and more, probably couldn't care less. Chelsea was adjusting to enough without worrying about the centuries of history she'd managed to miss.

She seemed to be adjusting well, at least. She shared Etienne's deep tan complexion, and her skin was glowing with health, which was a nice change from her exhausted pallor when we'd first met. She no longer wore unnecessary glasses to hide the copper-penny color of her eyes, and she was growing out her glossy black hair, which she had pinned back to either side of her sharply pointed ears. Her magic had been suppressed for a year in the process of saving her, and so she left no traces in the air; when the potion that bound her powers wore off, she would smell like smoke and calla lilies, and her training would begin in earnest. For now, she was getting a much-needed rest, and getting it in the company of both her parents.

Watching Raj size her up, his expression faintly wary in the way it always was when he was dealing with someone new . . . it made me wish we could have given that same luxury to all the kids I knew. "Here you are, sweetie, here's a year where you can't do anything for Faerie, and so it'll leave you the hell alone." It was a silly dream that could never be realized. That didn't keep me from having it.

Etienne's eyes narrowed as he looked around the room. "October," he said, in a tone which implied that he knew perfectly well he wasn't going to appreciate my answer, "where did your troublesome swain and your squire go?"

Guess Etienne hadn't received the "Quentin is the Crown Prince" memo. Good. That was supposed to be a secret, no matter how bad we were proving to be at keeping it. While Etienne was currently as powerless as his daughter, his sense of etiquette had always been top-notch, at least where the power structure of the Divided Courts was concerned. "Oh, they just went to do me a little favor," I said airily. "Don't worry about it. Quentin knows the servants' halls really well; they won't get caught."

"And what, precisely, is the nature of this 'little favor'?"

"They're getting the Duchess." Etienne gaped at me. I sighed. "Come on, Etienne, did you really not see that one coming? Luna was raised by two of the Firstborn. My mother is Firstborn. I need to talk to Luna."

"But why?"

"Because October believes the previously dead woman is actually the Firstborn of the Daoine Sidhe," said Raj, abandoning his study of Chelsea in favor of watching how Etienne took the news. "I am assuming she suspects herself of being resistant to Evening's manipulations because she had to learn to ignore her own mother, and wishes to verify this with the Duchess."

"Something like that," I said. Etienne was frowning at me again. I sighed. "Now what? I told you she was the Daoine Sidhe Firstborn."

"You're serious," he said. "You said that before, but I assumed it was some sort of strange jest. The Countess Winterrose may be an intruder, but she is *not* Firstborn!" He sounded affronted. I understood the feeling.

"Well, why not?" I spread my hands in a helpless gesture. "The Luidaeg lives here. My mom lives here. Blind Michael's skerry is anchored here. If the Firstborn are grouping together, it makes sense that there might be more than we've been able to identify." There were so many other reasons for me to be right—and I knew they were true, I *knew* it, just like I knew that this answered a dozen questions I'd barely recognized about why Evening's blood always tasted just a little different than the blood of the other Daoine Sidhe. I'd been too weak and too far in denial over my own nature to understand what was in front of me.

That wasn't true anymore.

Bridget returned through one of the open doors, a burgundy sweater over one arm and a pair of socks in her hand. "I hope this will fit you," she said, without preamble. "We're not much of a size, but you can wear your sweaters a little large, and it won't hurt you any."

"I appreciate it," I said, automatically dodging the "thank you" the sentence wanted to contain. "Can I leave my jacket here for a little while? I'm going to want it back." I hated to leave my jacket behind for even a short period, but wearing wet leather wasn't doing anything for my core temperature—or my sense of smell, since the pungent odor of tanned hide dipped in ocean was trying to overwhelm everything around it.

"There's a drying rack," said Bridget. "Now, what's so important that it's brought you here to visit us for the first time since we moved in? Not that we were ready for company, but we'd have been happy to have you regardless."

"I honestly don't know where to begin explaining

things," I said reluctantly. "I mean, I can *explain*, but so much of it is rooted in the history of this Kingdom and what happened before I met you—I guess the short version is that there's a woman here in the knowe who's supposed to be dead. I investigated her murder. I nearly died because she cursed me so that I'd be forced to find the person who killed her." Except that she'd never actually said that. She'd said I had to find the ones who "did this" to her. I'd done that. I'd found Devin, and while I hadn't been able to bring him to justice, vengeance has always served Faerie well enough, when necessary.

I'd fulfilled the terms of Evening's curse, and it was my fault that I'd always assumed I'd been solving her murder, not investigating a robbery.

"Dead woman, huh? Does that happen often?" Bridget looked to Etienne for confirmation. Apparently, she had learned to trust him to tell her the truth. Given that their relationship had been built on lies—most specifically the lie that he was human—this was a good thing. "Do I need to worry about dead folks popping up and asking me to do things for them?"

"For the most part, no," he said. "October is arguing that Evening was never dead at all. I feel we still need to confirm that the woman now holding Duke Torquill's attention is actually the Countess Evening Winterrose, and not someone pretending at her name and station."

"I tasted her magic, Etienne," I said wearily. "Just trust me on this one, okay? You can copy someone's face and body, but if they use magic around me, I'll know that they're not really who they say they are."

"Forgive me for being less confident than you are," he said, standing up a little straighter as he pulled his dignity around himself. "I do not share your particular skills."

"Don't put yourself back in the box, darling, it's not

good for you," said Bridget, pausing to kiss Etienne's cheek before handing me the socks and sweater. "I can't say I'll take her word over yours, but you've already admitted she has skills you lack. Maybe that means you should listen to her."

"I dislike the dead returning to life," said Etienne, his shoulders slumping again. "It's untidy and inappropriate."

"And that's Etienne in a nutshell," I said blithely. "Anything inappropriate should cease immediately, because otherwise it might disrupt the natural order in the course of killing us all."

Chelsea smothered a smile behind her hand. Raj simply watched, expression neutral. He was getting better at the Cait Sidhe trick of hiding his feelings behind a mask of vague disinterest.

"You say that as if it's a bad thing," said Etienne.

I was saved from needing to reply by Quentin running into the room. He was faintly out of breath as he said, "The Duchess will see you, but she'll only see you, and she wants to see you now." Tybalt ran into the room a few steps behind him, not as out of breath, but definitely more annoyed. Then again, Tybalt had less reason to be forgiving of the Torquills than Quentin did, and he knew how complicated my relationship with Luna really was.

"Let me change and I'll be ready," I said, holding up my dry clothes. I turned to Bridget. "Is there a place I *can* change without doing it in front of everybody?"

Most of Faerie lacks a nudity taboo, but I was raised human for several years, and sometimes it's nice not to strip in a room full of people. Luckily for me, Bridget understood my reluctance; she nodded and said, "Right this way," before starting toward one of the doors out of the kitchen.

"Be right back," I said, and followed her.

We walked down a short hallway to a half-open door.

Bridget pushed it the rest of the way open, motioning for me to go inside. "You can change here," she said. "Bring your wet clothes out with you, and I'll get them on the rack to dry."

"Okay," I said. I closed the door behind myself, leaving Bridget in the hall.

The room contained a large, perfectly made bed, a wardrobe, a desk loaded to the point that I worried about its structural integrity, and several bookshelves that made the desk look empty. More books were stacked on the bedside table. The one on the top of the pile was called *A Field Guide to the Little People*. I blinked, unsure whether I should be insulted or amused. This was clearly Etienne and Bridget's room; she couldn't be blamed for her reading material. Most of it was probably for class, and it was a good thing if she was teaching her students some things that weren't quite true. The last thing we needed was a bunch of overenthusiastic human college students showing up and asking to meet the local Fairy Queen.

It only took a few minutes to swap my wet shirt and jacket for the dry sweater, remove my wet shoes and socks, and wipe my feet dry enough to let me pull the new socks on. Putting my wet shoes back on over them sort of canceled most of the benefit, but I'd take whatever I could get at this stage in the game.

Bridget was gone when I emerged back into the hall; instead, Quentin was waiting for me, his hands shoved down into his pockets and a distressed look on his face. "What is it?" I asked.

"I don't like you going to see the Duchess by yourself," he said.

"Neither does Tybalt, I bet, so why are you the one telling me this?"

He shrugged. "Because he doesn't like the Torquills much these days—not like he used to—and he thought you'd be a little bit more likely to listen if it was coming from me."

I raised an eyebrow. "How much more likely are we talking here?"

Quentin raised his hand, holding his thumb and forefinger about half an inch apart.

"That may be a small exaggeration," I said, and started walking back down the hall to the kitchen. "I am going to go and talk to Luna because with Mom being . . . well, Mom, and the Luidaeg out of commission, Luna is the person most likely to be able to tell me more about Evening. Assuming she is who I think she is."

"And what if she is?" demanded Quentin. There was an anguished note in his voice that actually made me stop and blink at him. He shook his head, repeating, "What if she is? What if she's the *mother* of my *kind*, October? Do you honestly think I can stand against her? That I can side with you against the Firstborn of my entire race?"

"I don't know," I said quietly. "My mother is the Firstborn of my entire race, and I do pretty good standing against her, but my situation isn't the same as yours. I guess that if I'm right, we're going to find out whether or not you can be on my side when I'm going up against the root of your tree. But either way, you'll still be one of my best friends, and I'll still love you. So don't worry about it too much."

"Okay, Toby," he said, with a smile wobbling at the corners of his mouth.

"Besides, you know that if it comes to that, I'll go easy on you." I ruffled his hair before resuming my walk down the hall, leaving him to chase after me. It seemed like the only reasonable way to end the conversation. Because if I was being completely honest . . .

There are a *lot* of Daoine Sidhe in power in the Westlands, from High King Sollys on down. If Evening was the Daoine Sidhe Firstborn, and her descendants couldn't bring themselves to stand against her, I was in a lot of trouble.

SEVENTEEN

GETTING QUENTIN AND RAJ to stay behind was surprisingly easy after Chelsea revealed that she had an Xbox and a number of video games that allowed for cooperative play. The boys needed the break. Tybalt and I left Bridget and Etienne's quarters to the sweet sound of teenagers arguing viciously over who was going to drive the blue car. I smiled despite the situation as I slipped through the open hole in the wall and back into the servants' halls beyond.

Tybalt glanced at my expression and raised an eyebrow. "Something amusing?"

"Just the kids," I said. "I like teenagers. I never really thought I would."

"Ah," he replied. "Well, I suppose that's excellent luck on your part, as we're stuck with them for the time being. Teenagers turn out to be surprisingly difficult to get rid of."

"I'm pretty good at it."

"I meant for longer than the duration of an action movie."

"Yeah, that's harder." I shrugged. "But they usually bring me back popcorn, so I'm okay with it."

Tybalt snorted. "You are too flippant for your own good," he said. "October, what we are walking into . . ."

"Is dangerous, I know." I reached out and took his hand, lacing my fingers through his. "Luna sent me to face her father without telling me who she really was because she was scared. I know that. I also know that I haven't trusted her since then, and that her daughter is in an enchanted sleep because of me. We used to have this really straightforward, sweet relationship, and now it's like I'm afraid to be alone in a room with her."

"Growing up often comes at the cost of our heroes," he said.

I glanced in his direction, even though it was dark enough that all I could really see was the outline of his body. "So what does that say about my relationship with Quentin? I'm a hero of the realm now, remember?"

"You're his hero, but also his friend, and he idolizes you less than he used to," said Tybalt, with patient thoughtfulness. "Perhaps if you had never become his knight you would have betrayed his sense of who you were one day—and perhaps it would have been as bad as the betrayal the Duchess Torquill offered you. But you removed yourself from any pedestals he could build as fast as he assembled them. I don't think you'll break his heart. Not in that manner, anyway."

"I'm not planning on breaking any hearts any time soon," I said, giving Tybalt's hand a squeeze. "I'm going to talk to Luna, she's going to tell me what I need to know, and then we're going to figure out what happens next. Hopefully, it involves punching. All this skulking around is starting to get on my nerves."

"It's true, you've had few opportunities to bleed all over everything and ruin my best shirt."

"I can't have ruined your best shirt every time."

"Ah, but you see, each time you ruin one best shirt, another must take its place, and your aim is impeccable." Tybalt stopped walking. I stopped with him, dropping his hand as I reached out to feel the wall.

The servants' halls in Shadowed Hills are marked internally with wood carvings, little icons and patterns that identify where the nearest door will access the knowe. The carving here was of a stylized rose, with each of its petals made from a differently positioned crescent moon. I lowered my hand. We were standing outside of Luna's private quarters.

"I will wait for you here," said Tybalt solemnly.

"I'll be right back," I said, reaching into the dark until I found his shoulder and pulled him to me for a quick kiss. The contact was reassuring, and all-too-quickly broken as I stepped back, put my hand against the rose of crescent moons, and opened the door into Luna's quarters.

The rooms she shared with Sylvester were simple, all plain wood and unbleached linens. This room was like walking into a dream about a greenhouse. The walls were glass, held together by veins of silver filigree. Beds of flowers I couldn't identify by name were everywhere, filling the greenhouse with a riotous mix of scents and colors. I recognized each perfume, even when it belonged to a blossom I'd never seen in my life—the part of my mind responsible for identifying the scents of the magic I encountered was expanding its botanical database. That was a little bit disturbing.

Luna herself was standing next to one of the nearby flowerbeds, a pair of silver shears in her hands, clipping blooms off a long vine of fist-sized morning glories. Her long pink-and-red hair was braided—a concession to the number of branches and thorns around her—and her clothing was the simple, practical kind I'd always associated with her.

I paused, looking behind me. The wooden door I'd

entered through was gone, replaced by seamless glass and silver. That was going to be a problem.

"I've always been reluctant to allow the servants to come and go too freely here," said Luna. I turned again. She wasn't looking at me. All her attention seemed to be on the morning glories. "They might get ideas that could get somebody hurt. So I let them have their little doors, and let them think they can enter my spaces without my consent, but those doors never lead here unless I wish it. It seems a reasonable compromise, don't you think?"

"I guess," I said haltingly.

Luna raised her head, finally turning toward me. Her pink-and-yellow eyes were shadowed, making her look older than the lines of her face. "Hello, October," she said. "I didn't expect you to come looking for me."

"What *did* you expect me to do?" I crossed my arms, feeling obscurely naked without my jacket. It wasn't magical. There were no wards or protections built into the leather. It was still the armor I'd worn into almost every battle I'd fought in the last four years. "I need answers. They must have told you that when they came and said that I wanted to see you."

"Before that, I assumed that if you had any inkling of what was happening here, you would stay far, far away. But I suppose that was never an option, was it?" Her mouth twisted, expression going bitter as she turned away from me and went back to pruning her morning glories. "You came back to warn Sylvester. You'll always come back to warn him, no matter how much danger it could put you in, no matter what it costs you, because he cared for you when you thought you were nothing. You were never nothing. That didn't matter. Perception is everything in this world."

"I never wanted us to be enemies," I said. The words felt weak and insufficient even as they left my lips. I couldn't think of anything better to say. Luna had hidden her parentage from the world, wrapping it in the stolen skin of a Kitsune girl named Hoshibara. She had lost that borrowed skin and the safety that went with it, thanks to Oleander and Rayseline. I'd tried to stop them. I'd failed. That was on top of everything else I'd done to her, however accidentally.

It wasn't really a wonder she didn't much care for me these days. The miracle was that she didn't try to kill me every time I stepped into the knowe. "What you wanted doesn't matter that much, *October*," she said, stressing my name so hard I was almost afraid she would somehow snap it off. "What matters is what you did. That's what matters for all of us. Intention is meaningless—the people you cut still bleed, whether you cut them for good or ill."

I stared at her, aghast. "Luna, I . . ."

"Just ask whatever questions you have, will you? I'm tired." She dropped her shears in the dirt of the planting bed as she whirled toward me again, and I found myself more than a little bit relieved by the fact that she was no longer armed. "It's winter here, in case you hadn't noticed, and most roses do not fare very well in the snow."

That was the opening I'd been waiting for. "That's sort of why I'm here. Evening Winterrose is back from the dead."

"I am *fully* aware." Each word was sharply bitten off, more a staccato series of syllables than a proper sentence. "I felt her enter, with Simon like a poisoned thorn beside her. They have the run of the knowe, and I am here."

I blinked. "Luna, she's in Shadowed Hills right now. She has Sylvester wrapped around her little finger—oak and ash, she's the one who ordered Simon to kidnap you in the first place! Why are you here in the greenhouse, and not out there getting between your husband and that . . . that *bitch*?"

"Because I cannot touch her." Luna tilted her chin up, looking at me flatly. "Maybe I could have, before Oleander finished the process of stripping my stolen skin away, but all I have now are a Blodynbryd's charms, and those are *not enough*. You said it yourself: my husband is already hers to command. What would you have me do? Take up a sword and challenge her? My own true love would be her champion, and he wouldn't know what he'd done until he'd cut me down. Maybe were my father still alive . . . but no. He would never have raised a blade for my defense. Only to prune me back into a shape he could allow."

It took me a moment to find my voice again. Finally, once I could get my mouth to move, I said, "I've been looking at some of the things that have happened over the last few years, and some of the things that haven't happened—the ones that should have happened and didn't. Was Evening ever really dead?"

She narrowed her eyes and cocked her head to the side, studying me. In most people I would have called the motion "birdlike," but there was nothing avian about Luna. She was more closely related to her roses than she was to anything with a heartbeat, and she somehow made that simple motion into something alien. "That's not really your question, is it?"

"It is and it isn't," I said. "You say you don't have the power to stand against her. Is it because she's the Daoine Sidhe Firstborn?"

Luna blinked, looking faintly taken aback by the bluntness of my words. Then she straightened, drawing herself up as tall as she could go—and I remembered a time when she was shorter than I was, when we were friends, when her welfare mattered to me almost as much as Sylvester's did—and said, "If you want me to answer you, you'll have to do something for me, first."

"What's that?" I asked warily. I hate it when people

start the game of "if you want me to do this, you'll do that." It always ends badly. Most fairy-tale clichés are snares in disguise.

"She may have seized my husband's will for now, but she can't keep him forever. The roses will bring him back to me, even as they shield me here, out of her view. And while she plays her little games, my daughter is suffering." There was real pain in those words, and there was nothing alien about them. Whatever else Luna was or had become, she was a mother, and she loved her child. "Even in her sleep, she suffers. Your little oneiromancer says—"

"Wait," I said, my own spine stiffening. "You sent *Karen* into Rayseline's sleeping mind? She's barely fourteen years old! You have no right to do something like that!"

"I convinced her it would be useful in her training," said Luna, apparently unmoved by my protests. "Oneiromancers are rare. The last one before her died centuries ago. I don't know where she got such a wild talent, but there was no way I would let my daughter sleep for decades without at least finding an avenue into her dreams."

"And you didn't like what you saw there," I said, dropping my arms and glaring at her. "You sent Karen into a nightmare. You must have known."

"That my Raysel was suffering? I suspected. I had to know." She began walking forward. I resisted the urge to take a step back. Tone level, she continued, "I never expected to have children, October. Unlike your mother and her Firstborn's fecundity, I am a rosebush who dreams of being a woman. My offspring are rose goblins and prize-winning cultivars. It was only Hoshibara's stolen skin that allowed me to bear my little girl, and I nearly lost her several times before she arrived. She has suffered more than enough in this life without my being able to save her. Do you understand me? What I did, I did for a mother's love, and I'm not sorry."

"I do understand," I said. "You forget I was a mother, too."

Luna sniffed. "Only for two years."

It was funny. She had betrayed me with her silence; she had tried to forbid me to love Connor because she'd felt it would be inconvenient; she had been the one who'd roped Connor into a loveless, dysfunctional marriage in the first place. But until that moment—until those four words—I had never actually believed that I could learn to hate her.

"So what do you want from me?" I asked, balling my hands into fists to keep myself from going for her throat.

"I want you to take me out of her. Or her father. It matters little, as long as one of us is removed."

I blinked. "What?"

"I know what you did to the false Queen of the Mists. She was one thing, you put your hands on her, and she became another. I know what you did for Sir Etienne's child. I'm asking you to do the same for Rayseline."

Oh, oak and ash. I had considered offering the Torquills this very thing, but I had never been able to figure out the way to word it. "Luna, this will hurt her."

"I know."

"It'll hurt her *bad*, and it's not going to wake her up. You know that part too, right? All it will do is change her, and it can't be undone."

"Yes, yes, I know all that," said Luna, waving my objections away as if they were of no consequence. "She'll sleep until one of the alchemists finds a way to counter the specific blend they used on her, or until she's slept enough to satisfy the elf-shot. Either way, she'll wake up in a body where her blood is not at war with itself. She'll wake up with a *chance*. That's more than she has now."

When I first met Rayseline, she was a bright-eyed little girl who had yet to be kidnapped by her uncle. Her years of growing up in darkness were ahead of her, part of a dark and undreamed-of future. I loved her then. I would have done anything to protect her. Had that really changed, or had it just been buried under the bad blood and ill faith that stretched between us after she became an adult?

"I want Tybalt to be here," I said, before I could think better of it. "He knows how much blood magic takes out of me. And you have to tell me everything you know about Evening."

"But you'll do it," she said sharply. "Before you leave Shadowed Hills, you'll do it."

"Evening—if she is what I think she is, using that much blood magic could lead her straight to me. It could put Quentin and Raj in danger." I was less worried about myself and Tybalt. I was damn hard to kill, and he was more than capable of taking care of himself.

Luna smiled slightly. "I don't care about anything but my daughter. You'll change the balance of her blood, and then I'll tell you what you need to know."

I bit back a curse. "Fine. Open the door to the servants' hall. I want to tell Tybalt what's going on."

"It's behind you," she said, with a dismissive wave of her hand.

I turned, unsurprised to see the plain wood panel now set into the glass-and-silver wall. It slid open easily under my hand, revealing a distressed-looking Tybalt caught in mid-pace. He stopped when the light flooded into the hall, his head snapping up and his pupils narrowing to slits. Then he was through the opening and wrapping his arms around me, pulling me into an embrace as comforting as it was incomplete: his head stayed up the whole time, and I knew by the tension in his body that his eyes were fixed on Luna.

"Hey." I pulled away. He let me go, albeit reluctantly. The wooden panel was gone again, I saw, taking our only easy means of escape with it. "I have to do something before we can get the information we need. I'm sorry, but we're going to be here a little longer."

"What does she want you to do, pick lentils out of a fire?" he asked.

"Nothing so simple," said Luna. "Although I suppose the concept is the same."

Tybalt's eyes narrowed. "You must be joking."

"She's not, and I already said I'd do it," I said wearily. Maybe the confirmation of Evening's identity wasn't as important as I was making it out to be—but then again, if I was *right*, we needed to be prepared. There were only two ways to know for sure. This was one of them. The other involved trying to kill her and seeing if we could make it stick without using both silver and iron at the same time. For some reason, I wasn't all that excited about potentially breaking Oberon's Law again just to test a theory.

"I'm coming with you," said Tybalt. He didn't look happy, but to his credit, he didn't tell me not to do it. He knew better.

"I hoped that was what you'd say," I said.

Luna rolled her eyes. "Yes, yes, you're very sweet together, it's lovely to see a relationship so stable. Perhaps if you'd pursued each other rather than ruining my daughter's marriage, we wouldn't be standing here now."

I didn't have anything to say to that. Tybalt was not so restrained. "Much as I disliked the good Master O'Dell, his marriage to your daughter was dissolved, not through October's actions, but through Rayseline's. I believe she attempted to assassinate you, did she not?"

"She wasn't in her right mind when she did that," said Luna, drawing the tatters of her serenity around herself until it seemed almost believable. "She hasn't been in her right mind in a long time. Some of that is trauma, and will take a very long time to heal, but being what she is hasn't helped her."

"Being part plant probably does a number on your

sense of reality," I agreed, trying to keep my tone neutral. "Where is she, Luna? If you're going to make me do this, we need to do it now, before Evening comes looking."

"Didn't my husband tell you I was in mourning?" She waved her hand, almost carelessly, and the vines she'd been pruning this whole time writhed, twisting and pulling back to reveal the glass coffin at the center of the growth.

It was almost like a miniature greenhouse in its own right, designed to complement the architecture of the room. That said something about Faerie, right there: Luna had not only commissioned a coffin for her daughter, she'd made certain it wouldn't clash with her décor. Rayseline was lying inside, her hands folded on her chest in the classical fairy-tale position, her fox-red hair spread out across the pillow that supported her head. She was wearing a gown that appeared to have been made entirely from goose feathers, adding to the fairy-tale quality of the scene. She looked like something out of a painting, serene and pure and untouchable.

It was really a pity that I'd met her. "I need to touch her skin if I'm going to do this," I said. "Can you open the coffin?"

"Of course," said Luna. The vines writhed again, this time twisting and grasping until they had somehow lifted the lid entirely off of Rayseline's glass prison.

I breathed in, tasting the strange mixture of her heritage under the floral scents that dominated the room. Then, after one last uneasy glance back at Tybalt, I climbed into the still-writhing morning glory vines and started to wade toward Rayseline.

Luna might have wanted me to help her daughter, but the plants she controlled were nowhere near as sure about the idea. Vines tangled around my waist and legs, slowing my progress and threatening to send me face-first into the undergrowth. I gritted my teeth and forged on, trying not to break or uproot any of the individual tendrils as I made my way to the coffin.

"That's quite enough," said Luna. The vines let go of me so abruptly that I wasn't braced for it. I stumbled, falling forward, and caught myself against the coffin's edge. I glanced back. Luna was looking at me coldly. "Fix her."

"I'm not a switch, okay? You can't flip me on and off." I straightened, pulling the knife from my belt. "This is going to hurt her. I don't know whether people who've been elf-shot usually scream, but Gillian did, so there's a chance Raysel might. Scream, I mean. If that happens, you need to stay where you are. Don't try to touch her, and don't use your plants to try to throttle me. I have to finish once I start."

"If I think you're hurting her on purpose, you'll never be seen again," said Luna, and there was a coldness in her voice that I'd heard before from her mother, Acacia. It was impossible not to believe her.

And I couldn't let that matter. "You're the one demanding I perform blood magic on your daughter while she's unconscious and can't consent," I snapped. "Is it going to make her life better? Maybe. It'll stop her blood from warring with itself, and that's something anyway. But any pain she suffers is on you. Now are you *sure* you want me to do this?"

For a moment—just a moment—Luna looked fragile and uncertain, and in that moment she was more like the Luna I had known for most of my life than she had been since Raysel poisoned her. Then the moment passed, the shutters on her face falling closed again, and she said, "Yes. She is my daughter. She is lost. Now *save* her."

I sighed. "Right." I turned my back on her as I raised my knife and slashed the palm of my left hand in a quick, unhesitating gesture. Pain followed the blade, and blood followed the pain, welling up hot and red in my palm. I clamped my mouth over the wound, filling it before I could start to heal. The smell of my magic rose around me, cut grass and bloody copper overwhelming everything else.

When I had changed the Queen of the Mists, she had been awake and fighting me. It had been the same with Chelsea. With Gillian, though, she had already been elf-shot before I started to work my magic. I kept that in mind as I swallowed the blood, leaned forward, and pressed my lips against Raysel's forehead, starting to search for the tangled threads of her heritage.

Choose, I thought. *Tell me what you want, because I don't want to make this decision for you. Tell me what comes next.*

"What the hell are you doing?"

Raysel's voice came from directly behind me. I opened my eyes. Her body was still in front of me, but the glass coffin was gone, replaced by a bier of roses. I straightened, turned, and saw two women standing there.

Both of them were Rayseline.

One was shorter than the Raysel I knew. Her skin was a delicate shade of rose petal pink, and her hair, while still the color of fox fur at the roots, shaded paler and paler until it was white at the tips. She was her mother's daughter. The other was tall and pointy-eared, and there was a scowl on her overly perfect face. She had always looked predominantly Daoine Sidhe, but the edges of her had been ... blunted, for lack of a better word. That softness was gone now, replaced by hard angles and a subtly altered bone structure that spoke with absolute clarity to her heritage.

Tybalt and Luna were gone. We were standing in the middle of an endless riot of roses, real and unreal at the same time, until the two concepts ceased to have any meaning at all. There were three Raysels. This was going to be like Gillian, then: she was going to have a choice.

"Well?" demanded the Daoine Sidhe version. "What are you doing?"

"I'm here to offer you a choice," I said, trying not to feel self-conscious about my bloody lips and borrowed sweater. "Your mother asked me to."

The Blodynbryd's eyes widened. "Why would my mother ask you to do anything for me? I tried to kill her. I'll probably try again when I wake up." The statement was devoid of malice: it was just something she was going to do, whether she wanted to or not. It was inevitable. "She shouldn't be doing me any favors."

"Uh, she sent me here, into your . . . I don't know, dreams, whatever this is, so that I could pull you into a shared hallucination where I would ask you what you wanted to be. The end result is going to be a lot of pain."

"Way to candy coat things for me, Toby," said the Daoine Sidhe, actually looking slightly amused. I must have looked nonplussed, because she continued, saying, "I think a little more clearly here. I think it's because I'm not awake, so I can take my time figuring stuff out. You know how that is."

"I'll take your word for it," I said, and held out my hand. "I don't think we can stop being here if you don't make a choice."

"What kind of choice?" asked the Blodynbryd, as both of them waded toward me through the roses. "Are you here to wake me up or something? Because I have to say, you're not really my idea of Prince Charming."

I laughed despite myself. "No. I don't think you're going to be waking up for quite a while." Admitting that out loud sobered me right back up again. "But your mother thinks you'll have an easier road back to health if your blood isn't warring with itself. She wants you to be either Daoine Sidhe or Blodynbryd."

"She didn't just tell you what to turn me into?"

"She sort of did," I said, thinking back to Luna's

words to me in the garden. "But that was before I wound up here. Now that I can talk to you, I guess that means the choice is yours. What do you want to be?"

"Eight years old and not broken yet," said the Daoine Sidhe, without hesitation. She had finally reached me. She looked down at the version of herself who slumbered on the bier, and then turned, looking at the Raysel who was still struggling through the roses. "So that's what I look like if I take after Mom, huh?"

"Yeah."

"I'm really . . . pink." Raysel wrinkled her nose. "Like really, *really* pink. I thought that color was reserved for plastic toys. What's it doing on my skin?"

"Fae genetics are weird."

"I guess so." The Blodynbryd was speaking now. She stared at her Daoine Sidhe self and said, "I look like my father."

"Not entirely," I said. "You still look like yourself."

"So I'm just one more Torquill." She shook her head. It was starting to get hard to keep track of which one was speaking, impossible as that should have been. They were both her, and this was her dream, after all. "I don't think he wants me to look like him. I don't think he ever wanted me. You were the only daughter he needed."

"That's not true, Raysel. Your father loves you. He always has. He just doesn't know how to help you, and he's a hero. He doesn't deal well with not being able to fix things."

"I guess." The two waking Raysels looked at each other before turning to me. The Blodynbryd asked, hesitantly, "Which would you choose?"

I paused. "In your position?"

She nodded.

"Probably Daoine Sidhe. I've always been best at blood magic, even when I didn't want to be, so that would be the easier way for me to go. But that wasn't my choice.

It never has been." I lost a little more of mortality every time I had to make one of these decisions for myself, and every inch I lost carried me closer to my Dóchas Sidhe heritage. There had never been a choice about that, not where I was concerned.

"My mother loves me," said Raysel thoughtfully. "She always will, I guess, if she was willing to send you here after I almost killed her. But I think if I were a Blodynbryd, we'd always be a little bit connected. I don't know if I could take that. And I don't know if the parts of me that are broken and the parts of her that are broken would be able to coexist."

"That's definitely a risk," I agreed.

"My father doesn't know what to do with me, but he always tried to let me find my own way. There are more Daoine Sidhe in our world. It might be easier to learn how to be whole."

"That's true." I felt like all I was doing was agreeing with her, offering meaningless sounds that couldn't possibly simplify such an impossible decision. It was all I had.

Raysel bit her lip, worrying it between her teeth for a moment before she asked, "If you were in my position . . . what do you think my parents would want me to be? The royal, or the rose?"

"I'd say your parents both have their flaws, and you should be choosing for you, not for them. You'll have an easier time of it if you're Daoine Sidhe. There will be more people who can help you heal, and who'll understand the way your magic works."

"I'll have magic?" She sounded almost amazed, and I realized this, too, would be a big change for her: she'd never been trained, partially because her heritage was so strange that no one knew how to teach her, and partially because of her stolen childhood. She could disguise herself from human eyes, and that was about it. "Like my father?"

"If you choose to be Daoine Sidhe."

"But I'll be betraying my mother again," she said reluctantly. "I'll be leaving her alone."

I thought of Gillian, and the way she'd looked at me when we'd been standing together in her equivalent of this rose-strewn field. "You'll never leave her alone, and she knows it," I said. "Our mothers can betray us, and we can betray them, but they'll always be our mothers. Nothing takes that away."

The two Raysels nodded, very slowly. The Blodynbryd turned her face away as the Daoine Sidhe offered me her hands. I took them, smelling blood on the air, coiling like smoke through the mingled perfumes of a thousand roses.

"I choose Daoine Sidhe," she said.

I'd been expecting that. I still mustered a smile. "This will hurt," I cautioned.

"I know," she said. "And Toby . . ."

"Yeah?"

"Thank you."

There was no way I could answer that, and so I didn't try. I just reached into the cool, thorny field of her heritage, grasping the roots of what made her Blodynbryd, and yanked as hard as I could.

I was getting better with practice: I was able to keep going even when Raysel began to scream. Her blood didn't fight me, which made things easier. She had come to terms with what I was here to do, and even if she had never been much of a blood-worker before, every inch of her that turned fully Daoine Sidhe added a sliver more strength to her power. She fed that power into me, and I took it greedily, turning it back on her in a continual, cleansing wave.

The field of roses was blackening around the edges. The part of my mind responsible for keeping me alive noted dispassionately that it hadn't been that long since

I raised the dead, nearly drowned, and sobbed myself to the verge of dehydration, all without eating or sleeping or doing anything else that would allow my body to replenish its resources.

This will hurt, I thought again, and then the last thin tendrils of Raysel's Blodynbryd heritage snapped off in my hands, and I was falling down into the dark, and nothing particularly mattered anymore. Not even, I was relieved to discover, the pain.

EIGHTEEN

THE MIXED SCENTS of burning wood, warm fur, and roasting chicken assaulted my nose, drawing me up out of a sound sleep. I struggled to keep my eyes closed, dimly aware that as soon as I fully woke, I was going to have to start dealing with the world again—and given how long it had been since I'd slept, that wasn't something I was in a real hurry to do. My head was throbbing, but nothing else hurt. That was a nice change.

Even forming that thought was too strenuous to be safe. The shredded remains of sleep wisped away into a sigh as I pushed myself up onto my elbows and opened my eyes on the Court of Cats.

This was one of the smaller bedchambers, and it was different from most of the others I'd seen in that it only contained a single bed. It was a huge, four-posted thing, with a clean, if moth-eaten, canopy stretching across the top of it. I was in the bed, naturally, covered by a thick patchwork quilt. The center of the room was occupied by a small dining table. A fireplace took up most of the far wall. Tybalt was crouched in front of it, prodding at a chicken on a spit.

I took a breath and said the first thing that came to mind, which happened to be, "A chicken? A rotisserie chicken? Could you get any more Renfair cliché if you really, really *tried*, do you think?"

"I've never actually been to one of your Renaissance Fairs. I think it would be an amusing, if frustrating experience," said Tybalt, a relieved note in his voice. He twisted to face me without coming out of his crouch. "Welcome back to the land of the living, Sleeping Beauty—and before you protest the label, consider that I pulled you from a glass coffin in the midst of a riot of flowers. I believe a fairy-tale allusion or two is only fitting."

The last thing I remembered was holding Raysel's hands and yanking the Blodynbryd out of her one drop at a time. I blanched. "Oh, Oberon's balls, did I collapse on top of Rayseline?"

"Yes, and her howling like a Banshee the whole time," he said, twisting back to face the fire. He gave the chicken another experimental nudge with the fork in his hand. "There were a few moments where I thought you might actually awaken her from her enchanted sleep, simply because she was screaming so much. Alas, you did no such thing. That might have distracted her mother from the fact that you were lying on top of her like a sack of abandoned potatoes."

"That metaphor got a little mangled somewhere in the middle," I said, closing my eyes. My stomach rumbled. I ignored it as I asked, "So what happened?"

"Rayseline screamed, you collapsed, Luna shouted that you'd killed her daughter, I interceded before anything overly compromising could happen. I then stood between mother and coffin with you in my arms until she answered your questions." There was a scraping sound as he presumably took the chicken off the fire. "Once I had the information I needed, I carried you to Etienne's quarters, retrieved our charges, and brought you back here to the Court of Cats, where you would be safe."

Our charges ... my eyes snapped open, staring up at the threadbare canopy. "Quentin and Raj. Where are they?"

"They needed rest as much as you did," said Tybalt. "They are in the room next door, enjoying the chance to slumber without fear of discovery. I'll wake them after you and I have finished our conversation."

"Our—right." I turned toward him. He was standing next to the table, holding the roast chicken on a platter. "What did Luna say?"

"It's not what Luna said that should concern you at the moment: it's what I'm saying, and what I'm saying is that I'll tell you what Luna said as soon as you can get out of that bed, come to this table, and eat." His smile couldn't hide his concern. "You've run yourself to shreds today, and I simply cannot have that."

"I'm not that tired," I protested.

"Then push off the blanket, rise from the bed, and come to the table. I have seen how much you've bled today: you'll forgive me if I choose not to believe you." He took a seat, beginning to portion the chicken onto the plates he had already waiting—plates which appeared to contain potatoes and some sort of lightly dressed salad. He'd been preparing for me to wake up for a while.

Glaring, I attempted to rise to his challenge ... and failed as my jellied limbs refused to obey even the simplest commands. I tried again, with the same result.

Tybalt observed all this before commenting mildly, "I have seen you accomplish more under worse circumstances, but only when there was an immediate threat to be dealt with, an ally to be rescued or a life to be saved. The situation in which we find ourselves is unpleasant to be sure, and doubtless dangerous, but it is not, at the moment, life-threatening. Your body knows its needs better than you do."

"You're a jerk sometimes."

"I'm a cat, always," he said, and smiled. "At least you sound on the road to recovery. Stop thinking of rising as a way to gain access to information that will cause you to put even more strain on your body's ability to sustain itself, and think of it as a quick route to the sustenance I know you need." He picked up his plate and waved his hand over it, wafting the smell of the chicken toward me.

I was on my feet before consciously deciding to move, and my butt was hitting the polished bench across from where Tybalt sat before I had time to process what I was wearing. The growling of my stomach had become a roar. I shut it out for a moment as I looked down at my attire: black leggings, a white linen chemise that would need to be belted if I was going to wear it out of this room, and no shoes. No socks either. At least my bare feet were finally warm, courtesy of the bed and the fire.

"Your previous clothing still exists," said Tybalt. "It simply needed a good drying, and sleeping in it seemed mildly unsanitary."

"You know, there was a time when waking up to find that someone had changed my clothes would have been a surprise. When did I get used to this, exactly?" I finally reached for the plate that had been set in front of me, and asked a more important question: "Did you get my jacket from Bridget?"

"Yes, and it should be ready for you by now. Were you aware that the mortal world contained establishments called 'dry cleaners,' which are capable of working feats that previously only Bannicks had been able to accomplish?"

I raised an eyebrow. "Yes, I knew about dry cleaners. I'm a little surprised that you do."

"In this case, the credit for wisdom should go to your squire. Your precious leathers are pristine." Tybalt gave my food a meaningful look. "Now please. Eat, so that we may wake the boys and be on our way. I'm sure you'll want that, once you've recovered sufficiently."

The roaring in my stomach was almost impossible for me to ignore at this point. I still forced myself to hold it off for a few seconds more. "Tell me what Luna said."

He sighed. "Do you swear to eat your supper even once you have what you desire?"

"Yes. I promise that no matter what you say, unless it spells immediate disaster for someone I care about, I'll sit here and eat before I go haring off, okay? Besides. You took my shoes." And my knife, I realized: I was unarmed.

Maybe that was intentional. Tybalt took a breath, looked at me solemnly, and said, "Your suspicions are confirmed. The woman we know as Evening Winterrose was born Eira Rosynhwyr, called the Rose of Winter, first daughter of Oberon, King of Faerie, and Titania, the Summer's Queen. She did not return from the dead, because she never died. Of all the Firstborn, the Rose of Winter has been called the most difficult to kill."

"Ah." It wasn't as much of a shock as I'd expected it to be: I'd already been almost certain. This just confirmed it. "And Luna was able to resist her as much as she did because . . . ?"

"Because she was not there when Evening first arrived. She remained surrounded by her roses, as she said, which allowed her to resist any call that Evening might send. Further, she had already been exposed at such great length to her own parents, whose Firstborn nature would normally have overwhelmed her—but most of all, because Evening was not Luna's original. Any of the Daoine Sidhe would have trouble denying Evening if given a direct command." A smile tugged at the corner of his mouth. "I suspect that this was meant to make the Firstborn better able to control their descendants. I shall have to ask fair Amandine how well that has worked for her when I see her next."

"If my mother turns you into a lemon tree, I'm not going to yell at her," I said, somewhat numbly. My mind was far away, and my body took advantage of that brief absence to shovel several bites of chicken and potatoes into my mouth. I barely tasted any of it. Swallowing, I asked, "So why couldn't Grianne resist her? The Candela aren't descended from Titania."

"No, but Grianne swears her allegiance to Sylvester, who is Evening's to command."

"Etienne resisted. He swears his allegiance to Sylvester."

"I have no idea why he was able to achieve that state of grace. Wheels within wheels." Tybalt sighed. "It's all very troublesome."

"And it's just going to get worse," I said grimly. "Can we leave the boys here?"

Tybalt blinked. "Quentin is a friend of this Court, and is well chaperoned by the presence of my nephew, but you're generally loath to be parted from him. Why—"

"He's Daoine Sidhe. I don't want that bitch telling him what to do." There was a chance his exposure to so many other Firstborn—from the Luidaeg to Blind Michael—would make him resistant. I didn't want to risk it. I took a bite of salad before adding, "I'd hide all the Daoine Sidhe I know here, if that wouldn't be abusing your hospitality."

"I appreciate your concern for the limits of my charity," said Tybalt dryly.

"I try to be considerate," I said, before inhaling another few bites of chicken. My hunger wasn't abating. The magic I'd been doing had taken more out of me than I thought. At least the food seemed to be taking the edge off of my headache. "But yeah. I don't want Quentin near her. If he can be hidden here for a little while, that's for the best."

"He will object."

"He'll lose."

Tybalt raised an eyebrow. "You sound remarkably sure of yourself. Raj—"

"Is Cait Sidhe. Quentin is a squire and a prince of the Divided Courts. His upbringing was a little more hardcore on 'listen to your elders,' and while I'm aware that I've done a lot to damage his early training, I think some of it is still in there." I shrugged. "He's not going to be happy. He's going to give in."

"You speak of 'leaving the boys here' and carrying on with your current quest, but I admit, October, I'm somewhat unclear as to what that quest is." Tybalt leaned across the table to transfer half of his chicken onto my plate. I didn't object. "Simon is in town, and this is troubling. Evening is returned from the dead, and was never dead to begin with. The Luidaeg is injured. We know these things are connected, and we know that they are terrible, but none of them provides a clear or immediate course of action. Running to the Queen in the Mists seems logical, except that it might draw our enemies to her, and while Evening is not her parent and original, she's still no match for one of the Firstborn."

"I know. We need to keep at least one place aside from the Court of Cats safe for our allies, and since we know Evening could eat Arden for breakfast, that means we need to keep Arden off of Evening's radar for as long as possible." I put a hand over my eyes, taking comfort in the temporary darkness. "I'm happier when I have a bad guy I can hit. Okay. Let's look at this logically: both Simon and the Luidaeg were geased by Evening. We know that Evening was able to somehow know when the Luidaeg said something she wasn't supposed to—she shouldn't have been able to confirm that the geas had been cast by someone I knew. And when the Luidaeg broke the rules, Evening punished her for it."

We both paused for a moment. I had no doubt that Tybalt's thoughts were following the same dark path as mine, remembering the shattered condition of the Luidaeg's apartment, and the condition she'd been in when we found her. The Luidaeg was one of the most powerful people we knew. The fact that Evening had been able to take her out was terrifying.

"Wait." I dropped my hand, looking at him. "Evening is *Titania's* daughter."

Tybalt frowned. "Yes, and?"

"Raysel was able to make the Luidaeg stand down just by saying she was a descendant of Titania. The Luidaeg can't raise her hand against Titania's children. She's said so before, and she can't lie. That's how Evening was able to beat the holy crap out of her without bleeding all over the place and leaving me a trail to follow. The Luidaeg didn't fight back."

Tybalt's frown deepened. "If that's true . . . someone must have bound her so. Someone who did not much care whether she lived or died, given what I've heard about the treatment of the children of Maeve by the children of Titania."

"Yeah," I said. My plate was somehow empty again, and my stomach was no longer screaming at me. I took that as a sign that I was ready to get up, and stood, grateful to find that I was right: my legs took my weight without protesting. My headache was barely a throb. "I'm thinking it was either Evening herself, or her mother. I can't see Oberon doing that to one of his own kids. But it doesn't really matter either way, I guess: the Luidaeg is bound, and she couldn't fight back."

"So our Evening is not only a liar, but a coward." Tybalt shook his head as he stood. "Truly, it seems that I came into your life at precisely the correct moment."

I blinked. "Okay, you're going to have to take that one back a few steps for me."

"It's simple." He didn't walk around the table—he prowled, his feline nature surging to the forefront as he moved to slide his arms around my waist and pull me close to him. I wanted to object, to say that we were on a timetable. The trouble was, we didn't know what that timetable was counting down to. We still didn't know what Evening *wanted*, and so I couldn't think of a single objection to taking a moment and letting him hold me.

I might regret that later, but later would happen in its own time. At the moment, I was busy looking into Tybalt's eyes. He pulled one hand free, reaching up to tuck my hair back the way I so often did. His fingers lingered against the point of my ear, tracing the edges that had grown so much sharper in the past few years.

"You were clearly keeping company with the wrong sort of people before I decided to take an interest in your keeping," he said, as if it were the most reasonable thing in the world. "Anyone who would betray her own sister in such a manner is no fit friend for you."

"I have better friends now," I said, and leaned up to kiss him, letting him pull me closer. If someone had told me this would happen in the days that followed Evening's murder—excuse me, Evening's *disappearance*—I would have thought they were pulling my leg. Now, I stood in the embrace of a man I had once sworn was nothing but an irritation, and I didn't want to be anywhere else, ever again.

The bed I had so recently left beckoned, a silent reminder that he had been intending to let me sleep until I awoke, and that no one knew I was up—no one but him. We could spend a little time before things began to happen again. Like my unplanned nap, this was part of recuperation, and it mattered. It—

My phone started ringing. I pushed away from Tybalt, realizing how close I had just come to committing myself to a lengthy—if pleasurable—interlude, and began looking around for the source of the sound. There was a large oak wardrobe against the wall across from the fireplace that looked like a good bet. I strode across the room and hauled on the wardrobe doors, which opened to reveal my shoes and leather jacket, both clean and waiting for me. My underwear, jeans, and newly bloodstained shirt were in the bottom of the wardrobe, discarded like the trash they had become.

My jacket pocket was ringing. Stridently. I dipped my hand inside and pulled out my vibrating, ringing phone, bringing it to my ear.

"Hello?"

"Are you dead? I ask because I really want to know, and am interested in your response, and not because I'm planning to murder you myself for not answering the last three times I've called." May was using her murderously perky voice again, which meant that she was *pissed*.

"I was asleep when you called before," I said, directing a glare at Tybalt. He gave me his best innocent look, even going so far as to shrug, like failing to tell me that my phone had been ringing was no big deal.

On the other hand, if I'd been asleep enough not to notice the phone going off repeatedly, he might not have been *able* to wake me. "Uh, whatever, that's no excuse, even if you don't sleep enough," said May. "Where *are* you? Where have you been? Are you at Shadowed Hills?"

"No, I'm not at Shadowed Hills, I'm in the Court of Cats," I said. "I've been here for a while—not sure how long. I sort of ran myself ragged, and collapsed from overuse of blood magic, and then Tybalt put me to bed without asking me first." The fact that I'd stayed there, and hadn't even noticed being *put* there, spoke volumes.

I paused, finally parsing her last question. "Why did you ask if I was at Shadowed Hills?"

"Because they closed their wards like ten hours ago, and they're not letting *anybody* inside, not even when they come from the Queen," said May, sounding more bemused than frustrated. "I sort of assumed you were locked in a life-or-death struggle with Simon Torquill, and would eventually emerge bloody but intact. It's like eight in the morning."

"Okay, we are canceling the cable," I said. "If you think I'm behind a sealed ward fighting for my life, try calling someone other than me, okay? Like I don't know, Danny." He could ram the wards with his car.

"I guess," she said reluctantly. "It's still weird that the wards are closed."

"Not that weird," I said. "Evening's there."

"Winterrose?"

May didn't sound surprised. Of course she didn't sound surprised. She'd been among the night-haunts when Evening had "died." She'd probably known all along that Evening wasn't dead, but she hadn't realized it was important, and I'd never had any reason to ask her about it.

"Oak and ash, it's the phone book all over again," I muttered, before saying more loudly, "Yes, Evening Winterrose. She's not dead—which you apparently knew, and we need to have a *long* talk soon about what I'm assuming is true and you know is false—and she's got pretty much the entire knowe in her thrall."

"But how can she . . . ?"

"She's the Daoine Sidhe Firstborn, that's how." I paused to give May time to react. Silence answered me. I sighed, reading her lack of comment for what it was. "I'm sure, okay? Luna verified it. You need to tell Arden to keep her people in the knowe and close the doors. Evening can influence her descendants to do whatever she wants, and it doesn't just work on them. There's a good chance that anyone who gets too close to her is going to want to do what she tells them."

Except something about my words seemed wrong. Dean and his people certainly hadn't seemed inclined to do what Evening said, and Dean was half Daoine Sidhe. I was going to need to figure out what differed between Goldengreen and Shadowed Hills. Maybe it was something we could use.

Reluctantly, May said, "I'll tell her, but Toby, this sounds . . ."

"I know how it sounds, okay? Unfortunately, I don't have the luxury of only experiencing things that sound reasonable when you try to explain them to other people. Quentin is staying here in the Court of Cats. You and Jazz stay with Arden, where you'll be at least a little bit safer."

"Where are you going to go?"

I smiled thinly. "I'm going to go be a hero. Open roads, May."

"Kind fires," she answered.

I hung up, looking at the phone in my hand for a moment before I dropped it back into my jacket pocket and eyed my clothes with distaste. The dry cleaner had been able to work wonders on my leather jacket. Nothing was going to save my shirt and jeans, both of which were blotched with dried blood. Behind me, Tybalt cleared his throat. I turned.

"Was I really asleep for ten hours?" I asked. I ran a hand back through my hair, noting that it was soft and clean. Tybalt might not have been able to get the blood out of my jeans, but he'd been able to get it out of my hair. There was a time when I would have found that intrusive. Now it was just sort of sweet.

"I believe it was closer to nine," he said, looking obscurely relieved by the question. "I would have awak-

ened you, but when your portable telephone rang
without causing you to so much as stir, I realized how
much you needed the rest. I am a selfish man. I will not
have you kill yourself with exhaustion."

"There are much more entertaining ways for me to
die; don't worry," I said. "Is the Luidaeg—"

"My people are watching her. She has not stirred
since she was brought here, although she has continued
breathing, which I assume would have been your second
question," he said. "Gabriel has the current shift. He will
alert me if anything changes."

"We need to keep a very close eye on her," I said.
Things were beginning to fall together in my head, things
that had previously been kept apart only by my exhaustion and general feeling of being overwhelmed by everything around me.

Tybalt raised an eyebrow. "Why?"

"There were wards on the Luidaeg's apartment—
we're talking big time mega-wards. We could get in because she allowed us to get in, you couldn't access the
Shadow Roads if you got too close, all that fun stuff. Evening tore through them like they were nothing." I picked
up my jeans, giving them a disgusted look, and pulled
them on over the leggings. The denim, bloody as it was,
would add a little extra insulation when we inevitably
left through the Shadow Roads. Tucking the chemise
into my waistband did away with the need for a belt,
even if it was all a bit pirate-esque for my taste.

"All this is true, but I'm afraid I still don't follow, and
I certainly don't understand why you're putting your
trousers on," Tybalt said.

"We can't stay here forever, and I don't want to be
caught with no pants on when the alarm rings," I said.
"We brought the Luidaeg here on the assumption that
Evening wouldn't be able to follow, since Oberon gifted
this place to the Cait Sidhe. We know that Evening has a

measure of control over anyone that's descended from her. But what if it's not just them?"

"Meaning what, exactly?" asked Tybalt. A crease was beginning to form between his eyebrows, signaling his dawning concern.

"Not everyone in that hall would have been Daoine Sidhe," I continued. "There aren't that many Daoine Sidhe in the *world*. What if she gets absolute control over her descendants, but a measure of control over her relatives? There are Cait Sidhe who are descended from Titania." I took my scabbard down from its hook and strapped it around my waist before shrugging on my leather jacket. "We have to assume the Court could be compromised."

Tybalt stared at me for a moment, stunned into silence. Finally, he said, "I knew loving you would be dangerous. I had no idea *how* dangerous."

"Sorry." I grabbed my shoes and sat down heavily on the edge of the bed. I didn't have socks. That was really the least of my current concerns.

"Yes, well. I suppose this is my own fault." He laughed, a sharp, dry sound. "I will go and advise my guards that they should watch for any signs of odd behavior in their fellows. After Samson, they have started watching each other much more closely than they ever did before. If someone is compromised, they will know."

"Sounds good," I said. "When you get back, we'll figure out what happens next." I bent to start lacing up my shoes.

Behind me, the door opened and closed again, marking Tybalt's exit. I tried to focus, keeping my fingers as steady as I could. Tripping over my own shoelace and breaking my neck while I was trying to figure out how to stop a rampaging Firstborn would just be *silly*.

Evening was Firstborn, and more, Evening was angry. If she realized the Luidaeg wasn't dead—and I couldn't discount that possibility—she had to at least suspect that I was the one hiding her sister from her. That meant Tybalt's sense of duty would keep him in the Court of Cats until the Luidaeg was well enough to be moved; he wouldn't risk his people needlessly by leaving them there with her and not staying to come to their defense if Evening somehow got in. He also wasn't going to let me walk away and deal with things on my own, no matter how much I wanted to.

We were going to have to work this out, somehow. Evening had to be stopped, even if I still had no idea how to go about accomplishing that.

My phone rang again. I stood, moving to retrieve it once again from my jacket pocket, and blinked. The display listed the caller as "East of the Sun, West of the Moon," which was definitely not within the local service area. Sure that this was some sort of a trick—and not at all sure what I was supposed to do about it—I raised the phone to my ear.

"Hello?" I said.

"Please, I implore you, don't hang up."

Only two people had that voice, and there was no reason for Sylvester to be calling me from an unfamiliar number. "Hello, Simon," I said wearily. "How did you get this number?"

"Is that really what you want to know right now?"

"Given that you tried to turn me into a tree, and all the other antisocial crap you've pulled, yeah, it is. Did you hurt someone to get my number?" The door opened and Tybalt stepped back into the room just in time to hear my last comment. His eyes widened. I held up my hand, signaling for him to stay quiet. Just for the moment; just for now. "Answer me, Simon."

Simon sighed. "The Hobs at Shadowed Hills have your number written on a piece of paper posted next to the telephone. I copied it down. It's all very primitive there. I thought my brother would have made more strides toward modernity. He always thought of himself as a progressive, when we were younger."

"You didn't hurt anyone."

"No, I did not," said Simon. "Pray greet your feline swain for me, as he has clearly entered the room. You may stop ostentatiously using my given name and repeating everything I say. I promise, I am not calling to distress you."

"And yet you're managing it," I said. "What do you want, Simon?"

"I want to see you."

I laughed before I realized I was going to. "Oh, not just no, but *hell* no. That's not going to happen."

"But it must. Please. There are things we must discuss. I have . . . a small time, when I am not being watched. I don't know when this time will come again." Simon paused before saying, "I would have come to you, but I couldn't find you. I don't know where you have hidden yourself, and I don't want to. There's too much chance I could be compelled to tell."

He sounded sincere. I blinked. Simon really didn't want to know where I was, because he might have to tell Evening. He hadn't given me away when I'd called Shadowed Hills. He'd brought us the winter roses.

Maybe he was really trying to be on my side.

"Where are you?" I asked.

"Your home. I can linger for an hour. Please, come." The line went dead.

I lowered the phone and looked at Tybalt. "Simon Torquill is at my house. He wants to talk to me."

"And you have agreed to let him." Tybalt shook his head. "I suppose I should be upset, but we both knew it was only a matter of time before you resumed pursuing impossible quests and slaying dragons. Shall I wake your squire?"

"No," I said, walking over to offer him my hand. "Simon also said he couldn't find us here. If leaving Quentin behind keeps him safe, I can deal with him being pissed at me." I felt a small pang of guilt at the idea of leaving without saying good-bye to Quentin, but it was just that: small. Waking Quentin up would be selfish, and it would slow us down. We needed to get to Simon as quickly as possible. Part of me wanted to tell Tybalt that I didn't want to go; that if Simon couldn't find us in the Court of Cats, neither could Evening, and we would be safe here. The rest of me knew that was a lie.

"Take a deep breath," said Tybalt, and took my hands, and pulled me with him into the shadows.

Wherever we'd been in the Court of Cats, it must have been near the house, because we had only been running for a few minutes when we stepped back into the warmth of my kitchen. The lights were out, and the sky outside the windows was the clear, brittle blue of the early morning. I pulled away from Tybalt, reaching up to wipe the ice away from my face. The faint smell of oranges and smoke drifted in from the hall.

"October?"

I held up a hand, signaling for Tybalt to stay quiet as I sniffed the air. Simon's magic was the only thing I could detect. It had been long enough since dawn that even the ashy smell of my wards burning away had had plenty of time to clear.

"He's here," I said, lowering my hand and starting for the kitchen door. "I guess we're really doing this."

"I suppose we are," said Tybalt. He looked unhappy as he paced along beside me. I couldn't really blame him.

"If it looks like he's going to turn me into a fish again, you can gut him, okay?" I flashed a humorless smile. "As long as no one ever finds the body, there's no reason for anybody to know that we broke Oberon's Law."

"I am not sure whether I find this new viciousness enticing or terrifying," muttered Tybalt.

"Oh, trust me, sweetie: where Simon is concerned, this is nothing new." I pushed open the door, sniffing again as I stepped into the hall. The smell of Simon's magic was coming from the living room. I walked to the doorway and stopped, blinking at the sight of Simon Torquill sitting on my couch with Spike curled in his lap. He was running his hand down my rose goblin's thorny back, stroking with the grain rather than against it, and looked as if he'd been there for quite some time.

I must have made some small noise when I arrived in the doorway, because Simon looked up, eyes tired, and said, "I fed your feline companions, as well as this thorny fellow here. They were most insistent, and I thought you might appreciate it."

"I appreciate your concern," I said. I couldn't quite keep the bitterness out of my voice. "Why didn't you tell me Evening was alive?"

"I couldn't, could I? The geas under which I operate left me very little leeway for the telling of wild tales—and why should you have believed me? I, who should have been your father, and was your enemy instead." Simon chuckled. For some reason, it didn't sound mocking: it was more self-loathing, the laughter of a man who had looked upon his life and found very little to be proud of. "I did my best. I told you what I could, and prayed you would be smart enough to know what I'd been forbidden to say. It worked, to a point. You went to Goldengreen."

I blinked. "You knew that?"

"I saw you fall." There was no laughter this time. Just deep, crystalline sorrow. "You appeared in midair and dropped like stones, like you'd been slapped aside by the hand of Oberon himself. There was nothing I could have done."

"That explains your regret, coward," snapped Tybalt. "How could you have gone to your lady wife and reported that you'd watched another daughter die?"

"August isn't *dead*," snapped Simon. Tybalt and I both went still, watching him like we might watch a venomous snake. Simon blinked at us, looking surprised by his own outburst. Then he looked away. "My . . . my apologies. It's a sensitive subject."

"So sensitive you never mentioned it, even as you were turning your stepchild into a fish," said Tybalt.

"Much as I'm sure we all need the group therapy session, this isn't the time," I said. "Simon, what are you *doing* here? You're not my friend. You're not even my ally. Why are you in my *house?*"

"I knew the fall wouldn't kill you. I once saw your mother's throat cut so deeply that you could look at the bones of her spine. They were delicate, like coral, and washed with red." Simon kept stroking Spike. "An hour later she was laughing and asking when I would buy her a new gown to replace the one she'd ruined. You're not her equal—none of us are the equal to our First—but I thought you might have enough of her in you to let you make a miraculous return. I was right. As for your cat . . ." He shrugged. "I suppose some old wives' tales must be true, or else the old wives would stop telling them."

"I'm touched to hear that you had that much faith in me. Of course, a call to the Coast Guard would have been a little more useful. You called me, remember? Why did you call me *now?*" I crossed my arms. "What do you want, Simon?"

"You received my warning: you went to Goldengreen, even if you didn't fully understand the reason I was telling you to look there for your answers. You know now that Ev—" He choked on the first syllable of Evening's name, coughing for a moment before he spat, "You know *she* is still alive. That's more than you had before. You have seen her effect on my brother. I can help you."

"You can't even say her name. How are you supposed to help me?" I dropped my hands back to my sides. "You know what? Forget it. I came when you called, but I'm not ready to have this conversation. I'm going upstairs to change my clothes. Tybalt is going to watch you, and you're going to figure out how to make me believe a damn thing you say. Then you're going to leave. And we *will* be resetting the wards after this, so don't even ask whether I have a guest room."

"I wouldn't dream of it," said Simon. He remained where he was on the couch, continuing to stroke Spike with one hand. He flashed Tybalt a cool smile. "Will you be my keeper?"

"If you move, I'll gut you," said Tybalt.

"Whee," I muttered. "Play nice and don't kill each other. I'll be back." I turned and left the room before I could think better of leaving them alone, practically running up the stairs to my bedroom. Cagney and Lacey were curled up on the bed. They ignored my entrance, and continued to ignore me as I stripped out of my bloody and borrowed things, only to replace them with near-duplicates from my dresser. Only near: these were clean, save for a small bloodstain on the left cup of my replacement bra. Blood and cotton were best friends when they actually got the opportunity to meet, and getting the one out of the other was virtually impossible.

"These are not good saving-the-world clothes," I told the cats, as I retied my shoes—now worn over a thick pair of hiking socks. "These are cleaning-the-garage clothes. Maybe flea-market-in-Marin clothes. That's because I'm not a saving-the-world girl. They got the wrong person for the job."

The cats didn't reply. It didn't matter that I was dating their King: they were still cats, and they had better things to do with their time than engage in a conversation with their pet changeling.

I made sure to clomp as I descended the stairs, trying to give Tybalt enough time to let go of Simon's throat.

When I stepped back into the living room, however, there was no violence happening. Tybalt was leaning against the wall, looking at Simon with a combination of confusion and mistrust, while Simon remained seated on the couch, Spike in his lap and a resigned expression on his face.

"You don't trust me," he said.

I blinked. "Okay, that's getting straight to the heart of the matter. You're right, Simon: I don't trust you. You turned me into a fish. You *broke* Rayseline. You've done nothing to make me trust you, and a hell of a lot to make me hate you. Your point?"

"I did not . . ." He faltered before trying again: "It was not my intention to alienate you. I would have had nothing to do with you until I was free of my . . . commitments . . . so that I might become a part of your life that was welcomed. Wanted, even."

"But Evening had other ideas," I said slowly. "She told you to get involved with me, didn't she?"

He tried to speak, only to pause as no sound passed his lips. Looking frustrated, he took a deep breath and tried again: "I have chosen very few of my actions since I was foolish enough to give myself to . . . to the one who holds me. It's harder than I can express. I have struggled so long with the need to keep you safe and the need to obey my orders."

"And now here we are," I said. "What can you do for me, Simon? You're still bound, you're still *hers*, for all I know, you're leading her here — so what can you do for me?"

He stopped stroking Spike, but left his hand where it was, resting on the rose goblin's thorny back. "I can bleed," he said quietly. "I can let you see."

"Oh," I said, feeling my eyes go wide and round with surprise. "Yeah. I guess that *is* something you can do."

And here I'd been so pleased to be wearing something that wasn't covered in blood.

NINETEEN

MOST MAGIC FALLS into one of three schools. Flower magic—illusions and wards—is inherited primarily through Titania. Water magic—transformation and healing—comes from Maeve. Blood magic, the magic of memory and theft, comes from Oberon. There's crossover, but as a rule, no race will be strong in a school that isn't somehow connected to their First. As a descendant of Titania and Oberon, Simon had access to flower and blood magic. As a descendant of Oberon, and Oberon alone, all I had was blood ... but I was very, very good at using it.

"Are you sure?" I hated to ask. I wanted to grab him and bleed him dry, drinking any scrap of information he might have—but the line between me and the monsters was thin enough as it was. If I started taking instead of waiting for things to be freely given, I would cross that line. I needed his consent to be absolute. "Once this starts, I don't know if I'll be able to pull back. I've never drunk directly from a living person for the purpose of riding their blood. It could go anywhere."

Simon nodded. "Yes. I understand what you can do,

perhaps better than you do at this stage in your development. I give my full permission, and I will not stop you from learning the things you need to know. It's not like I could stop you anyway, once we've started. Words can lie. People can lie. Blood never can."

That was about as good as it could possibly get. I cast a nervous glance toward Tybalt as I walked across the living room and sat down on the couch next to Simon. Spike raised its head, making an inquiring chirping noise. I stroked its thorny ears. "It's probably going to hurt."

To my surprise, Simon smiled. "No, it won't. There's nothing in my blood for you to change; I am Daoine Sidhe to the core. My blood won't fight you."

That was new information. "Good to know," I said faintly, and drew my knife. "Give me your hand."

"No need." He pressed his palm flat against Spike's back, not hard enough to hurt the rose goblin, but hard enough to break Simon's skin in half a dozen places. The smell of blood flooded the room, and saliva flooded my mouth in a Pavlovian response that I *really* didn't want to think about. The sight of blood still freaked me out, but the smell of it promised answers: something I almost always needed.

Simon held his palm out toward me. The blood from the scratches was leaking out onto his skin, turning it an enticing red. I glanced to Tybalt. He nodded once, not moving from his position by the wall. Whatever came next, he would be here for it.

That helped a little. I reached out and took Simon's bleeding hand in both of mine, trying to ignore the way my stomach lurched.

"This may take me a moment," I cautioned.

"Take all the time you need," he said.

There was nothing I could say at this point to change what was about to happen, and so I brought my lips to his palm, and closed my eyes, and drank.

—believe she's really willing—
—looks so much like her mother—
—doesn't look like her mother at all—

Simon's thoughts slammed into me with the force of a hammer hitting a wall. I gasped, not opening my eyes, and tried to force my way through that top layer of active thought. I hadn't been expecting that, although I suppose I should have been; blood holds thoughts and memories, and Simon's blood was still a part of him, still connected to the rest of his body through the open wounds and the hot skin beneath it. Of course it was carrying more than I was used to.

Down, down, down, I thought, willing my magic to take me there. *Like Alice and the rabbit hole, come on, down . . .*

The thoughts faded into blurry unintelligibility, replaced by the veil of red that I was more accustomed to when I was working blood magic. I took a breath, only dimly aware of my body—of the fact that I had lungs I could breathe *with*—and pushed harder, until I broke through the blood, into—

She is so beautiful. She owns this room: all others might as well not be here, because no eyes are on them, not when Amandine walks in beauty. My brother loves her. He thinks I don't know, because he thinks I am foolish, but I am not foolish; I have seen the way he looks at her, the brave hero assessing the next tower he intends to climb. He won't have her. She deserves much more than Sylvester Torquill, and so much more than his younger brother, whose eyes follow her like all the rest. I have no chance with her. I have no choice but to look. She is so beautiful.

Seeing Amandine through his eyes was almost shocking enough to throw me out of the memory. She was wearing a long purple gown in a style that had been outdated for centuries but probably hadn't been outdated yet, not in that moment, and she was . . . there are people who say I look like her. Most of the time I'll just shrug and let them think that if they want to; it's not worth fighting over. But seeing her reflected in Simon's memory was enough to hammer home the fact that no, I *don't* look like her. No one with a drop of human blood could ever look like her, and that's a good thing, because her kind of beauty stopped hearts.

She was tall, with the kind of curves that would have made her a star if she'd ever cared to try her hand in Hollywood, and a face that looked like it had been refined by a hundred great artists before it was given to anyone to wear. Her white-gold hair was held away from her face with a simple circlet, and fell otherwise loose down her back, like a river of molten metal. I looked at her through his eyes, and wondered if the false Queen of the Mists had gotten her fondness for long, pale hair from my mother, who made it look like the only style worth wearing.

I hadn't seen her since I'd learned that she was First-born. Looking at the memory image of her, I couldn't believe I hadn't seen it from the very beginning. She looked nothing like the Daoine Sidhe. She looked only and entirely like herself.

Amandine looked around the room *(ballroom in the great palace of Londinium, and not a jewel in the Queen's crown could shine any brighter than her smile)* until her eyes settled on me/Simon. She started toward me/Simon, her smile broadening.

"Simon. I had hoped you would do us the honor of attendance this day. My lady, the Queen, has remarked often on your absence." She had an accent. Since when did my mother have an accent? She sounded Scottish, rolling her r's and burring her t's in a sweet, lilting rhythm.

She's never had an accent, I thought fiercely. The scene

took on a red tint as I resisted it. *Accents don't just disappear. Don't lie to me, Simon. Don't you dare.*

I can't. Not here, not in the blood. The thought was wistful, and almost intrusive in its immediacy. This was no memory: this was Simon answering me without saying a word. *Her accent faded, and then she put it aside like a toy she no longer wanted to play with. Centuries and the desire not to stand out as foreign when walking among the humans will work wonders on even the deepest habits. But when I first loved her, when she was Amandine of no particular family line, she was born in Scotland, and raised there for the better part of her youth.*

The ballroom had frozen, Amandine still smiling at Simon's memory of himself. This must have happened centuries ago. She hadn't aged a day.

Okay, I thought. *I believe you, but ... we can't linger here. I need to know what I need to know. The fact that you thought my mom was hot doesn't really matter.*

I felt his laughter. *Oh, October. The fact that I thought your mother was the most beautiful thing I had ever seen matters more than you can know. Let go. Come back.*

Letting go of my confusion and diving back into the blood memory was almost impossibly hard. The smell of smoke and mulled cider assaulted my nostrils as the ballroom scene blurred and disappeared around us, replaced, briefly, by Simon and my mother standing in front of a man that Simon's memory identified as the then-High King of North America, their hands joined, their eyes fixed only on each other. More than a hundred years had passed between those memories: I knew that, even if I didn't know how I knew. It was just ... obvious.

The scene dissolved. Amandine's tower appeared, the door standing open to reveal a garden riotous with color. Red roses, golden daisies, purple spires of love-lies-bleeding—it was like looking into an amateur version of one of Luna's projects, fiercely alive and just as fiercely beautiful. Mother's gardens had never looked like that while I lived with her ... but this memory was long before me, wasn't it? Because there was Amandine, her belly huge with a baby I had never met, smiling indulgently at Simon.

She chose me, she chose me out of everyone she could have chosen in the world, and I will not disappoint her; I will be the man she needs, and the father that our child deserves. I will always be there for her. I will be there for both of them. Nothing in this world or any other could make me fail them.

Another flicker, and the Amandine who raced through our/my field of vision wasn't pregnant anymore. The little girl she pursued had silvery braids that glimmered red, like the reddish gold I sometimes saw in wedding rings. Amandine pounced, and the little girl laughed, twisting in her mother's arms to bury her hands in the pale waterfall of Amandine's hair.

The scene froze.

"Even here, there are holes in what I can say." The voice came from beside me, not inside my own head. I turned. There was Simon—but he wasn't looking at me. His eyes were fixed on his wife and daughter, and there was a look of heartbreaking yearning on his face. I think that if I had killed him in that moment, looking at that scene, he would have died thanking me. "The bindings I am under are very strong. She made sure of that."

"You can say 'she' without flinching now," I said. "Can you tell me if I get something wrong?"

"I believe I can, yes." Simon sighed deeply. "We were so happy. What happened to us?"

"Near as I can tell, Evening Winterrose happened to you." I didn't mean to snark: it was almost automatic at this point. I still hated him for what he'd done to me—I wasn't sure there was anything that could make me hate him any less—but I was also starting to feel strangely sorry for him. Maybe that was a sign of growing maturity. Maybe it was a sign that I was just too tired to care. "She's the one who geased you, right? Just so we're absolutely clear."

"Yes." The scene changed. In an instant, the little girl was a long-limbed teen, sitting at the table with her mother, a smile on her face as they shared a plate of fruit and cheese. Looking at them, I felt sorrow, and an overwhelming jealousy. Amandine had never been easy with me. Not like that. Not like she was with the daughter that she'd lost.

"Did you know Evening was the Daoine Sidhe First-born?"

"Not at first." Simon's voice took on a new level of bitterness. "I had my suspicions—things she'd said, things she'd done. Even the way she looked at my wife. I asked Amy once if—" He stopped speaking.

The silence stretched on for long enough that I started to worry. I turned back to him, and he was gone, replaced by the tower wall. "Simon?" A red veil began to cloud my vision. Something was wrong.

Spoke too soon can't say can't say can't say her name . . .

The scene in the tower accelerated, the teenager becoming a young woman, arguing with Amandine, storming out; Amandine following her, and then the tower itself disappearing, leaving me floating in the endless red . . .

"Simon! It's okay, you don't have to say her name! Just focus, okay?" I tried to search through the red for the oranges and smoke combination of his magic, and as I did I realized that here, in his heart, there was no citrus sharpness or rot; just the sweet smells of mulled cider and extinguished candle flames. That was what his magic had been, once, before Evening corrupted him. "Come back to me." I pulled harder on the blood, calling on the thin line of his magic.

Beside me, Simon gasped. I turned to face him. We

weren't in the tower anymore: we were standing in the trees, vast evergreens reaching for the sky on all sides. He was breathing heavily, his hand pressed to his chest like he was trying to keep his heart from stopping.

When he recovered his composure, he said, "My apologies, October. That was somewhat more . . . bracing . . . than I had expected."

"I'll be more careful," I said. "Just breathe, okay?"

"I will do my very best," he assured me.

"Okay. So . . . you knew that Evening was Firstborn, or at least you suspected it. And this was after you and Mom were married. What changed? How did Evening get her claws into you?"

There was a long pause. Then, in a voice that sounded like it was breaking into a million pieces right in front of me, Simon whispered, "There she is."

I looked to the trees. The girl with the gold-red hair was stepping into view, wearing a dress the color of corn husks, a candle in her hand. I recognized its mottled calico pattern. She'd gotten it from the Luidaeg. She lingered for a moment, looking around herself like she was waiting for a sign. Then she continued forward, disappearing into the tree line.

"When August was . . . lost . . . we both dealt with our grief in our own ways," said Simon haltingly. His words sounded strange at first, until I realized there were traces of an almost British accent seeping into them, like some long-buried wound was being torn open. He was focusing so hard on what he was saying that he didn't have the energy to focus on how it was being said. "Your mother was . . . it's hard to be of the First, and she had it harder than her siblings, because she was born so soon before Oberon and his wives left us. Her father was not here to teach her how to manage her strengths, or how to compensate for her weaknesses. She was unprepared for the reality of a situation she couldn't change."

"Parental abandonment seems to run in the family." I couldn't keep the bitterness out of my voice. To be fair, I didn't try that hard.

Simon took a sharp breath. I waited for him to say I was being unfair, but he didn't; he just let it out again, and said, "Be that as it may, she couldn't handle the shock of losing our daughter. She began rattling at doors, making bargains, trying anything and everything she could think of in her mad quest to bring our little girl home. And I . . ." His voice trailed off, turning weak and broken.

The forest in front of us blurred, replaced by a room I knew all too well: the receiving room at Goldengreen, back when it had belonged to Evening. Back when it had been cold.

"I thought it was wrong to leave my wife—my love, my *Amy*—to sell her soul while I kept mine. So I went to the devil I knew, and I asked if she could help me." His voice dropped even lower. "I was a fool."

I hated to prod at what was clearly still an open wound, but I had to know. "Your daughter disappeared, and you went to Evening for help."

"Yes," said Simon. The word was soft, and somehow broken. His voice gained strength as he repeated, "Yes, I did, and I would do it again, even knowing her as I do now. What she offered me was worth the cost. I will not deny that."

"Was it?" I looked back to the empty forest. The faint smell of cider hung in the air. "Was it really? Because your daughter's still missing, and my mother's still on a one-way trip to wherever the hell it is her mind's been going for the past twenty years. It doesn't seem like you got anything out of the deal at all."

"I got power." The scene flickered, twisted: became the Japanese Tea Gardens. Any pity I had been starting to feel for the man dissolved, replaced by the sheer terror of returning to the place where my life had ended once already. I tried to step away. He grabbed my wrist, and the smell of smoke filled the air, mixed with a muddled combination of cider and rotten oranges. What felt like a rope of woven wind slithered around my throat and pulled itself tight—not choking me, but making the point that it could, at any moment, if that was required. Simon continued implacably, saying, "I got the strength to do whatever needed doing, and all I had to give up was my autonomy, my integrity, and the love of my brother, which I had never done a thing in my life to earn. There's something tempting about power, October. I know you know that. I can see it in your eyes. They're so much paler than they used to be. You're burning your humanity on the pyre of your ambitions, because we're so much stronger than they are, aren't we? Sometimes it's good to be the strong one."

"Let me go," I said softly. "Simon, you need to let me go right now, or Oberon help me, I'm going to see if I can make every drop of blood in your body come out of your eye sockets."

"You wouldn't."

"Wouldn't I?"

There was a long pause. The smell of smoke and oranges was so thick that it was becoming difficult to breathe. The smell of cider was completely gone. And then, to my surprise and annoyance, Simon started to laugh.

"Something funny?" I asked tightly.

"Peace," he said, and the ropes dropped away. "I simply wanted to test—"

I whirled and punched him square in the nose.

Simon stumbled back, looking startled. I hadn't been sure that would work. He was just a blood magic construct, after all. But then again, so was I, and magic is really remarkable sometimes.

"I'm not your daughter, Simon," I said quietly. "My father was a human man, and he died thinking he'd lost me forever, but he's never going to lose me, because I'm always going to remember him and honor his memory. I could never have been yours. Even if my mother had let you bring Evening's stinking corruption to her bed, I would never have been yours."

Simon's gaze hardened. Still, there was something satisfied there, like I was saying the wrong words with the right inflection. "I see."

"Here's how this is going to be, Simon," I said. "You have no allies. You've turned against Evening. Your own brother wants you punished for your crimes. Luna . . . I think Luna would gut you and use your blood to fertilize her roses if she got the chance, and hell, maybe Sylvester would give it to her. If you want to stay alive, you need to stay on my good side. That means no more tests. No more sneak attacks or attempts to test your boundaries. If you so much as think about using your magic on me, I won't stop myself from hurting you. And don't be concerned about the penalties we'd face for breaking Oberon's Law. That only applies when someone gives enough of a shit to report your disappearance to the authorities."

Simon touched his bruised nose and smiled. "You are your mother's daughter after all."

"And never say that to me again." I glared at him.

"As I was saying, power," said Simon, after a pause. "The Daoine Sidhe have always had the potential to be among the most powerful people in Faerie. It's simply that many lack the stomach for what must be done."

I knew what he meant. "You're talking about borrowing other people's magic through their blood," I said.

"Yes," said Simon. "Blood magic is so much more flexible than most could ever dream."

"Uh-huh," I said curtly. I knew full well what blood

magic was capable of. I had seen Duchess Treasa Riordan use blood magic to force Chelsea Ames to rip open doors in the walls between the Summerlands and Annwn. I had borrowed the teleportation magic of both Windermere siblings—Arden when she was being controlled by the false Queen of the Mists, and Nolan when Tybalt and I were at risk of dying in a room made almost entirely of iron. I could see the appeal of having all the powers in Faerie at your beck and call. I just wasn't sure the need to drink other people's blood was a worthwhile tradeoff.

"You think you know everything, October, but I assure you, you have so much more to learn. Things even your mother never took the time to learn. E—" He stopped before he even finished the first syllable of Evening's name, making a thin wheezing noise. Finally, the sound tapered off. Simon coughed and amended, "My benefactor taught me so many things that you could never even dream of."

"Was it worth it?" I cocked my head. "Because it sounds to me like you're trying to convince yourself almost as much as you're trying to convince me right now."

"I admit, things didn't go exactly as planned." Simon sighed. "I thought I would beg a boon of someone more powerful than I, and be asked to give my life—or at least my fealty—in exchange for what I received. Instead, I found myself indentured against future rewards. I did whatever I was asked to do. I was a willing slave, and every morning I went to sleep with the faces of my wife and daughter in my heart, reminding me of what I did this for."

"And uh, where does Oleander fit into your nice little story of nobility and self-sacrifice? Because for a married man, you seemed awfully fond of her."

"The Lady de Merelands—for she was a lady once, even if she left her title years and miles behind her—had been a servant of our mutual benefactor's for a long time. A service was apparently performed for her once: I do not know what it was. She never told me, and after a time, I stopped asking. It . . . amused Oleander to be with a man who had been with your mother, and by that time Amandine and I were separated. So I was asked to go to Oleander's bed, to warm her and to show that I was truly willing to do anything for the sake of my daughter's return." Simon spoke calmly, methodically, like he was giving a deposition in court. In a way, I suppose he was. "I won't claim not to have enjoyed my time with her. She was capable of her own form of sweetness, when she felt the need, and I have never done well alone. But I did not seek her out. She was given to me, and I to her, by the one who held our loyalty."

"Uh-huh."

"The circumstances—" began Simon.

I cut him off. "I don't give two fucks about the circumstances. Yes, it sucks that my sister," the words were still strange, "disappeared, but you don't *sell your soul* because your kid is missing. You find another way. You go to the Luidaeg. You ask Luna to appeal to her parents. You walk away the minute the person you're asking for help says 'sure, but you have to pledge fealty to me and sleep with this lady who we're pretty sure murders people for fun and also maybe some other stuff and the whole time your kid will *still be missing*, because I'm not getting her back for you until you prove yourself to me.' How did you even know Evening could do what she was promising you?"

"Not all of us are the darlings of the world's remaining Firstborn, and with Amy lost to me, I had few options," said Simon. There was a hint of bitterness in his tone. "I did what I had to do."

"Uh-huh." The throne room was beginning to blur around us, fading under a veil of red. The memories my magic could draw from Simon's blood apparently didn't extend to actually letting me see Evening's face. "Is there anything else you wanted to tell me before I lose my grip on this?"

"I am ..." He took a breath. "I know this isn't what you want to hear from me, October. But I am so proud of who you have become. I only wish I could have been there to help you grow." The smell of smoke and oranges was getting stronger.

My head was spinning. Something wet was on my lip. I raised my hand to touch my face, and my fingers came away bloody. Simon looked at me, eyes full of sorrow. I frowned. I wobbled.

"You tricked me," I said, and then I collapsed, and the world went from red to black before it went away entirely, taking Simon, and the smell of rotting oranges, with it.

TWENTY

I SAT UP WITH a gasp. The quality of light in my living room had changed, going from the brittle brightness of early morning to the deeper, calmer light of the afternoon. My lips felt sticky; I wiped them and my hand came away dark with blood. Still more blood cracked and fell away from my mouth, long since dried into a hard crust. I looked down. My fresh shirt was even bloodier than the last one had been, courtesy of what appeared to be a multi-hour nosebleed.

My brain was waking up slower than my body. I blinked at my bloody shirt for several seconds, trying to remember why a nosebleed that lasted for several hours was a bad thing—apart from the obvious dizziness and mess. Tybalt was going to be so annoyed when he saw that I had managed to get myself covered in blood *again*—

And just like that, I understood what was wrong. My heart plummeted into my stomach as I scrambled to my feet, looking wildly around the room. "Tybalt? Tybalt, are you here?" He wouldn't have left me voluntarily, he would *never* have left me voluntarily, not with me bleeding and Simon in the house. He had to be hurt, or missing, or—Oberon forbid—I couldn't even finish the thought. "Tybalt!"

"Pipe down, he's fine." The voice was familiar, yet so incongruous I couldn't quite wrap my head around it until I had finished my turn and saw the Luidaeg standing in the living room door. "Your kitty-cat is in the kitchen, sleeping off Simon's whammy. I tried to stop the bleeding a few times, and then I realized your body was purging whatever that Torquill asshole had done to you, so I let you be. You really shouldn't drink people's blood unless you're sure you're stronger than they are, October. That's what got you into this mess in the first place."

I stared at her, trying to figure out which of my questions I should ask first. None of them wanted to coalesce into anything coherent.

The Luidaeg frowned, the gesture calling my attention more properly to her face. She looked as human as ever, but her bone structure was subtly different, and her eyes were the driftglass green she normally wore when visiting her Selkie step-descendants. There was something different about the texture of her skin, and when I realized what it was, my eyes got even wider.

She no longer looked like she was on the verge of becoming something else. She looked, instead, like she was only and entirely herself. Somehow, she had settled in her own skin.

"Toby, are you listening to me? Tybalt is *fine*, but you've lost a lot of blood, and you need to eat. Come on." She turned and walked back out into the hall. I stayed frozen for a few seconds more and then hurried after her. The kitchen door was swinging, and so I pushed it open, stepping through.

The kitchen smelled of hot soup and fresh-baked bread. Tybalt was curled on the table in cat form, sleeping in a nest formed by my leather jacket. The Luidaeg was standing between us. As soon as the door swung shut behind me, she whirled, moving too fast for me to react, and clasped her arms around me, pulling me into a tight and uncharacteristic hug. I froze, blinking, unable to make myself return the gesture—unable to make myself do anything, honestly, except stand there.

"Thank you," she said, her voice muffled by my shoulder. My eyes got even wider, until it felt like they were going to fall clean out of their sockets. The Luidaeg pushed me out to arm's length, looking at me gravely. "You have no idea what you did for me. Thank you. I owe you a debt that I may never be able to repay. You understand that, don't you?"

I kept staring at her. Between the hug and the forbidden thanks, it felt like something inside my brain had broken.

"You need to say you understand," she said, some of the old familiar impatience seeping into her words. "That's how you accept the debt."

"I—I understand," I stammered.

The Luidaeg sagged, making no effort to conceal her relief. "Oh, thank Mom."

"Luidaeg, how did you . . ."

"I can't get into the Court of Cats under my own power, but I can get *out*," she said. "I thought you might need the backup. Since I got here to find you bleeding out and the cat unconscious on the floor, I was right. Do you know who you're up against yet?"

"Evening," I said. "She's not dead."

"She never was," agreed the Luidaeg, nodding enthusiastically, like a teacher trying to prompt a reticent pupil. "She can die—anyone can die—but Devin's method was never going to succeed. He didn't have certain information, and without it, there was no way he would have used the right tools for the job."

"He needed iron *and* silver," I said, eliciting another nod. "But . . . how can you tell me this? I thought you said the geas still held."

"Oh, it does, it does," said the Luidaeg, with almost giddy gleefulness. "I can't say her name. I can call her all sorts of unpleasant things, as long as they've never been her *name*. But I don't need to. You figured her out."

"I didn't have much of a choice," I said.

The Luidaeg sighed. "She's always been a pushy one. Most of my half sisters are, or were, but she was the worst of a bad lot. It's because her mother encouraged that sort of behavior. 'Prove you're worthy of my love' and all that crap." She walked over to the stove, where a large pot of something that smelled like rosemary and fish was simmering. "When's the last time you ate?"

"Tybalt fed me before we came here," I said.

She turned to give me an assessing look. "Uh-huh. And was that before or after you spent half a day bleeding on your living room floor? That shirt's ruined, by the way."

"You could have at least stuffed some tissues in my nose," I snapped, and walked past her to run a hand along Tybalt's side. He was breathing regularly, and stretched in response to the touch. "Hey. Wake up. I need to know that you're okay, and you need to keep me from killing the Luidaeg. Again."

She snorted in amusement. "I'd like to see you try. How did he get you to sit still and eat?"

"I fainted," I admitted. "I sort of did too much blood magic on too little sleep and even less food."

"I swear, October, my sister's not going to need to have you killed. You're going to kill yourself and save her the trouble." She took two bowls from the cabinet, moving as easily as if this had been her kitchen for years. "Wake up your kitty. You're going to eat while we talk."

"Because food is more important than stopping Evening?" I snapped.

The Luidaeg glanced at me again, a wave of blackness moving across her driftglass eyes like a shadow crossing the moon. Then it passed, and they were just eyes again. "No. Because when you're at war, you eat every time you get the chance. There's no way of knowing when you'll have another opportunity. Now sit, and I'll tell you everything the geas allows."

"We don't have time for this," I grumbled, and stroked Tybalt again. "Wake up."

He lifted his shaggy tabby head, opening his eyes, and blinked at me blearily. Then he blinked again and flowed to his feet, jumping to the floor where he became a man. A naked man. I'd seen it all before, but the Luidaeg hadn't, and she whistled appreciatively.

"Very nice."

Tybalt whirled. "Luidaeg! You're—"

"Go put on pants, please, for the love of Maeve, I cannot have this conversation if you are not *wearing any pants*," I snapped, pushing him toward the door before he could get over the shock of the Luidaeg's appearance and notice that I was once again covered in blood.

Tybalt glanced back, eyes narrowing. Oh, great. He'd noticed the blood. "I will return," he said ominously, and stepped into the hall.

"I hate this, I hate this—*why* wasn't he wearing pants?" I bolted for the sink and grabbed a handful of paper towels, attempting to scrub off the worst of the blood.

"Because for Cait Sidhe, transforming their clothes takes focus and will, and he didn't change forms voluntarily," said the Luidaeg, getting down another bowl. "I found him on the floor when I got here. I thought I would do well to keep an eye on him."

"Good plan," I agreed grudgingly, as I dropped my wad of bloody paper towels into the trash. My shirt was a lost cause. I slouched to the table and sat, too tired and dizzy to argue with her. "We need to be figuring out how to stop Evening, not sitting here and eating soup."

"If we don't sit here and eat soup, you're going to collapse," said the Luidaeg, setting a bowl of what smelled like fish chowder in front of me. "You lost more blood than you realize. You need to get your strength back up."

"It's been a bleeding sort of day," I grumbled, and took the spoon she handed me.

The kitchen door swung open as Tybalt returned, now fully clothed. "You are *covered* in blood," he accused, pointing at me.

"I noticed," I said.

"She noticed," the Luidaeg said. "Everyone noticed. Now sit down. You need to eat some soup."

Tybalt blinked at her, nonplussed. "I beg your pardon?"

The Luidaeg groaned. "You know, sometimes I miss the days when all I had to do was tell people to do something and they did it, out of fear that if they didn't, their skeletons would be outside of their bodies. The soup is going to help. Simon whammied you both, and his magic is all over you. This will purge it. It will also taste delicious, because I have been making medicinal chowder longer than either of your family lines has been alive. It's my own recipe. Toby, I used all your potatoes."

"Um, that's okay," I said, and took a bite of chowder. It was, as promised, delicious, sweet and savory at the same time, with chunks of potato swimming in the creamy broth. I thought I'd eaten too recently to be hungry, but my stomach roared at the taste, making it clear that my body had other ideas. Also, as promised, I started feeling better almost immediately.

"While you were asleep, I took the liberty of redoing

the wards on your house," said the Luidaeg. "My beloved sister won't be able to tell that I'm here. And you shouldn't need to recast them for a century or so."

"So your magic has returned?" asked Tybalt.

"My magic never went anywhere," said the Luidaeg. "I wasn't dead long enough for the spells I've been maintaining for years to collapse, thank Dad. There are some lovely palaces at the bottom of the sea that would have dissolved into foam, and at least one Cetacea who's currently enjoying life on two legs who would've stunned the crowds at Sea World. Until the night-haunts came for me, there was still a chance. My beloved sister did a great job of killing me. October did a better job of bringing me back."

"It's always nice to be good at something." I took another bite of chowder, swallowing quickly. "Luidaeg—"

"I don't think you understand what you've done." The Luidaeg pulled out a chair and sat down at the other side of the table, looking at me gravely. "It's been a long time since anyone in Faerie raised the dead. It isn't something we do often, or that should ever be done lightly."

"Technically this was my second time," I said. "Alex Olsen was dead too."

"That was your little Gean-Cannah?" she asked. I nodded. "That was different. He was a living man sharing a body with a dead woman. I was a dead woman sharing my body with no one. Bringing me back was a larger step than you could have known, or you might not have done it. Please, don't get me wrong," she held up her hand, palm turned toward me, "I'm grateful. I'd rather be alive than dead, and I have a great deal left to do. But you've tampered with the order of things. Keep that in mind, and don't let this become a habit."

I scowled at her. "How about you don't let dying become a habit, and I won't need to bring you back again?"

"Fair enough," said the Luidaeg. "About my sister.

She's harder to kill than anyone you've ever dealt with. It's part of her nature. She seems to die, and then she comes back stronger, like a weed."

"Well, right now, that weed is taking root at Shadowed Hills, and I need to know how willingly her descendants will follow her orders, and how much control she has over people who aren't descended from her," I said grimly. "Sylvester didn't bat an eye when she showed up and said that she wasn't dead and needed him to let her in. Dean Lorden was more resistant. He's also only half Daoine Sidhe. But a lot of the other people at Shadowed Hills who aren't Daoine Sidhe seemed perfectly willing to let her tell them what to do."

"My sister can control almost anyone if she puts her mind to it. As for Sylvester's people, she's playing on their fealty," said the Luidaeg. "They're sworn to Sylvester, Sylvester is of her line; all she has to do to control them is control him. Didn't you ever wonder why the Daoine Sidhe aspire to power the way they do? No other line holds so many thrones, or wants to wear so many crowns. The Daoine Sidhe would rule the world if they could, and all for the sake of that beautiful spider at the center of their web."

I frowned. "She told them to seek power?"

"Yes. Said 'if you love me, rule the world,' and then she walked away, leaving her descendants hungry for her love the way she had hungered for the love of her mother. I doubt many of them would remember her face — most of her children died young, in the questing for kingdoms to rule, and their children didn't live much longer. Your Sylvester's father was her grandson. She was already gone by the time he was born." The Luidaeg's expression hardened. "Some people should never have been parents."

"So she can control Sylvester because he's her descendant, and she can control the people who are sworn to him through their fealty," I said slowly. "Can she control me?"

"If you allowed her to, yes, but it would have to be your choice," said the Luidaeg. "You're too aware of her now. She'd have to work harder to have you, and if there's one thing she can't abide, it's hard work." She paused, appearing to finally realize that our little duo should have been at least a trio. Fear crept into her voice as she asked, "Toby, where's Quentin?"

"I left him in the Court of Cats," I said. "Even Evening is going to have trouble getting to him there. You would have seen him if you'd stuck around after you woke up."

"My Court was sealed to my kind by Oberon himself, and none among the Daoine Sidhe holds fealty over any of the Cait Sidhe. He will be safe," said Tybalt.

"He'll be safe until she finds a Cait Sidhe of Erda's line. Don't discount the part Titania played in the making of your kind. My sister has the most control over her own descendants, but anyone she shares blood with is vulnerable, to a degree," said the Luidaeg. Tybalt looked uncomfortable. She turned her attention to me. "You know my sister wants your squire."

"I do," I said grimly. Quentin was the Crown Prince of an entire continent. There was no way someone as interested in power as Evening apparently was could ignore the potential of a game piece like my squire. "But let's get back to figuring out her limits. What about Dean? Or Etienne? Shouldn't she have been able to control them?"

"Again, that would be harder for her," said the Luidaeg. "Etienne is descended purely from Oberon, which makes him more resistant to my sister's charms. If he felt he had something more important to defend, he'd be able to avoid her snares, at least for a time. As for Dean, he's only half Daoine Sidhe, and his fealty is sworn to the

Mists, which means Queen Windermere. She's Tuatha de Dannan, like Etienne, so my sister has no openings there. Before that, he would have been sworn to his mother."

"Who's Merrow," I said thoughtfully. "Got it. Blood makes him hers, but fealty doesn't, and we're back to hard work again. She'd have to want him enough to take him."

"Exactly," said the Luidaeg. "It's much better if she can push her hard work off on someone else. She probably didn't feel like she needed to make the effort for a half-breed son of a Merrow and a man who willingly gave up the chance at ever holding a position of his own. She's always been ... focused ... when she truly wanted something."

I looked at the Luidaeg, and then at the warm, homey kitchen around us, with the pot of chowder still bubbling on the stove. I'd never seen her look so domestic. It had to have come from somewhere. I hesitated, the question burning on my lips. She met my eyes and nodded marginally, giving me permission to ask what I needed to know.

"You told me once that one of your sisters betrayed you," I said slowly. "That she was the one who put the knives into the hands of the people who would become the Selkies."

"Yes, I said that," said the Luidaeg.

"Was it Evening?"

Silence followed my question. That wash of black danced across the Luidaeg's eyes again, crossing them so quickly that it was almost like she was blinking an eyelid made of nothing but darkness. Then, finally, she nodded.

"I loved my children. They loved me. They didn't want power, or to be part of any noble court, or anything but each other, and me, and the open sea." The Luidaeg leaned back in her chair, fixing her eyes on the ceiling. "I think that's what condemned us in her eyes. We were too happy, and nothing happy could ever be genuine. Not to her. She thought we were pulling some elaborate ruse . . . or maybe she was just jealous. I don't honestly know, and I've never been willing to ask her. I can't raise a hand against the children of Titania, after all."

"Why is that?" asked Tybalt abruptly.

"Because my children were slaughtered like animals, and the people who killed them kept their skins as souvenirs." The Luidaeg turned back to Tybalt. This time when the darkness flowed into her eyes, it didn't flow away again. "My darling *sister* went to our parents—they were still with us in those days, remember, and they still controlled so much of what we did—and cried that I was blaming her for the actions of the merlins. She said she feared I would harm her. My mother refused her. My father denied her. And her mother bound me. I was forbidden to spread lies—literally forbidden. If I try to tell a lie, my voice stops in my throat and my lungs burn with the need for honest air. I was forbidden to raise a hand against any descendant of Titania's line. And I was forbidden to refuse my favors to anyone who would meet my price."

"You became the sea witch because of her?" I asked, unable to keep the horror from my voice.

The Luidaeg spread her hands. "I am what she made of me. I wonder sometimes whether she's sorry. I don't think she is. I don't think she's capable of that. My mother . . . she took what vengeance she could. Do not ask me what it was. I can't tell you yet."

"Yeah, well." My chowder was half gone, and my bones no longer felt like they were made of Jell-O. I pushed the bowl away. "Evening is at Shadowed Hills. She has my friends. She has my liege. The wards are closed—no one can get in or out. How do I get them back? How do I . . ." I hesitated, the words seeming too large for my mouth. Evening had been my friend for years, or at least I'd believed that she was. "How do I kill her?"

"Honestly, Toby, I don't think you can." The Luidaeg stood, gathering our bowls and carrying them quickly to the sink. "But I'll come with you. I may not be able to fight her directly; I can help you at least a little. And we need to move now. The longer she has Sylvester in her thrall, the more likely it becomes that he'll never throw off her power. The man you know will be gone, replaced by a shell of loyalty and cold."

The idea sickened me. "She's had more than enough time already," I said. "I can drive us to the park, but I have no idea how we're going to get through the wards."

The Luidaeg's eyes narrowed in chilly amusement. "Oh, don't worry. There's more than one way to cross an ocean, and more than one way to crack my sister's wards. She thinks she's the smartest of us. She's not. She's simply the least scrupulous."

I looked at her for a moment before shaking my head and saying, "You know, just once, I'd like my life to be all about spending Sunday afternoon in my pajamas, instead of all about racing around the Bay Area trying to stop one of the Firstborn from committing a hostile takeover."

Tybalt put a hand on my shoulder. "To be fair, this is the first time this particular issue has reared its head."

"Somehow, not helping," I said.

The Luidaeg rinsed our bowls and turned, wiping her hands on a dishtowel that she summarily dropped on the counter. She picked up a rose stem that had been lying next to the dish drainer—all that remained of one of Simon's melted winter roses—and grabbed an apple from May's bowl of fruit. "Let's go. I'll help you get us there. And don't bother with disguises; no one's going to see either of you."

It was better not to ask when the Luidaeg said things

like that. I just nodded and followed her out the back door, Tybalt sticking close behind me.

The car waited in the driveway. The Luidaeg walked over to it and put the rose stem down on the middle of the hood, setting her pilfered apple on top of it. "Stand back," she suggested mildly. "Sometimes this doesn't work out exactly as I planned it."

"And it just keeps getting better," I muttered, pressing myself against Tybalt. "Well, it's been a while since one of my cars died horribly in the line of duty."

The Luidaeg clapped her hands together. All sounds from the street stopped. No horns honked, no birds sang. There was only the soft sound of the Luidaeg singing in a language I didn't know, but which sounded vaguely like the snatches of Scots Gaelic that I'd heard from some of the older fae I'd crossed paths with. The apple rocked. The air chilled. And then, like something out of a Disney movie, the apple and the rose stem dissolved into glittering mist that swirled around the car, etching what looked like patterns of frost onto the otherwise dingy brown paint job. Bit by bit, my car's true colors were concealed by an ice-white sheen. The smell of roses hung heavy in the air.

The Luidaeg stepped back and flashed me a smug smile. "Apples and roses. My sister's signatures. She'll never see us coming if we're surrounded by things she believes belong exclusively to her. Her ego won't allow it."

I stared. "That's . . ."

"I know." She turned to Tybalt. "I need a distraction, cat; I need her to think we're coming down a road she knows. Can you take the Shadow Roads and meet us in the parking lot?"

"Can you promise me that you will keep October safe?"

Her expression softened a bit. "As safe as I can. We both know that absolute safety and October are never going to cross paths."

He snorted. "True enough. Very well, then: I will go.

For all that I dislike what you ask of me, I will go." He turned to face me. With no more preamble than that, he grabbed me around the waist and pulled me close for a kiss that should probably have caused damage to the polar ice caps. He kissed me like he was never going to see me again, crushing his lips against mine until I tasted pennyroyal and musk under the veil of his desperate need for contact. I returned the kiss as best as I could, until he pulled away, leaving a void between us where his body should have been.

I must have gawked at him, because he smiled, the expression almost eclipsing the worry in his eyes.

"Now you will miss me," he said. "Let the sea witch care for you. I will see you in Shadowed Hills." He turned, stepping into the shadow formed by the corner of the house, and was gone.

I looked back to the Luidaeg. She was smiling, standing next to the open passenger side door. I guess First-born don't care whether something is supposed to be locked. I scowled and walked past her, the taste of Tybalt's magic clinging to my mouth as I slid behind the wheel. The Luidaeg got in next to me, slamming the door. She was still smiling.

"Don't say a word," I said, jamming the key into the ignition.

"I wouldn't," said the Luidaeg. "Love is love. It's rarer in Faerie than it used to be—rarer than it should be, if you ask me. If you can find it, you should cling to it, and never let anything interfere. Besides, he has a nice ass." Her lips quirked in a weirdly mischievous smile. "I mean, damn. Some people shouldn't be allowed to wear leather pants. He's one of them. He's a clear and present danger when he puts those things on. Or takes them off."

"And now you're creeping me out," I said. "It's a long drive to Pleasant Hill. Maybe you could save the creepy for the halfway point?"

"Oh, no," she said. Her eyes had gone black again, and as I watched, they faded to white, like the sun rising behind a bank of thick fog. Her smile remained. "We're going to take a little shortcut."

I fastened my seat belt, checking it twice before I asked, "Should I even bother starting the car?"

"It helps, believe me. Just drive normally and don't freak out."

"Oh, because people saying 'don't freak out' never freaks me out at all," I muttered, turning the key in the ignition. The car rumbled to life around us. I pulled out of the driveway, trying to focus on the road, and not on whatever the Luidaeg was doing in the seat next to me.

She wasn't making it easy. She began chanting under her breath in that same unknown language, and the smell of brackish marshes and cold, clean ocean air rose around her, filling the car. My own magic stirred in response to the flood, and was quickly drowned out by the power that the Luidaeg was putting into the air. Her ice-white eyes were fixed on the road ahead.

And then, with no more preamble than that, the road was gone, and we were driving through the dark with nothing beneath us or around us. It was like plunging into the Shadow Roads, and not like that at all, because it wasn't freezing cold, and there was still air; I could breathe. That was a good thing, since I let out a rather audible gasp when the transition occurred. The Luidaeg slanted me what I could only interpret as an amused look, despite her continuing chanting. The darkness *shivered*—there was no other word that could encompass the ripples that spread through the black, shadow on shadow and yet somehow still visible—and then fell away, replaced by an overgrown forest of creeping vines and heavy-branched trees that seemed to grab for our vehicle as it rocketed along the narrow horse trail that had replaced the road.

"Don't slow down don't look too closely don't stop the car for any reason," rattled the Luidaeg, her words coming staccato fast and without pauses between them. She chanted another line in that unrecognizable language before breaking back into English to say, more slowly, "This road was my sister Annis' once, to hold and to keep open. She died a long time ago. No one keeps the byways here anymore."

"And we're driving a forgotten road belonging to a dead Firstborn exactly *why?*" I couldn't stop my voice from cracking with half-contained panic at the end. This was the sort of situation that called for a certain amount of terror.

"Because it's the fastest way, and because no one can find us here, or stop us, or keep us out," said the Luidaeg. The smell of her magic surged again, filling the car until there was no space for anything else. "Let my frozen bitch of a sister hunt as long as she likes. She'll never be able to find the doors to this place, much less pry them open."

"Is it safe?"

The Luidaeg didn't answer me. She just laughed. That was somehow more unnerving than anything she could have said. I tightened my grip on the wheel and turned on the headlights, illuminating the rocky, hard-pressed dirt in front of us. Eyes peered out of the brush to either side of the road, shining in the reflected halogen glare. That didn't help. I didn't know what kind of creatures could or would exist in a place like this, and I was pretty sure that finding out would involve a lot of blood on my part.

"There's a left coming up ahead," said the Luidaeg. "Take it, and for my mother's sake, don't slow down."

"Oh, that's not helping," I muttered, and focused harder on the road, trying to spot the break in the trees. Even watching for it we nearly overshot our goal before

I could haul on the wheel and send us rattling down a second, even narrower trail. Thick ropes of thorns overhung this stretch of road, scraping against the roof and slapping the windshield as we drove.

"If we slow down, we could get stuck," said the Luidaeg, who either didn't know that she wasn't helping or—more likely—didn't care. "This isn't a place that's used to people anymore. We're a curiosity here. Something that can be kept and used as it chooses."

"Not making me feel any better about the situation!" I yelped, as I swerved to dodge a particularly hefty-looking branch.

"Wasn't trying to," said the Luidaeg. She dipped her hand into her pocket, pulling out a key that gleamed in the dimly-lit cabin with a faint rosy sheen, like it was an independent source of light. I glanced at it for only an instant, but an instant was long enough to tell me what I was looking at. It was silver, shaped from a single ingot and then inlaid with copper, bronze, and gold, until the rings of ivy and roses carved from its substance seemed to take on life of their own, chasing each other around and around the key's head and handle. They tangled like real vines, like living things, almost obscuring the shape of the key in their riotous overgrowth. But the key knew what it was. It had always known.

It had known on the day when I had taken it from the rose goblin that would become mine, the one that had been entrusted with the key's keeping by one of Evening's servants. The Luidaeg had claimed the key from me almost as soon as she had seen it. I'd traded her a game of questions for the prize, and I'd never really expected to see it again. I'd never really wanted to.

"Luidaeg . . ."

"Trust me," she said—and the worst part of it was, I did trust her. She was the sea witch. She was the monster under our collective beds. And it didn't matter, because

I trusted her, and I always would. She had earned it time and time again, even when she had no reason to.

She held the key up, its rosy light growing in strength. I could only see it out of the corner of my eye, and that was more than enough; I had the distinct feeling that if I looked any closer it would blind me, that it wasn't a thing intended to be seen by anyone but the Firstborn. Its glow grew stronger, shading from pink into red, until the car was filled with a bloody brilliance that made my eyes burn. I squinted, fighting to see the road. I didn't want to lose control of the vehicle. Not here, not now.

"Mother, if you can hear me, I've been very good," said the Luidaeg. "I haven't killed anyone who didn't deserve it, not even my sister, who should probably have been killed a hundred times over by now. I haven't stolen any hearts or broken any vows, and I'm only calling on you now because I need you more than I've ever needed you before. Mother, I am your oldest living child. I am your eternity made flesh. Now please, hark to me, heed me here, and open the door before we die a horrible and lingering death in the darkness."

The smell of her magic surged again, this time under-scored by roses like I had never smelled before—not the cold, snowy roses of Evening or the perfect hothouse roses of Luna; not even the bloody-thorned roses of my mother's magic, which used to define my entire world. These were wild roses, untouched by any gardener's shears and untamed by any horticulturist's design. They grew where they wanted, thrived where they chose, and would never be anything but their own truest selves, un-able to conform to anything else. They were the roses that had grown at the beginning of the world, and the roses that would grow at the end of it. There were a hun-dred other scents beneath the roses, loam and fresh-turned earth and the sweet decay that leads to new growth, but I knew that what I would remember was the roses. They would stay with me, because . . . because . . .

Because no one could smell Maeve's magic and forget it.

It took everything I had not to turn and gape at the key that had somehow torn a hole in everything I thought I knew about our world, calling forth the magic of our missing Queen. Instead, I watched the road as beside me the Luidaeg murmured, "Thank you, Mother," and raised the key to her lips.

As soon as they touched the metal, it exploded into light like I had never seen. The road, the trees, everything went away except for that glaring brilliance, which managed to be white and red at the same time, like it was bleeding as it purified. I slammed my foot down on the brake, fighting to keep control of the car as we reduced speed more quickly than the laws of physics would advise. The Luidaeg didn't want me to stop. I was not willing to drive blind into a landscape I didn't know.

I couldn't force my eyes to stay open. When everything went from white to black, I realized I had shut them at some point to block out that horrible brightness. They were still closed when the Luidaeg put her hand on my shoulder and said, "Hey. October. Open your eyes, I put the key away."

She couldn't lie to me—I knew that—but I still cracked my right eye open with caution, in case some of the light had managed to linger. Natural light can't do that, but that's the trouble with magic: it does what it wants, and screw the laws of nature.

The cab was reassuringly dim, and the world outside the window was visible, painted in late afternoon shades of green and brown and gold. I opened both eyes and blinked, twisting in my seat as I realized that we were at Paso Nogal Park, the spot where Shadowed Hills was anchored to the mortal world. We were parked in the main lot, assuming you used the term very generously, since the car was sitting slantwise across three spaces. I blinked twice, and then took my foot off the brake as I carefully navigated us into a more proper parking place and turned off the engine.

The Luidaeg was quiet while I parked the car, possibly because she recognized that my battered nerves couldn't take much more. Finally, once I was sure my heart wasn't going to burst out of my chest, I twisted in my seat and asked, "Did we just drive from San Francisco to Pleasant Hill in less than ten minutes?"

"I told you, shortcut," she said, sounding pleased with herself. "Let's go ruin my sister's day, shall we?"

"In a second." I undid my seat belt and slid out of the car, feeling better as soon as my feet hit solid ground. Maybe this was how Tybalt felt every time he had to take a ride. I'd have to apologize to him for not being as understanding as I could have been. Speaking of Tybalt ... "I don't want to go anywhere before Tybalt shows up. He'd freak out if we weren't waiting for him when he arrived."

"You *do* have a remarkable talent for getting yourself injured when your allies let you out of their sight," said the Luidaeg.

I shrugged. "I heal fast."

"Most of the time."

I didn't have an answer for that one.

Standing still felt obscurely like failing. Evening was a big enough threat that we should never have been allowed to stop long enough to take a breath, much less stand around a parking lot waiting for my boyfriend to show up. There was a time when I wouldn't have been able to take that pause. The need to be moving, to *act*, would have sent me running into the knowe, even if I knew that I was running into certain danger. "I guess I'm growing up," I muttered.

"No, but you're maturing, and that's more than I hoped for when we met," said the Luidaeg. I glanced at her, blinking. The bones of her face had shifted during the drive, going from what I thought of as her Annie-face to the one that I was more accustomed to. They were very similar; she could have been her own sister. They weren't quite identical. She met my eyes with a small shrug and said, "It's true. I don't lie to you, remember?"

"It took me a while to get used to that," I said. "How much danger are we walking into?"

"I honestly don't know." The Luidaeg shook her head. "She should still believe that she's killed me, which is an advantage for us: having me walk in will throw her off balance, at least a little bit, and that can't help but benefit us. At the same time, if she holds the knowe completely, she may be willing to do a little heavy lifting."

She didn't need to explain her meaning. "I'll fight her."

"It may not matter," said the Luidaeg. "Oberon was her father. That gives her a blood connection to you, even if it's not a strong one. That, in conjunction with your oaths to Sylvester, and the blood binding you once created between yourself and her, means there's an opening that she can exploit."

"Wait . . ." I frowned. "Luidaeg, your parents . . ."

"I am the oldest daughter of Oberon and Maeve," she said. "Which makes me their first-born Firstborn, but that's confusing, so we don't usually put it that way."

"And Evening is . . . ?"

"The oldest daughter of Oberon and Titania."

There it was again: the subtle sense that I was missing something. Frown deepening, I asked, "Who are my mother's parents?"

Much to my surprise, the Luidaeg smiled like I had just asked the five hundred dollar question on an afternoon game show. She leaned forward and tapped my chin with her thumb as she said, "Oberon's her father, making her the youngest of my siblings, but her mother is not my mother, nor my father's other bride. Who her mother *is* I can't say, but if you go looking, you might find some interesting truths hidden under some equally interesting lies."

"Can't, or won't?" I asked.

"Can't, can't, always can't," said the Luidaeg. "You should know the difference between those two words by now, especially as you've started wearing gold in your hair."

"I do, but—" The smell of pennyroyal drifted over on the wind. I stopped mid-sentence, turning to see Tybalt standing next to my car with a baffled expression on his face.

"How did you beat me here?" he asked, walking over to us. "I came as fast as I might, and expected to spend no small amount of time lurking in shadows, watching to see that the way was clear for your arrival."

"You know us, we'll put a girdle round the earth in forty minutes," I said airily. "Half the Bay Area in ten minutes is a piece of cake."

"I see," said Tybalt. He stopped next to me, offering a half bow to the Luidaeg. "I appreciate the fact that I left my lady with you and returned to find her neither bleeding nor running for her life. It's a charming change from what normally occurs when I turn my back."

"Don't get too used to it," I said. "We're all here now."

"Yes," said Tybalt. "I suppose we are."

We started up the hill, the Luidaeg in the lead. Getting into Shadowed Hills from the mortal side of things usually requires a complicated series of actions, all of them designed to be virtually impossible to perform by accident. The Luidaeg ignored them completely. She just climbed straight toward the summit of the hill, never turning, never looking back. We mimicked her. The worst that would happen was we would need to go back down and start over, but I didn't think that was going to be a problem. The Firstborn have a way of shaping Faerie to fit their needs.

When we reached the burnt-out old oak tree at the top of the hill, the Luidaeg stopped, sighed, and snapped her fingers. The sound was louder than it should have been, gathering echoes as it bounced off the trees around us and finally returned, remade by distance and the acoustics of the park into the sound of a key turning in a lock. The door to Shadowed Hills appeared in the hollow of the oak, swinging slowly open in silent welcome. The Luidaeg lowered her hand and smirked.

"See? All you have to do is know how to talk to them." With that she stepped through the open door and into the hall beyond. I followed her, and Tybalt followed me, both of us tensed against the potential for attack.

The hall was empty. The air still smelled of roses—the air in Shadowed Hills always smelled of roses—but the floral perfume was underscored by a hard, frozen note, like it had snowed recently inside the knowe. That would be Evening's doing. I could smell the traces of her magic everywhere, overlaid on the cleaner, less corrupt workings of Sylvester and his people.

The Luidaeg turned back to look at us, all traces of levity gone from her expression. Her eyes were solid black again, like the eyes of a shark. "From here, we must be careful," she said. "Remember what she is. Remember what she can do."

I didn't say anything. I just nodded once, tightly, and walked past her as I started toward the throne room where Luna and Sylvester received their guests. It seemed like the most likely place to find a power-hungry Firstborn who had instructed her children to go off and acquire glory in her name. The Luidaeg and Tybalt walked behind me, forming the other two points of our small triangle. Having them there made me feel a little better—I wasn't going into danger alone. Not this time.

There were no guards at the vast doors to the throne room. That didn't strike me as a good sign. I pushed the left-hand door open, trying to keep my arms from shaking under its weight, and started into the familiar vast, over-decorated space on the other side. My sneakers were silent against the checkerboard marble of the floor.

And there, on the other side of the room, in the throne that was meant to belong to Sylvester Torquill, sat Evening Winterrose. The sight of her took my breath away. Even seeing her in Goldengreen hadn't prepared me for this, for Evening in her element, strong and untouchable and restored to us, because even death couldn't hold her, not *Evening*. I'd been foolish to think otherwise.

A small part of me—the part that had struggled against the mists in Blind Michael's lands and the sweet spell of love cast by my Gean-Cannah almost-lover— screamed that the floor wasn't really falling away, that Evening wasn't really the most breathtaking thing I'd ever seen. This was all trickery, treachery, the sort of illusions that I'd encountered before.

She was wearing a red satin dress, the color of rose petals, the color of blood on the snow, the color of apple skins in the winter. It was a confection of floor-length layers and gathered falls. Her seamstress had been clever, because when Evening moved—even the slightest twitch—all that gathered cloth fluttered like feathers in the wind, revealing myriad small cuts and smaller dagger-points of deeper red silk, red as danger, red as dying. Against the cloth, her skin truly was as white as snow, and her coal-black hair seemed on the verge of bursting into flames. Then Evening looked at me and did the most terrible thing of all.

She smiled.

"There you are," she said sweetly. "I was wondering

when you'd find it in your heart to come and visit me. A little bird told me you'd stopped by the knowe and then left without even saying hello. Really, October, is that any way to treat someone who's been your friend for as long as I have? It seems uncommonly rude. I always thought you were more polite than that. It seems I over-estimated your mother's teaching of you."

The urge to abase myself was strong. I dug my finger-nails into my palms, bearing down until the pain allowed me to center myself and say, in a tense voice, "That's Sylvester's throne."

"What, this old thing? He said that I could borrow it for a time, since my own holdings have been closed to me." A frown flitted across her face. "That was really most unkind of you, to help that half-breed stripling take my place as his own. What must his parents have been thinking? Land and sea together, it's a mixture meant for disaster, don't you agree?" Her words were directed to me, but her eyes went to the Luidaeg, making it clear who her message was really intended to reach.

"That's Sylvester's throne," I repeated. "He didn't give it to you willingly. If you have to compel someone to give you what you want, it's not really yours."

"Isn't it? Because it seems pretty real to me." She leaned back in the throne, resting her hands on the arms like she had been sitting there for years. "It doesn't mat-ter how you get the things you own. What matters is that you keep them."

There was something very wrong with her logic. I swallowed hard, and asked, "Why are you here, Eve-ning? You weren't dead, but you let everyone in the Mists believe you were. You left us. Why are you back?" Tybalt and the Luidaeg were a silently reassuring pres-ence at my back. I wondered why they weren't saying anything, but only distantly; the bulk of my attention was reserved for Evening. Even though my head felt heavy and stuffed with cotton, I knew that taking my eyes off of her would be a terrible idea.

The smell of winter roses was so heavy in the throne room that it was cloying, worse even than the smell of the Luidaeg's magic in the enclosed cab of my car had been. I dug my nails a bit deeper into my palms, trying to find that pure vein of agony that would grant me laser focus, even if it made me suffer later.

"Come here, October," said Evening. "Let me see you."

I had taken two steps before I realized I was going to move. "Why should I?" I asked, stumbling to a stop.

"Because you don't want to make me come to you," she said.

That was so reasonable that I started walking again. I tried to make my legs stop moving, and they refused me; they had listened once, and it wasn't their fault if Evening made a better case than I did. My head was swimming, as much with the smell of roses and smoke as with the brute reality of her presence, and all too shortly I was standing on the dais in front of her, near enough that she could almost have reached out to touch me.

"Oh, rose and thorn, you've changed," she said, and stood, stepping forward so that we were almost nose to nose. It was startling to realize that we were virtually the same height. She had always seemed like she should have been taller than me when she was standing on her own. "Do you even know how much you've changed? Don't answer that."

To my dismay, I found that I couldn't. The Luidaeg had said that Evening would have to work hard if she wanted to have me; well apparently, I had been deemed worth the effort. Lucky, lucky me.

Evening reached out and ran her hands down my hair, the fingers of her left hand lingering on the tip of one sharply-pointed ear. Her skin was cool and faintly silky, like the petals of a rose that had been blooming entirely in the shade. Whatever masks she'd once worn for my benefit, they were disappearing now, washed away and replaced by the simple reality of what she was. Firstborn. Fairest of them all. "Look at you," she mused aloud. "I'd never catch you so easily now. Your arrogance is the same, but your blood . . . do you know what you are?"

The feeling of her hands on my skin made me want to submit, to bow down and do anything she asked of me. I was no descendant of Titania; I shouldn't have felt her presence that strongly, even through the bond of fealty I shared with Sylvester. *Her blood*, wailed that still, small place in my mind, the one that people like her never seemed to quite touch. *You drank her blood, and that makes her hold on you stronger.*

The things that voice was saying made me wish, more than anything, that I had a time machine and the ability to go back and punch my past self in the nose. I swallowed hard to clear the dryness from my throat and said, "I'm me."

"You? What a charming statement of identity. What, precisely, are *you?*"

The smell of smoke was getting stronger, setting off alarm bells that weren't connected to any specific danger. I swallowed again before I said, "I'm Toby. October Christine Daye, Knight of Lost Words. Hero in the Mists."

"New titles won't impress me, child. You're telling me who you are—or who you think you are—but you're not telling me *what* you are."

I took a hard breath. "Changeling." I had to get away from her. I was drowning in her eyes. Obedience is a hard habit to break, and her hands had held my strings for much too long, even before I had tasted her blood and given her another way of controlling me. There had been a time when I *enjoyed* being her plaything. At least she'd treated me like a person, most of the time. I was coming to see that all of that had been a lie, and it was the real Evening who stood in front of me now, in this room that smelled like smoke and roses.

Wait—smoke? Evening's magic didn't smell like smoke. But Simon's did.

"Changeling?" asked Evening mockingly, yanking my attention back to her. "Born of Faerie and human both? Is that what you are?"

"Yes," I managed.

"Can you even remember what humanity felt like anymore?" she asked. The danger in her tone was impossible to ignore, and it triggered the part of me that was more interested in staying alive than anything else. I jerked away from her like I'd been stung, nearly falling off the dais.

At least that got her hands off of my skin. "I'm still part human! I remember my humanity."

"How can you remember something you've never had? Humanity has never been your cross to bear, and as for the contamination in your blood, you've been giving it up freely, more and more with every day that passes."

I took another step backward, my eyes narrowing. "I didn't give it up freely."

"Didn't you?"

Her clear amusement made me pause. Had my humanity really been stolen from me, the way I told myself it was? The first time, when I was elf-shot and dying, maybe I hadn't had much of a choice. When the options are "die" or "become a little harder to kill," well. I'm not completely stupid. The second time, it had been to save myself from the goblin fruit that was eating me alive. I'd only changed to survive.

Standing a little bit straighter, I said, "It doesn't matter. I'm myself. That's who I've always been and who I'll always be, no matter what my blood says about me." The universe could do whatever it wanted to me—it would anyway, whether or not I gave it permission. But I always knew who I was.

Evening frowned sharply, and I fought back the impulse to cringe. She had always been commanding. Now, stripped of whatever illusions she'd used to make herself fade into the fabric of Faerie, she was terrifying. "Will you really be your own creature?" she asked.

I forced myself to meet her eyes, and not flinch as I watched frost spreading across her pupils. "I am Amandine's daughter, and I belong to no one."

"Things change, October. You belong to me. You used to be better about accepting that, but I suppose I left you without a leash for too long, didn't I? I'm sorry about that. I know how confusing that sort of thing can be." She smiled. "There's no sense in fighting me. It won't do you any good. Your fealty belongs to me, through the chain descending from your liege, and I have long since taught you to obey me."

Pain is the body's way of telling you to stop doing something. I dug my nails still deeper into my palms, and felt that glorious moment where the skin gave way and the pain became ten times more intense. The smell of blood assaulted my nose an instant later, strong and hot and all the better because it was my own.

I hate the sight of my own blood, and I've never been that fond of the taste, but when I brought my bleeding hand to my mouth, it tasted like freedom for the first time. I drank as deeply as I could before the wounds started closing, and then whirled, Evening still staring at me in slack-jawed disbelief as I flung myself from the dais—

—only to freeze when I saw Simon Torquill standing behind Tybalt, his hands raised in a gesture that I recognized as a spell in progress. Tybalt's back was rigid, his arms pressed down at his sides like they were held by some invisible rope, and he looked like he was choking. That explained the smell of smoke. What it didn't explain was the Luidaeg standing only a few feet away, a snarl on her lips and her hands curled into helpless fists at her sides.

I started moving again, running toward them with my bloody fingers outstretched. I'd ripped one of Simon's spells to pieces already. I could do it again, if I could just figure out how to begin. I never got the chance. One of those wind-ropes drew suddenly tight around my ankles, and I was moving too fast to stop myself; I lost my balance, and gravity carried me down to the marble floor. I tried to raise my hands to catch myself, and discovered that I couldn't move my arms, either.

That wasn't as smart a move as Evening probably thought it was. My face bore the brunt of the impact, and I felt the squishy crunch as the cartilage in my nose gave way. Between that and my lips being smashed up against my teeth, there was suddenly more blood than I needed for any single spell right there where I wanted it: flowing into my mouth.

"Really, October," said Evening, her words accompanied by the soft sound of slippers on marble. "You do get *so* worked up over things. What good did you expect this little rebellion to do? You're not going to save your friends. You can't even save yourself."

Swallowing the blood that was seeping from my lips was easier than swallowing the blood running down the back of my throat from my battered nose: I almost gagged, but kept gulping. The pain was enough to keep me from falling back under Evening's spell, at least for the moment. I knew it wasn't going to last. I needed to gather my resources fast, and whatever I was going to do, I needed to do it before I stopped bleeding. Time to gamble.

"You're not allowed to move against the children of

Titania, but you *are* allowed to come to the aid of the children of Oberon!" I shouted, lifting my head off the floor and focusing on the Luidaeg. Her eyes widened slightly, despite whatever spell Evening was using to bind her. Now I just had to pray that I was right. "He's my grandfather! Help me!"

Her lips moved, but no sound came out.

I've never been a lip-reader. I took a split-second to think about what she might be saying, and then shouted again, "Help me!"

The Luidaeg coughed. It was a small sound, almost obscured by Evening's scoffing and the slap of her shoes against the marble. She was almost on top of me. I was running out of time.

Then, voice almost inaudible, the Luidaeg said, "Ask me again."

I smiled, showing bloody teeth. Third time's the charm, especially in Faerie. "Help me," I said.

And the Luidaeg moved.

There was nothing violent about the way she crossed the marble floor; she didn't descend like an avalanche or strike like a thunderstorm, but there was something so primal about it that for those few seconds, she didn't look like flesh—she looked like nature itself coming to life and stepping in to intervene. She was a wave on the ocean, she was a ripple on a pond, and it only seemed to take the blink of an eye before she was in front of me, leaning down and offering her hand.

"You are my niece, and I am your aunt, and when you ask my help, it is within my power to give it," she said, smiling. Her teeth weren't bloody, but they were sharper than they had any right to be, more like the teeth of some deep and unspoken sea beast than anything that should be allowed to wear a human shape and walk in human cities. She spread the fingers of her outstretched hand a little wider. "All you have to do is let me."

"Sure thing, Auntie," I said, and slid my fingers into hers.

If touching Evening had been like touching a cloud, touching the Luidaeg was like touching a corpse. She was cold and felt waterlogged under my clutching hand, as if bearing down too hard might cause her to burst open and melt across the floor. She pulled me easily to my feet, Evening's ropes of wind dissolving back into the air that they were made from.

The Luidaeg smiled at me again as we straightened up, our eyes almost level with one another. Those terrible teeth still distorted the shape of her mouth, although they didn't seem to be making it any harder for her to talk. Her eyes were the same as they usually were, warm and very, very human. If not for that, I'm not sure I could have kept looking directly at her.

Then Evening's hand caught my shoulder, whirling me around to face her. The Luidaeg hissed, yanking me back, out from under Evening's hand. Evening sniffed dismissively, her eyes traveling from my bloody face to the blood-soaked front of my shirt before finally settling on the Luidaeg.

"I see you're just as beastly as ever, Annie," she said. "Didn't it ever occur to you that it's easier to be beautiful in this world? Beauty opens oh so very many doors."

"I never wanted those doors to be opened in the first place, Eira," snarled the Luidaeg.

"Then it's a good thing that what you want has never mattered to me, isn't it?" Evening shook her head. "I was here first, darling sister. Do yourself a favor, calm yourself, and remember your place."

"I was there before she chose Faerie," said the Luidaeg. "Can you really claim to have beaten me to her cradle?"

Evening's smile was a terrible thing to behold. I shrank back against the Luidaeg, suddenly glad for her terrible teeth, for the solid *beastliness* of her. She was something I could understand, and if she wore her knives on the outside, that just meant that I was better able to see them when she finally chose to use them on me.

"I was at her christening, dear one," said Evening. "I saw her father hold her in his arms, little red-faced screaming thing that she was, and say that they could call her Olivia when she got older, if the other kids teased her too much about her name. I saw pretty, simpering Amy playing faerie bride, and when she asked if I believed that she was mortal, I told her yes, yes, oh, yes, my darling, you are *so* believable as something frail and temporary. I beat you to October by a matter of years. You have no claim here."

The Luidaeg's hand tightened on mine. "That's for October to decide, don't you think?"

"She's a changeling. She has no decisions on her shoulders. Only duty." Evening focused on me again. "She'll work herself to death to be what I order her to be."

"No, I won't," I said, licking my lips to get the last of the half-dried blood and the strength that it promised me. It wasn't nearly enough, but it still helped me keep my grip on the Luidaeg's hand, even as the part of me that remembered the taste of Evening's blood murmured about loyalty and legacies and why I needed to go to her now, before she grew angry with me.

"You see, this is why I didn't want her anywhere near you," said Evening, throwing up her hands in a gesture of frustration that was as familiar as it was out of place in this setting, in this scene. She should have been wearing a business suit when she threw her hands up like that, not a dress better suited to the wicked queen from a fairy tale. "You always spoil everything, Annie. That's your entire role in my life. The spoilsport."

"I've been called worse," said the Luidaeg. She gripped my hand even harder. "Don't trust her, Toby.

Don't let her take you back. She's not worth it, and you're worth so much more than she is."

"Oh, leave her alone, Annie. She doesn't know me. She never did. You told her, and she thought she heard you, but she didn't understand. They're so frail, these changelings, and so slow to catch on to what's happening around them. Leave her alone. She belongs to me."

"No, she doesn't." The Luidaeg gripped me even harder, until a small gasp escaped my throat, summoned by the pain of her nails against my skin. "If she doesn't know you—and you're insisting that she doesn't—then she can't give herself to you. You know the rules."

"Oh, yes, the rules," said Evening mockingly. "Mustn't forget the rules. Who branded those rules across your heart, dearest sister? Who made you what you are to-day?"

"And don't think I'm not intending to kill you for that when I get the chance," said the Luidaeg.

"You'll have to catch me first," said Evening. She returned her focus to me, smiling so sweetly and so warmly that my heart leaped in my chest like a salmon trying to swim upstream. She looked like safety. She looked like *home*. "October—Toby. I know you missed me while I was gone, and I'm so sorry that I had to leave. Can you forgive me? Can you just come over here, come to me, and forgive me?"

"I—" The sentence dissolved into a wordless yelp as a sudden, piercing pain lanced through my hand. I looked down and saw that the Luidaeg's nails—which were more like talons, really, making a matched set with her teeth—had gouged into my flesh, opening cuts that ran all the way down to the brutal whiteness of bone. "What the hell, Luidaeg?" I jerked my hand away, sticking the side of it in my mouth as I sought some small measure of relief in that most mammalian of gestures.

The taste of blood hit my tongue and I froze, the

scene around me suddenly becoming clear. Still sucking on the open wound I turned to Evening, eyes wide. She didn't look like home anymore. She looked like the deep, dark wood where little girls and boys went to find wolves of their very own, the place that no one returned from. Her coloring was as fairy-tale extreme as ever, but it didn't seem comforting or familiar: it was alien and garish, her lips too red for her skin, her skin too pale for anything that wasn't dead.

I took a breath, scenting out the magic in the room. It had all faded away under the taste of blood and the compulsion that was rolling off of Evening like a wave. Now that I was looking, though . . .

The smell of ice and roses was everywhere, nearly burying the smell of marsh water and the sea that rolled off the Luidaeg. My own cut grass and copper didn't stand a chance. Neither did Tybalt's musk and pennyroyal, but the fact that I could taste it told me that he was still fighting. That was a good thing. If she'd hurt him, if she'd *killed* him, I would have been forced to find a way to kill her. I wanted time to think about that before I actually tried to do it.

"I'm not yours," I said. "I won't be yours. I refuse you and everything that you stand for. Now get the fuck out of my liege's knowe before I get mad."

"You really think it's going to be that easy?" demanded Evening. "You drank my blood, you stupid little mongrel. You're *mine*."

"Oh, is that all?" I turned to the Luidaeg. "How much of your blood have I consumed since we met?"

The corner of her mouth turned upward as far as her terrible teeth would allow. "At least a quart. You're a thirsty little vampire when you want to be."

"Uh-huh." I turned back to Evening. "I am not a descendant of Titania. I am not yours by blood. I have tasted your blood once, and once only. I am not yours by mistake. And while Sylvester Torquill may be my liege, I am a hero of the realm, so named by Arden Windermere, the Queen in the Mists. Kingdom trumps Duchy. I am not yours by fealty. I refuse your claim on me."

She blinked, looking briefly surprised. Then she rolled her eyes. "It's not that easy, October. It never has been."

"See, I think it is. You've been arguing about this with me for a long time now, and you've sort of blown your cover—you were dead, then you weren't dead, then you were trying to take back Goldengreen, then you were holing up at Shadowed Hills—even if that didn't show a major lack of planning on your part, it would tell me one thing loud and clear: you're desperate. You can't go back to being Evening Winterrose, harmless Countess. Not after coming back from the grave." Anger suddenly bubbled in my chest, and I let it, making no effort to swallow back the words that spilled from my lips: "You *died!* You left me, you left me with no allies and no idea of what to do and . . . and . . . and now I find out it was your *fault?* You're the one who sent Simon after me, who *ruined* my *life?*"

"You seem to have done fairly well for yourself," said Evening, looking taken aback. "You have your friends, your house, your little squire—where is the boy, anyway? I can't wait to introduce myself to him properly."

"He's where you can't touch him, and it doesn't matter if I've built myself something better, because you're the reason that I *had* to," I snapped. "I shouldn't have been forced to do that. You were supposed to be my friend."

"I never said I was your friend, October," she said, all traces of bewilderment fading. "I said I was your ally. I was, at the time. I never harmed you directly."

"Because you weren't *allowed*," snapped the Luidaeg. "Don't pretend your limitations are some kind of altruistic gesture."

"Why not? You do it all the time." Evening looked past us to where Simon was holding Tybalt in wind-wrapped thrall. "They're not going to listen to reason. Kill the animal, and come here."

"Yes, milady," said Simon. I whirled in time to see him slant a regretful glance in my direction, and then he waved his hands in the air, a simple, almost graceful gesture.

Tybalt screamed.

TWENTY-ONE

I HAD NEVER MOVED so fast before in my life; I may never move that fast again. Tybalt's scream was still gathering strength as I launched myself across the room, drawing the knife from my belt and charging straight for Simon. Behind me, I heard Evening shouting; I heard the Luidaeg shouting even louder, until their words blurred together in a senseless mass of sounds and syllables. None of it mattered. The only things in the world with any meaning to them were the men in front of me, one red-haired and frowning, the other screaming in evident agony.

My knife wasn't weighted for throwing, and even if it had been, I'd never thrown a knife before; I wouldn't have known how to begin. So I settled for what I knew, flipping the blade around and slashing open my own palm as I ran. The wound flared pain up my arm. I ignored it—I've gotten surprisingly good at ignoring little things like that—and instead used the blood to call as much of my magic as I could summon from the marrow of my bones, calling and calling until the air around me was thick with the smell of cut grass and copper, burying all traces of roses and snow, smoke and oranges.

Tybalt was still screaming. I was still running. All of this had taken seconds, barely enough to register on a clock's face. It had been enough to accomplish one thing, however: it had been enough to get me close enough to Tybalt that I could slam my still-bleeding hand flat against his chest, transferring all the momentum of my run into his body. He rocked backward, held up only by the ropes of wind that still bound him, and I rocked with him.

Simon cursed. I allowed myself a flickering instant of satisfaction. As I had hoped, when I hit Tybalt, the shock of the impact had transferred back to the man who cast the spell.

That man was going to have to deal with me in a minute. Right now, I needed to deal with Tybalt, whose screams were tapering off as he choked and gasped for air. I pressed my palm down harder against his chest, praying that the wound would stay open long enough to give me the blood that I needed, and closed my eyes. *Please let this work,* I thought. *Please let me remember how . . .*

Glowing orange-and-gray lines snapped into view on the inside of my eyelids, carefully and precisely twisted around each other in a net that a master craftsman would have been proud to call his own. They looked almost diseased to my mind's eye, like they had been infected with something that might never come clean.

"Sorry," I murmured, not opening my eyes, and slashed my knife along the worst of the lines.

The silver was coated in my blood, and my magic was sizzling in the air. When the blade hit the edges of Simon's spell they withered, snapping and fraying with every pass. My headache—gone, but not forgotten—flared back to life, and I ignored it. I couldn't be entirely sure that I wasn't hitting Tybalt at least a little, but I hacked away at the center of the spell without allowing myself to hesitate. Better a few bandages than a single coffin.

Simon cursed again, and more of the lines sprang into view, slithering to fill the spaces left by the ones I had cut away. I responded by changing the directions of my cuts. Instead of slashing at the spell, I brought the knife down on the inside of my arm, opening the skin from wrist to elbow. The blood came fast and dangerously heavy then, but I ignored the implications of that as I dropped the knife, covered my hands in sticky warmth, and began shredding the spell by the fistful, ripping it away like there was no tomorrow.

When I yanked the threads from Tybalt's throat he breathed in—a huge, whooping gasp of a sound—and the lines on his chest began to move as he panted. I took that as a good sign and ripped away chunks of spell even faster. The threads stung my fingers when they got through the insulating layer of blood. I didn't care. I could handle a few small abrasions better than I could handle my boyfriend's death.

Then enough of the strands had broken for Tybalt to fall. He hit the ground hard enough that I heard the impact, and I opened my eyes, sparing only a brief glance down to see that he was on his hands and knees, not crumpled in an unconscious heap. Then I raised my head and looked at Simon, my teeth bared in a snarl.

Simon Torquill, my personal bogeyman and unwanted stepfather, took one look at me and realized that he had finally gone too far. He didn't say a word. He didn't try to defend himself. He just turned around and ran.

The wound in my arm was healing, but not as fast as it would have if I hadn't lost a lot of blood, used a lot of magic, and generally exhausted myself. My head felt like it had been used as a punching bag. The sound of blood dripping from my fingertips to the floor punctuated my movements as I turned and knelt next to Tybalt. He raised his head as soon as I crouched beside him, and a pained smile crossed his face. There were red welts on his throat, and blood seeped through his shirt where I had misjudged my slices and cut shallow gouges in his chest. At least none of those wounds looked serious.

"I am beginning to feel as if we do not save each other in equal measure," he said wearily, voice rasping a little from the strain he had put on it with all the screaming. "Next time you must let me save you, or I will start to feel I am not contributing to this partnership."

"I'll try," I said, taking his hand and pulling him with me as I straightened. He didn't shy away from the blood on my fingers. There was something to be said for loving a man who came from a part of Faerie that still settled its battles the old, brutal way.

Speaking of battles . . . I turned back to where I had left the Luidaeg and Evening, and was disappointed but unsurprised to find that both of them were gone.

"Oh, Oberon's ass," I muttered. "Tybalt, how are you feeling? Do you think you can walk?"

"I can walk, and I can fight, as long as I'm not caught in a coward's snare again," he said, before coughing in a way that gave the lie to his words. He looked sheepish. "It would, however, be best if I could refrain from fighting for a time."

"Again, I'll try. We're missing two Firstborn. I think we might need to find them before somebody else gets hurt." Find them, and find Simon. Even when I had no clear goals, it seemed I was still doomed to be forever running after *something*.

Tybalt stilled, expression going neutral as he sniffed the air. Then, with the solemnity of a man passing judgment, he said, "They are not here."

"I can see that."

"No. That isn't what I meant." He closed his eyes and

rubbed the side of his face with one hand, smearing blood across his cheek in the process. I didn't say anything. It wasn't his blood, and that was really all I cared about. "The air smells wrong."

"A lot of blood and a lot of magic just happened here."

"The air smells like somewhere else. Somewhere that does not follow the rules of here. The air on the Shadow Roads is similar—it is air to the Cait Sidhe, or we would die when we ran there, but it smells of silence and of stillness, if you have the nose for it." He opened his eyes. "They aren't *here*."

That changed things a little—but not as much as it once would have. "Right," I said, digesting his words. Then: "Follow me."

I made it halfway across the ballroom before I realized Tybalt wasn't following. I stopped and turned just in time to see him crumple to the floor.

"Tybalt!" I shouted, running back over to him and dropping to my knees. The few spots on my jeans that hadn't already been saturated with blood soaked through. I was too panicked to care. He was lying face-down and not moving, but when I fumbled for his neck, I found a strong, if somewhat irregular, pulse. Shock and blood loss, then, and not anything more serious. I breathed a sigh of relief . . .

. . . and froze as the point of what felt like a spear was pressed against the back of my neck.

"Speak and explain," said Grianne, her voice like the creak of a rusty gate in the still air. One of her Merry Dancers zipped past my face, the globe of animate light circling us once before it rose to hover somewhere overhead.

"Grianne." I relaxed a little, although not completely. "Evening's gone. Her hold on you is broken. That's fantastic. Where is Sylvester? I need him to ask Luna to open a Rose Road for me, and I need Jin to take a look at Tybalt." I kept my tone level and reasonable through all of this, as if I were making my requests while standing and facing her, and not while kneeling in a pool of blood.

"What?"

The Candela didn't talk much: for her, that single word was virtually a speech, especially coming on the heels of her demand for an explanation. I rolled Tybalt onto his back, stroking his hair away from his face as I said, "Evening Winterrose is the Daoine Sidhe Firstborn. She used your fealty to Sylvester to make you do what she said, which is why I went to get the Luidaeg and see if we could somehow interfere with Evening's ability to control her descendants. Only Evening brought Simon as backup and he used a nasty choking spell to nearly kill Tybalt, hence the blood everywhere—although most of it is mine, as per usual—and then she got away while I was dealing with him. Tybalt said they were somewhere 'else' before he collapsed, and the Luidaeg and I used a shortcut to get here, so I'm hoping that Luna can somehow open me a Rose Road that goes where I need to be and seriously, Grianne, I don't mean to nag or anything, but my boyfriend is hurt and needs medical assistance, and Evening is just getting farther away while I sit here explaining myself to you. Please, can you just go get Sylvester for me?"

"I'm already here," he said wearily.

I turned my head, the point of Grianne's spear scraping against the back of my neck and adding a fresh line of blood to the coagulated mess around me. My liege was standing next to his faintly glowing knight, his hands dangling by his sides and a weary expression on his face.

"Hi," I said. I twisted back toward Tybalt, bending to kiss his forehead, before I climbed to my feet and turned to face Sylvester. I was all too aware of his pristine condition, and how it contrasted with the bloody mess I had become. I was starting to feel like I'd been bleeding on his behalf for much too long. "Uh. How much of that did you hear?"

"All of it," he said. His expression didn't change.

For one heart-stopping moment I was afraid I had gotten one thing wrong: that Evening's control *hadn't* snapped when she left the knowe, and I was about to be forced to choose between fighting my liege and abandoning Tybalt while I ran for my life. Sylvester was the man who taught me how to use a sword. He'd mop the bloody floor with me without even breaking a sweat. And if he came at me, I'd stand my ground.

Then he sighed, weariness growing even more pronounced, and asked, "Can you forgive me for being so easily swayed?"

"She's your *Firstborn*, Sylvester, and she's a bloodworker. I don't think there's any way that you could have resisted her." I ached to throw myself into his arms and be held, even if it was only for a few seconds. But there wasn't time, and touching me would have ruined his clothes—and also, I was more and more aware that the part of me that needed his reassurance was small, and weak, and frightened. She was the girl I'd been, not the woman I had finally become. "I need to talk to Luna. I need her to open a door for me."

"A door won't do you much good without a map," he said, before turning to Grianne and saying, "Go tell my lady she is needed here. Then go to Jin, and tell her the King of Cats is injured, and to Ormond. Tell him . . ." He glanced to the pool of blood around me. "Tell him to bring several mops, and more hot water than he expects to need."

Grianne nodded. Then she jumped into a small fold of shadow that had been formed by the intersection of his foot and the floor, and was gone.

"They didn't leave me a map," I said, bending to retrieve my bloody knife. As I bent, something in my right pocket dug into my hip. I reached in, intending to adjust whatever it was, and stopped as my fingers hit a familiar curved shape. I straightened, still holding my knife in one hand, and pulled the twisted metal key out of my pocket. It caught and bounced back the light when I held it up for examination. "Okay, I stand corrected," I said. "They *did* leave me a map after all."

"What is that?" asked Sylvester.

"A key. Evening gave it to me, although I think she expected to get it back when she returned; the Luidaeg took it from me almost as soon as I got it. And now I have it again. The Luidaeg must have put it in my pocket when we were in the car." She'd known we were going to be separated, and that I was going to have to follow her. She'd known, and she'd done nothing to stop it. We were going to have words about that.

After I got her home safely. I crouched down next to Tybalt, the key held loosely in one hand, and watched Sylvester to see what he was going to do next. He watched me, expression remaining tired and grave.

Finally, he took a breath and said, "I'm sorry. I have not been a proper liege to you."

My head snapped up. "You've been a great liege," I said fiercely. "You defended me when I needed defending, and you've given me enough rope to hang myself when I asked you for it. You've been a resource without being a hindrance. We both know that you could have put a lot more demands on me than you have these past few years. I give you a hundred percent in the liege category. It's the friend category where you've been falling down a little." I looked down at the blood obscuring the checkerboard marble floor, and sighed. "It's where you've been falling down a lot."

"October . . ."

"The Luidaeg not telling me things I can sort of understand. She's Firstborn, she's under all these geasa, and she didn't meet me all that long ago. I like to think we're friends now, but I didn't grow up with her. You, on the other hand . . ." I raised my head again, meeting his eyes. "Why do you keep secrets from me, Sylvester? You've been the closest thing I've had to a father for most of my life. I would have died for you. I almost did die for you, more than once. And you kept things from me, and those things keep getting the people I care about hurt. Hurt bad, in some cases. Why?"

He sighed. "I'm sorry," he said again.

I waited almost a minute before I realized he was done: that was all he intended to say. My eyes widened. "That's it? You're sorry? Nothing else? No reasons or justifications or explanations? Just 'I'm sorry' and we're done?"

"Yes," he said, raising his chin. "I'm sorry I hurt you. It was never my intent. But I don't feel any need to justify myself."

I stared at him. "Maybe you don't," I said finally. "Maybe that's the only answer you have to give me. But oak and ash, I'd hoped for more."

The doors swung open, saving me from needing to hear his response, and Luna walked into the room. She was moving with a calm sort of serenity that made me want to shake her and demand to know why she was wasting my time when she knew that I needed her help. Jin came in after her, and she was running: the petite Ellyllon was moving as fast as her legs allowed, which was almost comic, given her 1940s pin-up girl looks and the gauzy mayfly wings on her back. They buzzed constantly, speeding her along.

"I need to introduce you to my friend Mags," I said when Jin got close enough to hear me. I straightened up, stepping aside. "Tybalt got blasted with a spell that tried to choke the life out of him. I managed to cut it off, but he suffered some minor wounds in the process, and—"

"What do you mean, 'cut it off'?" she demanded, even as she sank to her knees in the puddle of semi-coagulated blood and began ripping Tybalt's shirt off. Normally, I took great interest in things that involved removing Tybalt's clothing. Under the circumstances, I moved aside and let her work.

"I used my knife to slice the knots holding the spell together, and then I ripped the rest of it away with my bare hands," I said, aware as I spoke that my words probably sounded like absolute nonsense. My headache wasn't helping.

"Was he still wrapped in the spell at the time?" asked Jin. Her wings snapped open, sending a spray of pixie-sweat over the three of us.

"Yes," I said.

"He's got magic poisoning. Back away and let me work." The way she turned her head made it clear that she was done talking to me: Tybalt was her patient and her first priority, and the rest of us could go hang.

I closed my eyes for a split-second, allowing myself a silent moment of gratitude, before opening them and turning toward Luna. She was standing next to Sylvester, as pristine and untouched by the chaos around her as he was, while Tybalt, Jin, and I were surrounded by blood. There was probably something about the symbolism there that I should have caught on to sooner.

Live and learn, I guess. "I need you to use this key and open me a road," I said, thrusting it toward her. "I think your Rose Road can get me there, if you follow the map."

Luna blinked, her pink eyebrows rising toward her hairline. "Opening roads is difficult," she said. "I've done it for you before, but never without cost. Why would I do this for you now? I owe you nothing."

"You owe me nothing but your life," I corrected harshly. "When I saved you from the salt poisoning—you remember the assassination attempt that *your daughter* thought was a good idea—I didn't ask for any reward, because Sylvester is my liege and it was the right thing to do. Well, that assumed that everyone was playing fair. Turns out no one here was playing fair but me. I saved your life, Luna Torquill, and more, I killed your father. I set you free. Now open this door for me, or I will make you sorry that you even considered refusing my request."

She looked at me for a moment with those strange, pollen-colored eyes, and in that moment I could almost see the Luna who had loved me, once, before things got so complicated between us. Then she extended one bone-white hand and said, "Give me the key."

I straightened, walking away from Jin's murmuring and Tybalt's silence. Every step I took left another bloody smear on the ballroom floor, and that seemed somehow exactly right. I held the key out in front of me; Luna took it, turning it over in her hand.

"This belonged to my grandmother," she said.

"Which one?" I asked.

Luna's head snapped up, eyes narrowing for some reason. Then, with no further fanfare, she shoved the key into the air between us. The bottom half vanished, like it had been placed in a lock I couldn't see.

"My debts are paid," she said, and turned the key sharply to the left, pulling at the same time.

What opened wasn't exactly a door, but it wasn't exactly a portal either: it was a hole in the world. Through it, I could see darkness. Not blackness—blackness would have implied an absence—but darkness, green, wet, *living* darkness, where things could slither unseen by the eye and unknown by the heart.

"You asked for this," said Luna. "Now go."

I held out my hand.

She narrowed her eyes as she pulled the key out of the air and slapped it into my open palm. "I hope this is everything you think it's going to be, because it has cost you more than you can know."

"If you mean I'm no longer in your good graces, Your Grace, I've known that for a while." I pocketed the key. "Love you can spend like currency isn't really love. Take care of him, Jin." I glanced back over my shoulder to Jin and Tybalt. "I'll be back soon."

There was no way of knowing what the air would be like on the other side of the not-a-door still hanging open in the air. I took a deep breath, shoving the key into my pocket, and jumped through into darkness.

TWENTY-TWO

MY FALL WAS shorter than I expected; I'd only been dropping through space for what felt like a few seconds when my feet hit the spongy ground and I fell, rolling out of control until I slammed up against what felt like a stone retaining wall. The impact knocked the wind out of me, something that even my accelerated healing couldn't prevent. Wheezing, I used the wall to pull myself back to my feet and peered into the dark, trying to see what was around me.

At first, I couldn't see anything. Then, as I blinked and strained, the darkness seemed to pull back, growing lighter and lighter until it had achieved a sort of midnight quality, still unlit, but somehow bright enough to let me see. There was no color in the world. I would have needed to be less human to rate color, given the circumstances.

The forest around me was overgrown, the trees fat with sap and dripping with moss, creeping vines, and thorn briars of a type I'd never seen before. Some of them had spines more than two inches long, making them look less like plants and more like torture devices waiting to be used. The air—and there *was* air, breathable and ripe with the smell of the growing world—was hot and humid. For the first time, I found myself glad not to be wearing my leather jacket. It would have been unbearable, and I would have been afraid to take it off. I had the feeling that when things were lost in this forest, they tended to stay that way.

For a moment, I held perfectly still, breathing in deep and trying to filter through the myriad scents of this unfamiliar place, looking for the familiar smells of marsh and ocean breeze, of snow and roses. Evening had no way of knowing that I'd followed them here. The Luidaeg had been counting on it. They wouldn't be hiding themselves from me.

Standing frozen in a place I didn't know, where I had previously been instructed not to slow down my car for any reason, was not the easiest thing that I've ever done. I breathed in even deeper than before, trying to ignore the fact that I could be eaten at any moment. This place used to belong to the Luidaeg's sister. The Luidaeg was a fabulous monster and, unlike most of Titania's children, she at least tried to play fair. She wouldn't have left me the key if it was just going to get me eaten.

I hoped.

It helped that we were in a place that wasn't the sea, and that was definitely not in the middle of its own private winter. The native scents of the land around me were hot and green and growing. Life scents, decay scents, but not sea scents or snow scents. So when the smell of roses addressed my nose through the tangled perfume of the land, I knew I was on to something. My eyes snapped open, and I turned, sniffing as I tried to determine the direction the smell was coming from.

West. I don't know how I knew which way was west, but I did—I just knew—and Evening's magic was coming from the west.

"Hold on, Luidaeg," I murmured, and broke into a run.

Running through an unfamiliar forest filled with thorns is half an exercise in masochism, and half an obstacle course from the deepest reaches of Hell. I kept one arm up to block my face, letting it take the brunt of anything sharp that dangled overhead, and kept the other arm out in front of me, fingers spread to find the trunks of surrounding trees before I ran straight into them. The smell of snow and roses urged me onward, ebbing and surging with the force of whatever spells she was casting, but always there, a thin ribbon of poisoned sweetness to urge me onward into the dark.

Unfortunately for me, no amount of positioning my hands to reduce my potential danger could level out the ground under my feet. I was running down what I had taken for a slight incline when everything dropped out from beneath me, and I was plummeting like a rock. I had time to squeak my surprise and wrap my arms around my face. Then I hit the tree line, and developed a whole new set of problems to worry about—like how to keep myself from getting hung up in the high branches, forcing me to fall even further after I recovered.

My right arm hit a tree trunk on the way down. There was a loud "crack" followed by shooting pain. I'd broken at least one bone, if not more than one. I made a sound that was halfway between a gasp and a scream, and then finally landed on the ground in an untidy heap. My broken arm was pinned beneath the rest of me, making sitting up more difficult than it should have been. Eventually, I managed to roll into a position where I could use my unbroken left arm to push myself to my feet.

"Shit," I muttered, folding my right arm to my chest. I could feel the bones starting to knit back together. I just prayed that they were healing straight, and that I wasn't going to need Jin to rebreak my arm when I made it back to Shadowed Hills. At least I wasn't bleeding all over everything for a change. Something told me Evening would be able to pick up on blood that was shed in her presence the way that I could follow the scent of a person's magic through dark forests that would have been better left abandoned. And I did *not* want to give her any more warning than I had to.

I hurt myself a lot, but I don't tend to break many bones, and I didn't know how long my arm would need to heal. I moved forward more slowly now, feeling out the ground with my toes before stepping into shadows. I would probably survive breaking my neck. I would probably even recover from it. But it would slow me down even more than my broken arm already had, and I didn't have time for that.

The smell of snow and roses was stronger now, interlaced with the smell of cold wind blowing over an open sea. I could probably have followed it with my eyes closed. I was glad I didn't have to—anything that would make this a little bit easier was good, especially given that I was injured and relatively unarmed. You need iron *and* silver to kill one of the Firstborn.

The signs really *had* been there from the beginning. I'd been a fool not to see them: a fool blinded by my own preconceptions of the world and my place in it. It was the same blindness that had prevented me from seeing that Tybalt loved me, or that I wasn't what my mother had always told me I was. You'd think I'd know better by now.

Voices drifted through the wall of thorns ahead of me. I stopped where I was, barely daring to breathe, as I strained to hear what they were saying.

"—the only one who's suffered? You're very wrong about that, *sister*." Evening's words were punctuated by the sound of wood stiffening and breaking off with a crack. A gust of frozen roses washed over me. I fought the urge to sneeze.

"No one had to suffer at all," countered the Luidaeg's voice. "This has always been on you, Eira. You were the one who couldn't be patient, who couldn't see the value of waiting on the greater good."

"I've killed you once since I came back," spat Evening. "Don't think you can stop me from doing it again."

That was it: I'd heard enough. I shoved my way through the thorns with my good arm, ignoring the way they pierced and tore my skin—now that I was revealing myself to Evening, a little blood could only help me—and into the clearing on the other side of the wall.

I found myself standing at the middle of a large clear space in the forest. Not naturally clear, if the broken trees and shattered stumps were anything to go by, but that wasn't the worst problem currently facing me. No, that honor was reserved for the two angry Firstborn who were now flanking me. The Luidaeg was to my left, her clothing torn to reveal the dark green scales that were now covering her skin. Evening was to my right, her red dress dyed even darker by sweat and water and blood.

"Uh, hi," I said.

"What are *you* doing here?" Evening spat, eyes narrowing as she took in my bedraggled appearance and motionless right arm. "You can't reach this place. It is forbidden to your kind."

"You're a little off the mark there, Eira," said the Luidaeg. She actually sounded like she was enjoying herself. That made one of us. "The Thorn Road wasn't forbidden when Annis died, it was sealed. There's a difference. If someone can open the doors, they're welcome to commit suicide by walking through them."

Evening's head whipped around, her narrow-eyed glare transferring to the Luidaeg. "Stay out of this, Antigone."

"I would, if you hadn't dragged me here and kept trying to kill me." The Luidaeg folded her arms. "That's what you always do, you know. Drag me places and try to kill me. You should really get a new routine. Something more interesting and modern than sororicide."

I blinked. The Luidaeg could be hard to deal with sometimes, and I'd never known her to take a challenge lying down, but she didn't sound like herself. The way she was mouthing off to a greater power made her sound more like, well, me.

She caught me looking at her and winked broadly before adding, "Maybe you could take up needlepoint. You know, a nice handicraft that wouldn't leave bodies scattered everywhere when you were finished."

Evening made an incoherent sound of rage as she whirled and hurled a blast of ice at the Luidaeg. The Luidaeg didn't dodge: she just raised her crossed arms, and the blast rebounded off the air in front of her, freezing the nearest patches of thorn solid. I blinked again, this time with understanding. Whatever fight they'd been having before I arrived, it had changed when I entered the scene. The Luidaeg was trying to protect me, and if there was one thing my method of dealing with a greater threat was good at, it was drawing focus.

Too bad I couldn't let her die again for my sake. "Evening, stop," I said. "Just stop. I don't understand why you're doing this, but I know that you're not a bad person. You're just . . . I don't even know. You're my friend. Friends don't do this sort of thing."

"Your *friend?*" Evening turned back to me, an astonished look on her face. "Is that really what you think, October? That we're *friends?* We were never friends. I wouldn't lower myself to form that sort of bond with someone like you."

I raised an eyebrow. "Someone like me?"

"You're a half-breed. A mongrel. You should never have existed, in this world or any other. I knew Amandine was perverse, but I had no idea she would lower herself to lying with a human before the day that news of your birth was brought to me. As if it were something to celebrate! As if I should have rejoiced in a new niece who carried the stink of mortality in her veins." The air around Evening's hands began to crackle with cold. "You should have been killed in your cradle, rather than allowed to live and taint our bloodline with your filth."

"Huh," I said. "That's funny, because I mean, you had the hope chest. The whole time, you had the hope chest. You could have pulled the human out of me while I was still a baby, and I would never have known any better. But you didn't. You left me the way I was, and you let Mom have me. It seems weird."

Evening's lip curled in a snarl. "Don't talk about things you don't understand."

"What, the hope chest? I understand it. I've used it, several times. It knows me." I held out my good left hand, fingers spread. "This is not the skin I wore when you left me, Evening. You really should have made sure I was dead. You should have killed me yourself, if that was what it took."

"She can't!" crowed the Luidaeg, her joy coloring her words until they were like fireworks in the dark forest night.

I turned toward her. "What?"

"She can take you, if you let her, but she can't touch you. Can you, Eira?" The Luidaeg began walking toward us. She was limping slightly, although she was working hard to conceal it, much as I was trying not to show how badly my broken arm still hurt. "Our father made sure of that before he left, because he recognized that maybe leaving a sociopath in a position to wipe out the competition was a bad idea."

"What are you talking about?"

"She can't touch Amy either," said the Luidaeg.

"Shut your mouth," spat Evening.

"She doesn't like being limited," said the Luidaeg.

"I said *be quiet!*" Evening whirled, hurling another blast of ice at the Luidaeg. Again, the other woman deflected her attack—but this time it seemed to take more out of her, leaving her shoulders drooping while Evening began to fill her hands with cold for a third time. "You are not a part of this. You should have stayed dead."

"I've never been good at 'should haves,'" said the Luidaeg.

"I'd like a time-out here," I said. "Does someone want to explain what's going on? Because this whole situation is getting damned difficult to follow, and I'd really appreciate some footnotes." I drew the silver knife from my belt with my uninjured hand, shifting so that I was holding it behind my back. I wasn't sure what good it would do me—no matter what I did to Evening, I couldn't kill her—but holding it made me feel a little better.

"She's sowing dissent, that's what, the same as she always has," said Evening. She turned to face me, a cool wind blowing between us and carrying the scent of snow and roses. Roses. That was another clue I should have caught. When I believed that my mother was Daoine Sidhe, the fact that they both smelled of roses made perfect sense. Once I learned that Mother was something else entirely ... but ah, Evening was speaking, and I needed to pay attention to that. I always needed to pay attention to her.

"My sister is the sea witch," said Evening, taking a step toward me. The skirt of her torn and dirtied dress swayed around her legs, and I felt a pang at seeing such beauty disturbed. "She is the darkness under the waves and the bargain you fear to make. Of course she's a troublemaker. Of course she wants to turn you against me, October, can't you see? I've been your friend for years. I've always been your friend."

The Luidaeg can't lie and this woman just said in so many words that she could never be your friend, whispered the part of my mind that was distant enough from Evening's spell to hold itself separate. Sadly, that part of me was outweighed by the sweet, cloying scent of her magic as it rose around me.

"I was the one who came for you when you returned from the pond," said Evening, taking another step toward me. "I was the one who told you how your human family would react to your return. I tried to save you so much pain. Don't you remember?"

I frowned, trying to find the line between what she was saying and what I knew her words actually meant. It had been so clear only a few seconds before, but now it was blurred and difficult to see. She had been my friend for so long. She had allowed me to enter her presence and treated me like I was almost worth something, despite my human heritage. She had hired me to do the things she didn't want to do herself. She had . . .

She had ordered Simon Torquill to kill me. She had orchestrated the kidnapping of Luna and Rayseline Torquill, tearing wounds in the fabric of their family that would never really heal, just scab over and fester. She had treated me like dirt and, because I was a changeling, desperate for any sign of acceptance, I had allowed her to do it.

"You're not my friend," I mumbled.

"What's that?" asked Evening.

"I said, you're not my friend." I forced my right hand into a fist, sending bolts of clarifying pain through my broken arm. It cleared the fog out of my thoughts as I raised my head, forcing myself to look at her. The air around her head crackled with the power she had gathered around herself, splintering and refracting the faint light until it seemed like she almost glowed. "You were never my friend. You were just using me until you didn't need me anymore. I don't know if you still need me. But I don't need you."

Evening smiled languidly. "You will," she said, and let

all that gathered power go, directing it straight at me, and at the thin cord of my fealty. What had been a faint glittering in the air exploded into true light, virtually blinding me. She was perfect, she was untouchable, she was above reproach, she was undying, she was everything I had ever wanted to be and everything I could never approach, she was—

—*she was casting a spell, she was casting a spell on me, and spells could be broken*—

Shaking from the effort, I forced my hands up, one balled into a fist and coated in my own dried blood, one holding Dare's silver knife. My broken arm howled in protest. The pain was still helping me focus, no matter how much damage I might be doing to myself. I squinted into the brilliance, finding the individual threads of Evening's compulsion. Then, before I could think about it too hard, I opened my right hand, grabbed a fistful of threads, and yanked them tight, slashing my knife down across them in the same gesture.

Evening shrieked with pain and surprise. The spell snapped, casting the clearing back into its previous darkness. And the faint smell of smoke drifted out of the trees across from me. That was my only warning before Simon Torquill stepped out of the tree line, a longbow in his hands, and fired the arrow that he had been aiming during our confrontation.

It flew straight and true, and would have embedded itself solidly in Evening's back, had she not turned as fast as a striking snake, raising her hand in an imperious gesture. The arrow froze in midair, becoming completely motionless.

Simon's eyes widened and he dropped the bow, turning to run. Not fast enough. With a small gesture, Evening sent the arrow flying back to him. He yelped with pain as he fell. I didn't see the arrow strike, but I didn't need to.

I could smell his blood.

"Simon!" He'd tried to kill Tybalt. He'd nearly killed me. But he was also Daoine Sidhe, and I had seen first-hand just how hard it was for Evening's descendants to tell her "no." When the chips were down, he'd tried to change sides. In that moment, in that place, that was good enough for me.

I ran across the clearing, heedless of the fact that I was putting an angry Firstborn behind me. Let the Luidaeg distract her; Simon needed me.

He was facedown in the brush when I reached him. The arrow protruded from the top of his left arm. I dropped to my knees, pushing him onto his side with my left hand. "Simon? Simon, look at me."

"October." His eyes were closed when I first rolled him over, but he opened them, offering me the most honest smile I had ever seen on his face. "Even now you're trying to be a hero. Let it go, and run. Save yourself." His eyes drifted closed again.

A horrible certainty stole over me. "You were trying to hit her with elf-shot, weren't you?"

"Mmm," he said. "I'd been meaning . . . to rest . . ."

"Simon!" I shook him. "Don't go to sleep. You have to fight this."

He chuckled. "As if elf-shot can . . . be ignored. You are your mother's daughter. Too stubborn . . . by half." He yawned again. "You should have been mine," he murmured, and went limp. The elf-shot had him. He'd wake in a century, if he woke at all.

I stayed frozen where I was for a few precious seconds, trying to make sense of things. Then, moving slowly and methodically, I reached forward and shoved the arrow through his arm, causing the already-crowning arrowhead to break out into the open air. A literal gush of blood accompanied the motion. I let go of the arrow and washed my hands with it, covering my fingers in as much of the wet redness as I could. Then I wiped them on my knife, until both my hands and my blade were completely covered. My arm throbbed. I ignored it.

"Sleep well, Simon," I murmured, and stood, turning back to Evening. "He's gone."

She had gathered the shreds of her glamour while I was distracted: she was once again beautiful, perfect, untouchable, so much better than me that it was a wonder I was allowed to look at her at all. I locked my eyes on her face as I started across the clearing, noting the small, smug smile that she wore.

"Good," she said. "That means it's just us, at last. You've been very bad, October, but I can forgive you, if you'll let me."

"I've been very bad," I agreed. I cheated my eyes to the side. There was the Luidaeg, standing apart, bound by the injunction that she not harm Evening. At least she could defend herself now. I returned my attention to Evening before she could start to question, and said, "He was yours."

"He was flawed," said Evening. "You can be better."

"I can be better," I agreed. There were only a few feet between us. Could it really be this easy? Was she really that sure of herself?

"But first, put down the knife," she said.

Apparently not. Damn. "Right," I said, and lunged for her.

I expected a bolt of ice to catch me in the chest. Instead, she danced backward, trying to evade me. There was what looked like genuine fear in her eyes.

Several things suddenly started making sense. "Luidaeg!" I shouted. "What you said before, about her not being able to touch me. Is she allowed to hurt me?"

"No," called the Luidaeg. She sounded almost smug. "She can't."

"Good," I snarled, and lunged again. This time, I

didn't let fear of reprisal hold me back. I slammed my shoulder into Evening's stomach, bowling her to the ground. She screamed. I shoved her down, straddling her, and raised the knife covered in Simon's elf-shot-riddled blood in my left hand.

"Don't," she begged.

"Sorry," I said, and stabbed her in the shoulder.

It wasn't a mortal wound, but Evening stiffened all the same, eyes going wide with shock and pain before they clouded over in what looked very much like exhaustion. "You can't kill me," she said, punctuating her words with a yawn. "I'm . . . the First . . ."

"I don't need to kill you. I just need you out of the way."

". . . be back . . ."

"Promises, promises."

Evening closed her eyes.

I stayed where I was until her breathing leveled out, becoming deep and slow. Then I crawled off of her, watching warily for some sign that she was going to wake up. The Luidaeg walked over to stand beside me, and we watched her together.

Finally, after several minutes, the Luidaeg said, "You can pull your knife out now."

"Soon," I said.

She put an arm around me, pulling me close. I let myself be pulled, sagging against her as my own pain and nonmagical exhaustion threatened to overwhelm me. We stood there, watching Evening sleep, and I had never been so tired in my life, and I had never felt so far away from home.

TWENTY-THREE

WE LEFT HER THERE, naturally. What else were we supposed to do? She was Firstborn; there was no telling how long the elf-shot would keep her under, and not even the Luidaeg was powerful enough to bind her. The best we could hope was that being stranded on a road that had been intended for use by Maeve's children would slow her down when she finally woke up and decided to come after us. It wasn't a good solution. Under the circumstances, it was the best one that we had.

Sylvester was waiting in the ballroom when the Luidaeg and I stepped back through the hole in the air, Simon carried limp between us. He didn't say a word. He just put his arms around me while Grianne and Etienne took Simon and carried him away into the knowe. Another glass coffin for the collection; another sleeper to wait for. I hoped the brothers would be able to make peace when Simon finally did wake up. I hoped they could forgive each other.

I wasn't sure I could forgive them—either one of them, even as Sylvester led me to Jin and held my hand while she broke and reset my arm. The pain was bad. The fact that I didn't want to be with my liege was worse. There was a chasm between us that had never been there before, and I didn't know how to cross it. From the way he was looking at me, neither did Sylvester.

I was Jin's last patient of the night. Tybalt was already patched up and waiting for me in the Garden of Glass Roses. When he saw me, he laughed and said, "To the last, covered in blood. Now I know we're on track to solving the world's problems." I'd managed to smile at that, only somehow my laughter had turned into tears, and he'd had to hold me until they stopped. And then he, the Luidaeg, and I left Shadowed Hills, and walked back down the hill to my car, and went home.

I don't remember washing off the blood, only that I must have done it before I went to bed, because I woke up the next evening clean and dressed in a fresh nightgown, with Tybalt curled possessively beside me, his arm around my waist. I raised my head enough to sniff the air, and found no traces of foreign magic. No one here but the people who were supposed to be here, and that was good. That was the way that things were meant to be.

Tybalt stirred beside me.

"Hi," I whispered. "Are the boys home?"

"Mmm?" He raised his head, blinking sleepily before he caught my meaning. "Yes. I went for them last night, after you had gone to sleep. May and Jazz are home as well. I believe May is intending to make waffles to celebrate everyone's unexpected survival."

"Good." I closed my eyes again. "No emergencies today."

"No emergencies," he agreed, and kissed my shoulder. "The Luidaeg left a message for you."

"What's that?"

"She said to thank you again, and that you should do your best to reduce the hazard I present by keeping me separate from my greatest weapon." He sounded confused. "What is she talking about?"

I sighed. "She's being creepy because she thinks it's fun. I don't think you should wear leather trousers to her place anymore."

"Ah." He kissed my shoulder again. "You were very brave."

"I didn't die. I'm going to call that good enough."

"October?"

There was something about his tone—some tight, querulous thing—that made me open my eyes and roll over to face him. He was shirtless, propped up on one elbow as he looked at me. "What's up, Tybalt?"

"I woke in a guest room at Shadowed Hills and was told that you had pursued two Firstborn through a hole in the wall of the world," he said. "You were not guaranteed to return. I could not go after you. I would prefer you not do that again."

"I'll try not to," I said.

He inclined his head. "I appreciate that. I was ... quite concerned. My fear caused me to realize that there was something I had neglected to ask you."

I frowned, sitting up the rest of the way. He moved with me, until we were both sitting on the bed, disheveled and tangled up in sheets. "What?"

"October Christine Daye—my dearest little fish—you are probably going to die horribly one day in the process of doing something you feel is absolutely necessary, and can be done by no one else. Given that this limits our time together in a way that is quite unfair, I feel that patience has ceased to be a virtue, and has instead become an indulgence. I dislike indulgences. They have their place upon the stage, but all they really do past a certain point is pad the scene."

My frown deepened. "You're being flowery again, Tybalt. You know it's a little hard for my non-

Shakespearean-era brain to follow you when you do that, right?"

"I do. But some questions are difficult for me to frame without becoming somewhat, ah, 'flowery.'" Tybalt sighed, running a hand through his hair and putting his stripes into brief disarray. "I am aware that my position is a difficulty. I believe it is one we can work around if we are so motivated, and I am more than motivated. And so . . . October, will you marry me?"

I blinked. I blinked again. And then, slowly, without any conscious intent, I began to smile. The smile grew until my lips hurt. Tybalt was watching me anxiously. It occurred to me that I should probably say something before he really started to freak out.

"Yes," I said, in a small voice.

Tybalt blinked. Then he started smiling, too. "Yes?"

"Yes. I'll marry you. Yes." I laughed disbelievingly. "I . . . yes."

"Yes!" Tybalt pounced on me, driving me back down into the blankets. I wrapped my arms around him. He kissed me, and I kissed him back, and everything else in the world ceased to matter, at least for a little while. Maybe I had lost the family I'd counted on when I was a child; maybe Sylvester wasn't the man I'd always thought he was, maybe Evening was my enemy, maybe Luna and I would never make peace with each other. All of that was terrible, and yet I wouldn't have taken back what I had if I'd somehow been granted the power. I was building something better.

I was building something real.